Some de[...]

"SMART AN[...]"

"LASHNER KEEPS THE READER SPELLBOUND."
Harlan Coben

"AN EXTREMELY GOOD CRIME NOVEL."
Booklist (*Starred Review*)

"TOUGH, FAST-MOVING." *San Antonio Express-News*

"BIG AND BEAUTIFULLY WRITTEN." *Publishers Weekly*

"A WINNER." *Palm Beach Post*

"Well worth the time."
Providence Journal

"Thoroughly enjoyable . . .
[Lashner] is better than most.
Victor Carl is one of the more interesting
series leads in mystery fiction,
mostly because you usually feel a little
uncomfortable rooting for him, since you
know he's going to do things he
probably shouldn't."
National Post (Canada)

"William Lashner is a remarkable . . . writer—
quick, witty, funny, and authoritative."
Nelson DeMille

"[Lashner] will keep you turning pages."
Philadelphia Daily News

"Brilliant, poignant, provocative, humorous,
suspenseful, and highly readable . . .
Victor Carl is one of the most surprisingly
engaging characters in fiction today . . .
There's not a single throwaway line,
and that alone is a marvel . . .
This is one thriller you won't want to miss."
Newmysteryreader.com

Books by William Lashner

Past Due
Fatal Flaw
Bitter Truth (Veritas)
Hostile Witness

And New in Hardcover

Falls the Shadow

WILLIAM
LASHNER

PAST
DUE

HarperTorch
An Imprint of HarperCollins Publishers

Grateful acknowledgment is made for permission to reprint lyrics from the following:

"Mambo Italiano," written by Bob Merrill. Copyright © 1954, 1982 by Golden Bell Songs. Reprinted with permission from Music and Media International, Inc.

"Wild Thing." Words and music by Chip Taylor. Copyright © 1965 (Renewed 1993) by EMI Blackwood Music Inc. All rights reserved. International copyright secured. Used by permission.

"Day-O (The Banana Boat Song)." Words and music by Irving Burgie and William Attaway. Copyright © 1955; renewed 1983 by Cherry Lane Music Publishing Company, Inc. (ASCAP), Lord Burgess Music Publishing Company (ASCAP) and DreamWorks Songs (ASCAP). Worldwide rights for Lord Burgess Music Publishing Company and DreamWorks Songs administered by Cherry Lane Music Publishing Company, Inc. International copyright secured. All rights reserved.

HARPERTORCH
An Imprint of HarperCollins*Publishers*
10 East 53rd Street
New York, New York 10022-5299

Copyright © 2004 by William Lashner
ISBN: 0-06-050819-1

First HarperTorch paperback printing: May 2005
First William Morrow hardcover printing: May 2004

HarperCollins®, HarperTorch™, and ♦™ are trademarks of HarperCollins Publishers Inc.

Printed in the United States of America

Visit HarperTorch on the World Wide Web at www.harpercollins.com

10 9 8 7 6 5 4 3 2 1

For Martin and Rosalie

CHAPTER

1

There is something perversely cheerful about a crime scene in the middle of the night, the pulsating red and blue lights, the great beams of white, the strobes of photographers' flashes. Festively festooned with yellow tape, a crime scene at night is a place cars drive slowly by, as if before an overdone Christmas display with bowing reindeers and whirling Santas. In the uniformed workers busily going about their business, in the helicopters spinning madly overhead, in the television vans with their jaunty microwave disks, in the reporters giving their live reports, in the excited onlookers excitedly looking on, in all of it lies the thrilling sense of relief that the arbitrary finger of desolation has squashed flat this night a total stranger.

Unless the corpse within the tape is not a total stranger. Then, suddenly, the crime scene at night is not so cheery.

I didn't yet know why I had been summoned to the crime scene at Pier 84 on Philadelphia's dank waterfront, or whose death was the subject of this swirl of activity, but I knew the deceased was not a total stranger or I would never have been called, and that was enough to turn the cheeriness of the scene into something bleak and icy. The possibilities flitted through my mind like bats through a dusky sky, an endless swarm, each swoop or swerve carrying its own name and causing its own jolt of fear.

"I was called by McDeiss," I told one of the uniforms standing as solid as a Roman sentry at the gated entrance to the pier, his arms crossed, his thick leather jacket zippered tight. Far behind him, lying between two huge shipping containers, surrounded by cops and technicians, slipping out of a strange dark puddle, was a lump of something covered by blue.

"You a reporter?" said the cop.

"I'm a lawyer."

"Even worse. Yo, Pete," he called out to a young cop standing a few feet away. "What's more trouble than a lawyer?"

"Two lawyers," said Pete.

"Go tell Detective McDeiss to hold on to his wallet, there's a lawyer here to see him."

"Who died?" I managed to get out.

"Talk to McDeiss."

"What happened?"

"Some guy got an early good-night kiss."

Until then I hadn't known if the victim was man or woman, now the possibilities narrowed. Half of the swooping bats dissolved and disappeared, yet that didn't seem to help at all.

The pier was a flat sheet of cement, jutting out into the wide, slow Delaware River, just north of the Walt Whitman Bridge. Rail lines crisscrossed its length and an arcade-style warehouse squatted in its center, with trailers hitched at the bays in front like puppies sucking milk from their mother's teats. Chocolate milk, because Pier 84 was the primary cocoa-receiving facility in the entire country. On Pier 84, burlap sacks, unloaded from heavy cargo ships, were thrown into shipping containers and hauled by rail and truck to the gay little chocolate town of Hershey, Pennsylvania. You would expect you could smell the sweet rich flavor of the chocolate even on the pier, but you'd be wrong. All you could smell that night was the wet of the river, the oxide of rusting metal, and something dark and desolate and sadly familiar beneath it all.

The warehouse now was in shadow, the river itself a thick black void. At the entrance to the pier, brown and low, squatted Frank's, a lunch shack with tables out front and a blue sign reading: COLD BEER. To my right was the great steel bridge named after America's most American poet. I hear America singing, yeah yeah yeah. Not tonight, Walt, not with all the racket from the helicopters, not with that lump of something beneath the blue tarp. And to my left, the oddest sight, the red tilting stacks of what appeared to be a great ocean liner fallen on hard times. The red paint on the funnels was streaked and flaking, the metal was rusting, the lighting was desultory at best, making it seem as if the great ship was sagging in the middle like a tired old horse. It looked as if it had suffered some foul disease and had crawled into the Philadelphia waterfront to die. Well, it had picked the right place.

This visit to Pier 84 was for me the start of the strange case you read about in the papers, the one with the Supreme Court justice and those pictures of the naked woman, the one with the dead client and the kidnapped lawyer and the rotting old ship and the ghost reaching back from the dead to exact his revenge. That one, remember? But for me it wasn't yet a headline, it was just a call in the night that had sent me scurrying to the water's edge, and so the strange sight of that rotting old ocean liner was just that, a strange sight, nothing more. A fading remnant of a far brighter past, it sat there, dead in the water, like a warning I couldn't yet hear.

"Victor Carl," came a rich voice from within the cordon of the yellow tape. "Why am I not surprised when your name comes floating up in the middle of a god-awful mess? Let him in, Sal."

The cop with the crossed arms stepped aside.

Detective McDeiss, Homicide Division, was wearing a long black trench coat, a gray suit, a black porkpie hat tipped low. His large hands glowed strangely blue, covered as they were with latex gloves. He was a big man, broad shoulders, thick legs, the cheeks of one who savored his wines and preferred his sweetbreads rare.

"Thanks for coming out, Carl," he said. "The deceased's wallet is gone and there's no quick way to make an identification, but lucky us, he had your card in his back pants pocket."

"My card?"

"You sound surprised. You don't toss them to the multitudes?"

"Just to passing ambulances and old ladies who fall and can't get up." I took a deep breath to steady my nerves, smelt the coppery tang of spilt blood, suppressed a gag.

"You all right there, Carl?"

I wasn't, not at all, but I turned away from the covered thing on the ground and tried not to show it. "So let me get this right, Detective. You have a dead man, you don't know who he is, but he had my card, and you took a flyer on seeing if I could identify him."

"If it's not too much trouble."

"Can I stand back a bit when I do it?"

"Please. These are new shoes."

McDeiss laid a gloved hand on my shoulder and squeezed before stepping toward the lump of something covered by a blue tarp twenty yards away. The crowd surrounding it stepped back. At McDeiss's instruction a sharp white beam was focused on the tarp and the puddle.

McDeiss leaned down, grasped the edge of the blue sheet of plastic with his gloved hand, looked at me.

I swallowed and nodded and stepped back still farther as McDeiss lifted the corner of the tarp.

I caught a glimpse, that was all it took, even bleached by the bright white light it took only a glimpse of the face rising out of a thick puddle of dark blood, only a glimpse, and I knew without a doubt. A single bat swooped low, aiming for my head. I flinched and turned away.

Joey Cheaps.

CHAPTER

2

Joey Cheaps.

I was sitting in my office, hoping something lucrative would come along and save me from bankruptcy court, when Joseph Parma, Joey Cheaps as he was known in South Philly, phoned. This was that very morning, about ten-thirty, and I wanted to tell my secretary to take a message, but I didn't. What we needed just then was something lucrative and Joey Cheaps was not something lucrative. Joey Cheaps was the opposite of something lucrative. Joey Cheaps was a monetary black hole. When he entered a bank, the share price dropped ten percent. When he walked down the street, parking meters flashed red one after the other. Every time I so much as said his name I lost money. Joey Cheaps. There went five dollars. See? He was a client and he owed me money and that was the only reason I took his call, so I could tell him he owed me money. He knew he owed me money, he didn't need me to tell him he owed me money, and yet still I couldn't help myself. It was that sore tooth thing all over again.

"Joey," I said. "You owe me money."

"Yeah, I knows. I'm working on it. It was genius, what you pulled in court. I owe you."

"Yes, you do. You owe me thirty-five hundred dollars."

"Well, you know, Victor, some things you can't put a price on."

"But I can put a price on what I did for you, Joey. And you know what the price is? Thirty-five hundred dollars."

"Hey, you know me, Victor. I'm good for it."

"Yeah," I said. "I know you."

"Listen, Victor. I got something going on what's going to make me flush, going to take care of everything. But before I does anything I got a question, a legal question."

"Then you should find a lawyer."

"That's why I called you. Just do me the favor, all right, Victor? I'm asking as a friend."

"I'm not your friend."

"We're not no friends?"

"I was your lawyer, you were my client. And now you owe me money. That makes me your creditor."

"Victor, the way my life is now, the only friends I got is my creditors. Everyone else I owes too much money. But I'm thinking of coming clean. I'm thinking of paying what I owes and starting new. Right after this thing. And I got reason to. I found someone."

"Joey."

"Shut up."

"Joey in love. Who is she?"

"Shut up, it don't matter. But first we needs to talk, I needs to talk. To someone."

A line of desperation like an ominous riff of bass, rose from beneath the rough melody of his voice. I thought about it. I wanted to say no. My accountant, had he been in my office, would have insisted I say no. But there was that line of desperation in his voice that to a lawyer is as seductive as a purr. "What's it about, Joey?"

"I needs you to tell me, Victor, about that statue of limitations."

"Are we talking art or crime?"

"What do I know about art?"

"Considering your record, Joey, you don't know much about crime either. What you are asking about is the *statute* of limitations. The law doesn't want you running scared your whole life about something you might have done wrong years ago. If the prosecutor doesn't bring the case within a set amount of time, then he can't bring it at all."

"How long he got?"

"Depends on the crime."

"Let's say drugs or something?"

"Possession only? Two years."

"How about theft?"

"Simple theft? Same two."

"How about with a gun?"

"Robbery? Five."

"How about you beat some moke with a baseball bat?"

"Aggravated assault. Still five."

"And what if the moke you beat with the baseball bat goes ahead on his own and dies?"

"Joey."

"Just answer the question, Victor."

"There's no statute of limitations for murder."

"Shit."

"Yeah."

"But it was twenty years ago."

"It doesn't matter."

"Double shit. We needs to meet."

"How about Thursday?"

"How about now, Victor? La Vigna, you know it?"

"Yeah, I know it. But why the rush?"

"Now, Victor. Please. I'll pay you to show up."

"You'll pay me?" I said.

"I'm scared," he said. "I'm scared to death."

And he was, was Joey Cheaps, scared enough to offer to pay me, which for him was scared as hell, and I suppose, based on what I saw beneath the blue sheet of plastic, he had every right to be.

3

But that was the morning and now, in the deep of the night, I sat on a curb at the crime scene, about twenty yards from Joey Cheaps's corpse, and held my head in my hands. I held my head in my hands because it felt like it was breaking apart.

I had already given a full statement, identifying the victim, identifying myself as his lawyer, indicating I had seen him that very afternoon at a restaurant on Front Street. I told what I knew of his vital statistics, age, place of birth, rap sheet. And before I sat down on the curb I told the police where his mother lived. I could imagine the scene, the police detective stepping inside the dark house, the near blind woman offering coffee, offering cake, offering to heat up a piece of veal. The officer declining, asking the old woman to sit down, telling the old woman he has terrible terrible news. The way her face collapses as she learns the truth. If I had courage I would have done it myself, but I've never been accused of having courage.

"You look like a sick puppy" came McDeiss's voice from in front of me.

"He was a client," I said.

"Why don't you stand on up so we can talk some more."

"If I stand I'm going to puke."

"You keep on sitting, then." He hitched up the pant fabric at his knees and squatted beside me and I couldn't help but wince.

"Your knees sound like walnuts cracking in a vise."

"I've been younger, I admit it," said McDeiss.

We didn't get along so swell, McDeiss and I. We'd had a piece of business together in the past which had turned out poorly: a couple of dead bodies and a bad guy who in the end had gotten away. Still, I couldn't help but admire McDeiss. He was Ivy-educated but he didn't show it off, he was a righteous cop but he didn't preach, he was better at his job than I was at mine. And to top it off, he knew all the best restaurants.

"The first cops on the scene found your card on him," he said. "When the captain called out the case your name was prominently mentioned."

"And because of that you volunteered?"

"We picked straws. Mine was seriously short. Mine was the runt of the litter, the jockey of straws. So lucky me, here I am to interview you. This afternoon you were with this Parma at a restaurant?"

"That's right. La Vigna."

"When?"

"About eleven."

"What did you have?"

"The cheesecake."

"Ricotta?"

"Absolutely."

"Any good?"

"Not good enough that I want to taste it twice."

"When did you last see him?"

"It was about eleven-thirty when we left."

"You and Parma just met up for an early lunch?"

"Something like that."

"Simply a friendly chat?"

"Sure."

"What did you two boys chat about?"

"He was a client."

"You're claiming privilege," said McDeiss, nodding his head. "I have a great respect for constitutional privilege, yes I do. I would never do anything to trample on privilege." Pause for effect. "But your client is dead."

"It doesn't make a difference."

"Don't be a dickhead."

"Tell it to the Supreme Court."

"We already know they're dickheads. But, see, I'm a little puzzled with you claiming privilege. We checked his record. You had just gotten this Parma off the burglary rap, some sleazy trademark Victor Carl maneuver from what I understand. But Parma wasn't up on anything else. No pending charges, no parole violations. What I'm wondering is what kind of trouble was he in which required him to consult with his criminal defense attorney at eleven in the morning?"

I didn't answer, I just lifted my head out of my hands and stared at the detective.

"Anything that might have gotten him hurt?"

I said nothing.

"The killing was apparently done somewhere else, a knife through the throat, in a car maybe, and then he was dropped here. Forensics will check him for fibers, see if we can match a make and model. Wherever he was killed, there'll be a whole lot of blood. And it looks to us like he was beaten too. His eye, for example, was pretty busted up. How'd he look when you saw him?"

"His eye was busted up already when I met him."

"That you can tell me?"

"It's not privileged information. When you talk to the waiter at La Vigna, a guy named Louis, he'll tell you the same thing."

"But you won't tell me anything else?"

"Sorry."

"Because right now, Carl, we don't have a clue as to what actually happened here tonight. His wallet was missing so it could have been a robbery, but his Timex is still on his wrist and word is this Joey Parma never had anything worth stealing. So was this a mob execution? Was this drug-related? Was he stepping out with someone else's wife? Did he owe someone money? Anything you can tell us would be mighty handy."

"Joey was never part of the mob. A wannabe maybe, but that's it. And the drug conviction was well in his past. Best I could figure, he was trying to go clean. But his street name was Joey Cheaps, which means he owed everybody money."

"Anyone in particular?"

"Me."

"Oh, I bet he did. Anyone else? Anyone mad enough to extract it in blood."

"Not that I know of. But as to what we talked about, there is nothing more I can tell you."

"He's your client, Carl. Doesn't that matter?"

"Clients die, Detective. It happens all the time. Rich old ladies with wills to probate. Cancer-ridden smokers waiting on their suits against the tobacco companies. For criminal lawyers there are good ways to lose a client and bad ways to lose a client. A good way is for a client to die in his bed, surrounded by his family, receiving last rites from a priest. A bad way is for a client to be strapped on a gurney with a line in his arm, as the victim's mother stares stone-faced through the viewing window. I don't know why Joey was killed, but it wasn't the state that killed him, or a fellow con with a prison shiv, and so I figure this falls on the right side of my line."

"All righty then," said McDeiss without rising from his crouch. "I suppose then there's nothing more to be done."

"I suppose so."

"Thanks for all your assistance."

"It was nothing," I said. "You need any help getting up?"

"I'll manage."

We should have been through, I should have stood, kicked the curb, left, gone on with my life. I should have, yes, but that thing I had said about clients dying all the time, that whole cynically hard-boiled little speech, was an utter lie. They didn't die all the time, and when they did, I couldn't just shrug it off. So I didn't stand, kick the curb, and go on with my life. Instead, I said, "Before you go, Detective, I wonder if you could do me a favor."

"A favor. Is this related or unrelated to what happened to Mr. Parma?"

"Unrelated. I wonder if you could check your files to see if any unidentified floaters turned up about twenty years ago in the Delaware River. And maybe you could also see if you have a file on a missing man named Tommy, who disappeared twenty years ago and was never found."

"An unidentified floater and a missing person, name of Tommy."

"Or Thomas. Or Tom."

"Twenty years ago."

"Approximately."

"And this is unrelated to your friend Parma."

"Unrelated."

"But you just happen to ask me this favor after your friend Parma meets with his criminal defense attorney for no apparent reason and then gets dumped between two rusting shipping containers with his throat slit and his blood flowing into the Delaware."

"Just happenstance."

"And I should do this why?"

"Because I'm a sweet guy."

"You make it hard to want to help you, Carl."

"Nothing worthwhile is ever easy."

We stayed at the curb, me sitting, my head still in my hands, the nausea turning the edges of my vision pale, McDeiss still in his squat. We stayed there for a while until McDeiss said, "Know what I got a strange hankering for right now? Ossobuco. You ever had a great ossobuco?"

"Do you mind? I can still smell the blood."

"Veal shank braised in a wine sauce till it melts at the touch. And then, at the last moment, the secret ingredient is added, the *gremolata,* minced garlic, chopped parsley, and a dash of lemon zest. There's a place on Seventh that makes a killer ossobuco."

"Perfect for a homicide detective, I suppose."

"I'll consider if the information you sought is worth pursuing."

"That's all I can ask." I paused for a moment, thought about what he had just said. "And maybe," I continued, as if struck with a plan out of the thin of the air, "if you find something, we can discuss it over dinner."

"What a wonderful idea."

"There's a place on Seventh Street I've been told about."

"Sounds intriguing."

"A little expensive, I'm sure."

"Yes it is," he said, letting out a soft groan as his knees popped once again and he stood. "But worth every penny."

"You'll keep me informed of what you find about Joey?"

"Why?"

"Professional interest."

"Don't worry, Carl, one thing you can be sure of is that you'll be hearing from me."

By the time I left the scene the coroner's van had shown up, the body had been scraped off the tarmac, the arc lights taken down. The immediate scene had slipped back into the innocent darkness, but there was still the stain on the ground, still the remnants of what had been lying there not thirty minutes before. There wasn't anything more I could do about Joey Parma's legal problem—it's amazing how quickly death cleanses the docket—but that didn't mean he and I were through.

CHAPTER

4

When I came home from the crime scene I
sat on the couch in my living room, too weary and sick at
heart to even take off my jacket or loosen my tie. I sat in
the dark, and listened to my breathing, and felt a bleak
hopelessness fall about my shoulders like an old familiar
cloak.

My legal practice was failing for want of paying clients
and my partner was thinking of bolting to greener pastures.
My last love affair had ended badly, to say the least. I had
been summoned to Traffic Court for a myriad of moving
violations that were really, really not my fault. My mother,
to whom I hadn't spoken in a number of years, was drinking her life away in Arizona. My father was deathly ill,
awaiting the operation that would prolong, but not save, his
life. And worst of all, my cable had been cut off because I
had fallen behind on my bill.

And now Joey Parma had come to me for legal advice
and had ended up dead. We had met at La Vigna, at a table
in the back. His eye had been swollen, his hands had been
sweaty. And at that back table, just hours before his death,
Joey Cheaps had given me something. It was something I
didn't want, something I had no use for, but he had given
it to me all the same. He had given me a murder.

"This was twenty years ago," said Joey Parma. He

leaned forward, his voice was soft, he spoke out of the side of his mouth to ensure privacy. "An old buddy brought me in, told me to bring a bat, sos I did. Nothing was supposed to happen. Just a little rough-up, is all. Three hundred for a rough-up. Some guy. Tommy something. I never knowed beyond that. He was coming to a pier on the river with a suitcase. There was supposed to be a boat or something waiting. But before he got to the boat we was supposed to take the suitcase. We was supposed to take the suitcase and teach the guy a lesson at the same time.

"It was dark, deserted, cold as shit. The lights on the pier was out, but the moon was this bright thing in the sky. We was standing in the shadows, smoking, we was waiting, see? And the bat cold as it was in my fist, and the chill seeping through our jackets. Little leather jackets, like Travolta in that movie, that's what we all was wearing then. And so we was waiting and then we was waiting and then the guy I'm with, he stamps out his cig and says, 'There's the bastard, right on time.' And I look up, and there he is all right.

"Just a shadow. Coming closer. And when he gets close enough, with that crazy moon glowing down on him, we get a pretty good look-see. He's about our age, tall and lanky, his hair a mop of black that falls over his eyes. He wears jeans and a black turtleneck, he carries the suitcase. It's a hard shell Samsonite thing like they had back then, and the light of the moon, dying on his dark clothes and hair, catches the shiny surface of the suitcase so that it sort of glows on its own. We can tells that it's heavy, it pulls down his right shoulder so the whole angle of him is tilted, as he walks toward us.

"And then he senses something wrong. He stops, turns, calls out, something like 'Johnny' it was, and he calls it out again, but he gets no answer. When he turns around again we done stepped out of the shadows.

"There's a moment when he figures out what is happening and then the strangest thing. You'd think he'd run, or come out swinging, or something. I was worried that maybe he'd be carrying and me, all I had was that stupid bat. But there's this little smile comes on his face and he starts talking to us, you know, being all friendly. 'How you guys doing? Nice night, isn't it? Think we can work something out?' Like he's charming us, like he's going to talk us out of it. But he's not, is he? The other guy, he says to me, 'Shut 'im up, Cheaps.'

" 'Shut 'im up, Cheaps.' And sos that's what I tries to do. One-handed is all, I don't mean to hurt him much, I want to get him in the arm, shake him up. I bring the bat back with one hand and give it a swing. And I get him in the arm and he starts cursing at me and he swings that suitcase at me and he slams me, he slams me. He gets me on the shoulder and it hurts, and I get pissed at this little pissant and I want to shut him up. Sos I grab the bat with my other hand and I take it back and I was never much with a bat and sos I figure I better put some oomph into it. And so I does.

"And he ducks, and it's like he ducks right into it.

"In Little League I couldn't hit a basketball with a rake, but this time, with this swing, I get him flush on the face and something gives, I feel it, and down he goes, as if a string keeping him up had been cut, down he goes, like a magic trick. Except it isn't magic, is it? I give the bat a swing and it smacks up against his head and the string is cut and he's on the ground and there's blood, shit. And then we see, see that, see that he's, that he's . . ."

"Say it," I said.

"Fuck you, Victor."

"You sure?"

"No doubt about it. Blood everywhere."

"What happened to the body?"

"Splash, man, if you get the picture. Hey, don't look at me like that. I been sick about it every day from the time it happened. It wasn't supposed to be like it turned out. We was just supposed to take the suitcase from him, is all."

"What was inside it?"

"I wasn't supposed to know, we wasn't supposed to open it. But we did, didn't we? His keys was in his pockets, we was supposed to get them too, and so when we found them we opened the thing."

"And?"

"Loaded to the gills."

"With what?"

"Cash."

"Joey."

"And it was heavy, too."

"What was this guy doing with all that cash?"

"Who knows? But he wasn't up to no good, that's for sure. Just the way he tried to charm us, the bastard, you could tell he was into something and thought he knew how to handle himself. Son of a bitch, if he just hadn't of ducked."

"What happened to the suitcase?"

"We was supposed to hand it up to the guy what hired us. But you see all that sitting in front of your face, what are you going to do? We'd been taking all the risks, and all for a measly three hundred each. Shit, Victor. The two of us what had done the thing loaded up our pockets, our crotches, our shirts, just stuffed in as much as we could. We ended with about ten grand apiece and you couldn't really tell there was nothing missing, it was still that full. Then we locked it up again, and the guy what brought me in, he lugged it away."

"Who was he?"

"Just someone. I don't want to say. We go back."

"To get out of this, you might have to tell his name to the DA."

Joey shrugged.

"And this guy, he lugged the suitcase to where?"

"Don't know. That was the job, to take the suitcase and deliver it on up. But the guy I was with said it would have to be buried after what I done with the baseball bat. That was twenty years ago and for twenty years there's been silence. Until now."

I leaned forward. "Tell me."

"Last night. Late. They came around asking me about it, demanding answers, wanting to know who else was involved. They knew about the pier, they knew about this Tommy that we offed. And, Victor, they was looking for the suitcase. Two men, a sour face with a Brit accent what did all the talking, and some other, shiny-faced freak who stood stiffly with a cigarette in his fist and said nothing, not a freaking word."

"What did you tell them?"

"Nothing. They wanted the name, too, but I gave them nothing. That's why I got this decoration round my eye. But I always been stand-up, Victor. You know that."

"Sure. Stand-up. So how'd they know about you?"

"I don't know. I don't know. But I'll tell you this, ever since it happened I ain't said a word about it to no one. No one, understand? I ain't like one of those peacocks strutting around, proud of who they offed. It made me sick, the whole thing. I look back, whatever I turned out it wasn't what I was intending. You think I planned what I became. You think I planned three jolts in the joint. I was young, I didn't know what I wanted. But after that, I couldn't want nothing decent, you know? All I was fit for was what I ended up doing, small-time nothings with the occasional spectacular screw-up. But I thought this thing what happened was long over. I thought I was past it. And then, twenty years later they're looking for the suitcase? What the hell's that all about, Victor?"

I didn't have an answer for him then—my advice had been to make a deal, to give the story and the name of his old pal to the DA, to pay the price and put the thing behind him, a suggestion he said he'd have to think about but that I figured he'd ignore—and I didn't have an answer for him now, but I would find one, yes I would. On the last day of his life, Joey Parma had given me a sordid piece of his sordid past, and now that his throat had been slashed I couldn't just give it back.

Joey Cheaps might have been a sad sack no-account who still owed me my fee, but he was a client. That means something, to be a client. It means he gets my loyalty, whether he deserves it or not. It means he gets my absolute best for the price of an hourly fee. It means in a world where every person has turned against him there is one person who will fight by his side for as long as there is a battle to be fought. And the final battle, far as I could see, was just beginning. So, I couldn't just ignore what had happened, I couldn't just ignore that my client was dead, that his killer was free, that his past had risen to swallow him whole. My life was imploding in on itself like the fizzling core of an atomic bomb, but a client was dead and something had to be done. Yes, something would have to be done.

But first things first.

CHAPTER 5

"You want some veal, Victor?"

"No, ma'am," I lied. "I'm fine, thank you."

"I made it last night. The whole family came. But I prepared too much. I have it left over. I will just have to throw away."

"All right then," I said. "If you're just going to throw it away."

"Good. Sit. And some baked rigatoni? And a sausage? You want me fry a sausage?"

"No, thank you, Mrs. Parma."

"Are you sure? No trouble."

"Well, if it's no trouble."

"Sit. You'll eat and then we'll talk. Like civilized people. Sit."

I sat. It was no use arguing with Joey Parma's mother when she decided you needed to be fed. You would eat and you would enjoy.

Mrs. Parma's house was dark, the curtains drawn, the lights low. I could barely see my way into the kitchen to the little Formica table to the side, but Mrs. Parma, in a long housecoat and slippers, bustled about her territory with an assuredness born of long practice despite her failing sight. When she opened the refrigerator and bent down to feel for the platter of veal, the light illuminated the lines on her cheek, her lean prowlike nose, the dark circles beneath her eyes, the stoic tragedy of a woman who lost her son years ago and had just now gotten around to burying him.

She hummed as she cooked, pouring olive oil into the pan, dropping in breaded pieces of veal that sizzled with excitement, placing a square of baked rigatoni in the oven, slicing a sausage and adding it to the pan. She took fresh greens from the crisper, brought them to her nose and then held them gently in her gnarled fingers as she sliced the greens roughly, chopped the garlic, fried it all up together before splitting a lemon and reaming it over everything. It filled the kitchen, the smell of meat and garlic, the spices, the sizzle of oil, the delicious clatter of her knives and pans and dishes, the sound of her soft humming.

"You want maybe wine with your veal, Victor?"

"No, ma'am, that won't be necessary."

"I have a bottle already open."

"Will you join me?"

"I'm not hungry. Who can eat after all these years? But I'll have some wine, if you don't mind."

"Mrs. Parma, it would be a treat to share some wine with you."

She reached into a cabinet, pulled out two plain water glasses, filled them with a dark Chianti. She lifted her glass. "To my Joey," she said.

"To Joey."

She took a drink and seemed to slump for a moment, the outline of her body beneath the housecoat sagging before she recovered, pressed a hand to her forehead, returned to the stove.

"Mange," she said as she put the plates in front of me.

I manged.

She sat with her third glass of wine, leaning on an

elbow, as I put the empty plates in the sink, rolled up my sleeves, turned on the faucet.

"I'll take care that, Victor."

"No, you won't," I said. I filled the sink with water and soap, scrubbed the plates and pans clean, rinsed, left everything on the rack. I cleaned the counters with a sponge, I put away the garlic and oil, the salt. As I worked, she sat heavily at the table. She was a small woman, short and thin, weighed maybe ninety pounds, and still, to see her at that table was to see the force of gravity work on some huge awful weight.

"My Joey was an altar boy, Victor. Did you know that?"

"No, ma'am," I said, drying my hands on a dish towel.

"In his little white robe, with the other boys, swinging the incense. Oh, he was angel. Sweet as marzipan. I have picture, do you want to see?"

"Yes."

She started to rise, sighed, and sagged back into her chair. "One moment, please." She took a sip of her wine. "He was good boy. In his heart. But that don't matter much in this world. It wasn't easy being Joey Junior. Joey Senior was a man, my God, Victor, yes he was. Just the stench of him, coming home after a hot day wrestling with the meat, it made my head swim. Did you know him?"

"No, ma'am."

"Let me tell you, it was no easy thing being his wife. It was harder being his son. You needed to be smarter and stronger to survive him. I was. Look at me, the size I am, he was twice as big as me, and still I was stronger than him every day of his life. But Joey wasn't. My little Joey. Forever trying to prove himself and proving nothing. Though always sweet, Mr. Carl. Always. Did you see how they came out for the viewing?"

"Yes, ma'am."

"Lined up around the block. Such a crowd. They came out of respect for Joey Senior, and they came for me maybe, but they was also there for my baby. People loved him. He could have taken the shop, turned it into something for himself. Politics maybe. But that would have meant standing behind his father six days a week. So he became something else, even if what he became was crap. One day it was like a switch was turned, first he was just a sweet kid, and then he was ruined. Sad, desperate, stupid. Not a good combination. But as a boy, such a face on him."

She put her hands to her eyes as if to cover her sorrow. A thick golden ring shone on her forefinger, with a diamond chip in the center.

"That's a beautiful ring, Mrs. Parma," I said.

Her face lifted. She smiled as she bent her hand toward me, like a young woman showing off an engagement diamond. "Pretty, yes. You like? I wear it all the time. To me it is special. Joey gave to me years ago. A birthday gift."

"May I see it?"

"Of course," she said as she twisted the oversized ring off her finger. "He could be so sweet. He was an altar boy, did you know that? In his little white robe. I have picture. Do you want to see picture?"

"Yes, ma'am."

She pushed herself up from the table, successfully this time, and rubbed her back as she left the kitchen.

While she was gone, I examined the ring. It was heavy, it felt solid, masculine. I nipped the bottom with my teeth and left a small mark. Nice. On the inside were the initials TG. I tossed it in my hand and then placed it gently on the center of the table.

When Mrs. Parma returned to the kitchen a few moments later she was carrying a picture in a frame. Three boys in white robes, young boys, eight or nine, posed in front of a church, butcher boy cuts with bangs hanging down. The boy on the right was chubby, happy, with a smile that could melt butter. Joey? Was Joey ever that happy? He was leaning against the boy in the middle, a broad, sturdy lad with a fierce smile and dark eyes. To the left was a tall thin boy, standing apart from the other two.

"Such a face," said Mrs. Parma, sitting back at the table, twisting her ring back on. "If only he could have stayed like that. But boys grow up and disappoint, every one. That is the way of it. Even you, Victor. Is your mother proud? Truly, in her heart? Joey Senior was just a boy himself when I first set eyes on him. Striding down the street in his uniform. Who could tell what was inside of him?"

"I wanted to again say how sorry I am for your loss."

"I know you are. You took care of him that last time, when he told me he was falsely accused. My Joey, always a bad liar, but he couldn't help himself. He was allergic to the truth. But things were turning around for him, so he said."

"Is that what he said?"

"That night, before he went out. He said he had a plan would turn things around for him."

"Did he tell you what the plan was all about?"

"No. Never. My Joey never told me a thing. In fact, the policeman who came, he asked the very same thing. The black man with the Irish name."

"Scottish name," I said. "McDeiss."

"That's it, yes. I made him some veal. A man his size, he eats a lot of veal. He asked about you as much as he asked about Joey. But I knew nothing about Joey's business. I knew enough to know not to know. He was my son, Victor, my boy, and I loved him like he was still my little Joey, but I knew what he was. And for that they killed him dead?"

"Who's they?"

"Who knows? I don't. But he was never very smart with money."

"Joey told me he had a girlfriend."

"That's a lie. Not my Joey. He was never one for the girls, had no handle on them. Not like his father, who knew how to have his way. For my little Joey there was only me." She twisted the ring on her finger. "I was his girl."

"Do you know why he was going out the night he died?"

"He was going out, that's all he said. Over to Jimmy T's, that craphole, like his father before him. I used to send him there to bring his father home. He hated when I did that. His father would smack him each time. Never went on his own when his father was still living. But after, it became his place. Your mind can go crazy trying to figure it out. Jimmy T's and that Lloyd Ganz, who was stealing from us every day of his life." She spit between her fingers. "Whatever money Joey Senior earned, he took half of it, the thief. One hand is all you need to steal. Joey knew I'd never call there, so he gave me another number to call if I needed him."

"What number?"

"He had a number where he could be reached if I needed him. I was to leave a message and then he would get back to me. Made me memorize in case something happened with my heart like the last time."

She recited it to me. I took out a piece of paper and had her recite it again.

She sighed, took a sip from her wine. "Tell me, Victor, what kind of trouble was my Joey in this time?"

"It was about something he did long ago, that's all I know."

"Is that why he was killed?"

"I don't know, Mrs. Parma. I don't know why he was killed. He might simply have been in the wrong place at the wrong time."

"Joey was always in the wrong place at the wrong time, but that's no reason to be dead, is it?"

"No, ma'am."

She picked up the framed picture of the three altar boys. "Take this."

"No, Mrs. Parma. I can't."

"Take this. You remember him." She jammed the framed photograph into my hands. "Take. Look. They killed the boy too, not just the man. Everything he ever was, it fell to the ground with the blood. The man, to be truthful, wasn't worth much, even I'll admit that, but the boy. Like marzipan. He would run from his father, snuggle on my lap, bury his head in my neck. The warmth of his tears, his sweet tears. You do me favor, Victor?"

"Anything." ·

"Find out what happened to my boy."

"I don't know if I can, Mrs. Parma. The police—"

"I don't want to hear about police. What have police ever done for my Joey? You done, you the only one. You find out what happened to my boy. You."

"I'll try."

"Good. And when you find who did it, you let me know, okay?"

"I will."

"You let me know and I take care of it. Like I took care of Joey Senior. Just get me the name, Victor. My knives are sharp. Whoever it is I'll cut off his balls, slice them thick, fry them with garlic, feed them to the rats."

"Mrs. Parma."

"I shock you, maybe, Victor? He was my boy. You know what is vendetta?"

"Yes, I do. But—"

"What is wrong, Victor? You think I'm not entitled?"

"Of course you are entitled. And no, Mrs. Parma, you don't shock me. It is just that I think we can do better than feeding the rats."

"What are you saying, Victor?"

I reached into my jacket pocket, pulled out an envelope. "Have you ever seen, Mrs. Parma, a contingency fee agreement?"

CHAPTER
6

I didn't know what it was about hospitals that pressed their weight upon me with a physical force the minute I entered one, whether it was the information lady with her perky smile, the doctors walking casually among desolation and death, the smell, the stuffy framed portraits of long-vanished healers, the sick, the really, really sick, the smell. Did I mention the smell? You know what I mean, eau de mortality, a fragrant mixture of rubbing alcohol, ammonia, green beans, false cheeriness, false hope, urine and sweat and lime green Jell-O. Whatever it was, I had the usual mordant sensation as I walked into the lobby of Temple University Hospital smack in the middle of North Philadelphia. Or maybe it was the fact that my father was on the fourth floor. Any building that housed my father, whether the decaying little bungalow in which I was raised or the sprawling multilevel inner-city hospital in which he now lay, had the same effect on me, something akin to dropping down down in the deep sea and feeling my chest compress from the weight.

He had collapsed on the steps of his home away from home, the grand and glorious Hollywood Tavern, in his sad suburban enclave of Hollywood, Pennsylvania. There was blood coming out of his mouth and his breath was wet, and in the ambulance they had enthusiastically pumped him

full of drugs. By some miracle he had survived the trauma
of the ambulance and, when he had been stabilized at Holy
Redeemer Hospital, he had been transferred to Temple.
The religious symbolism was deliciously inapt, but Temple
was the only hospital in the area that performed the delicate yet brutal surgery his condition required. Now they
were treating the pneumonia that had invaded his lungs and
were waiting for him to gain enough strength so they could
open up his chest and kill him proper.

"Hi, Dad," I said with as much pep as I could muster.

"You're back," he said, matching my pep with his normal tone of bitter resignation. "You was just here. What, is
your cable out?"

"Don't be silly. I came to see you. But I do seem to remember the Sixers might be playing Orlando tonight. Do
you want me to put it on?"

"What for? I seen enough gunners in the damn army to
last me, I don't need to see that Iverson bum."

"He's good. I like watching him play."

He waved his hand in disgust. He could barely move,
my father, lying on his bed, his face gray and drawn and
unshaven, only sixty years old but looking like he'd already been buried twice as long. A clip bit into a finger of
his waving hand, reading the oxygen level in his blood,
now a paltry ninety-three percent. He barely had enough
energy to breathe, sure, but he was never without enough
energy to give the world a dismissive shove. "I seen
Chamberlain play. Greer. Cunningham coming off the
bench. After what I seen, he's nothing."

"So how are you doing?"

"I'm dying, how do you think I'm doing?"

"You're not dying."

"Yes I am, and it's not such a bad thing neither. At least
I earned it. I didn't earn much in my life, but I earned this."

I took off my coat, sat down beside his bed. "Nice to see you in a good mood for a change. What's going on?"

"What the hell do you think is going on? I lie here and they stick things in me. Bloodsuckers, is what they are."

"And you, of course, are being your normal, personable self."

"You try smiling as they play voodoo with your body. If the sickness doesn't kill me, they'll do it themselves."

I smiled indulgently. "Why so cheerful this evening?"

"They got this thing up my dick."

"To help you pee."

"Sixty years I didn't need no help."

"Want me to adjust it for you?"

"Stay the hell away from me, you bastard," said my father. "So there's that. And, I don't know, I been thinking about things."

"Oh, Dad, don't do that," I said. "That's the wrong thing to do. Especially here. No good can come from it. We've both made it this far precisely by not thinking of things."

"And look where we are." He tried to shift in the bed, struggled to take a breath. His face enlivened brightly with pain. "Hell," he said.

"Why don't I turn on the game?"

"I been thinking about things," he said. "I been thinking about . . . things."

"The Sixers?"

"A girl."

"Should I turn it on?"

"A pleated skirt."

"Ah yes, pleated skirts. I've always liked them myself. Very flattering to the hips."

"I need to tell you."

"Sure, Dad. That's fine. But how are you feeling? It looks like you're in pain. Are you?"

"What do you think? Whenever I breathe. I haven't slept in days."

I jumped up. "Let me find a doctor." Before he could reply, I was out the door.

"My father's in a bit of agony," I told the nurse behind the desk. "You think he could be given something to ease it for a time, maybe let him sleep." The nurse told me to wait a moment as she went off to find the intern, and I stood dutifully at the nurses' desk, playing the part of the dutiful son, glancing uneasily at the door to my father's room, just down the hall.

I didn't want to hear that he had been thinking of things, my father. I didn't want to hear what he was thinking about. And I really really really didn't want to hear about the girl in the pleated skirt that had suddenly popped into his consciousness as he stared unblinking at his own mortality. The girl who got away, the girl who broke his heart, the girl, that girl, the girl, the one. It was all too sad and ordinary. It didn't take much to imagine it all in one sad swoop. The shy glances, the sweet romance, and then the cheating, his or hers, it didn't matter, the cheating and the recriminations, and then the breakup that left him sad and wounded, that left him weak and unguarded, like a boxer ready to fall into an exhausted embrace with the first girl who came along, even someone totally unsuited to him, even someone certifiable, someone like, well, like my mother, from which all his ruin and misery had come, including his only begotten son. No, I didn't want to hear how with the girl in the pleated skirt everything would have been different, how with the girl in the pleated skirt life would have been more than a sad burden to be shouldered through to death. Because it wouldn't have been different, my dad's life, and we both knew it. My father was someone who trudged through life while others floated, a man who set a course of low expectations for himself and then mercilessly failed to meet them, a man who chose bitterness and anger because they just came naturally, dammit, and what do you know anyway, you little bastard.

"Are you Mr. Carl's son?"

I pulled myself out of my self-absorption to see a set of scrubs and a chart and a woman wearing and holding them both. She was young and thin and her eyes, though tired, were very blue. And she was a doctor, Dr. Hellmann.

"Like the mayonnaise," I said.

She smiled thinly as if she hadn't heard that more than a thousand times before and then went right to the chart. "You said your father has been in acute distress, is that right?"

"Yes."

"We don't give opiates to COPDers."

"Excuse me?"

"Chronic obstructive pulmonary disease. It's what your father has, it's why he's here. But there is something maybe I can prescribe to ease his pleuritic pain. It won't put him to sleep, but it will let him sleep if the pain is keeping him up. I'll need to talk to him first."

"Sure," I said as I followed her down the hall. "How's he doing?"

"We're waiting for the antibiotic to work."

"Maybe you should pump in some Iron City. That's his usual medication of choice."

She looked at me with her eyes narrowed. "Is that a joke?"

"Yes," I said.

"Try harder next time."

"How long have you been on duty?" I asked.

"Thirty so far."

"Maybe after thirty hours nothing is funny."

"Maybe," she said, as we reached my father's door, "but I couldn't stop laughing at the evening news. That Peter Jennings, he was just cracking me up. You, on the other hand . . ." She gave me a jolt of her baby blues as she backed into the room. "Wait here."

I waited. She spoke to my father for a long while and came out, writing on the chart. "The nurse will be back in a moment with the Toradol," she said. With a toss of her hair, she walked toward the desk without giving me another glance. Hellmann, Dr. Hellmann. Like the mayonnaise.

I stuck my head in my father's room. "Good news, the nurse is going to bring you something for the pain."

"It won't do nothing," he said. "Whatever they give me, it won't work. Nothing works. It's just something else to charge the insurance company."

"I'm going down to the cafeteria to get a bite. You want anything?"

"Get me a beer."

"I tried," I said, "but the cute doctor said no way."

"She ain't that cute."

"Remember old Doc Schaefer you took me to when I was a kid?"

"With the nose hair and the mole?"

"Well, she's cuter than him. I'll be right back."

I went down to the cafeteria, bought a cup of coffee, a soggy egg salad sandwich, a bag of chips. I sat down at a table and had my dinner. I took my time, I was in no hurry. I chewed the egg salad very carefully. I ate the chips one at a time instead of in handfuls. I spent a long while deciding on which color Jell-O for dessert.

When I slipped back into my father's room, he was lying peacefully, asleep, his wet breaths rising and falling softly like the waves of a distant ocean. I spoke to him and he didn't respond, but I didn't want to leave him just yet. I turned on the television. The Sixers' game was in the third quarter, they were up by three. It looked to be a pretty good game, a game I couldn't get on my currently cable-free TV. I sat back in the chair, propped my foot on my father's bed, watched the telly, wondered when Dr. Hellmann might check back in so I could flirt a little more.

It was turning out to be a rather nice visit with the game on and my father asleep and Mrs. Parma's signed contingency fee agreement in my briefcase. It had worked out just as I had hoped when I went to the nursing station to complain of his pain because I didn't, I didn't, I didn't want to hear his story about the girl in the pleated skirt. There are some things a son just doesn't want to hear from his father, and his story of the girl who got away was, I was sure, just such a thing.

And I was right, yes I was, right at least about it being a story I didn't want to hear. But I was wrong when I thought I had dodged it, because my father, for some perverse reason of his own, which I was only to discover much later on, was determined that I hear it, every damn breath of it, and I would, yes, yes I would.

And in its own peculiar way, his story told me everything I needed to know about the plague that had reached out to kill Joey Parma, the plague of slavery to the past that had doomed Joey's life, and maimed my own life as well.

CHAPTER

7

"**What are we** supposed to do with this?" said Beth Derringer, from behind her neatly organized desk, holding the Parma contingency fee agreement in front of her like a floppy piece of moldy bologna. We were having a firm meeting, which meant that I had strolled into her office, the two of us comprising the whole of the less than prosperous law firm of Derringer and Carl.

"Investigate," I said. "Isn't that the first part of our three-part motto? Investigate, sue the bastards, collect gobs of money. I wonder what that would be in Latin. *Vidi, vici,* contingency fee?"

"Did you get a retainer?"

"Mrs. Parma is seventy-something, she can barely see, she lives off her husband's Social Security. How was I going to ask for a retainer?"

"Victor," said Beth, shaking her head, "we need money."

"Who doesn't?" I said.

"But we need it now. Immediately. We need money or it's over. The rent is long past due, Ellie has been two weeks without pay. I just got off the phone with the bank and they won't extend our line. We're in trouble."

"Let's go out and get a drink."

"This is serious."

"That's why I want to go out and get a drink."

"Victor, you're avoiding."

"Of course I'm avoiding. What sane person wouldn't avoid what I'm avoiding. I don't have enough money. I'm not getting laid. I have a glove compartment full of traffic tickets and a date in Traffic Court, where I'll most likely be stripped of my license. I'm stuck every night or so visiting my father in the hospital and watching him die. And did I mention they shut off my cable? How is it possible to lead a meaningful life, I ask you, without the Golf Channel?"

She looked at me with almost pity in her eyes.

"Yes, it's true," I said. "No Golf Channel."

"How is he?"

"Who?"

"Your father."

"They want to slice him open and chop up his lungs. But I'd rather talk about business. What about our accounts receivable?"

"The accounts receivable, I'm happy to say, grow by the hour. But receivables don't pay the rent. Guy Forrest still owes us for his murder trial. Why don't you give him another call?"

"He can't be reached. Whatever he had he sold and put in a trust for his kids. He says he'll pay us when he can, but who knows when that will be. Now he's hit the road. Bali. Tibet. Off to find himself."

"Wow," said Beth, spinning in her chair. "That sounds nice." She took a moment to imagine herself walking through an exotic marketplace, bargaining over batik, or hiking high into the Himalayas.

Beth was more than my partner, she was my best friend, and I loved practicing law with her, but our long-term goals were quite dissimilar. I had a fierce ambition to succeed and prosper and rise, which made our struggles all the

more despairing for me. But Beth, Beth always had the attitude that she was just passing through. She didn't seem to
have long-term goals. She saw the legal profession as a
helping profession, God help her, and was pleased to be of
some use. But she could also see herself trying something
else, going somewhere new, dedicating herself to some
other life. She sometimes mused about the Peace Corps.
Really, she did, which, like, boggled my mind. I mean, my
life had turned bleak because my cable had been cut off.
Cold showers, long hours, no golf on TV, porridgy gluck
masquerading as dinner? Philadelphia was too tough for
me, how would I handle the Peace Corps? But she was
right, I was avoiding, avoiding the whole precarious perch
of our practice. For her, bankruptcy would have meant a
new beginning, which I think she secretly found attractive.
For me, the idea of bankruptcy was too brutal to even con-
template. If I wasn't a lawyer, what was I? It would take
some deep soul searching to figure that out and, frankly, I
firmly believed my soul, like certain biohazard properties,
was better left unsearched.

"Are you ever tempted," she said, "just to go off and
find yourself?"

"God no. I might succeed."

"Yes, that would be frightening. And isn't it weird to
think that you might be somewhere out there to be found.
Can you imagine the poor sap who goes off on a walkabout
to find himself, climbs the highest peaks, the widest val-
leys, and when he gets to the final spot what he finds, instead of himself, is you?"

"We were talking about accounts receivable," I said
drily.

"I suppose we should cross Joseph Parma and his thirty-
five hundred dollars off the list."

"He was never good for it anyway."

"So why'd you take the case?"

"He needed someone. But don't put it all on me," I said. "You brought in Rashard Porter."

"Yes, that," she said, nodding her head. "I know his mother, she's a wonder, and he's basically a good kid. But I got a retainer for that."

"Three hundred dollars, which didn't cover the arraignment."

"She's a single mother paying half her salary in rent. The three hundred itself was a struggle for her."

"His suppression hearing is day after tomorrow."

"How's it look?"

"Not good. The joint they found lying next to him on the front seat was the size of a small dog. Mr. Magoo would have seen that spliff from across the street. But I have a plan."

She sighed, turned again to look out the window, saw, I was certain, not the grimy strip of Twenty-first Street visible from her office but the great Plateau of Tibet at the base of the Himalayas.

"Without some paying clients," she said, "we're not going to survive through the summer."

"Oh come on. We'll make it, we always do."

"Struggling to pay the rent was charming when we were first out of law school," she said, "but it's getting old."

"Don't go south on me, Beth. I have a hunch about the Parma case. I think there is money here."

"You always think there's money here, but it always ends up being there, not here. What was Joey's nickname, Victor?"

"Joey Cheaps."

"And he died owing us thirty-five hundred dollars. What makes you think a man whose life was so devoid of value he earned the moniker 'Cheaps' could suddenly become a cash cow in his death?"

"It's that image from his story, the one I can't seem to shake. A moonlit night on the waterfront. A man lies dead. Joey Parma holds a bloody baseball bat in his hand. And in the distance, Joey's partner in crime is walking away with a suitcase full of cash."

"Victor, wise up. The suitcase is empty. The money's long gone. Cash gets spent, that's the beauty of cash."

"Maybe, but twenty years pass and then two goons show up, beat the hell out of Joey, and then start asking about the suitcase? That same suitcase? Joey was scared out of his wits, scared enough to call me, and then twelve hours later he's dead. There's a connection here between Joey's death and that suitcase. I think it's still around, I think it's still in play. You find that suitcase, you find a murderer, Beth. A murderer with a pile of money."

"And how do we do that?"

"McDeiss is looking into Joey's homicide, but we know things he doesn't know, things we're not allowed to tell him. Maybe we should do what we can to help his investigation. Twelve hours passed from the time I met with Joey at La Vigna to the time of his murder. If we can suss out those twelve hours, we'll be far on the road to finding our killer. We know Joey saw his mother in the afternoon. And we know he was one other place for sure."

"Where?"

"Let's go out for a drink. Let's you and I step out for a drink at Jimmy T's."

CHAPTER

8

They say Philly is a city of neighborhoods,
but it's really a city of neighborhood taps. There they sit,
one on every corner, with the same hanging sign, the same
glass block windows, the same softball trophies, the same
loyalty among their denizens. When you're a Philly guy
you can count your crucial affiliations on the fingers of one
hand; you got your mom, you got your church, you got
your string band, you got your saloon, you got your wife,
and the only thing you ever think of changing is your wife.

Jimmy T's was just such a neighborhood joint. When
Beth and I stepped inside we were immediately eyed, and
for good reason. We were strangers, we were wearing
suits, we had all our teeth.

The dank, narrow bar was decorated like a VFW hall,
Flyers pictures taped to bare walls, cheap Formica tables,
a pool table wedged into the back, a jukebox in the corner
with its clear plastic cover smashed. Someone had made an
unwise selection, maybe something not sung by Sinatra.
Workingmen of all ages slumped at the bar, leaned on the
tables, wiped their noses, sucked down beers, complained
about politics, the economy, the Eagles, the cheese steaks
at Geno's, the riffraff moving in from the west, their girlfriends, their wives, their kids, their lives, their goddamned
lives. Before we stepped in, it had been sullenly loud, but

the moment we opened the door it had quieted as if for a show. It didn't take long to realize we were it. I figured we might as well make it a good one.

"You sure yous are in the right place?" said the bartender, a crag of a man with a great head of white hair and a missing arm. The thief, Lloyd Ganz, I presumed.

"We're in the right place," I said. "I'll have a sea breeze."

Ganz blinked at me. "Say what?"

"A sea breeze. It's a drink."

"Hey, Charlie," said Ganz without looking away, "guy in the suit says he wants something called a sea breeze."

A slim-jim at the end of the bar, long, brown, and desiccated, said in a rasp, "Tell him to drive his ass on down to Wildwood, face east, open his mouth."

I turned away from the derisive laughter swelling behind me. "You don't know how to make a sea breeze?"

"Are you really sure yous in the right place? We don't got no ferns here."

"Careful," I said. "My mother's name is Fern."

"Really?"

"No, not really. Do you have grapefruit juice?"

"It's late for breakfast, ain't it?"

"Cranberry juice?"

"You kidding me, right?"

I let out a long disappointed breath. "Why don't you then just inform me as to the specialty of the house?"

Lloyd Ganz blinked at me a couple times more. "Hey, Charlie. Man here wants the specialty of the house."

"Give him a wit, Lloyd," said Charlie.

"A wit?" I said. "Something Noel Coward would have ordered, no doubt."

One of the guys behind me said, "Wasn't he the councilman up in the Third District, caught with that girl?"

"Yes, he was," I replied. "All right, Lloyd, let me have a wit."

Lloyd took a beer glass, stuck it under the Bud spigot, pulled the spigot with his stump, placed it before me.

I looked up at him, puzzled. "That it?"

"Wait."

He took a shot glass, slammed it on the bar next to my beer, filled it with tequila. When I reached for the tequila, he slapped my hand away. Then he lifted the shot glass, hovered it over the beer, slop-dropped it inside. The beer fizzled and foamed and flowed over the edges of the mug.

"What the hell's that?" I said.

"A guy comes in," said Lloyd, "sits down, says, 'Lloyd, let me have a Bud,' he gets just the beer. But he says, 'Let me have a Bud wit,' then this is what he gets." He leaned forward, cocked his head at me. "Mister, it's the closest we got to a specialty of the house."

I stared at the still foaming drink for maybe a bit too long, because an undercurrent of laughter started rising from behind me.

Beth reached over, snatched the beer with the shot glass still inside, downed it in a quick series of swallows, slammed the empty glass back on the bar so the shot glass shook. She wiped her mouth with the back of her hand, swallowed a belch.

"How was it, missy?" said Lloyd.

"It's not a sea breeze," said Beth, "but it'll do."

I took a twenty out of my wallet, dropped it on the bar. When another wit sat before me, boiling over, I lifted the glass high, turned to face the crew watching me from among the tables, said loudly, "To Joey Cheaps," and downed my drink.

It roiled in my stomach like a pint of sick. I shook my head, gasped out a "God, that's bad."

I expected a jiggle of laughter at my discomfort with the drink, I expected a few expressions of surprise that I had mentioned Joey Parma, I expected maybe a few murmurs of assent to my toast, a few sad exclamations of poor bastard as they remembered the man who had turned Jimmy T's into his local tap. I expected something different from what I got, which was a dark, glum silence.

It took me a minute to figure it out, but I did.

"So," I said, "how much he end up owing you guys when he died?"

There was a moment more of quiet, and then one of the men said, "A hundred and six."

"Thirty-eight," said another.

"Fifty," said a third.

"How about you, Lloyd?" I said. "What was his tab here?"

"Two hundred, thirty-six, and fifty-nine cents," said Lloyd. "Approximately."

"Well, we got you all beat," I said. "Three thousand, five hundred. Approximately."

There was a moment of stunned quiet and then someone, barely suppressing his glee, said, "Oh, man, you got hosed," and then a wave of nervous laughter hit the bar.

"What were you, his bookies?" someone said.

"Worse," I said. "We were his lawyers."

The entire tap then collapsed into laughter, loud belly-grabbing laughter. Even Charlie at the end of the bar turned his sour gape of a mouth around. "His lawyers," he said in rasp. "What a pair of saps."

"It would have been quicker you just let him burn your money," said another.

"Joey's lawyers. What a perfect pair of saps," said Charlie.

"Hey, Joey's lawyer," said a man, "how'd it feel to be getting it up the bum instead of giving it for a change."

As the laughter spiraled and swelled, I joined in and

then I said loudly, "You know what we need to soothe our empty wallets?"

"What's that?"

"We need to have ourselves a proper wake for our debts. But not on wits, no more wits for me."

"What yous got in mind?" said Lloyd Ganz.

"Why don't you send someone to the Wawa for some juice," I said, "and then, Lloyd, let me teach you how to make a sea breeze."

It didn't end with a conga line, but it came close.

The first taste Lloyd took of a sea breeze made his lips twist. You could tell he didn't take to it right off.

"Close your eyes this time," I said.

Lloyd's eyes blinked shut, the crowd came closer.

"You're on a tropical island. Beyond your lounge chair, the ocean is lapping. A cabana girl, tawny and lean, wearing a lot of nothing"—catcalls, whistles—"has handed you your drink. She leans over, her breath is sweet, redolent of coconut, conch."

"Conch?" said Lloyd, eyes still closed.

"Conch. And she leans ever closer and her warm breath now is in your ear and she whispers, her voice smooth as the white sand beneath her bare feet, 'How is the drink, Lloyd? Is it okay? Is it, Lloyd? Is it okay?' "

Lloyd took another sip, swilled like a swell, considered carefully. "Better than a stick in the eye," he said finally, and a cheer went up and we were off and running.

The jukebox with its smashed plastic was plugged in and the volume jacked, Sinatra bypassed for a few novelty numbers from the bottom of the list. I was behind the bar, jacket off, tie loose, shirtsleeves rolled, making up the sea breezes as fast as Lloyd could take the orders and get me the glasses filled with ice. Two jiggers cranberry juice, one jigger grapefruit juice, one jigger house vodka, a slice of lime. Maybe not perfect but close enough, and they were going as fast as we could set them up. An empty peanut basket had replaced the till, two dollars a pop for the drinks, all cash, all of it earmarked for the Joey Cheaps bar tab memorial fund. The kid we had sent to Wawa to buy the juices and the lime was sent out two times more.

Glasses clinking, shouts called out. *"Hey, mambo,"* sang Rosemary Clooney, *"don't wanna tarantella. Hey, mambo, no more mozzarella. Hey, mambo, Mambo Italiano,"* and then the guys shouted out the next line along with her, *"All you calabraise do the mambo like-a crazy."*

Beth sat on the bar, legs crossed, leading the singing, her pink drink sloshing over the sides of her glass. "Hey, Lloyd," she said, "turn up the heat."

"Why?"

"Let's make like Jamaica."

He did, and soon the jackets came off, and then some shirts, which would have been better left on, and the drink orders came in even faster than before. Guys were hogging the phone, calling their wives and girlfriends, sometimes both, telling them to come on down to the party. Guys were stopping in, drawn by the noise leaking through the steadily opening door, asking what the hell was going on.

"It's a wake."

"Who died?"

"Do it matter?"

Hell, no, it didn't matter. The crowd grew, grew louder, more frantic. "Two more, Lloyd," said a man with both hands already filled with drinks. "Let me have some more of this pink crap," said another, "but this time wit."

Charlie climbed himself up top the pool table as the jukebox sang, *"Day-o, day-ay-ay-o, daylight come and me wan' go home."*

"I always liked that Sidney Poitier," said someone.

"Hell of a singer," said another.

Lift six foot, seven foot, eight foot bunch.

"Two more sody pops, Lloyd," shouted Charlie on the pool table just before he collapsed on his back, his head banging off the felt like an eight ball.

Daylight come and me wan' to go home.

Just as I was running out of cranberry juice for the third time, when the beat cops had stopped in for the second time, when we were listening to "Mambo Italiano" for the fifth time, someone called out, "Frank," and it turned into a chant, "Frank, Frank, Frank," and someone else banged the jukebox, skipping off Rosemary Clooney before he punched in a number by memory and soon enough the sweetest voice that ever was came pouring out like liquid regret. The place immediately calmed, Sinatra sang Paul Anka's surly anthem to individuality, we leaned one against the other, and listened and sang along badly and when Frank had let out his final *"My way,"* Lloyd raised up his sea breeze and said, "To Joey Parma."

A razzing of Yos and Hurrahs.

"We all knew his dad," said Lloyd. "The best damn meat man in the city. I remembers when Joey was just a kid, coming in here to pull his dad home. They weren't on the best of terms, yous remember, but that's the way it is with dads and sons. He wouldn't come here when his dad was alive, but as soon as Joey Senior died, Joey Junior, he started showing up. He said to me, he said, 'Lloyd, there ought always be a Parma at Jimmy T's.' And there always was, though I guess, unless that battle ax shows her face, there won't be none no more. But let's give Joey his due. Can't say the man wasn't consistent. He went out the way he lived his life—in debt. To Joey Parma."

"To Joey Parma," came the response from the congregation.

"Good," said Lloyd. "Now somebody want to scrape Charlie off the pool table?"

"Tell me about Joey's last night," I asked Lloyd when the money had all been stashed, the glasses cleaned, the jukebox unplugged, and the place every bit as quiet and sullen as it had been when we first stepped inside. He stood behind the bar, leaning on his arm, talking to us as Beth and I each sat on a stool. He had seemed like a dour old coot when first we met, but our sea breeze party had opened him up like a steamed clam.

"Nothing to tell, Victor," said Lloyd Ganz, my new best friend. "A cop came in asking the same thing and I had nothing for him, neither. A big black fellow with some Swedish name."

"McDeiss?"

"Yeah."

"It's Scottish."

"Funny, he don't look Scottish."

"He doesn't look Swedish either. Just tell me anything you can remember."

"He was the same as always, came in, ordered a Bud wit, felt around in his pockets, and then told me just to put it on his tab."

"And you did?"

"Yeah, I always did. When I got out of the VA and my pension wasn't enough to take care of the family, his dad took care of me, you know. I always had meat on the table. A lot of shit you can eat in your life when you got meat on the table. So with Joey, out of respect for his dad, I let the tab run."

"He promise to pay it off?"

"Sure. Always. With Joey, the big score was just around the bend. And that night was no different. He was jumpy, you know, bouncing around, telling everyone that he was on to something."

"Did he say what?"

"Nah, and truth—no one cared. It wasn't like we hadn't heard it all a hundred times before, him and his pipe dreams. And it didn't look so promising, him coming in with that mouse on his eye. I asked him about it, he just said it was a wake-up call."

"A wake-up call?"

"Yeah." Ganz looked both ways, lowered his voice. "So he's in here, drinking and talking, telling everyone he was getting ready to pay thems all off, when he gets the phone call."

I looked at Beth. "Phone call?"

"From the woman who was always calling him here. Some dame never set foot in the place."

"Joey's mother?"

"Nah, she don't call here. Every time she sees me she spits between her fingers, like I'm giving her the evil eye. First I was getting free meat and then, when I got enough to buy this place, Joey Senior spent more time here than at home, not that you can blame him, her and her knives. But this other dame was always calling here, and Joey, he was always this little sheep on the phone, baaing out yes, yes, yes."

"Sounds to me," I said, "like he was falling for a girl just like the girl that terrorized dear old dad."

"Don't it though. That last night, same call, same yes, yes, yes, and then he's slapping the bar, hiking up his jacket, shooting his cuffs on his way out the door."

"He say where?"

"He said he had a meet."

"He say with who?"

"He said with money. Like that was ever a possibility with Joey. Poor sap. You know, he wasn't a bad kid, but he never had a clue of what was what."

I had a sudden thought. "Beside me, who did he owe the most?"

Lloyd leaned close. "What I heard, he was deeper than he ought to have been with Teddy."

"Teddy?"

"Teddy Big Tits."

"Are they?"

"Oh yeah."

"Why was Joey borrowing money from some big-breasted loan shark?"

"Maybe for the wolf on the phone," said Lloyd. "He was stupid enough, wasn't he?"

"Where does Teddy drink?"

"The Seven Out, on Fourth Street. You know, Victor, them drinks you was making, us all remembering Joey, the toasts, it was almost nice."

"Yes, it almost was," said Beth.

"What do you think, Lloyd?" I said. "You got yourself a new specialty of the house?"

"Fugettabout it," said Lloyd. "Guys don't come in here for the fancy cocktails. They come in here to get blurry fast and cheap. Tomorrow it'll be back to the wits."

"Does that mean no ferns?" said Beth.

Lloyd snorted, took his rag to wipe the far side of the bar.

"Who was Joey meeting?" said Beth, softly.

"I don't know," I said, "but it doesn't sound right. That morning he's scared witless and by nine-thirty that night he's all gussied up for a big money meet."

"Maybe he wasn't as scared as he let on."

"Or someone changed his mind. I'd sure like to meet that new girl of his. Maybe baby needed a new pair of shoes. And maybe Joey got a line on the suitcase. Whatever it was, it had something to do with the man Joey killed twenty years ago, I'm certain of it."

"Who was he? Do you have any idea at all?"

"His name was Tommy," I said, "and his initials were probably T.G."

"How do you know that?"

"It has a ring to it, is all. But as to who he really was, I don't have a clue."

Except I was lying when I said that last little bit. Because I did have another clue. I had the envelope. And inside the envelope was something that would come to haunt my very dreams.

CHAPTER

9

The envelope.

It was yellowed, worn, one of its edges was ripped halfway down—twenty years will take its toll on even the finest bond—and on the top left corner was a dark black smudge over the preprinted return address: The University of Pennsylvania School of Law. Joey Cheaps had given the envelope to me at the same time he had given me the murder. And if I didn't tell Beth about it, I had my reasons.

"You take anything off the dead guy?" I had asked Joey Cheaps. "Anything that could help us figure out who he was?"

"You think I would strip the dead like that, Victor? He was dead, there was blood. What do you take me for?"

I didn't have to say anything, I just stared for a moment. Joey's eyes peeled away.

"A watch I pawned over at the Seventh Circle on Two Street."

"Dante's place?"

"Yeah."

"Brilliant." Earl Dante then had been a lower-level mob guy with middling prospects, now he was *nùmero uno*, with a *pallòttola* next to his name. "Anything else."

"A ring, gold, what I gave to my mom."

"Jesus, Joey."

"It was her birthday."

"She still have it?"

"Never takes it off."

"How gruesome is that?"

"Tell me about it. And something else. It was in his jacket, in an envelope."

"Go ahead."

"Photographs." His eyebrows rose. "Dirty photographs."

"You give those to your mother too?"

"Shut up. No, them I kept."

"Did you bring them with you?"

He sat still for a moment and then bobbed his head as he reached into his jacket and pulled out the envelope, old, worn, thickly filled. And here it was, now, in my hand, that selfsame envelope. The University of Pennsylvania School of Law. One of the many fine institutions of higher education that had rejected my application. So our dead Tommy G. was a law student, or a professor, or a clerk, or knew someone related to the school. That was one clue. But the other, more interesting clue was inside.

The first time I had opened the envelope was the night after my meeting with Joey Cheaps. This was just before McDeiss called me to the crime scene, when I still thought I could do something to get my client out of his mess. I had opened the envelope, pulled out the pictures, leafed through them quickly, looking for a clue as to who my client had killed twenty years before, looking for the face of a dead man.

But there was no face. No face at all.

And after moving through them once, quickly, I moved through them again, slowly, and then again, even more slowly, my astonishment growing by the second. They weren't dirty, as my client had described them, they were anything but.

A single breast, soft and full. The curved arch of a foot. The taut lines of a neck. Fingers posed like dancer's. A wisp of dark hair over an ear. And then, what was that, with the substance of flesh over long curving bone? A thigh? A hip? It was soft and smooth and supremely abstract. Oh yes, now I saw it, the arch of a back as it moved gently toward the shoulder.

In my hands were pictures of a woman's body, perfect and strong, young, open. Pictures of a body only, no face, parts of the body separated into their own distinct curves and lines. A body, young and miraculous, universal, dividing itself until each inch of flesh became its own framed landscape with a mysterious, primal pull.

The rise of the clavicle. The run of the scapula. A distinctive mark on the areola of the right breast. The sharp climb of the calf.

They hypnotized me that first time I examined them, fascinated me still, and as I went through them now, once again, for the nth time, I found them burning themselves into my brain. Sitting on my beat up, old red couch, the lamp beside my head the only light in the apartment, a circle of brightness fell from the lamp straight onto the photographs and then through the photographs into a different time and place, into the very past.

Every inch of the woman was worshiped by the camera, every speck highlighted as if a marvel of nature. The landscape of these photographs was pristine. And they hadn't just captured one woman's body, they had captured the photographer too, his passion, his utter devotion. In every photograph, as clear as the woman's flesh and bone, was the picture of an obsessive love guiding his eye as he made his study, like Ansel Adams, drunk with nature, capturing the unblemished beauty of a wildland at dusk.

The jut of the hipbone from the smooth line of her side. The sweet rippling ridge running through the narrow valley of her back.

I made the calculation. When these photographs were taken I was maybe nine or ten. I never had a chance. And yet, why did I feel, as I went through them, that I had missed my opportunity? Why did I feel the familiar pang of regret fostered by the sight of a woman whom I spy once in the street and who captures me wholly and who then disappears from my life without a trace. Some great gap existed in my life and these pictures somehow sounded out its depth. That was why I hadn't given them to Beth. I was protecting them, and myself, at the same time.

One picture showed the woman's torso, frontally, at ease, one leg languorously bent, a picture from the knees to the shoulders with the dark triangle, luxurious and mysterious, at its center. She was tall, thin, athletic, unselfconscious. Her hair was dark, her legs long, her breastbone high, her fingers delicate and smooth. It was intoxicating, that picture, that center, that mystery. I couldn't turn away.

Was it poor dead Tommy G. with the suitcase and the ring who had taken these photographs? It seemed likely, yes. And so who was she to him? More than a model, that was clear. A girlfriend, still maybe pining for her lost love? A wife, still mourning her missing husband, still waiting for him to return? Well, he wasn't returning, was he? Maybe I should find her, tell her what had happened so long ago, see if, maybe, she wanted to go out for coffee.

How pathetic was that?

Yet, still, there was something to it. Joey Parma had finally broken free of the world that had failed him as much as he had failed it, but I was still around to shoulder the burden of his past, and these pictures, that girl, was part of it. If I was to find out who had reached out from decades past to slit poor Joey's throat, then I could find worse places to start than her. Worse places indeed.

CHAPTER

10

"**I had seen** her before," said my father between rasps of breath. "But this time she walked by me. South Street. She walked right by me. And I smelled her. Christ, I can still smell her."

I had fought to avoid it, this telling of my father's sad lovesick tale. I had turned on the television, I had made calls from his phone, I had tried to start a conversation about the Eagles. In Philadelphia, if a guy comes at you with a shiv in his hand, demanding your wallet, just say something like "How about them Eagles," and next thing you know you'll be in a bar, drinking wits together, debating the merits of the stinking West Coast offense. But even the Eagles couldn't derail my father. Once, when he started again with his story, I jumped out of my chair and intercepted the lovely Dr. Mayonnaise, whom I had been scheming to run into all night, and beguiled my way into escorting her downstairs to the cafeteria for a cup of joe, on me, no, no, I insist, please, you're already doing so much for my father.

I carried the tray to a table in the corner and set out the cups and napkins and spoons like a fussy bald waiter at a French bistro. We talked about my father's condition and then slipped into the short and imperfect histories two people give when they're first eyeing each other. She winced when I told her I was a lawyer, but it was the kind of wince that let you know she didn't really mind, that lawyerdom fit her notion of an acceptable vocation, not as good as an accountant but better than grave-robbing scum, which only showed how little she knew of the profession. Her name was Karen and she was from Columbus, Ohio. I had never before met someone from Columbus, Ohio, but I figured it must be very sincere out there in the heart of the heartland because Karen Mayonnaise was a very sincere person. She sincerely cared about being a doctor, she sincerely cared for her patients, she was sincerely concerned about the state of the world. But despite all that I kind of liked her and when she had to leave she gave me a smile that I took to be an invitation to call.

So I was feeling pretty cheery when I stepped back into my father's room and sat down. And then he began again about the girl in the pleated skirt.

"Dad, really, I don't want to hear it. Is that okay? I just don't."

He stayed still for a moment, breathing noisily in and out. I reached for the television remote control, hanging by a cord from the wall, but he yanked it away with surprising strength for a COPDer. "They're going to kill me," he said.

"Who?"

"The doctors. With their knives. They're going to slash out my lungs."

"That's the procedure. It's lung reduction surgery. They explained it all, didn't they? Something about tidal volume and residual volume. The upshot is that the surgery should increase the amount of useful air your lungs breathe in."

"I know what they say. But they're going to kill me."

"Dad," I said, "no, they're not," but even as I was saying it I was thinking that yes, yes they would.

"You should know about her before I die," he said. "You

need to. About her, about what we did, about what I buried."

"Dad."

"Dammit, just listen for once in your life. Can you? Just listen without being a smart-ass? I don't ask for much, do I?"

He was right, my father. He didn't ask for much, he had never asked for much. That was maybe his greatest strength and greatest flaw. He had never asked for much and so was accepting of all that he had never received. He had never asked for much from me and gotten exactly that. If I had a strength it was that I could accept the truth when it flopped into my face like a dead reeking fish. He never asked for much but he was asking for this, he was asking me to listen. And not just to listen, but to listen actively, to listen in a way that gave full expression to a story his weakened lungs wouldn't allow him to flesh out by himself. I could do that. The least I could do for my father, my dying father, was to do that. And heaven knows the least from me was the most he could ever expect.

"All right, Dad," I said. "Go ahead, tell me about her, tell me about the girl in the pleated skirt."

"I had seen her before," said my father between rasps of breath.

He had seen her walking down the street, on Locust or Spruce, always dressed prim and proper in an era where that stood out. And he had seen her drive by in the passenger seat of a long burgundy car with a high chrome grill, the girl staring forward, stiff and formal in that beast of a car, luminous, unobtainable. She was like something from a different era with her combed hair spilling behind out of a white hair band, her back straight, her pleated skirt.

Things were just starting to break down then, the social

mores of his own boyhood. Hair was getting longer, kids
were wearing dirty jeans and sandals, some just let themselves completely go and were proud of it. It was like
clothes and hair and cleanliness, everything that once
marked a man or woman, didn't matter anymore. But for
my father, they still did. My father was a throwback, like
he too was from a different era, with his hair greased and
combed back nattily, his pants pressed. Frankie Avalon,
Bobby Rydell, Fabian, the Philly kids who had made it big
on the left coast set the style and that was the way the boys
on my father's block dressed and acted before he did his
tour in Germany. When he came back he saw no good reason to change. So he had noticed her when he had spied
her, walking on the streets or driving by in that car, because
of the way she dressed and the way she carried herself, like
a dream from an age that was already passing him by. And
of course, she had the face of an angel.

"But this time she walked by me. South Street." South
Street in the sixties. I hadn't ever thought of my father
cruising South Street in the sixties. By then the song had
already been written, the song had already hit the charts:
Where do all the hippies meet? South Street. Sure, but the
conversion isn't total yet. There is a clash of cultures, the
old-style Philly boys and the new-style hippies, and it is
that very clash that gives the street its frisson. Two very
different generations cruising the same strip, eyeing each
other warily with the future at stake. And then he sees her
again.

"She walked right by me." In her tight blouse, her
pleated skirt, her long slim legs, a shimmering vision in
white. "And I smelled her." The cleanliness of her silky
hair, the soft floral scent that stings him with its subtlety
and sends him careening after her like a bee chasing a but-
tercup. "Christ, I can still smell her."

He follows her, gains on her. He is a big man, my father, his body strengthened by his bout in the army, his skin dark from his work outside cutting suburban lawns for Aaronson. And he knows all the right lines, if he learned anything in the damn army it was the lines, the lines to give to the German girls hanging outside the base, the lines to lay on the neighborhood girls with their hair teased high. He has his lines ready, but when he finally reaches her, when she finally turns around as if to find the address she had passed, when finally he is there, with her, on the street, face-to-face, the lines all skitter and fly away, a frightened flock of birds.

He says something clever, like Hi. She looks through him, as he was certain she would, but then, she looks at him, directly, and he feels it, like he is back in the ring, boxing for the base team and getting a shot in the gut.

What's your name? he manages to say.

None of your business, she says, but then a sly smile. What's yours?

Jesse, he says.

Okay, Jesse. I guess I'll be seeing you, Jesse.

Where? he says.

Wherever.

When I see you, what will I call you?

Whatever you want.

She nods at him and then walks past him and he watches her, watches her walk away, watches her stop, turn around, come back toward him, smile.

What do you want to call me? she says.

I don't know, he says, flustered. Angel Face or something.

Oh, Jesse, she says, you can do better than that.

How about just Angel?

She sticks her chin out for a moment as she considers it,

sticks her chin out and then a smile breaks through. Okay, she says. I'll be seeing you, Jesse.

I'll be seeing you . . . Angel, he says back to her. And as she walks away, her pleated skirt swaying with each step, he repeats the name to himself, again and again.

The next time he sees her she is not a pedestrian on the street, she is instead sitting once again in the long burgundy car, sitting up front, her back straight, her eyes forward. He shouts to her, but she doesn't respond, doesn't move a muscle, as if she hadn't heard. Then he notices the old man in the backseat of the car, his great swath of white hair, his long pale face, his black eyes turned toward my father with a strange intensity as the car slides by and my father chases after it calling out, Angel, Angel, Angel.

I couldn't sleep that night, there was something about my father's story that rattled in my brain. Maybe it was the image of him, strutting down South Street, young and arrogant, full of life, still in the great human pursuit of something special around which to shape his life, something which he, sadly, never found. Or maybe it was the sight of him calling out after a woman, calling out like a lovesick puppy. Some people you can't ever imagine other than as they are now, and my father, old and bitter, with a life restricted by his own failings, was just such a person. I couldn't reconcile the man I had known my entire life with the young and questing hero of his story. But whatever my father was or had been, he was not prone to flights of fancy. So I had to wonder what could have changed him so irrevocably. And the only answer I could come up with was the answer he had apparently come up with too: the girl in the pleated skirt, his Angel. Or maybe it was the sinister chap staring out at him from the back of the long burgundy car.

I climbed out of bed, went to my desk drawer, took out the envelope, turned on the lamp. The photographs, the sight of her limbs, her flesh, the arch of her back, the openness of it all. Whatever my father was feeling as he watched Angel drive away, the photographer was feeling when he took these photographs and maybe I was starting to feel as I pored over them, not only now, but the night before, and the night before that, and the night . . .

And I had a thought just then, a wild guess that made sense only while I felt myself still in the spell of emotions cast by my father's story, the emotions evident in the photographer's worship of his subject, in the emotions I felt as I stared ever deeper into the black-and-white world of this strange and wondrous body and felt something missing from my life. If it was the emotions stirred by that woman in the pleated skirt that ruined my father, maybe it was the emotions evident in these pictures that led this boy, this Tommy, to his murderous rendezvous with Joey Parma on the waterfront.

I didn't know how to prove, one way or another, this wild speculation. I was waiting still on McDeiss with the information I had requested, whether or not it would lead to anything concrete. The number Mrs. Parma had given me was not listed in the reverse directories on the Internet and my calls were not being returned, no matter how often I left a message. The story of Joey Parma's last night, told me by Lloyd Ganz, had only confused me further. I was at a loss, stumped.

And then fate did its dance with me, its lively little two-step, and a lovely woman with tawny skin and bright high heels stepped into my life and set me on a truly twisted trail to the truth.

11

She was dressed for the part of the woman trailing trouble, a tight, bright dress, hair done just so, lips painted dark, a mad glint in her eye. I noticed her in the back of the courtroom noticing me. I noticed her noticing me and I liked it.

We are popinjays, all of us, we trial lawyers, puffing out our chests and playing to the crowd, even when the courtroom is empty of all but a strange woman in the back row. I glanced her way, caught her smile in my heart, and turned back to the cop on the stand and the business at hand, a motion to suppress.

Rashard Porter was a good kid, talented and sweet-natured, none of which precluded him from driving around in a stolen car with a joint the size of a megaphone on the front seat. The car was lent to him by his cousin, he explained to me. He didn't know it was stolen, he explained to me. And the spliff was something he bought to impress this girl he had a thing for, he explained to me. His explanations might have been true, but they didn't mitigate that he was driving around in a stolen car with a joint the size of a megaphone on the front seat. He had been stopped, the joint had been spied, the car had come up on the computer as stolen, and Rashard was neck-deep in the outhouse.

But that's what I do. I'm a lawyer. I shovel crap.

"Now your testimony, Officer Blackwood," I said to the cop on the stand, "was that you were parked on Parkside when you saw the defendant drive by."

"That's right."

"And he was driving the Lexus, right? Silver. Sharp."

"He was driving something."

"Did you recognize it as a Lexus when he drove by?"

"I suppose."

"How far from Wynnefield Avenue were you parked when you saw him?"

"About fifteen yards."

"Forty-five feet back, so the passing cars couldn't see you until it was too late."

"That's right."

"Sitting there in your stakeout, looking for scofflaws."

"That's right."

"And you testified you noticed my client because of his high rate of speed."

"Yes."

"How fast was he going exactly?"

"I don't know, exactly."

"Did you have the radar on him?"

"No."

"No radar?"

"I was working on something else at the moment."

"Wiping the powdered sugar off your uniform, no doubt. And then you saw him run the red light."

"That's what I testified to, yes."

"From forty-five feet back, you saw him run the stop-light not on Parkside, but on St. George's Hill."

"That's right."

"How far away was that light?"

"About forty yards."

"One hundred and twenty feet? And wasn't there a tree in your way, a big old sycamore?"

"There was a tree, but I could see around it."

"It's a big tree, isn't it? Thick?"

"It's a tree."

"A big old sycamore. And from forty-five feet back on Parkside that big old sycamore was blocking your view of the intersection. I have photographs that will show this to be the case."

"So maybe it wasn't exactly forty-five feet."

"Oh, so maybe not exactly forty-five feet. But whatever it was, as he drove by your stakeout, you could see my client's face through the window, right?"

"I suppose."

"A young black man driving by in a fancy silver Lexus."

"Objection."

"Sustained."

"And that's why you chased after him, not because of the high rate of speed or because of the traffic violation, which you couldn't possibly have seen, but because of his color and because of the make of the car?"

"Objection."

"Sustained."

"Your Honor," I said. "This question is at the heart of our motion. The officer couldn't see the intersection but he could see the driver, a young black man driving a fancy car, and that's why he zoomed out of his stakeout and chased my client."

"The officer testified he could see the intersection," said Judge Wellman, a large round man with a small head and a high tinkling voice.

"It's a big tree, Your Honor. My investigator, Mr. Skink, who is in the courtroom and ready to testify, has all kinds of photographs showing that big old tree blocking Officer

Blackwood's line of sight. The reason he stopped my client
was that my client fit a certain profile, which the Supreme
Court of this state has repeatedly called an improper basis
for a stop, violating my client's Fourth and Fourteenth
Amendment rights and making the seizure of the stolen car
and the drugs found therein fruit of the poisonous tree."

"I understand the argument, Mr. Carl."

"Obviously not, Judge, if you're sustaining the objection."

"Let's wait a moment," said Judge Wellman. There was
a long pause. "Do you know what I'm doing now, Counselor?"

"What's that, Your Honor?"

"I'm counting, quietly, to myself. My doctor has told
me my blood pressure is too high and my wife has been
teaching me to restrain my temper by counting to ten. I am
now at twenty-four and my temper is not restrained. My
wife will be very disappointed."

"She's not the only one, Judge."

"Here's some advice, Mr. Carl. Be quiet, be very quiet.
Don't say another word while I am still counting. And as
for you, Miss Carter, does the District Attorney really want
a potential profiling issue running up to the Superior Court
on appeal? Is that what the District Attorney wants to see
in the papers, knowing, as you do, Mr. Carl's penchant for
free publicity?"

"The one thing, I like to say, that money can't buy."

"Didn't I tell you something, Mr. Carl."

"I'll zip it, Judge."

"There you go. Now, I'm going to take fifteen minutes
and continue counting in my chambers. If that doesn't
work, I'm going to take a pill and go home. While I'm
gone, see if you two can take care of your business. Ms.
Templeton?"

The judge's clerk, a short squat woman with weight lifter's arms, stood and said, "Yes, Judge."

"Wait here with our friends, please. When they settle their differences let me know."

"Oh, I certainly will," said Clerk Templeton, turning toward us, crossing her arms, giving us the look. You know the look, what lunchroom ladies give to fifth graders who complain about the mystery meat.

After Judge Wellman fled the bench, I had a conversation with the Assistant District Attorney and then sat down beside my client. Rashard Porter was tall, handsome, with his hair shaved so flat on the top of his head you could shoot pool on it.

"The DA's willing to drop all the charges having to do with the stolen car if you plead to misdemeanor drug possession."

"What does that mean?"

"It means you probably won't go to jail. She promised to make a no sentencing recommendation to the judge. Judge Wellman acts like he's a hard guy, but he's not likely to give you more than probation. It would be a lock without your priors, but still I think you'll stay out of jail."

"I don't want to go back to jail."

"I know."

"I thought you said it was a bad stop."

"I said I'd argue it was a bad stop. The cop says he saw you go through the red light and the judge appears willing to believe him, no matter what my investigator says. If we lose this motion you'll get rung up on the auto theft felony in addition to the drug thing and jail time is a real possibility. We can appeal, but you'd be in jail while it's argued."

"I don't want to go back to jail."

"I know you don't, Rashard. Did you get that application you sent away for?"

"Yeah."

"You going to fill it out?"

"We don't got no typewriter or nothing."

"Bring it to my office. I'll have my secretary type it up for you."

"I don't know, bunch of geeks talking about a bunch of dead guys."

"Welcome to the wonderful world of higher education, except the students at Philadelphia College of Art aren't geeks and they spend most of their time drawing and painting, not talking. You like to draw, don't you?"

"Sure, yeah, but, you know, that ain't real."

"Who says? Are you letting your boys on the corner tell you what's real? I'll do what I can to help you out with the school. They have scholarships. You're talented, Rashard, you should be doing better things with your life than driving around in stolen cars and buying drugs to impress girls."

"I told you, I didn't know it was stolen."

"You know they have nude models at that school."

"Get out my face."

"It's the truth, Rashard."

"What do you think I should do, Mr. Carl?"

"Take the plea, apply to school, take a chance on yourself."

"You think I can do it?"

"Yes, I do."

"Aiight, Mr. Carl. Aiight."

I walked over to Clerk Templeton to give her the news.

"It took you long enough," she said.

"The wheels of justice are not always swift."

"And from what I can tell, neither are the lawyers. I'll tell the judge."

Judge Wellman nodded as he took the plea, sending

Rashard home on his own recognizance, setting the sentencing date for three weeks hence so the judge could get a full presentencing report. By that date, with any luck, Rashard would have some good news to tell the court. No judge would send a kid to jail on a drug misdemeanor when he had solid plans for the future. I explained all this to Rashard and made him promise to show up at my office first thing next week so that my secretary could help him with his application.

As I watched Rashard saunter out of the courtroom, my eye, like a shirtsleeve on a nail, caught again on the woman in the back. She tossed me a smile, stood, and began walking toward my place at the defense table. Her head bowed forward seductively, her arms swung freely, leather portfolio rising and falling, her smile inched wider. She was like a model on a catwalk until she stumbled in her shiny high heels and fell onto her face.

CHAPTER

12

Before I could reach her she had scrambled back to her feet and was straightening herself.

"Oh my God, I can't believe I just did that. I am sooo clumsy. And these shoes are mad hot, but who can stand in them? Hi. You're Victor Carl, right? Your office said you were here at the courthouse, and I asked around and found you, which is good because I could have been here all day going from room to room to room. There are so many courtrooms here, it's slightly ridiculous. How many do they need? What they should do is knock down some walls and build a food court. A food court for the courthouse. Couldn't you go for an Orange Julius right about now? Okay, okay, okay, let me get settled first before I begin."

She took a deep breath and, as her outstretched hand fanned her chest, I examined her more closely. Her skin was smooth and flawless, her eyes bright and unlined, her neck taut. She was dressed like a corporate killer but she was far too young for the role.

She reached into her portfolio and pulled out a card. "Here, let me give you this first, so you know who I am. That's the first thing we should do, right, exchange cards? Does that mean you're supposed to give me yours?"

"You already know who I am," I said.

"Oh yeah, duh, right." She slapped the side of her head.

I tore my gaze away from her pretty eyes to read the card. It had a name: *Kimberly Blue*; a title: *Vice President*; and three phone numbers: office, cell, and fax.

"So you're Ms. Blue?"

Her smile was near to incandescent. "Isn't that something? I've never had a card before, I mean a real card. They have those things you can print up on the computer, and one of the girls made us each some at the sorority with our phone number and the pretty floral border, which we would sometimes give out if the boy wasn't a total loser, but this is quality, isn't it? You can feel the printing. It's raised. Feel it. See?"

"And you're a vice president."

Her eyes widened with a joyous disbelief.

"Vice president of what?" I said.

"External relations. Let me see, how did he explain it? I'm the one who interfaces with everyone outside that does stuff for my boss, like caterers, dentists, computer guys, cleaning staff, lawyers."

"In order of priority."

"Exactly. I'm supposed to keep track of everything, make sure everyone knows what needs to be done, make sure everyone is happy."

"And who is your boss, Kimberly?"

"The thing is, Victor . . . It's okay to call you Victor, isn't it?"

"Sure."

"Good. I haven't dealt much with lawyers, other than on TV, so I don't know if you're supposed to be all formal or if it's okay to say just the first name like you're a regular person. My daddy always said after you shake hands with a lawyer you ought to count your fingers so you can probably figure we did our best not to have much contact with the legal profession."

"Most people avoid us until they have no choice. But you were going to tell me who your boss is."

"Yeah, well, the thing is, Victor, the thing of it is . . ."

"Go ahead."

"I'm not allowed."

"Not allowed?"

"No, but he does want to hire you, really. He's heard only good things. Says you're quality. He wants you to work on something really important."

"But who would I be representing?"

"There's a company. I own some shares, not much, but really now. How cool is that?"

"Quite cool. And who in this company would I be dealing with?"

She tilted her head and looked at me as if I were an utter idiot. "Helloo. I'm the vice president in charge of external relations."

"Listen, Kimberly, I don't—"

"Maybe you should call me Miss Blue, seeing as I am, like, an executive now."

"What is this all about?"

She looked around the courtroom. Judge Wellman had retired to his chambers for the day, the bailiff and court reporter had left their posts; of the official members of the court, only sullen Clerk Templeton was in the courtroom, giving us that look as she worked on her files. Other than the clerk, just my investigator, Phil Skink, was still around, sitting in the back, watching our conversation with an amused smile on his scarred face. She noticed him too—Skink was so ugly he was impossible not to notice—and then she turned to me and nodded her head in his direction, trying subtly to let me know he was there.

I flexed a finger and Skink slunk out of the courtroom.

"It's private enough," I said.

She looked back at the empty spot where Skink had been sitting. Now convinced, she opened her portfolio and rummaged around and came out with a stenographic pad, the pages of which she flipped through before finding what she needed.

"Joseph Parma," she said softly.

I stared at her for a long moment. "He was a client."

"Yes, we know."

"Mr. Parma died ten days ago," I said.

"Right."

"Murdered."

She stretched her mouth as if she had just knocked over a vase. "Sorry about that. Such a thing. Brutal, eh?"

"Yes it was."

"They find out who did it?"

"Not yet."

"We might be able to help."

"Excuse me?"

"Maybe we should talk someplace more private, do you think?"

"If you know anything about the murder, you should tell the police. Did you know Joey?"

"Me, personally? No. Though I heard he was quite a quality fellow. But we were just kind of wondering if maybe you had any sort of conversation with Mr. Parma before he died?"

"He was a client."

"Helloo. I know. That's why I'm asking."

"I can't tell you anything he told me. He was a client."

"I don't get it."

"It's, like, a rule."

"But he's dead."

"It doesn't matter."

"That's a stupid rule."

"Tell the Supreme Court."

"Why would I tell them?"

"How old are you?"

"Do you think that question is appropriate?"

"I was just wondering?"

"I'm twenty-one."

"And already a vice president."

"Doesn't that totally rock? Isn't that just the best?"

I glanced at my watch. "Right now I have to be upstairs in another courtroom. Why don't we meet next week in my office, we'll talk about everything, Joey Parma, the company you work for, and your boss."

"I'm not allowed to talk about him, remember?"

"Sorry, I must have forgotten. And you said you also had a case for me?"

"Yes, Victor, we have a case we'd like you to handle."

"And it involves Mr. Parma?"

"Indirectly."

"If I do elect to take the case, I'll need a retainer."

"Orthodontia? Are we talking orthodontia here, Victor?"

"Talk to your boss, he'll know what I'm talking about. My office, Monday. Let's say ten?"

"Fine. I have the address written down here somewhere."

"See, I told you you didn't need my card."

I walked with her down the aisle and held the courtroom door for her. She gave me a smile and shook my hand. Her skin was remarkably soft and there was an awkward moment, as if she thought we should air kiss or something. The firm and distant business handshake was not yet part of her repertoire, but the blinding smile certainly was. She grasped her portfolio to her chest like a high school girl before starting down the hallway.

I was watching her leave as Phil Skink sidled up to me. "Who's the twist?" he said.

I handed him her card.

"Nice-looking thing, no doubting that," he said.

As she continued down the hall one of her heels wobbled and she almost fell before catching herself. Without looking back she continued on.

"She's twenty-one," I said, "and a vice president."

"They're minting them vice presidents younger and younger these days, ain't they."

"Seem to be."

"You ever been a vice president, Vic?"

"Not even of the chess club in high school."

"So what's our little miss vice president of?"

"Follow her and find out."

"Ah, it's like that, is it?" he said. "You owes me three-fifty for today."

"I know."

"And this'll be more."

"I'm good for it."

"I hopes so, Vic. A man gots to eat."

I gave him a quick glance, up and down. "From what I can tell you're doing fine. But as for the girl, don't let her know what you're up to. Find out what you can about her and her employer. I put her off a bit so you would have some time. Let me know before ten on Monday morning. She mentioned Joey Cheaps."

"The one what got his throat slit down by the river?"

"Our vice president seems to think she knows why."

"Interesting. And if she does?"

"I know an old woman who is sharpening her knives."

CHAPTER

13

    "Ossobuco," **said Detective** McDeiss, his rich voice rolling over the rounded syllables like a thick gravy. "I like the sound, the way it falls trippingly off the tongue. Ossobuco. The name, if you are interested in these things, which I am, is derived from a Tuscan rendering of the Milanese dialect. Osso for bone. Buco for the cavity within the bone holding the marrow. Ossobuco. Ossobuco. You can't say it without smiling. Give it a try, Victor."

"Bone hole."

"That's the spirit."

"Can we go over what you found now?"

"What's your rush?"

"Don't you have to get home? Isn't your wife waiting on you?"

"Not tonight. She has her book club meeting."

"What are they reading?"

"The usual crap, father has an insidious disease, mother brings the family together for one final Christmas, heart-warming redemption for all. But they'll be talking for hours, that's the way it is with her ladies and their book club. They might even talk about the book. So you see, Victor, there is no reason to rush." He leaned over, refilled my wineglass with dark red wine. "Sit back. Enjoy yourself. It's not every day we sup in a place such as this."

McDeiss was right about that. We were in a large expense-account restaurant with a sharp wooden bar stocked with well-dressed business types and valet parking out front. I had checked all the restaurants with a Seventh Street address to find the place that McDeiss had not so subtly referred to, a place that served a killer ossobuco, and that place turned out to be the Saloon. Wooden walls, deep chairs, fresh linen tablecloths, a menu with prices that could blanch asparagus without the boiling water. It was McDeiss's show and so I let him order, a Caesar salad for two, *due* ossobuchi, and a liter of Chianti.

When the waiter brought the main course, McDeiss rubbed his thick hands together. Two large bowls with a circle of risotto and in the middle, sitting within a pond of rich wine reduction, the veal shank, a well-browned snap of bone surrounded by a thick wheel of meat.

With his fork, McDeiss pulled a small section of meat off the bone, swirled it in sauce, brought it carefully to his mouth. His eyes widened and his head did a little dance as he swallowed. And then he looked at me and said, in a voice overcome with joy, "Ossobuco."

"Did you taste the lemon zest?" he asked, after our plates, empty of all but the bone and a smear of sauce, had been whisked away from the table.

"Is that what it was?" I said, trying not to show how much I enjoyed the entrée. "I thought the wine had gone sour. Can we do this now?"

"You're so anxious," he said.

"Yes, I am."

"Why don't we discuss it over coffee and dessert?"

"You want dessert after all that?"

"There is a mixed fruit tart I have my eye on."

"No wonder your knees shoot off fireworks when you kneel."

"Are you calling me fat?"

"Let's just say you have a physical presence."

"Damn right, I do. In my job that's an asset. Nothing like a big sweaty black man leaning over a suspect to get a tongue to start wagging."

"Can I get you gentlemen anything further? Coffee perhaps?"

"Two coffees," I said. "And the fruit tart my friend has his eye on."

"Very good."

"And perhaps an aperitif," added McDeiss, "just to settle the stomach."

I thought about saying something, the price of the dinner was rising with every word and the bill would come barking like a rabid Chihuahua when my statement arrived at the end of the month. But then I figured if I was facing bankruptcy, and I surely was, I might as well enjoy the fall.

"Make that two," I said.

"*Very* good."

"All right, Detective," I said after the waiter left. "Let's have it."

He leaned forward, his elbows heavy on the table. "The information you asked for wasn't easy to get. The files from two decades past are in external storage. I had to send an intern to do the search, it took him three days."

"Okay, so the dinner's paid for."

"Unidentified floaters approximately twenty years ago. The time frame was loose, so I gave us four years of leeway on either side, eight years total. We came up with four bodies. Of the four, one was female, one was a child—an unidentified child, is that lousy or what?—which leaves us two. One was a black man of approximately sixty years of age. I have a picture, but that doesn't sound like who you're looking for. The other was a white man approximately twenty to twenty-five years of age, hauled out of the Delaware, not far, as a matter of fact, from where we found Joseph Parma. No identification was on the floater's person."

"Do you have a photograph?"

"Yes, but you won't like it. His face was missing."

"Missing?"

"Taken off, most likely by a boat propeller, and his teeth were smashed too."

"Good God."

"Fingerprints gave us nothing, and this was before DNA, so identification proved impossible."

"Do you have the file?"

He reached beneath the table, opened his briefcase, took out a stack of files. He slid a thin manila folder across the table to me like he was dealing giant playing cards. "I anticipated your interest and made a copy for you. Don't open it here, even a bad photocopy of the photographs could put a passerby off his appetite."

I pushed the file to the side of the table and left it there. "What about the missing persons?"

"Same eight-year time period. Only unsolved missing persons with the name of Tommy or Thomas or Tom. You'd think that would be rare enough, but you'd be wrong. Seventeen. I brought them all. I think I have a few that might interest you."

"Go ahead."

"Thomas McNally, small-time bookie and numbers runner, just by chance happened to grow up on the same block as Joey Parma. Left his mom one night, said he had a date. Mom was excited. Thomas McNally didn't date much and I suppose this date wasn't so successful. Never returned."

I took the file, gave it a quick glance. It didn't feel right.

Whoever the Tommy was whom Joey Cheaps had killed, he had certainly not been small time, not with that suitcase, not with that money. Besides, the initials were wrong, and if the kid had grown up on Joey's block, Joey would have recognized him for sure. "Who else?"

McDeiss tilted his head and closed one eye. "You don't like that one?" He took out another file, opened it. "Tommy Barone, age fifty, very connected, a right-hand man to Scarfo when Little Nicky still ran things. A long record of violent offenses, did a stint in a federal prison. Left one night to meet the guys and play a little high-stakes poker. His regular game at some dusty storefront men's club right up the street here called the Sons of Garibaldi. Barone was a good card player, supposed to have been lucky, but not that night. Never returned."

Some middle-aged mobster, not even close. "Who else?"

McDeiss ran his tongue up and down the inside of his left cheek. It looked like a hamster was doing calisthenics in there. He leaned down and took out another file. "How about this. Tom Grand, seventeen, turned tricks on Twelfth and in Fairmount Park, at the bathrooms. He was reported missing by some of his fellow hustlers, who hadn't seen him working the park for a while. A few weeks before, he told them he had a sugar daddy that was keeping him fat and then he disappeared. Never found."

That didn't seem right either. The initials worked, T.G., and he might have been able to steal the money, who knows what goes on between a hustler and his sugar daddy, but what about the pictures of the naked woman? Tom Grand? Don't think so. "Who else?"

"Who else? Is that what you're asking? Who else?"

Just then the waiter came with our coffee cups, two little aperitif glasses, and a bottle of Courvoisier. While a busboy poured the coffee, the waiter filled our fancy little glasses with the golden brandy.

McDeiss picked up his glass. "To Victor Carl, a son of a bitch who is holding out on me, as usual."

We both drank to that. Lovely.

"If you give me more information," he said after he put his glass down, "maybe we could move this parade along."

"Just give me a brief rundown of the rest."

"This isn't right. You have information that might be of material interest to a current homicide investigation."

"Maybe I do."

"You're playing games with me, boy. I don't like games."

"Oh, look, Detective McDeiss, they've brought your tart."

The waiter laid out a small tart covered with glistening slices of bright fruit.

McDeiss picked up his fork as if to threaten me and then attacked the tart instead. The tension in his face eased as the fruit and the custard and the pastry mixed together in his mouth.

"Well what exactly is it you're looking for?" he said calmly after finishing. He took his glasses out of his pocket, put them on, peered at me over the frames for a moment, and then went quickly through the files. "Is it the baker, never showed up for his morning bake? Is it the family man with three children and a load of debt? Is it the truck driver on a haul from Maine to Florida? Is it the law student who slipped away from his failing grades? Is it the mysterious handyman who just showed up one day and then two months later was gone? Is it the podiatrist who broke into his—"

"Where was the law student a law student?" I said.

McDeiss stopped, gave me a careful look, went back

through the files until he found what he was looking for. "University of Pennsylvania."

"What was his last name?"

"Greeley," said McDeiss.

"That's the one," I said, my hand out for the file, which he ignored.

"Tommy Greeley," he said, reading now. "Twenty-four. A third-year law student at the University of Pennsylvania. Reported missing by his mother in Massachusetts, a place called Brockton. Hadn't been to school in weeks when the report was filed. Lived alone. No sign of him at his apartment. The girl that was supposed to have been his girlfriend, according to his mother, didn't even know he was missing. School said he was failing out. It looked like life wasn't working out for him and so he just up and ran away. It happens."

"That's it?"

"That's it. You want to see?"

"Yes."

He took off his glasses, handed me the file. "You sure the guy you're looking for isn't that Tommy McNally? He seems a more likely candidate. I figured if Joey Parma was involved it had to be a lowlife that was missing. Not a law student, for God's sakes."

"Are you implying, Detective," I said as I examined the file, "that not all lawyers are lowlifes?"

"There are a few I've met that seem decent enough. Mostly retired folk."

The file contained write-ups of the mother's initial report and the cursory follow-ups done by a police detective. Once he found the girlfriend's evident lack of interest and the failing grades, the detective figured he had figured it out. No reason to listen to the harping of a distraught mother in a distant state when there were more pressing matters. Not much there, to be sure, but this was my boy, Tommy Greeley, I could feel it. The initials matched the ring, the Penn Law connection was clear, and there was a girlfriend—I leafed through the file—a Sylvia Steinberg. I made a mental note of the name. But how would a law student end up with a suitcase stuffed with money? How would a law student be so calm and cocky under the pressure of a midnight rough-up? There was something missing still, a second shoe that needed to drop.

"So, Carl," said McDeiss, "you think maybe this missing Greeley and the floater without the face are one and the same?"

"They seem to match up," I said.

"Yes they do. And you're interested because . . ."

I raised my hand to catch the waiter's attention. When he looked my way I pretended to scribble and he nodded.

"You're not going to tell me," said McDeiss.

"Can I keep this?" I said.

McDeiss took off his glasses, looked at me for a moment, and then shrugged. "A twenty-year-old missing persons file? Knock yourself out."

As I continued looking through the file I said, "You get anywhere on Joey yet?"

"We're getting somewhere."

"You should know I now represent Joey's mother and am investigating a possible wrongful death claim against his killer. Anything you can tell me about the status of your investigation would be most welcome."

"I knew you chased ambulances, Victor. I didn't know you chased coroner's vans too."

"I find my business where I can and sometimes where I can is at the morgue. Funny how that sort of puts us in the same boat. Any leads?"

"Some."

"Fibers on the body?"

"Gray polyester from the interior of a car."

"Make?"

"Late-model Toyota."

"That narrows it down like not at all. Have you gotten around to tracing the phone call he got at Jimmy T's before he stepped out for his meet?"

McDeiss's eyes bulged and his cheeks swelled and he looked for a moment like he swallowed his tongue.

"Nice little double take," I said. "You could have been in pictures."

"The investigation is proceeding apace and we'll keep you informed to the extent we see fit. But just so you know, the owner of the fine establishment you mentioned wasn't so cooperative."

"You should have made him a sea breeze."

"Excuse me?"

"Go on."

"We learned enough to get a warrant for a search of his phone logs and we believe we found the call you may be referring to."

"A woman, right?"

"Isn't it always?"

"You mind giving me the address?"

"Yes, I mind. But I will give you some advice, Victor. You don't want to be interfering with an active homicide investigation. Trust me, you don't."

"I don't want to interfere, Detective. I want to help. I heard Joey was in a little too heavy with a loan shark by the name of Teddy Big Tits."

"Oh yeah?"

"He hangs out at a saloon called the Seven Out."

"Is that right?"

"It seems Joey might have been borrowing to keep the

party at that number happy to see him walk in the door. Don't know for certain, but I'm just trying to help."

"We always appreciate help."

"And I wouldn't mind asking that same party some questions so long as you don't think it will hinder your investigation." I was just about to close the Tommy Greeley file and stuff it in my briefcase when something stopped me.

"What's this right here?" I said, pointing to a small yellow slip fastened in between two longer sheets of paper.

McDeiss shoved his glasses back onto his face, brought the file close. "It says the active investigation was closed after the initial inquiries and a discussion with . . . with S.A. Telushkin, and then it gives a phone number."

"Who is S.A. Telushkin?" I said.

"I didn't notice this before."

"Who is he?"

McDeiss took off his glasses, pursed his lips. "Remember when I said you could have the file?"

"Yes."

"I was mistaken." He shut the file, jammed it into his briefcase, and grinned at me. "Believe it or not, I might want to look at it again. In fact, I might want to reopen a decades-old missing persons case. Would you have a problem with that?"

"Would it make a difference?"

"No."

"Then I've no problem, no problem at all."

"Good," said McDeiss. "Later on maybe I'll make you a copy, send it off to your office. But right now I have a sneaking suspicion that this old file might prove to be more interesting than I first thought. You know, Carl, I suddenly am wondering whether this old file might link up to one of my open cases. What do you think about that?"

"I think you're a hell of a detective, Detective."

"Yes, I am."

"Who is S.A. Telushkin?"

"I think he's retired now, but I had some dealings with him early in my career when I was doing fraud. An interesting character. Easy to underestimate."

"McDeiss."

"His name is Jeffrey, Jeffrey Telushkin."

"So what's the S.A. part?"

"Special Agent," said McDeiss.

"Aaaah."

"Special Agent Jeffrey Telushkin of the FBI."

Did you hear that? Did you? There it was, the kerthump of the other shoe dropping smack on my head.

CHAPTER

14

Phil Skink was a long walk off a dank pier. Phil Skink was as ugly as a Salisbury steak but his teeth were pearly. He smoked cigars that smelled like the New Jersey Turnpike. He bought his suits wholesale from a guy named Harry. His cholesterol level was a national tragedy. The sight of him on the beach with his shirt off was enough to stun a jellyfish. Phil Skink played golf in a straw hat and old wingtips, and on the city course he played once a week he would take your money, guaranteed. He would have been the world Jumble champion if there was any money in it. He could have starred in the Lon Chaney story without the makeup. He played the "Star-Spangled Banner" through the gap in his teeth. He was a bad enemy, a good friend, a free man. Just by looking at him you would never figure he was smarter than you, but he was, guaranteed.

I had met Skink when he was working the other side of a murder case, working the other side, that is, until we realized we had the very same intentions and so we started working together. He was a licensed PI, and every lawyer needs a PI, and so I hired him, when he was available, to PI for me. He was smart, like I said, and he was fast.

"She's working for a company called Jacopo," said Skink over the phone as Kimberly Blue, Vice President of External Affairs, sat in a plastic chair set up in front of our secretary's desk. "Some la-di-da outfit what is renting a town house smack on the southwest corner of Rittenhouse Square."

"What do they do?"

"Everything and nothing."

"Who owns it?"

"A couple of shell corporations I traced to the Caymans where the traces, they disappear."

"You're slipping, Skink."

"Yeah, well, maybe I am. You want to send me down there for a few days, I could maybe dig a little deeper."

"And work on your tan in the process."

"They gots golf courses down there look like brochures."

"Forget it."

"Thought to check with the rental agent on the town house. Tough bird, she is. Constant cigarette, voice like a lawn mower. Insisted on a personal guarantee on the lease, and got one too. Signed by a man of substance name of Edward Dean."

"Edward Dean. Okay. Now we're getting somewhere. Tell me about our little Miss Blue."

"Grew up in South Jersey, just over the bridge, Bellmawr. Father ran a liquor store. Cheerleader, no surprise there, right? Graduated this year from Penn. Didn't have the grades or SATs for an Ivy, but slipped her way in and survived. Was a marketing major, seems that's what they major in if they don't know what the hell to major in. Found her current position on a bulletin board at the job office at the school. Lots applied, this bird pulled it down. Good for her, right?"

"How'd she get it?"

"No one knows. There was better-qualified applicants, top of the class, Wharton grads even. But she's a looker, ain't she. I had my choice between some little owl with a four-point-oh and our little Kimberly, I'd take Kimberly too. Now she's living in a walk-up with some of her school chums but she ain't there much, if you catch the drift. No steady boyfriend since she broke up with a basketball star last year, least not what her flat mates know of."

"Anything else?"

"She's an orphan."

"What?"

"She's an orphan. Her moms died when she was still in diapers, her pops died last year. And every now and then, ever since her pops died, she just goes off and cries."

"Come on, Phil. What am I supposed to do with that?"

"I thought you should know, is all."

"You like her."

"I been keeping my distance like you wanted, never spoke to her once."

"But you're sweet on her all the same."

"Yeah, maybe I am. But not in the way you're thinking. I spent some time with her mates. Nice girls, though two beers and they can't stop their yapping. But Kimberly, she was working that night, like she works almost every night. Like she worked her way through a college that was too hard for her, like she worked her way into this job that ain't like any job a girl like her should grab hold of. You get a sense of a girl giving her the tail. Our Kimberly, she's been in over her head every day of her life and she keeps going on, doesn't she?"

"Except when she's home crying."

"There you go. Anything else you want?"

"Not just yet, Phil. But keep your phone on, I sense I'm going to need you sooner rather than later."

Today Kimberly Blue was wearing a different version of her corporate outfit, this one bright red, with matching pumps and lipstick. Very nice. She smiled when she saw me, but I gestured her to wait for a moment.

Rashard Porter was standing behind my secretary, Ellie, as she typed out his application to the Philadelphia College of Art.

"How's it going?" I said.

Ellie looked up, seemingly exasperated. "He keeps changing his answers."

"They got more questions than the probation lady," said Rashard. "I mean my address and high school stuff is no problem, but like this here. They want to know why I want to go to art school. Should I tell them the truth, Mr. Carl? I don't think they want to hear the truth, being that the truth is me liking the idea of spending the day staring at naked ladies and needing to get in to keep my butt out of jail."

"Except that's not the real truth, is it?"

"It isn't?"

"If you could do anything with your life, what would you do?"

"Blow dope and play X-Box?"

"Really?"

"Nah, man."

"So then tell them what you really want to do. And tell them why. Tell them about the newspaper thing you did at the high school. From what I understand, with these places the most important thing is your portfolio."

"Mine's like a piece-of-crap cardboard thing."

"Not what it's made of, Rashard, what's inside of it. I've seen your stuff. You'll do all right. Just be sure to show them your best. Keep at it, but I have a meeting."

With that I nodded at Kimberly Blue and led her into my office.

15

She dropped into a chair, pulled at the hem of her skirt, straightened the fabric on her lap, removed the stenographic pad from her leather portfolio. We chatted a bit, about the weather, about the city, about law school. She had been thinking about law school, she said, before she got a job as a vice president. "Now, being a lawyer would be a step down, don't you think?"

"Absolutely," I said. "So, where were we?"

She glanced at her pad. "You want me to start the whole thing over again, beginning with the card? Have you seen my card?"

"Yes I have. It's quality, for sure."

"It is, isn't it? Did you notice that the printing is raised?"

"Yes, I noticed. Why don't we begin where we left off in the courthouse. You said you had a case for me."

"Yes, yes, okay. Okay. Here it is." She calmed herself, looked at her pad, and then punched her fist in the air like a peewee soccer coach exhorting her troops. "Victor, we need for you, Victor, to collect a debt."

"Collect a debt?" I said.

"Yes. A debt."

"That may be a problem, then, Kimberly, because I don't do collection work anymore."

She looked at her tablet, riffled through it quickly. "Are you sure?"

"Quite sure. Last collection case I ended up with a bullet in my ribs."

"Oogly," she said. "Did it hurt?"

"Oh yes."

"Why would someone want to shoot you?"

"Well, Kimberly, take away a man's money, he gets upset. Take away a man's wife, he gets down right pissy. But take away a man's car, then you've got trouble on your hands."

"Still, someone has to do this case and we figured you were just the man for the job." She gave me another exhorting punch.

"What is that, that fist in the air thing you do?" I said.

"You don't like that?"

"No. It's something they do to old men before they wheel them off to get their prostates removed."

"Helloo. TMI. Can we avoid the prostate metaphors? I don't even want to think about mine. So okay, my bad, no more of the fist thing." She did it again. "But let me show you what we have." She reached into her portfolio, pulled out a legal-sized document, handed it to me with great care like it was the Magna Carta itself.

A note, executed by one Derek Manley, promising to pay the First Philadelphia Bank and Trust one hundred thousand dollars, plus interest, plus collection fees, plus court costs if required.

"Is this the Derek Manley who owns the trucking company down by the stadium?"

"Do you know him?"

"Only by reputation, and most of it bad, by the way. But this debt is owed to First Philadelphia."

"Mr. Manley has already . . . What's the word for failing to pay?"

"Defaulted."

"No, that's not it. Whatever, my boss bought the note and now wants you to collect it." She gave me a frozen smile before reaching again into her portfolio. "Here is the transfer document."

I looked it over. It was dated about a week ago. A firm named Jacopo Financing had bought the note at a steep discount, which probably wasn't steep enough, considering Manley had already failed to make a number of payments and was probably flat-on-his-back broke. The note allowed the holder to confess judgment without filing a legal case in the event of a default, which meant the only issue facing Jacopo was finding Derek Manley's assets and seizing them.

"It looks pretty straightforward, but like I said, I don't do collections anymore."

"I have the retainer thing you said you needed."

"It doesn't make a difference."

"Is there a magic word or something I need to say?"

"No."

"How about please? Please take the case."

"No."

"Please, please, please."

"Well, Kimberly, in that case . . . no."

She stared at me for a moment, something welling in her eyes. "What about Joseph Parma?"

"What about him?"

"I thought he was your client."

"He was."

"And you're just going to sit there and do nothing?"

"I don't understand. Are Joseph's murder and this collection case somehow related?"

"I'm not allowed to say."

"You just did."

"Did not."

"Yes, you did, Kimberly. And if you want anything from me, you are going to have to tell me who you are working for, why he cares one whit about Joseph Parma, and how all of that is related to this Derek Manley. Whatever game is being played is no longer amusing. Tell me what I need to know or go home."

She looked at me for a long moment and her jaw trembled, just a bit, but still it trembled, and her eyes glistened, and I remembered what Skink had said about her. I felt like a cad. And then, like a faucet was turned on, the water started running.

"I am in so much trouble," she said, after the tissues had been brought in and the fluids had been wiped away. "I am so dead. And it's not just you. I'm the vice president in charge of external relations and external relations are a total poodle. The caterer got the order wrong and brought in salmon saté when my boss is, like, deathly allergic to fish, and he thought it was chicken and his head swelled so much it almost exploded. Then the carpet cleaner used a chemical that had my boss breaking out in hives and scratching like he was a dog with fleas. And now he gives me one more simple thing to do, hire you to collect a simple debt for a ten-thousand-dollar retainer, and you won't take the case."

"How much was that retainer?"

She just waved her hand as if it didn't matter, as if the amount wasn't even worth discussing in the midst of her failures.

"You have to tell me more, Kimberly," I said.

"Ten thousand dollars," she said, glancing up to track my reaction.

"You have to tell me more about the case."

"I can't. He didn't tell me anything more. I am so fired.

I'm going to be, like, the vice president of external relations at McDonald's. Can we super-size that for you? Oh God. For this I could have gone to a party school."

"Maybe I can help, but you need to help me too. Let's start with this. I know you work for a man named Eddie Dean."

"Huh? How did you—"

"So the question is, does Mr. Dean speak with a British accent?"

She stared at me for a moment. "No. Why would he? Helloo. He's from California." Her hand slammed into her mouth. "But don't let him know that I told you or—"

"What is the relation between Mr. Dean and Joey Parma?"

"I don't know. He didn't tell me. But it's something that happened a long time ago, I got that."

"Is it about a suitcase?"

"No. That's ridiculous. What would luggage have to do with anything?"

"That's what I'm asking you."

"I never heard anything about luggage."

"Okay, one final question. What does Derek Manley have to do with any of this?"

"He called him."

"Who did?"

"Mr. Parma. He called him. Derek Manley. Mr. Parma called him right before he called you."

"And Mr. Dean got hold of the phone records and found this out."

"Yes."

"And bought this note from First Pennsylvania."

"Yes."

"Now I understand," I said. And I did, understand. I understood exactly why Eddie Dean had bought Derek Manley's debt and why Eddie Dean's vice president of external affairs had brought that debt to me and why Kimberly Blue had broken down to great effect in front of me all so that I would take this little collection case that was not so little and not so much about a collection after all. I didn't know yet the why behind all the whys, but I knew what Eddie Dean wanted from me and I was ready, now, to give it to him.

"All right, Kimberly," I said. "I'll take that check."

"Does that mean?"

"Just hand it over."

"Oh, Victor, Victor, I am soo . . . soo . . ."

"Kimberly, let's play like the shampoo, all right? No more tears. You don't need them anymore, they did their job already. Just give me the check and wait here for a moment."

A check for ten thousand dollars, from the account of Jacopo Financing, signed by Kimberly Blue, made out to Derringer and Carl. Ten thousand dollars. I held it in both hands as I soberly left my office, closed the door, and then skipped like a bunny over to Beth.

"Will this do?" I said to her after I dropped the precious little paper on her desk.

She picked it up, examined it closely, let an expression of wonderment lift her features. "How'd we get this?"

"A retainer. For a collection case."

"We don't do collections anymore."

"I made an exception. It has something to do with Joey. We'll both be working on it, doubling up the billables."

"Are you sure?"

"If you and I, with a steady effort, can't blow out this retainer before the first of the month, then we ought just give up law and become orthodontists."

"How very nineties of you, Victor."

"Why don't you take this to the bank and then pay Ellie and Skink and the landlord. And if there is still something left over, maybe I can pay the cable bill. I miss my ESPN. This is just the start, Beth. Didn't I tell you? Didn't I?"

When I returned to my office, my expression was suitably somber, the tone of my voice was suitably businesslike. "All right, Miss Blue. We have decided to accept Jacopo's representation."

"Oh, Victor, thank you. I am so relieved."

"Yes, I'm sure that you are. Tell your boss that I am on the case. I'll confess judgment right away, just like the note provides, and I'll set up an expedited deposition of Mr. Manley and I'll have him in here within the week and I'll ask him all I need to ask him. Tell your boss I am on the case and I will take care of everything."

CHAPTER
16

I was feeling chipper about things when next I visited my father. I had actual leads in the Joey Parma investigation, I had a paying client in Jacopo Financing, and, for the first time in weeks, there was money in my bank account. Not enough, yet, to get the cable back on, but it was close. I could barely suppress my excitement.

Let me tell you something true: There's not much in this life that can't be cured by the cable guy.

And then to top it off, I had engineered another run-in with Dr. Mayonnaise, the chance meeting in the hospital halls that was not chance at all. But I did it subtly, oh so subtly.

"What are you doing on this floor, Mr. Carl? Your father's on four."

"This isn't the fourth floor?"

So we had gotten to talking and, since she was new in town, we had gotten to talking about restaurants.

"You know a good Chinese place?" she had asked.

"Sang Kee Duck House," I said. "In Chinatown."

"Do they serve anything besides duck?"

"I think so. You want to, maybe, I don't know, maybe, try it sometime?"

"With you?"

"That would be, sort of, the point."

"I suppose."

Is that a ringing affirmative, or what? So I was feeling pretty damn chipper when I sat down beside my father in his hospital room.

"You look like crap," I said.

"It's not getting better," said my father.

"What did the doctor say?"

"She's going to try a different antibiotic."

"I'm sure that will work."

My father just grunted. He was sure it wouldn't, his natural pessimism demanded nothing less than despair, and, as was often the case with my father, maybe it was warranted. His oxygen absorption level had dropped to ninety-one percent and his breaths were coming faster now, even with the plastic tube feeding oxygen into his nose.

"Hey," I said. "I'm going out with that doctor."

"It won't go nowhere."

"Why not?"

"She ain't your type."

"What the hell does that mean?"

"First, she's a doctor, so she's too damn good for you. Second, she's from Ohio."

"Nice," I said, though, as usual, I worried that he was right.

"Did I tell you how I found her?" said my father.

"Who? The doctor?"

"The girl. The pleated skirt. Did I?"

"No, Dad," I said, settling in, resigned to hearing more. "You didn't."

"It was the car," he said. The long burgundy car. My father roams all over the city, looking for it. He has a motorcycle, my father, he had seen Marlon Brando in *The Wild*

One and he liked the look, so out of the army he took what pay he had saved and bought a motorcycle. It was a used 1951 Indian Roadmaster Chief, I knew, because it had been a part of my childhood, the motorcycle, sitting amongst the weeds in the backyard, a rusting relic of a faded past collapsing in on itself. But then, in my father's youth, it is bright blue and killer loud and perfect. Sitting on its wide black-leather seat, hands gripping the handlebars, he tears through the city, street by street, canvassing the possibilities, searching for a car.

He doesn't spy it parked outside at the curb like any common family sedan, no. But he gets lucky one evening, sees it out and about, the long burgundy car with the high metal grill. A Bentley Mark VI, impeccably maintained. He follows it back to its lair on a small fashionable street not far from Rittenhouse Square, a spacious garage attached to a double-wide town house with a big red door.

"And once I knew where he lived, it wasn't nothing to ask around." The old man is well known in that part of the city, with his fancy Bentley and his colored chauffeur and his secretary. The old man's money is inherited, his great interest is in collecting collectibles, little things with much value, stamps, coins, rare manuscripts, and, so they say with their snide smiles, pretty secretaries that are maybe more than secretaries.

"But I didn't believe that none," my father said. "I seen her eyes, her angel eyes."

So he waits for her. He gets off work early, cleans himself up nice and sharp, Brylcreems his hair back, takes the bike down to that fancy street, parks smack in front of the house, and waits. And waits. He sees a curtain twitch, someone knows he's there, good, he figures. And he waits, waits until darkness falls and the streetlights start to glowing and night covers the city like a blanket. It is midnight when he leaves, but the next evening he is back, parked in the same spot, waiting. Waiting.

"And then I saw her."

The big red door opens, she steps out, closes the door carefully behind her. She is dressed again all in white, but there is none of the brash confidence in her face now. She is nervous, worried. She walks toward him, glancing back once and then again at the house. A curtain is pulled slightly aside. The old man is watching, my father knows, and my father doesn't care.

You can't be here, she tells him, her gaze down at her feet.

I came for you.

You have to go.

Come out with me.

I can't. I have to go back.

Tomorrow night, then, he says.

No.

I won't go until you agree.

She raises her face. Her eyes are red, and there is a darkness on the ridge of one cheek. A bruise? he wonders.

I can't, she says.

Tomorrow night.

Not here, she says.

I'll park around the corner. Tomorrow night.

She doesn't say anything, she stares at him for a moment and then moves her head slightly, an almost imperceptible nod. Before he can respond, she turns back to the house, runs back across the street, up the steps, through the big red door. Gone.

But the next night, as he promised, he is waiting around the corner, waiting for her, and as she promised, she comes. She doesn't say a word, she simply climbs onto the seat behind him, grabs him around the stomach, leans her chin on his shoulder. Together at last, they roar off into the night.

"And that's how it started," said my father, lying on his bed in the hospital, his eyes closed, either from the pain of his condition or the sweetness of his past.

"Did you see her a lot?" I said.

"It went fast. I knew places to dance, to drink. She liked to drink."

"And when your dates were over?"

"I took her back."

"To the house. To the old man?"

"Yes. Back. By ten. Every night." And every night he shudders as he watches her walk along that same narrow street, up those same stone stairs, through the same red door, into the blackness of the old man's house. Whenever he asks about the old man, she won't answer. She is his secretary, is all she says. The bruise? She was clumsy. The reason she only would meet him around the corner? She likes to maintain her privacy. He begs her to quit, to get a new job, to do something else, someplace else, so they can be together alone, without her fear. She only shakes her head sadly, shakes her head and says it is time for him to take her back. Back to the house. By ten. Back to the darkness. The old man. Every night. Until one night.

"I did it on purpose," said my father.

They are drinking, dancing. She is holding him close. He can feel her body pressed against his, her breasts, her knees. Her flesh and bone seem to melt, to mold into his so that nothing can fit in between. She leans her head on his shoulder. Her eyes are closed, her breath is warm on his neck. There is a clock on the wall. He knows it is time to leave, they have to leave now to make her curfew, but he doesn't tell her. They continue dancing, song after song as the minute hand spins its way slowly on and the hour slips past ten.

When she notices, finally, he expects her to be scared, distraught, angry. But she simply blinks and swallows and asks for another drink. And it is that easy, like stepping over a line painted on the road, crossing the line and not looking back. That night he doesn't take her to the old man's house. He takes her to his apartment, a small walk-up hovel in a failing North Philadelphia neighborhood. The place is just off Broad Street, not six blocks from the very hospital where now he lay, fighting for his life.

He closed his eyes in the hospital bed and remembered, the feel of her skin, the taste of her mouth, the way her tongue brushes his, gently at first and then more roughly, more urgently. This he didn't tell me, this he didn't have to, its reality lived in the very pain scrawled across his face. She unbuttons her shirt, steps out of her white pleated skirt, unhooks her garter. Even as he lay there, struggling for breath, his emotions leaving him unable to speak, it was not so hard to see. The first time with a true love is different in every way from what my father had experienced in those brothels in Germany, or the quick blow jobs from local girls between the trash cans in North Philly alleys.

He let out a soft gasp. "Perfect" is all he said. "Perfect."

And it was, it always is, in the remembering. And in the quiet after, as her head rests on his chest and she murmurs in her sleep, he knows this is what he wants, my father, the feel of his angel's hair on his chest, the feel of her body leaning upon his, rising and falling with each delicate breath she takes, the taste of her tongue still intoxicating his brain. This is what he wants, all he wants, for the rest of his life, forever.

"Oh God," he said, remembering, perhaps, his prayer as he lies awake through the night with her, staying awake to savor it all, desperate not to lose a second. He had never been a religious man, my father, he always claimed he left the mumbo jumbo to his own pious father, a cobbler who spent his life pounding on the last or praying at the neighborhood shul, but here, now, in this room, this bed, with his true love sleeping on his chest, he prays. My father prays that this night, this perfect night of true and unyielding love, will never end. My father prays that he and this girl, this angel asleep on his chest, will be together, forever.

"Oh God."

My father lay on his hospital bed, alone except for the son who never forgave him for being what he had become, lay with his eyes closed remembering, I was certain, remembering his prayer and the night God failed him for the final time.

CHAPTER

17

When I was a kid, we used to head out to the creek by the railroad tracks, catch crawfish, stick them in a cup, prod and poke them for no better reason than to satisfy our sad, sadistic impulses. That's sort of the idea behind a legal deposition.

"I understand, Mr. Manley," I said, "that you own a partial interest in a strip club on Columbus Boulevard called the Eager Beaver."

Derek Manley sucked his teeth. "Just a small piece."

Derek Manley was quite a big man to own only a small piece. Tall and thick and looking like he had swallowed a basketball, he leaned heavily onto the oaken table of our shabby little conference room, his meaty hands rubbing one against the other. He had the air about him of a guy who had secrets, who had connections, who lived life hard. And to say his bulbous nose was mottled was to say Hoffa was hard to reach. His nose was a Jackson Pollock painting.

Manley sat beside his lawyer, a small bespectacled man named John Sebastian, who looked like a scared lion tamer sitting next to his big cat, unsure what unspeakable piece of horror his pet would unleash next. Beth and I sat across from them, perfect prodding position. Between us was a pitcher of water and a fetid plate of Danish. At the head of the table, taking down every word, was our court reporter, a nice old lady with blue hair and fast hands.

"How small a piece of the club do you own?" I said.

"Just enough sos I can tell the girls I'm an owner," said Manley.

"Be specific, Mr. Manley. How much stock?"

"Who knows from numbers. Ike said I would get a third of everything, but that's been a third of nothing. And that was before the IRS started chewing on his butt."

"Is the club liquid?"

"We got ourselves a liquor license, if that's what you're asking."

"If you requested Mr. Rothstein to buy you out, could he accommodate you immediately?"

"Nah, the club ain't got no cash flow. Truth be told, a club like that is worse than a boat. I thought the only thing swallowed more money than a vagina was a boat until I got involved with Rothstein and his club. But I never done it for the money, I only done it for the girls."

"And how did that part work out for you, Mr. Manley?"

"Don't answer that," said John Sebastian.

"Not so good," said Manley, ignoring his lawyer, as clients are wont to do. "A couple of hand jobs is all."

"Keep quiet, Derek," said Sebastian. "I object to the question. The purpose of this deposition is to search for assets, nothing more."

"On advice of counsel," said Manley, "I ain't gonna say nothing more about the hand jobs. But is that what yous looking for, Victor? Would that make yous happy?" He leaned forward, raised an eyebrow. "Ever see that Esmerelda down at the club? They call her the Brazilian Firecracker. That I can maybe set up, but the money, forget about it. By the way, I got regards from a mutual friend. Earl? Earl Dante? He said I wouldn't have no trouble here. Sos I don't understand why yous coming down so hard."

"That was off the record," said Sebastian.

"Like hell it was," I said.

"Let's go off the record and talk this through," said Sebastian.

"Absolutely not. Keep typing, Mrs. Mumford. Your client just mentioned his connection to an alleged organized crime figure. I take his mentioning that connection as an implied threat and believe any such implied threat should be on the record."

"Well, ain't you the blue-nosed son of a bitch," said Manley. "I was just passing on a hello."

"And thank you for that," I said. "Now, there's a Cadillac registered in your name. Where is that located?"

"I don't know."

"You don't know?"

"I lost it."

"A black 2002 Eldorado? You misplaced it?"

"One day it's there and then I can't find it no more. The day before I lost my keys. The next day I lost my reading glasses. Funny, ain't it?"

"I'm sure the judge will find it hysterical too. But you do own the Lincoln you drove up in today."

"Well, that one, you can check the papers, it don't belong to me. It belongs to my girlfriend."

"What about the luxury apartment you live in on the waterfront?"

"My girlfriend's."

"And the time share in Florida?"

"Same."

"This is the girlfriend who works as your secretary?"

"Office manager."

"You must pay a hell of a wage."

"Actually, the wage ain't so much, really, but the benefits . . ." He waved his thumb at me.

"What about Penza Trucking?" I said. "You own that, don't you?"

"Not really no more. It's the bank what owns it now, with the thing mortgaged like it is up the wazoo. First Pennsylvania gave me this loan yous got without any security. Things was a little more flush then. They decided I was good for it. Too bad for them, huh?"

"Is there anything more?" said Sebastian. "It's been four hours already. I think we've covered everything."

Beth leaned toward the lawyer, opened her eyes wide, and said, "Are you sure you're not the singer John Sebastian?"

"Positive," he said.

"Woodstock?" she said. "The Lovin' Spoonful? 'Summer in the City'? Ring a bell?"

"Stop it now," said John Sebastian.

I looked around. It was time. Manley was hot, his lawyer was bothered. The whole deposition had been leading to this moment. Sometimes you get right to the point, sometimes you dance around a bit, get everyone hot and bothered before you spring, with an innocent tone of voice, the crucial question. By then the guard is lowered, by then sometimes, against all odds and counter to all intentions, the truth slips out.

"All right, Mr. Manley," I said. "Just one more topic. You started with Penza Trucking when?"

"Geez, I was just a kid. Seventy-eight, seventy-nine."

"And what was your position?"

"I drove. Penza, what owned the place, always hired young kids 'cause he could pay 'em squat."

"So what was your pay?"

"I think the most it went up to was like six an hour."

"And when did you become the owner?"

"A few years later. Penza was getting old, his daughter wanted nothing to do with the business. He was looking to get out."

"And so you got in?"

"Yeah, imagine that. Like Horace the Algerian, it was."

"Horatio Alger?"

"Who?"

"How much did you pay for the business?"

"Not much, really. It wasn't worth much, the trucks was old, the accounts was small. He almost gave it away."

"Fifty thousand dollars."

"What?"

"Mr. Penza is living in Boca. He said he sold the company to you for fifty thousand dollars. Ten thousand down, the rest on a note."

"How is the old guy?"

"Tanned."

John Sebastian piped up, "Is this relevant?"

"Are you instructing him not to answer?" I said, my voice exploding in finely aged indignation. Sebastian's head snapped back with such force that I wondered if it was my breath. "Because if you are, I'll call the judge right now. I'll get on the phone right now. I'm entitled to ask this."

"You don't have to go ballistic on me."

"I'm entitled to ask this."

" 'Do You Believe in Magic?' " said Beth.

"Excuse me?" said Sebastian.

"So the question I have, Mr. Manley," I said, having set Manley's lawyer back on his heels, "the question you need to answer here, is where did you get hold of the ten-thousand-dollar down payment you paid Mr. Penza?"

"I don't know. I saved up."

"On six dollars an hour?"

"Time and a half for overtime. And I was living at home."

"But you weren't a monk?"

"I had some times, sure."

"And some girls?"

"What, are you kidding me?"

"I heard that your girlfriend at the time, who later became your first wife, was expensive. She liked nice clothes, jewelry."

"Who told you that?"

"She did. I assume the bulk of the six an hour went to her."

"Whatever you assume, you ain't assuming the half of it."

"So from where did the ten thousand come?"

"I don't know. I did a guy a favor, maybe."

"Who?"

"Just a guy what I knew."

"Give me a name."

"I don't remember his name right off."

"What kind of favor did you do for this friend?"

"Nothing. I don't know. Let's forget about it."

"Where was this favor done?"

"I told you to forget about it."

"I want to show you a picture. Let's mark this as plaintiff's nine for identification. It's a photograph of three young boys, altar boys. Do you recognize the boy in the middle?"

"Is that me?"

"How old were you there?"

"Truth be told, I can't ever remember being that young."

"Who's the boy on the left?"

"It was a long time ago."

"It's Joey Parma, Joey Cheaps, isn't it?"

"Where'd you get this?"

"And it was Joey Parma with you that night at the waterfront?"

"What night?"

"The night with the moon shining overhead. The night where the two of you waited in the shadows to do that favor for your friend."

"I don't know what you're talking about."

"Who was the friend who asked for the favor?"

"I told you I don't remember." He lifted the pitcher, poured a shaky stream of water into a plastic cup, took a sip. "Is it getting hot in here?"

"You and Joey Cheaps, with a baseball bat, waiting in the shadows."

"Never happened."

"For the guy with the suitcase."

Manley's head tilted down, his eyes turned hard beneath his brow, his voice lowered into a growl. "Watch yourself, Victor."

"The baseball bat and the guy with the suitcase who was hit in the face and then the splash. Do you remember the splash?"

"Shut the fuck up." Manley stood, threw his plastic water cup at my face. Lucky me, the water landed mostly on my tie. Isn't polyester a wonderful thing?

"This deposition is over," said John Sebastian.

"That's what you and Joey discussed on the phone the morning before he died, isn't it?" I said. "What you did together that night at the waterfront?"

"Are you deaf," said John Sebastian, standing himself now. "It's over."

"What did you do with the suitcase, Derek?" I said. "What happened to the money in the suitcase?"

Derek Manley, his face crimson, his nose fluorescent with rage, leaned over and jabbed his finger at my face. "You don't know shit about what happened."

"And what did you do twenty years later to Joseph Parma?"

"Yo," he shouted. "I didn't have nothing to do with whacking Joey. He was my friend."

Sebastian put his hand on Manley's shoulder as if to comfort. "Don't say anything more, Derek."

"On the advice of counsel I'm shutting up for good. But let me give you some advice, Victor. You like your bowels? You find it convenient having them sitting there between your mouth and your asshole?"

"Let's go, Derek," said his lawyer, the hand on the shoulder now pushing him out.

"You shut up about what it is yous asking about or I'm gonna reach down your throat, pull out them bowels, toss them against the wall so they stick, you understand, you little pissant? You don't watch out you'll be shitting out your ear. Don't think I won't."

"This was totally inappropriate," said Sebastian after Manley had stormed out of the room. "The judge will hear about this and so will the Bar Association."

"Don't leave, John," I said, as he made his exit too. "There's still Danish left."

"They seemed to have marched off in a huff," said Beth.

"What does that mean anyway, 'in a huff'? A huff. It sounds like one of those short fur jackets."

"Is that what you wanted?" she asked.

"Close enough," I said. And it was. Manley had as good as admitted to being there that night with Joey Cheaps when the bat had slammed into Tommy Greeley's face. And he had as good as admitted that he had been there on the behest of a friend. It was the friend's name I needed; all

I'd have to do was squeeze a bit to get it. It wouldn't be so hard. I was a lawyer, my entire professional training was in the art of the squeeze.

And it wouldn't end with Manley. I fully expected word would get out about what I was looking for; I fully expected someone other than Manley would start to feel the pressure. I just didn't expect it to happen so fast.

CHAPTER

18

    I had a date the very night of my deposition of Derek Manley with Dr. Mayonnaise of the serious mien and the pretty blue eyes. She was everything I was supposed to want in a companion, the moral and financial rock upon which I could securely anchor my flailing existence. And she was a doctor, a doctor to bring home to my Jewish mother, if I had one to whom I still talked and who gave a damn about more than her next drink. So I decided that I would work at this one, that I'd see if I could build, with the good doctor, something akin to a healthy relationship. It was not something I was good at, building healthy relationships, but I was determined to give it the old community college try.

    We met at my favorite restaurant in Chinatown, with its barbecued mallards hanging in a row at the entrance, and everything should have been right with the world. Yet, as I pawed with my chopsticks at the tofu stir-fry, tofu because Karen, which I discovered to my utter delight, was a vegetarian and we were sharing, I found myself scheming of ways to get the hell out of there.

    Maybe I was simply a coward. Yes, I was afraid of committing myself to a healthy relationship, whatever that was, and yes, I was intimidated by anyone with a richer past and a brighter future than my own, which included most of the known world and certainly included a doctor, and yes, I was paralyzingly afraid of earnestness and sincerity. I was a coward, that was undeniable, but maybe what really got to me was the sight of the heaping platters of duck and beef and chicken and shrimp passing by our table as I pawed at the tofu. This is what I have learned of life from eating in Chinese restaurants: The meal that would make me most perfectly happy is always being served at the table next to mine.

"After dinner," said Karen slowly, seriously, as if making a statement of great portent, "let's say we go back to my place."

I punched my chest as a soft piece of soy curd caught in my throat. "Excuse me?"

"I want you to meet my little family."

Her family? Back at the apartment? Waiting to meet me? "Don't you think it's a bit premature?"

"I don't hide anything from them. They saw me getting ready to go out, they've been wondering where I've been."

"You live with them?"

"Of course."

"They came from Ohio to live with you?"

"Why wouldn't they. I'm sure they'll like you, and, if they approve, we can all cuddle together."

I stared at her and the furrow between my eyebrows must have canyoned out because she said, her voice ever serious, "Victor, I'm talking about my cats."

She had four of them, and they swirled around her like she was a great piece of catnip and she spoke to them like they were cute little babies. I forced a wide smile onto my face as she told me their names, their idiosyncrasies, the adorable things they did. I sneezed when one of the little critters hopped on my lap and when Karen offered to show me her photos I sneezed again. Later, as I tried to wile my way out of there, she held one close to her face and snuggled while making big baby eyes at me and I wondered if maybe the Chinese didn't have it right after all.

I was walking home from Karen's apartment in the art museum area, heading south along a deserted commercial stretch on Twenty-third, beneath the Kennedy Boulevard overpass, when I spotted the car, long and black, following me slowly; about fifty yards behind but matching my pace. I sped up my step: the car sped up too. I began to sprint, looking behind as the car gained on me, and turned my head just as I ran smack into a broad expanse of bright green broadcloth.

I bounced off an elbow to the ribs and fell back, threw out my arms to protect myself, jammed my wrist hard as I hit the pavement. I looked up at a big piece of beef in the green sport coat, his jaw huge, his nose pinched, his short black hair sticking up from his head as if repelled by the dim but violent thoughts careening around his cranium. I knew this guy and he knew me.

"How are you doing there, Leo?" I said.

Leo leaned down and flicked my forehead.

I let out an "Ow."

"You going somewhere, Victor?" he said.

"Home?"

"You asking or telling."

"Telling?"

"Then say it like you mean it."

"I'm going home."

"Good. We'll give you a ride."

"That's not really necessary, Leo," I said. "I can walk, but thanks, awfully, for the offer. It's been a real treat seeing you again. And congratulations on your win at Augusta. The jacket looks marvelous."

A long black Lincoln slid beside me, the back door opened. A voice came out of the back of the car, a soft voice with the slightest lisp. "Shut your mouth, Victor, and get in."

I couldn't see a face in the gloomy interior of the car, but I didn't need to. "You didn't waste any time," I said.

Leo, in the Masters' jacket, grabbed my shoulder, hoisted me off the sidewalk, shoveled me into the car, where I ended face-to-face with Earl Dante.

A few years back I had found myself in the middle of a war for alleged control of the alleged mob. It was all very medieval and unpleasant but I survived, which, believe me, was no sure thing. The winner of the alleged war was a pawnbroker with a shop on Two Street, the Seventh Circle Pawn, the very shop where twenty years before Joey Cheaps had pawned a stolen watch. The broker was a black-suited figure of the macabre, with a sharp dark face and small white teeth. It was the kind of face you expect to see when the door opens after that final elevator ride takes you down down down and the smell of sulfur fills your soul. The door opens and the man with that face and those teeth smiles darkly and says, *"How grand that you've come. We've been expecting you for ages. Right this way, please. And don't forget your baggage."*

Earl Dante.

"I thought I cleaned you off the bottom of my boot, Victor, but here we are again," said Earl Dante as we cruised slowly south in his big black car. Leo was in the front passenger seat. A short pencil-necked man with a long, sharp nose was driving. "I am not happy with your lawsuit against Derek Manley. I am not happy with what happened today in your office. I am not happy to see Derek Manley in a state that can only be described as apoplectic. I am not happy."

"They have pills for that now."

"Shut up. This is not a dialogue. Derek Manley and I are partners of a sort. He owes me money that he cannot possibly repay. As a result he performs favors for me. How valuable it is for a man who sends his trucks to department stores all over the northeast to owe me favors is impossible to overstate."

"I am collecting a valid debt."

"I don't care about your valid debt. But tell me this. Who is behind the debt? Who is behind the questions?"

"It's confidential."

"Give me the name."

"I can't. Professional ethics."

"Ever the comedian, aren't you? Jacopo. You know what Jacopo means in Italian? It means fool. Or it means dead man. It all depends on the intonation. This thing that happened twenty years ago, this thing you brought up today, I want to hear no more about it. Nothing, do you understand? It is not your business."

"Joey Parma was a client."

"Yes. Poor Joey. It was a shame what happened, a crime."

"Twenty years ago he pawned a watch at your shop."

"I remember."

"I had no doubt but you did. Twenty years ago he pawned a watch and twenty years later, because of how he got that watch, he was killed. I'm going to find out why. He was a client. I have an obligation."

"You make me weep with your obligations."

"Do you know his mother?"

"Her veal Milanese is extraordinary."

"I represent her. I'm going to sue the hell out of whoever it was who killed him."

"A jealous husband, I heard."

"Is that what you heard?"

"Or maybe I heard something else. But you have a different theory, is that it? You think it was Derek Manley behind it?"

"I'm just asking questions."

"Let me say this about your questions, Victor. Derek Manley doesn't piss unless I tell him to unzip, understand? Derek Manley asks my permission each time he gives his girlfriend the pump, understand? May I ejaculate on her tits, Mr. Dante? No, Derek, not today. Then I won't, Mr. Dante, thank you for your guidance, Mr. Dante. That's the way it is between Derek Manley and myself. Derek Manley didn't take out Joey Parma because he didn't ask me first. Mr. Raffaello kept the peace by controlling the violence. It is a lesson I have taken to heart."

"How is the old man these days."

"He's painting. Seascapes and flowers. Awful things."

"And how's it going for you, Earl, how does power taste?"

"Pretty damn good. Like a perfectly grilled sirloin, charred on the outside, raw and bloody on the inside."

"You should try tofu. It's good for the heart."

"Do you understand what we discussed here? Are we finished with this nonsense?"

"It's not that simple."

"Oh yes, it is, Victor. Yes, it is. What happened to Joey Parma is a matter for the police only. What happened twenty years ago is of no concern of yours. Derek Manley's trucking company is to be left alone. What could be simpler?"

"There is a debt. I need to collect something."

"What do you want?"

"He owns cars. Can I take his cars, at least?"

Dante sucked his teeth for a moment and then shrugged. "Knock yourself out."

"Thank you."

"Do you know how a zero coupon bond works, Victor? The interest on a debt isn't paid out yearly, it accumulates, accumulates, grows ever larger until the note becomes due."

"This financial message brought to you by . . ."

"Joseph never reclaimed that watch. I still have it. I consider the pawn price an investment. What happened twenty years ago is a tragedy for some, but for me it is a zero coupon bond. Don't get in the way of my payout, Victor. Gerald, stop here. Victor will walk the rest of the way home."

The car stopped, Leo jumped out, my door opened, Leo's hand alighted on my lapel. I don't know if I stepped out or he pulled me out, but I was out.

"Before you go, Victor," said Dante, from inside the car, "tell me one thing. Here we were, sitting in a long black car, dividing up another man's life—you take the cars, I take the business—carving him up like a roasted goose. So this is what I want to know. How did it taste?"

Back in my apartment, I stripped off my clothes and turned the shower on as hot as I could bear it and I let out a yelp as the water flayed my skin and brought the blood to the surface. I rubbed my sore ribs, my sore wrist. I tried to think it through.

As soon as Derek Manley mentioned Dante's name at the deposition I knew Dante would be around for a chat. And funny thing, I believed him about Manley having to ask permission before he unzipped his fly. So Manley hadn't been behind Joey Cheaps's death. Then who was? And what was that financial lecture on zero coupon bonds all about?

I stayed in the shower until the water cooled and then I stepped out and roughly toweled myself down.

Clean now, and ruddy from the heat, I walked over to my desk, dropped into the chair, opened a drawer, took out the envelope. They were inside still, the photographs of the naked woman found in a dead man's pocket. I went through them one by one by one, the images so haunting even though they now were so familiar. The taut skin, the long legs, the beauty mark on the breast that seemed to glow in my imagination. Stare at something long enough and it becomes the model for perfection. Dr. Mayonnaise, despite all her evident qualities, was not the woman in the photographs. Dr. Mayonnaise had a face, she breathed and moved, she had the kind of daily concerns the woman in the photograph seemed to never know, and maybe that was the core of my disappointment in Karen, not the tofu or her sincerity or the cats, but her very concreteness. Right now, I was certain, I'd be disappointed in anyone other than her. The her of the photographs. Her.

Looking through the stack I had a strange idea. I rose and went to the area beside my bed and quickly pinned one of the photographs to the wall. A thigh, gently curving as it rose toward the rear. Then I pinned up another, a calf. Then a foot. Then a hip. Then a breast. One by one I pinned the photographs to the wall, in a rough order. There was no real shape to it, the photographs in no way matched up, each was as individual as a flower, but I did my best, reaching for a photograph, examining it carefully, twisting to pin it in its proper place, as absorbed in the task as a painter before a giant canvas. Picture by picture I created a sort of cubist montage of perfect body parts. And as I worked, something miraculous happened, the disparate parts came together in my mind, this ankle, that shoulder, that finger. As I put the parts of her body together, in my mind, I saw the body move and stretch and turn and bend.

When I was finished, when all the photographs were

arranged on my wall, I sat on my bed and stared, and as I did, fear dropped like a black crow onto the base of my spine, sending out spurts of adrenaline that set me to shaking. There was something coming down on me, something handed to me by Joey Cheaps and kept alive for me by some strange unknown entity, something bigger than I ever could have suspected that first day in La Vigna when Joey Parma disclosed to me the darkest spot in his muddied past. It had cost Joey his life and sent Kimberly Blue my way and caused Earl Dante to threaten me in his smooth hissy lisp. It was huge and I was in the middle of it, for good or for ill, and I had to find my way into its heart before it swallowed me whole. And it seemed, somehow, that these pictures would lead me there.

These pictures, yes, and something else, a question, the question that Earl Dante had asked, trying and failing to hide the keenness of his interest. *Who is behind the debt?* he asked. *Who is behind the questions?* He wanted to know, and so did I. It was time to find out. It was time to meet Eddie Dean.

But before I did, I needed to know exactly what I was dealing with, I needed to peer into a dead man's past.

CHAPTER

19

"I had been warned you would darken my doorstep," said Jeffrey Telushkin as we sat in his time warp of a living room.

"Detective McDeiss informed you of all my faults, no doubt," I said.

"And more, I can assure you," said Telushkin, his eyes bright, his hands coming together in a clap of glee. "He was positively savage. All of which, of course, only peaked my interest. So I made inquiries of my own, just to learn what I could."

"Nothing too awful, I hope."

Telushkin didn't respond, he just chuckled and sat back in his chair. Telushkin was nothing like I expected for a former special agent of the FBI. He was short, round, with a bristly gray mustache, circular black glasses, and very shiny, very small black shoes. And he was cheerful, oh my yes, so very cheerful.

"You've come to talk about Tommy Greeley, from what I understand," he said.

"That's right."

"Any particular reason?"

"His name has come up in a case I'm involved with, concerning something that happened many years ago."

"Can you give me a clue, at least, as to what it's about?"

"No, I'm sorry, there is a privilege I must abide, but anything you can tell me about Tommy Greeley will be much appreciated."

"Tommy Greeley, the one that got away. Can I get you some tea? Maybe some Earl Grey?"

"That would be wonderful," I said.

As Telushkin bounded to his kitchenette, I took a swift gaze about and then stood to get a closer look. I was recovering from the night before, but slowly. The bruise on my ribs had turned a fine shade of yellow violet, my wrist still ached whenever I pressed it back, so I pressed it back constantly to be sure it was still aching. But I was here on business, so I tried to ignore the pain as I examined Telushkin's living room.

The walls were covered with familiar Picasso prints, a colorful outline of a rooster, the silhouettes of Don Quixote and Sancho Panza, along with original and badly painted abstract and cubist paintings of naked women, paintings whose colors had dimmed over time. I peered at one of them more closely. Yes, of course, a tiny J.T. painted in the corner. There was a spinet piano wedged into one section of the modest one-bedroom but the rest of the furniture would have been considered stylish fifty years ago, rounded chrome legs and arms, square cushions, thin slabs of wood. Henry Miller, I assumed. And Henry Miller was on the bookshelves too, the other Henry Miller, along with Joyce and Bellow, Mailer, Anaïs Nin, Samuel Beckett, early Updike, early Wouk, a massive biography of Ben Gurion, oversized picture books on Surrealism, the Impressionists, Picasso, Picasso, more Picasso. I recognized the decor and the ambiance, yes I did. I could imagine old copies of the *New Yorker* stacked thigh-high in the bathroom.

There were bunches of photographs in silver frames

scattered here and there on side tables, on the piano. A younger Telushkin and a prim little woman, undoubtedly Telushkin's wife. A middle-aged Telushkin with the same wife and some children, presumably his own. Assorted wedding pictures as the children hitched one after the other under the chupa. An older Telushkin alone with his grand-children. A widower now, or had the wife simply had enough of the Henry Miller and just upped and left? Along with those family mementos were the expected trophy photographs of a man who had spent his career in public service one way or the other: Telushkin with Robert Kennedy, with Johnson, with Carter, with Clinton. Was I detecting a pattern?

"Ah, Mr. Carl, yes." He brought in a wooden tray with a ceramic teapot, two cups on saucers, a sugar bowl with sugar cubes, a small milk pitcher. "How do you like your tea?"

"Just plain," I said, sitting down again.

"I like mine with milk and sugar, in the British way. There now, how is that? Yes." He stared at me over his teacup as he took a sip, as if he were sizing me up for some unknown purpose. "So. Mr. Carl," he said, continuing his appraisal. I grew uncomfortable under his stare, looked around.

"Nice place," I said.

"Thank you. I try to keep modern."

"You said that Tommy Greeley was the one who got away."

"Yes, I did. Of them all, he was the only one not to pay the piper, don't you see? Which is unfortunate, since he was the main target all along."

"Target of what, Mr. Telushkin?"

"Jeffrey. Call me Jeffrey. I'm retired now, no need to stand on ceremony any longer. The target of my inquiry.

My great success. It was I who stumbled on it all." He looked at me, waited for admiration to show on my face, was disappointed. "How much don't you know?"

I took a sip of the tea, dark and biting. "Pretty much everything, I'm afraid."

"Well, let me see. Perhaps I'll begin at the beginning, a novel idea, no? It started with Babbage, Bradley Babbage. A noted entrepreneur, young and successful and much the hit with the ladies. You must have seen his picture in the paper at the time. He was a star at all kinds of political and civic functions." His eyebrows rose with a genuine merriment. "He raised money for Rizzo, Specter, and then for Reagan."

"Unless he was in *Highlights for Children,* which was all I was reading at the time, I would have missed him."

"Well, too bad then, he put on quite the spectacle. But things in the Babbage empire were not entirely as they seemed. There were questions about the profitability of a building he owned, and another enterprise he ran, a limousine service actually, and about a small publishing house he had purchased that was slow in paying its royalties. It was the complaining authors that put us on the track, imagine that? Babbage was claiming losses in everything, so no taxes were paid, and yet he was constantly buying and expanding. It seemed, well, peculiar. It seemed to deserve looking into, yet it seemed also to be an avenue not so interesting for the agency to vigorously pursue. And, because of the administration then in power and the subject's connection to it, not an investigation designed to enhance the career of any agent who took it on. So they gave it to me.

"I was with the department then, of course, but I was mostly considered a mid-level drone, ushered into a corner cubicle and ignored. A bit of excess waste kept on by civil service regulations," he said, his eyes trying to twinkle but unable to hide the angry pride underneath, "not up to normal department standards. You see, I was never one of those agents who charged about with my gun drawn. It is the hero types who get the press, the big cases, who rise to heights in the department. Yes, I understood that, but that didn't always make them the most effective agents, despite their swaggered steps and deep voices.

"Do you know how Rockefeller became the richest man in America?" he asked. "He kept his books more carefully than anyone else. He bought and sold things, that is all, but he knew to the penny the profit on each and every transaction and made his decisions accordingly. You can change the world with an eye on the books, you see. I am an accountant by training. I was not thought much of by the hierarchy or the heroes, but I could read the books better than anyone. And when they gave me the Babbage case I started with the books and that's how I discovered him."

"Discovered who?"

"The secret investor. There had to be a secret investor. Babbage was losing money, but he was still buying businesses. So slowly, carefully, I traced the money that was keeping Babbage afloat, traced it back from one account to the next, the whole trail. I found the checks, the shifting accounts, the wired deposits, traced it all back to the source. Cash deposits, you see. Some were made by Babbage himself, receipts from his business, he told the bank. But the receipts didn't match the books, they were higher than his cash flow could have possibly allowed. Something was wrong. And then there were others, from other accounts, cash deposits straight into the bank, all less than ten thousand dollars, the amount that triggered financial reporting, but adding up, when you took them as a whole, to far far more. That is a crime, you know, Mr. Carl, dividing up a

single cash deposit into many to avoid reporting require-
ments. So it was a snap to get the warrant to find the name
behind it all, the hidden investor who was laundering his
money through Babbage. And there he was, as if his picture itself was painted in the various columns of the various ledgers."

"Tommy Greeley?" I said.

"Yes, of course. He was a law student, that was all. His
family was once firmly middle class but it had fallen on
hard times, so you would expect him to be struggling to
pay even his tuition. But tuition was paid, he had a condo-
minium apartment, a fancy car, a beautiful girl, a huge circle of friends. He took his friends on vacations in Hawaii,
was well known in the casinos at Atlantic City for throwing lavish and risqué parties. It was all too obvious to ignore. When I brought it to my superiors, they added three
agents and a prosecutor to the case, three hero types and a
lawyer with a fetish for free publicity, all of whom tried to
elbow me out. That is the way that type works, but you see
I wasn't so easy to get rid of. They began presenting the
case to the grand jury, they thought they could do it themselves, but they were wrong. You see, I had something they
needed. I had the books.

"More tea, Mr. Carl?"

"I'm fine," I said. I watched Telushkin carefully as he
poured himself another cup, dropped in one sugar cube,
then another, swirled in the milk. Something about him
riled me. Maybe it was his utter fatuousness, or maybe it
was the way his voice colored judgmental as he talked
about everyone else in his story. There was a not-so-hidden
subtext to all his comments, as if he assumed, for some
reason I could very well imagine, that he and I were so ide-
ologically simpatico that much of what he wanted to ex-

press need not be said. His very discretion seemed to put us in the same jolly conspiracy. His self-satisfaction was so evident, I wanted to knock his glasses off.

"I brought in Babbage and his lawyer," Telushkin continued. "His understandable position was to say not a thing, to plead the Fifth. He was there only to listen, said his lawyer. So I showed them both what I discovered in the books, the raw numbers that had told me everything. Page by page, entry by entry, I went through it all, and when I was through, both he and the lawyer realized with absolute certainty that Babbage was caught. Tax evasion, of course, and money laundering, yes. But then, when I told him in my quiet way that there was more, that I could twist my reading of the books to tab him with being an integral part of whatever Tommy Greeley was part of, and when the penalties of that became clear, he blanched. And he turned. And he exposed everything that had been going on."

"And what was that, Mr. Telushkin?" I said.

"Call me Jeffrey. Please. I insist. And I'll call you Victor, is that all right?"

I smiled at him like we were in a league together and nodded and gripped my teacup ever tighter.

"It was drugs, of course," he said. "Cocaine. Massive amounts brought up from Florida and distributed through Pennsylvania, New Jersey, as far north as Boston, as far west as Phoenix. It was more than a business, Victor, it was an empire. We thought we were seeing all the enterprise's profits being run through Babbage, but he was only working with some of the money from only one of the participants, from Tommy Greeley. But there was another leader too, and others were taking out huge amounts of money. They were selling sixty million dollars a year of drugs, Victor. Sixty million dollars. A year. And it had been going on for half a decade."

I put down my cup because it had started to shake atop its saucer. This was big, bigger than I had ever imagined, and it fit perfectly with what Joey had told me, about what Tommy was carrying when he was killed, and the cool way he handled the threat before Joey's first swing with the bat. And something else, the thing that made my cup shake on the saucer. There was suddenly more than the suitcase at stake. Only Tommy Greeley's money had gone through Babbage. Where was the rest of it, and was that the reason Tommy was killed? And was that the reason Joey too, twenty years later, was killed? My contingency fee agreement with Mrs. Parma began to glow with a fabulous heat.

"But, as could be expected, Victor, even with all that business, the heroes were having trouble breaking into the organization, the heroes were finding themselves stymied. This was more than a business organization, all the participants were friends, comrades. They had, all of them, made each other rich. And they weren't talking, not a word. The grand jury was getting nowhere. They couldn't prove up the drug charges. We would get some of them for tax evasion, yes, but it was looking like only a tax case. Until I brought Babbage into the grand jury room.

"I can't tell you everything he told me, Victor, or what he told the grand jury, that would be improper, not to mention illegal, but he broke it open, did our Mr. Babbage. His testimony was like the wedge that split everything apart. The indictments are public record, and the results were well publicized in the press. There were two indicted as so-called kingpins, eligible for stiff sentences without parole. One was a fellow called Prod, Cooper Prod. He is still in jail, don't know when he gets out. The other was Tommy Greeley."

"The one that got away," I said, almost pleased that this

trophy had eluded Telushkin even though I knew what had really happened to him.

"Yes. I had wanted him especially, with his high living and his haughtiness. You know, once when I went to talk to him, to see what I could see, he laughed at me. He laughed, as if it was inconceivable that someone like me could corner someone like him. And then he leaned over and quietly, in my ear, said, 'You're not smart enough.' I wasn't sure I had caught what he had said, I asked him to repeat it, it was too much to believe that someone could be so arrogant. But he just laughed at me and walked away."

"What happened to him, do you know?"

"Of course I know."

I peered at him closely. "What?"

"He ran," he said. "He took what he could and he ran. But he didn't get far."

"How do you know?"

"He was a troubled man dealing with dangerous people. There was a tremendous amount of money involved and he owed as much as he was owed. Not a healthy situation. When someone runs away he always slips up somehow. After a few months, or a few years, his arrogance gets the best of him, he thinks he has won, he has escaped, that his pursuers have lost interest. He will make contact with old friends, with family, he will make a mistake. But Tommy Greeley never did. I spent the rest of my career searching for him, checking the mail to his parents, his girlfriend, keeping tabs on those of his friends released from jail. It became something of an obsession. Call me Ishmael, I suppose."

"It was Ahab obsessed with the whale," I said.

He clapped. "So it was. So it was. But there was nothing, nothing. Tommy Greeley wasn't clever enough or modest enough to pull it off. All that time searching for him was not wasted, it gave me the certainty that I sought, the certainty to conclude that something happened early on, that somehow his run to freedom failed at the start. He got his, along with the rest, only he got it worse. Well now, Victor. Anything else? More tea?"

"No thank you," I said, standing. "I appreciate your time. One more question. This Babbage, the informer. What kind of sentence did he get?"

"Seven years probation."

"Sweet."

"It was a necessary evil, I assure you. He was offered witness protection but he refused it, said he didn't need it. And he did quite well after everything passed. Apparently there was some money unaccounted for, which he discovered after the case was over. But pursuant to the terms of his cooperation agreement, there was nothing we could do about that. I still don't know how we could have missed those moneys," he said, even as his wink let me know that he certainly did, that the man who had studied Babbage's books with the care of a Rockefeller knew where every penny had been buried, so the money left to be discovered was all part of Telushkin's deal for his prize witness's testimony. "He had a nice plastics business later on, did Babbage, recycling, with a big house and a pool in Gladwyne. Was still political, but had been turned by his experience, I suppose. Became a great supporter of Clinton, if you can believe that?"

"I'd like to speak to him."

"That would be quite difficult, Victor."

"Excuse me?"

"He drowned."

"My God."

"Just a few weeks ago. In his pool. He took a swim every morning, a few dives, a few laps. But I suppose he took one dive too many. They found him floating face-down."

"Did the police investigate?"

"Ruled it an accident. Apparently he had a heart attack, right in the pool. So it goes. You know, Victor, cracking that case was the highlight of my career, the highlight, actually, of my professional life. I worked on many white-collar cases, tax cases, fraud, but that was the biggest win. And all from a careful examination of the books. I guess I'm not so different from Rockefeller after all."

"Give or take a billion dollars."

"Yes, I suppose," he said, at a loss for a moment before his unctuous smile returned and he gestured me toward the door. "If there is anything else I can help you with, please let me know."

"Oh I will," I said, still thinking of Babbage, floating facedown in the water.

"By the way, Victor, one thing you might want to know." His eyebrows rose and his face took on the expression of self-delight that seemed to be his trademark. "Our Tommy Greeley. Believe it or not, his best friend in college and in law school was not his business partner, that Cooper Prod. It was someone else. We couldn't link him with any of the wrongdoing, and he was never indicted, but still it is quite an interesting association."

I looked at him. He wanted me to help him out, to pressure it out of him for some reason, as if that would put us further in league together, but I knew if I waited long enough he would spill, he couldn't help himself. His smile was expectant for a moment before it turned exasperated and then he couldn't hold it in any longer.

"Straczynski. Jackson Straczynski. They were the best of friends. Isn't that something?"

"Yes," I said, and it was. I swallowed with surprise at the name, but I tried not to show it.

His hand moved solicitously to my back, like he was pushing me out now that he had told me exactly what he had wanted to tell me, led me exactly where he had wanted me to go. I didn't mind leaving, but I didn't like being pushed the way he was pushing me.

At the doorway I stopped, turned around. "Thank you so much for your help."

"It was nothing. Nothing at all. I was glad to be of service."

"I suppose he was, wasn't he?"

"Who?"

"Tommy. You said he got away, never paid the piper. So I suppose maybe he was too smart for you after all."

His puckish expression dropped for just a moment and what was left was all the arrogance and intolerance that I had heard beneath his jovial voice, and then the smile returned. "Good day, Mr. Carl," he said, closing the door before I had the chance to turn away.

It was all a swirl for me as I walked back down the hall toward the elevator. The squirrelly FBI special agent who brought down an empire, the money launderer who did a spectacularly bad job of laundering Tommy Greeley's cash, the grand jury investigation, the sixty-million-dollar-a-year cocaine enterprise, the indictments, the dead informant, the dead informant who died in a strange swimming accident not two weeks before Joey Parma got his throat slashed. All of it swirled around me as I tried to make sense of it, but then a name popped out of the swirl, a name that Telushkin had made sure to tell me for reasons I could guess, oh yes.

Jackson Straczynski.

I knew the name, every lawyer in the city, in the country, knew the name. Jackson Straczynski, State Supreme Court Justice Jackson Straczynski, one of the most respected conservative legal scholars in the country and the first name on a very short list to fill the next open seat on the United States Supreme Court.

Whatever I had thought I had been getting myself into before, I had just fallen into the big leagues.

CHAPTER

20

"**What I heard**," said my private investigator Phil Skink, "is this Edward Dean, he made his money out on the Coast in some Internet con job what he sold afore the bubble burst. Or he was involved in some complicated investment scam the coppers are still trying to unravel. Or he invented the thingamajig what goes in the whatchubob what they stick into every computer comes off the line."

"In other words," I said, "you've learned nothing."

"This is crucial data, it is, culled from the most respected sources nationwide."

"Zilch."

"Pretty much, yeah."

It was approaching midnight in Rittenhouse Square, the residential heart of Philadelphia's high society. The park was dark, deserted except for the occasional couple strolling home from the bars and clubs on the east side of the square, or the occasional cop strolling from bench to bench to roust the homeless. Beth and I had arrived at the park first. Skink came after, assuring us that we hadn't been tailed by Dante's boys. Now we three sat on a bench in the middle of the square, staring at an imposing town house just to the west of the Ethical Society, with a curving stone staircase and granite pediments and wrought-iron grates over its first-floor windows. The town house, dark now except for a bright light falling from the third-floor window, was currently home to the various and sundry Jacopo businesses, along with their principal shareholder.

"You pick up any other useless information about him?" I asked.

"He's a charitable sort, so long as his name's prominent on the donor list. Gives to plastic surgeons what are curing hair lips in China. Gives to groups pushing literacy in the inner city. Gives to an organization committed to saving some old boat on the waterfront."

"Excuse me," I said.

"Some old oceangoing liner."

"With the two huge red funnels?"

"That's the one. The owner wants to scrap it. This group is trying to save it, turn it into something like a hotel, or a floating museum, anything to keep it intact."

"That's peculiar," I said, remembering the sight of that same boat, looming not far from the pier where Joey Parma's lifeless body was tossed. "So, is he inside?"

"The limo pulled around back at nine, most likely with this Dean inside. The hard-act what keeps watch and runs errands, name of Colfax, he showed up around nine-thirty. And then she showed up a little after ten."

"Kimberly Blue."

"That's right, our Kimberly."

"So you think . . ."

"I ain't thinking nothing."

"Why did we wait until so late?" said Beth.

"Knocking at a reasonable hour would be expected," I said. "I'd rather shake him up a bit."

"Are we treating him like a client or a suspect?" said Beth.

I thought on that one for a moment. We had, after all,

taken Jacopo's money and paid our bills with it and we were, after all, pursuing Jacopo's claim against Derek Manley. And yet, there was something about that old rotting boat and its proximity to Joey's corpse that convinced me.

"Suspect," I said.

"Attaboy," said Skink. "You sure you don't want me inside with you?"

"The law firm of Derringer and Carl can handle this for now. No need to show Mr. Dean everything we have. I'm saving you for later. You're sure about that Eldorado being at the club?"

"I ain't seen it with my own eyes, but it's somewheres there. You just might have to poke around a bit. When you getting it?"

"The sheriff is scheduled for day after tomorrow," I said. "All right. You ready, Beth?"

"Ready," she said.

"If we're not out in half an hour," I told Skink as I pushed myself off the bench, "send in the dancing girls. Not that I'm worried or anything, but I always like a good show."

We walked together, Beth and I, south through the park and then west to the town house and our meeting with the mysterious Eddie Dean. Who was he? Where did he come from? Why had he magically appeared in Philadelphia? And why did an apparent high roller like Edward Dean have any interest in the death of a four-time loser like Joseph Parma? It was those very questions that impelled us up that curving stone staircase toward the ornate wooden door.

I pressed the buzzer and pressed it again.

After a long stretch of time, a voice came through the little black squawk box beside the door.

"Who the 'ell are you two and what are you after?" The voice was harsh, dismissive, and, surprise surprise, British, like a London cabbie on a wet morning with the traffic snarled and a poodle making puddles on the backseat.

I stepped away, scanned the wall left and right of the door, found the small camera staring at me, smiled and waved like a beauty queen.

"We've come to see Mr. Dean," I said into the box.

"Bugger off."

"We're his lawyers. We have something to deliver that I think he'll be anxious to see."

"Do you know what 'our it is?"

"Late? My bad. Just tell Mr. Dean his lawyers are here and they've brought for his perusal the deposition of Derek Manley."

We didn't have to wait long before the door opened and the gate was unlocked. A man in sharp black pants, loafers without socks, and a gray V-neck sweater, all apparently quickly thrown on for our benefit, scowled before leading us into the house. He was medium height, medium build, nothing too threatening there, but his hair was razored close to his skull, his nose had been broken and reset badly, his eyes were cold and gray and frankly scary.

He led us through a central hallway and then left, into a large sitting room, with urns and red walls and stiff French furnishings. There were paintings of horses. There was a fireplace the size of a Yugo. There was a wall of old leather-bound books in matched sets. A huge grand piano, its cover raised jauntily, sat expectantly in the corner. It smelled of must and ashes and perfume, that room, it smelled of money stashed in boudoir drawers.

"Wait 'ere," said the man. He slid a heavy wooden door closed behind him after he left the room.

A leather-topped table by the window caught my attention. Small, precisely carved pieces of wood were scattered across it, some painted, most not. I picked up a large conical piece, painted red and white and black. It looked like something, yes it did, and then I realized what. It was the stack on that decaying ship in the harbor. He was building a model of the old ocean liner, trying to put it all back together, but he hadn't gotten far.

Beth strolled along the bookshelves and ran a finger across a row of spines, leaving a trail in the dust. "I suppose Mr. Dean is not much of a reader," she said.

"Why don't you open one and check if the pages are cut."

"The collected works of Victor Hugo. The collected works of Charles Dickens. The collected works of Alexandre Dumas."

"Quite a collection. Anything appear like it's been read recently?"

"Here's one a little bit out of place. The collected works of William Shakespeare. Volume Three, the Tragedies. And there is a silk page mark in . . . *Hamlet*."

"To be or not to be?"

"No, actually. A different speech of Hamlet's, with the last line underlined. 'O, from this time forth, my thoughts be bloody, or be nothing worth.' "

Just then the door slid open.

"Helloo? Victor? Have you gone postal or something? What are you doing here?"

Kimberly Blue was standing in the doorway, a thick white robe clutched tightly closed. Her hair was loose and in disarray, her face clean of makeup, her feet bare. She looked impossibly young and impossibly lost amidst the stuffy moneyed decor of the house. She appeared, just then, despite the anger twisting her features, like someone who needed to be rescued. Behind her, glowering, stood the man who had let us in.

"We came to visit the CEO of Jacopo Financing," I said. "We came to see Mr. Dean."

"Are you forgetting? External relations? Everything goes through me? I thought you understood that. This is such a poodle. And why didn't you return my calls? I called, like, five times to find out about the deposition. I wish you had let me sit in. How did it go?"

"It was very interesting."

"Colfax said you had the deposition transcript. Why don't you just leave it with me and we'll talk about it tomorrow? When people are, like, awake?"

"I want to hand the deposition to Mr. Dean personally."

"Victor. No. You can't. This is totally bogus. I am the vice president of external relations—"

"And now we know how you got that job."

"Oh, shut up. That is so uncalled for. You have so little idea of—"

"You want, Miss Blue," said Colfax, "I can just take it from 'im. It won't be so 'ard, 'andling a twig like that."

"Like it wasn't so hard handling Joey Parma?" I said.

Colfax smiled. "That was a piece of wedding cake, it was, and you'll be ever more a snap, you septic little fuck."

"Hey. Hey. Hey. Hey. Hey," said Kimberly, each exclamation growing louder. "Just cool your tools and get over yourselves. It's not all about you boys, okay? Victor, what are you really doing here?"

"Mr. Carl has some questions," said a voice from behind Kimberly, a bray of a voice with a sharp Boston accent. "And he thinks himself entitled to some answers."

Kimberly and Colfax both stepped aside and Edward Dean entered the room.

He was a tall, overly dramatic man, wearing a silk paisley gown over his silk pajamas, an ascot at his throat. His left hand, held like a claw in front of his stomach, gripped a cigarette between two middle fingers. His long blond hair was combed back, his teeth were big and bright, his eyes were shining. But it wasn't the teeth or eyes or hair you noticed first about Edward Dean, and it wasn't even his absurd anglophile lord-of-the-manor getup. What you noticed first was his face, shiny, stiff, smooth, strangely expressionless, somehow unnatural, almost like a mask glued over his features. As if he had suffered a Botox overdose and never recovered.

"I have wanted to meet you for some time, Mr. Carl," said Dean, his mouth carefully forming the words, the one live thing among the stillness of his strange dead face. "Kimberly has said some very complimentary things about you." He stiffly swiveled his neck toward Beth. "And who is this you brought along?"

"Beth Derringer," said Beth.

"The Derringer of Derringer and Carl?"

"The same."

"I'm frankly stunned. I pictured you as an aging lion, mentoring Victor in his bruising legal career, not a lovely young woman. How did your name end up first on the letterhead?"

"Talent," said Beth. "I was admiring your books, Mr. Dean."

"Call me Eddie. And they're not mine. They came with the rental of the house, along with the piano and the paintings of horses."

"I love paintings of horses," I said. "Especially when they're playing poker."

"I couldn't help but notice," said Beth, "that you were reading *Hamlet*."

"Was I? Maybe yes. I find him inspirational."

"Shakespeare?"

"The Dane. Despite all his inner torment and his dithering, in the end he gets the job done, doesn't he? Avenges his father's death, restores his mother's honor. So yes, I was rereading *Hamlet*. I love to read. I still remember picking up my first thick novel, feeling its heft, holding it with such fear and wonder, as if it held all the truths of the world."

"What was it?" asked Beth.

He walked over to the shelf, searched for a bit, picked out a book. "Dumas. How many times my best friend and I were sent to the principal for sword fighting with wooden yardsticks I couldn't tell you. I think back and it's still the best book I ever read. A great influence to be sure. What was the book of your youth, Ms. Derringer?"

"*To Kill a Mockingbird*," said Beth. "I read that while still in grade school and knew who I wanted to be."

"Atticus Finch," said Eddie Dean.

"Exactly," said Beth.

"And you, Victor?" asked Eddie. "What was your earliest great literary experience?"

"A beat-up old paperback of *The Godfather*," I said. "Page twenty-seven."

"Page twenty-seven?" said Beth.

"Sonny Corleone," I said, "a bridesmaid, and a door."

Dean barked out a laugh at that. "Well, I'm delighted you've come too, Miss Derringer. The room needs some brightening, but I thought I was dealing just with Victor." He swiveled to look at Kimberly. "My staff didn't inform me you were on the case too."

Kimberly's face turned red.

"She didn't know," said Beth, "but helping each other on our cases is what it means for us to be partners. Although I am puzzled as to exactly what this case is?"

"Why, it's a case about a debt."

"More than that, isn't it?" I said.

"Oh, there is always more. Here, there is betrayal, deceit, murder, the usual, but it's still about a debt."

"You're talking about Joseph Parma's murder," I said, nodding.

"Yes. I suppose. That too. I am told, Mr. Carl, that you come bearing gifts. How fared Mr. Manley? Did you dig the dirt?"

"I found some assets I believe I can seize to start to pay off the note."

"I hope you found more than mere assets."

I tried to read his mask of a face, but it was impossible. Still I knew exactly what he had wanted from the deposition, and it had nothing to do with an apartment in New Jersey owned by Derek Manley's girlfriend or a car stashed somewhere at his strip club.

"Manley was part of it too," I said.

"Did he admit it?"

"No, but his reaction was clear as a confession."

"And who else? Did he name names?"

"He said he was doing a favor for a friend, but he wouldn't divulge who."

"Not unexpected. Start seizing his property, bit by bit, and see if that pricks his memory."

"That won't be so easy. Mr. Manley has an ally. A mobster. He is protecting Manley and he already tried to scare me off the case."

"Are you scared?"

"Yes."

"Enough to stop."

"Not yet."

"Good. You are as I expected you to be. When things grow difficult for Mr. Manley, tell him I'll trade the note for a name. That might open his lips."

"What's this all about, Mr. Dean?" said Beth. "Why do

you care what happened to Joey Parma, or what Joey Parma and Derek Manley might have done twenty years ago? What is your stake in all this?"

"It's about living up to an oath," he said. "It's about not forgetting the past. It's about paying one's debts. *Hamlet,* I suppose."

"I don't understand."

"Sit down, all of you." He glanced around him. "Kimberly, Colfax, make yourselves comfortable. This may take a while. I have a story to tell. Sit down, please."

Dean moved toward the fireplace and leaned on the mantel. Beth and I took seats beside each other on a stiff blue couch. Kimberly Blue curled into a wide aubergine wing chair to the right of the fireplace while Dean, with a careful impassive gaze, watched her every movement. Colfax remained standing by the door, guarding the exit.

"Good, now, are we, all of us, comfortable?" He lifted the cigarette to his mouth, inhaled, blew out a plume as if he were about to give a soliloquy on a great stage set to a packed house of adoring fans. "A long time ago," he said, "I had a friend. His name was Tommy Greeley."

Tell me why I wasn't surprised.

CHAPTER

21

"**Tommy Greeley was** the kind of friend you only find when you are six or seven and then only if you are very lucky," said Eddie Dean. "We were a unit, he and I. Fric and Frac, Tweedledee and Tweedledum, Eddie and Tom.

"This was in Brockton, Massachusetts, where I grew up, famous as the Shoe City of the World. We played baseball in the church yard like we were Yastrzemski and Fisk. We hung out by the railroad tracks. We swam at the lake. We spent long summer days in a tree house we hammered together deep in the park. He was closer to me than my family, closer to me than my own skin. I would have done anything for him and he me. When Frankie McQuirk took a shot at me it was Tommy who stepped in and got the broken nose. No big thing, but the kind of thing you never forget. Never.

"He came from a difficult family, nothing that ended up in the paper, but it had its effect. The Greeleys were rich by Brockton standards, country club people. They belonged to Thorny Lea Golf Club, where the boys I grew up with could only hope to caddie, and they lived in a huge stone house on Moraine Street, the best street in town, and on the best part of Moraine too, just north of West Elm. But when you stepped in the house it smelled wrong, like some crime had just been committed. The mother was cold, distant, more interested in her martinis than her son. And the father, Buck—everyone called him Buck—was big and bluff with a bright streak of anger at everyone and everything, an anger that grew to monstrous proportions when the shoe manufacturer Buck worked for went bankrupt and Buck found himself on the street, looking for work in an economy that was shedding jobs by the thousands.

"One afternoon—we were about eight by then—Tommy came out to the tree house with a black eye and split lip. He wouldn't tell me what had happened but he didn't have to tell me, I knew. It was Buck. The violent undertone of his bitterness, which had been there all along, was finally unmasked. And right after that, Tommy's mother left the house, moved up to Framingham where she had a sister. And she didn't take Tommy with her. The maternal instinct was not strong in Mrs. Greeley, killed off, I suppose, by massive quantities of gin.

"That beating was only the first Tommy took that summer at the hands of Buck—God that name, how purely it fit the hulking brute. It got so bad, Tommy took to hiding in that tree house in the woods and I, with my mother's permission, hid out with him.

"One night, in the park, we built a fire. We smeared lipstick on our faces like war paint. We concocted a strange Indian ceremony. And then we swore each other an oath. That we would be friends for life, together forever, the brotherhood of the woods. That we would take care of each other no matter what. That if something happened to one, the other would chase the wrongdoer to the ends of the earth to see justice done. This last bit was insisted on by Tommy and I understood exactly what it was about: Buck. Tommy wanted protection, for himself and his mother, if something happened to him, and he thought that in some strange way I could give it. But Buck was a big, hard man and I knew I could never do a thing against him. Still we sliced our palms like in the movies and clasped hands and, with solemn voice and full heart, I promised to protect him with my life."

He looked down at his right hand, stroked something on his palm, as if stroking out a memory.

"What happened?" said Kimberly, leaning forward now, sitting on the edge of the wing chair.

Eddie Dean turned his face to her, that same careful, impassive gaze directed her way, as if this story had some special meaning for her, as if it was directed at her and her alone. And then, as much as it was possible with that face of his, he smiled.

"Nothing. Buck found a job of sorts and Tommy's mother moved back and the danger in the Greeley house receded. Six months later my father was transferred to the West Coast office in Sacramento. And so we moved. And that was the end of it. I never saw Tommy Greeley again."

I cocked my head, looked at Beth, looked back at Eddie. "So?"

"So, a couple years ago I was having my . . ." Eddie Dean took a long drag from his cigarette, another quick glance at Kimberly. "Episodes. I made too much money too quickly and found too many ways to spend it. There was a fire—we're in Richard Pryor territory here—a fire which paradoxically saved my life, and I ended up where all the foolish rich end up, in rehabilitation. It's the same old story. But in this program, you were supposed to tally up all the obligations that you failed in the past, as a way to gain a grip on how you ended up addicted in the first place. Step seven it was. And that's when I remembered my oath with Tommy Greeley. Friends for life, together forever, the brotherhood of the woods. So I started looking for him.

"It's easy now, right? Just check the Internet. Everyone's on the Internet, but not Tommy Greeley. I called his mother in Brockton. And she told me this. That twenty years ago, Tommy Greeley had been living in Philadelphia, studying to be a lawyer, and then one day he simply vanished. Gone. Disappeared out of thin air.

"I had two choices, forget about it or pursue it. I probably would have forgotten about it, friendships die, that is the nature of things, and so do friends. But I had begun to see the wisdom in the program. If I couldn't be faithful to the dearest friend I had ever had, how could I be faithful to myself? A promise had been made, an oath had been taken. If something happened to one, the other would chase the wrongdoer to the ends of the earth to see justice done."

"So you decided to solve the mystery on your own?" said Kimberly.

"It sounds silly, I know."

"No it doesn't," she said, and something in Dean's immobile face lit with a deep pleasure.

"I had a contact in Los Angeles," he continued, "a police detective. I am a donor to a number of charities, including one with which he was intimately concerned. A tragedy involving his son. With his eyes welling in gratitude at my generosity, he had told me to call him if I needed help on anything, anything at all. I took him up on the offer. He made a request to the Philadelphia Police Department for any information they had on Tommy Greeley. There was a file. A missing persons file. And in the file was a memo about an offer from a jailhouse snitch. He said he knew why the person was missing. He said that Tommy had been set up, that a valuable suitcase had been stolen, that Tommy had been murdered. He said he would tell who had done the killing for a reduction in his sentence. The memo ended with a notation about the snitch being murdered in a fight in the yard. There was nothing more to be done. But the snitch had given something to the police, a tidbit of what he could offer if given a deal. He had given a name: Cheaps."

"Joey," I said.

"It didn't take much to find him, his nickname is unique enough, or to confirm that Joseph Parma and the jailhouse snitch were incarcerated at the same time in a prison called Graterford. I sent my man Colfax east to rent suitable housing and to hire a staff. When I arrived, Colfax and I paid a visit to Mr. Parma.

"He denied everything. Despite our entreaties, both firm and generous, he denied everything. He never heard of Tommy Greeley. He never was involved in anyone's disappearance. He never told a thing to the jailhouse snitch. It was all exactly as I expected. But it wasn't what he would tell me on which I had pinned my hopes, it was on who he would call afterward. My detective in Los Angeles obtained the phone logs. Two calls of interest. And this is where you came in, Victor. One call was to a Derek Manley, and the other was to Joey Parma's lawyer."

"So you used me to put pressure on Manley," I said, "based on information you believed Joey Parma might have disclosed to me."

"I *hired* you for that reason, yes. I had hoped my vice president of external affairs would clue you in to what I was after and she didn't disappoint. I realized from the start that Joseph Parma was at the bottom of a chain. He was nothing more than a tool, and so was the Derek Manley of twenty years ago. My obligation required me to rise up the chain, step by step, to find the person ultimately responsible. Because there was more to Tommy Greeley's disappearance than a mere accident of crime. The snitch said he had been set up. Someone close to Tommy, for some reason, had wanted to do him harm. Someone close to Tommy was responsible for his disappearance. He is the one I intend to find."

"And what are you going to do when you find him?" I said. "The same thing you did to Joey?"

He tilted his head at me, the only form of puzzlement his frozen face allowed him to display, and as he did his vertebrae cracked. "We were rougher with Mr. Parma than I would have liked, yes, but it was more for show than anything else. We meant him no real harm, we only wanted him to be afraid enough to take some sort of action."

"Slicing his throat was just for show?"

"Excuse me? Oh, I see. Victor, no, you have it wrong. I had nothing to do with that. In fact, I had been hoping you would convince Mr. Parma to go to the police with what he knew. What happened to Mr. Parma was a major setback."

"That still leaves the question of what you are going to do if you find the man responsible," said Beth.

"Turn over all that I've learned to the proper authorities. What else? Victor, do you have the name of a detective who could prove useful?"

"I might indeed," I said. I glanced down at my hands, and then peered directly at Eddie Dean when I said, "You did know, didn't you, that Tommy Greeley was one of the leaders of a million-dollar cocaine enterprise?"

Eddie Dean didn't flinch, his immobile face was unable to perform such gyrations, but he did glance to the side, to where Kimberly was still curled on the chair. My gaze followed his. Kimberly was watching carefully, surprise clear on her face.

"Yes," he said, finally. "My police detective in Los Angeles informed me of the indictment against him. Never proven in a court of law, of course, so I choose to presume him innocent. Maybe I'm being overly gallant toward my old friend, but my protector from the ravages of Frankie McQuirk deserves at least that from me, don't you think?"

"Depends on how tough McQuirk really was?"

"Oh he was a beast, believe me," said Dean. "Four-foot-six, sixty-four pounds, at least. So, that is my story. Have your questions been answered? Are you willing to continue my collection action and learn what you can from Mr. Manley?"

I looked at Beth. She shrugged. It was my case, she was leaving it up to me. I pursed my lips and pretended to be impressed, even though I knew his story to be a total crock.

You might imagine that I was angry at being lied to, that I would storm out of that house in righteous indignation. But, frankly, if I waited for a client I believed one hundred percent I would starve. In no relationship are the lies more blatant, excepting perhaps the marital relationship, than the relationship of a client to his lawyer. Clients lie, it's what they do, that clients lie to their lawyers is the first of three immutable laws of the legal profession, and so I wasn't shocked, shocked that Eddie Dean would be lying to me. What surprised me was the forethought of the lie. Eddie Dean had created a marvelous, intricate, Gothic lie, a touching story of childhood friendship and adult remorse and pledges unfulfilled. I was flattered, frankly, that he cared enough to craft such a fine full lie, and puzzled too, that he would think it mattered enough to go to all the trouble, even though something about its ornate nature indicated it wasn't quite manufactured for me. But a lie still it was. For Edward Dean could not have known that I had seen the missing persons file, but I had, and there was no note from a jailhouse snitch with details of Tommy Greeley's murder and the name "Cheaps" prominently displayed.

I looked at him for a long moment, his masklike face re-

vealing nothing, and then looked at Kimberly. Eddie
Dean's story was a lie, yes, but it seemed to me just then
that it wasn't told for my benefit, it was told for hers. Why
would he care? What did she have to do with anything? I
remembered what I had thought when I first saw her in that
house, her feet bare, her robe clutched close.

"So, Victor," said Eddie Dean. "Can I count on you?
Are you willing to help me pursue the ends of justice? Are
you willing to help me solve the murder of Tommy Greeley?"

CHAPTER

22

"That doctor came in again," said my father, after I had slipped into his room, trying to avoid that very same doctor.

"Which doctor?" I said with sincere disingenuousness.

"The cute one."

"I thought you said she wasn't so cute."

"Cute enough. She came in again. She asked about you."

"Wonderful," I said, my smile tight.

"What's the matter."

"She's a vegetarian, Dad."

"Oh."

"And she's got cats. A swarm of them. She takes their pictures."

"See, I told you."

"Yes you did."

"Ohio."

"How are you feeling?" I said, though the room itself provided my answer. Two new monitors had been installed. One showed the rate of his breaths, now at nineteen per minute, which I knew already was dangerously high. The other monitor showed the beating of his heart, one hundred and nine beats a minute, his heart struggling to keep up his respiratory rate. Things were not going well for my father.

"I feel like crap," he said, wincing as he shifted on the bed, "which is good."

"Why is that good?"

"Because as soon as I start feeling better they're going to open up my chest and cut out my lungs."

"That's true."

"You don't got to be so damn cheery about it."

"I just want you to get well."

"Why?"

Good question, why indeed? What wondrous marvels of life awaited my father as he stepped out of the hospital with his lungs slashed in half? My father had always been able to cut through the noise and ask the telling question, which was one of the things I couldn't stand about him.

"Where am I?" he said.

"Dad?"

"Where? Where am I?"

I felt tender toward him for a moment, an old ill man who had completely lost his bearings. "You're not well, Dad," I said. "You're in the hospital."

"I know that, you idiot. In the story."

"Of course," I said. "The story."

"Oh yes," he said, closing his eyes. "Now I remember. Yes. The morning after."

The morning after the night before. The world seems new, cleansed somehow. He doesn't get up before the sun this day, not with his newly minted love still asleep on his chest. Aaronson and his damn mowers can get along without him for once. He lies there, staring at her, feeling her hair tickling his chest, waiting for her eyes to open, for the expression of pleasure to brighten her features when she sees that it is him there, that his body is the pillow beneath her head. And they do, and she does. And my father didn't say it, but I knew what also he was waiting for, waiting for her to awaken so he can kiss the sleep from her eyes, to lick the film from her teeth, to reach again for the perfect closeness, the perfect urgency of the night before. And the way my father's eyes widened at the memory told me it was just as perfect, and maybe, my God, even more.

"I said it," he told me. It. "And she said it too." It. The word that had so pained my father that he had been unable to pronounce it more than a handful of times for as long as my entire life, and I had an inkling now of why. They say it, back and forth, it, and the it he proclaims is not the rote mewings of habit or the smooth lies of the Casanova, no. For my father it is a declaration that cements for all eternity the swirl of emotion that has overwhelmed him and defined him anew. I love you. I love you too. Yes I do. Me too. Oh yes. Yes. I love you I love you I love you. There, in that most unlikely of places, that narrow bed in that cramped decaying apartment in North Philadelphia, there my father and the love of his life promise the world and their hearts one to the other.

Tell me we'll be together forever, he says.

Together, she says.

Promise me, he says.

Forever, she says.

Promise me, he says.

I promise. You and me, Jesse. Together forever. I promise and now you promise too.

I do, he says. I promise.

And so it is asked and answered, promised, sealed. The crucial most difficult steps have been taken with remarkable ease. The rest are mere details. Details, where, according to the sages, both God and the devil reside.

Let's go somewhere, he says.

Okay, where?

I don't know. California maybe.

They are lying on the bed, the morning sun is now slanting in the window, a soft cloud can be seen floating by in the distance. His arms are behind his head, the future rolls ahead of my father like a long lazy river to be savored and explored together with this girl, this naked girl in his bed, their love the raft keeping them dry and buoyant.

California sounds nice, she says.

San Francisco, or maybe Los Angeles.

Hollywood? she says.

Sure, Angel, anywhere you want.

Hollywood then. Anywhere, really, so long as it's away from him.

The cloud drifts across the sun and the room suddenly darkens.

Who is he? he asks.

Nobody.

So why does he matter?

Because of who he is.

And who is he?

He is rich, greedy, grasping, she says. He is a soulless spider. And then she tells my father of how she became entwined in his web.

"Her mother had been sick," said my father, fighting now for breath as he struggled to explain. But he didn't have to struggle so hard. As soon as the sick mother was marched to the fore all the other elements fell in behind her. The financial need, the golden opportunity, the lifesaving stream of income, the financial dependence. And once the dependence was settled upon her shoulders like a yoke, the more unusual secretarial requests. The personal letters. The inventory taken side by side on the large dining room table. The late hours. The working dinners. And then the rainy evening, the roads awash. You mustn't try to go home in this weather. It isn't safe. I insist you stay the night. I simply insist. And so there she was, tossing awake in the big iron guest bed, as the sounds assaulted her from every side. The lashing of the rain against the windows, the wind scraping the tree limbs across the stone facing, the old house settling down upon itself. And then something different, the creaking of the floorboards, the whispered entreaty, the low whine of the door as it slips open, only the long bony fingers visible at first. "Her mother had been sick," said my father, which was explanation enough for all that followed, the gasp in horror, the calm voice of age and authority, the tears, the sobs, the ultimate submission as the old man rutted atop her like a bearded billy goat, while she stared at nothing and thought only of her mother, her sick, old mother, and the medical bills that were piling against their door higher and higher with every visit to each new specialist.

My father had always been quick to anger, anger being his natural state, so it wasn't hard to imagine his reaction, the bile flowing through him at the thought of the old man taking advantage of his love, the old man turning his love into something ugly, something unclean. "I wanted to kill him," my father said and of that I had no doubts. He wants to smite him as the defilers were smote in the olden days, to stone him to death for what he did to her, to his love.

No, she says. You can't. No. Let's just go away.

What about your mother?

She passed away, her illness, she was too weak even with the specialists.

When?

A month ago. Maybe two.

So why are you still with him?

Where was I to go? I had no place else. No place else, Jesse, until I met you.

She would have kissed him then, kissed him hungrily,

urgently, sucking the air from his lungs. And I knew how he would have reacted, how her kiss would have dissolved his anger, banished his questions, how it would have stiffened his devotion, I knew all of that without him telling because he and I were of the same blood.

All right, he says, the sweat pouring off of him, her taste like an opiate on his tongue. All right, let's just go, go away somewhere. Let's go.

Okay.

To California.

Hollywood?

Sure.

Okay. Yes. Let's go.

I love you, he says. I'll love you forever.

Yes, she says. Me too. Yes. But first, before we go away, we have to go back.

To the old man's house?

Everything I own is there. All my belongings. We have to go back.

Forget them.

All I own is there, and more. He owes me, Jesse, don't you see? There are unpaid wages . . . and there is more. He owes me. We can't get started, she says, we can't live the way we deserve until we get what he owes me.

"What he owes me," said my father, from his bed, his voice now merely the softest of whispers riding over his wet sucking breath. "Only what he owes me."

He was right, my father, once again. He wasn't getting better. The new antibiotic wasn't any more efficacious than the old one, and his lungs remained flooded with poison. They would have to try something new, some other wonder drug to cure his infection, though I sensed as I watched him fall into a pained sleep, with the words "What he owes me" on his lips, that there wasn't any new wonder drug that could cure what was truly ailing him. Maybe I had been right before when I had suggested they pump him full of Iron City beer, because that was what he had been using all these years, I recognized, to keep these memories at bay. But they were coming out now, one after the other, pulled from his throat like a rope of knotted kerchiefs, as if he were some second-rate magician and I an audience of enraptured schoolkids. And as each one passed it left its own virulent strain of bitter disappointment in his blood that no antibiotic could ever hope to destroy.

The only answer was to pull it to the end, to get the entire story out of his gut, to tell it and maybe in the telling to free himself of the past, which was killing him day by day, and which had been killing him, I now believed, since long before I was born.

CHAPTER

23

"He's late," I said.

"He works for the city," said Beth, sitting next to me in my parked car.

"But he is going to come?"

"On his horse, most likely."

"Yeah," I said. "What is up with that?"

"He thinks he grew up in the North Country."

"North Kensington is more like it. It's the name of the office that gets to them. Every little boy wants to grow up to be sheriff. But he's generally reliable. What time is it?"

"Three minutes later than the last time you asked. Why are we still doing this, Victor, if our client is lying?"

"The CEO of our client is lying, true, but there are other Jacopo stockholders to consider. Kimberly, for instance."

"Ah, now I see," she said.

"What?"

"And now I see why you agreed to let her accompany you as you look for Tommy Greeley's killer."

"I had my reasons."

"She's mighty pretty."

"Yes she is, but that's not why I find her so interesting."

"Why then?"

"Because Eddie Dean hired her. And because he seems overly concerned with her opinion of him. That lie he told night before last, I don't think it was for us. I think it was for her."

"Is he sleeping with her?"

"Gad, with that face I hope not."

"He's dangerous, Victor. And so is that Colfax thug he's got with him."

"Where do guys like Dean find guys like that anyway?"

"You should ask him sometime."

"I will."

"What do you think he's really after?"

"Maybe the suitcase."

"Stop it already."

"Answer me this, Beth. Why is there so much interest in something that happened so long ago, interest that would prompt a murder, maybe two if you count the unfortunate drowning of Bradley Babbage, a threatened disembowelment from Derek Manley, a warning from Earl Dante, and now Eddie Dean's intricate and fabulous lie?"

"You always believe money's at the root of everything."

"And I haven't been wrong yet. If everybody wants to take a look inside that damn suitcase, then I want to peek inside it too."

"How do we do that?"

"Maintain the pressure on Derek Manley, dig up what we can about Tommy Greeley, and keep little Kimberly close."

"Like I said, she's mighty pretty."

"Yes she is."

"You going to hit on her?"

"Nah. She's too young for me too—I don't know—innocent?"

"Maybe she's not sad enough."

"What does that mean?"

"Nothing. Or maybe you're just getting old."

"Tell me about it. But truthfully, the only desire she invokes is the desire to keep her out of trouble. And you want to know the sorriest thing? Whatever is going to come down, it's going to come down on her, and I won't be able to do a damn thing about it. Look sharp, here he comes."

The tow truck pulled beside us in the parking lot off Oregon Avenue, followed by a white Lumina with police lights on top and a Philadelphia Sheriff's logo on its side. A short, wiry man with a uniform and a gun climbed out of the Lumina and hitched up his pants. His legs were splayed and bowed like he had just climbed off his quarter horse. Beth and I stepped out of the car to meet him.

"Howdy, R.T.," I said.

R.T. stuck a cowboy hat on his head, pushed its brim up as if to survey the far prairie. "Victor," he said, nodding at me. "Beth."

"Thanks for coming," I said. "You're looking spry this morning."

"Healthy living," said R.T. "And soy curds. You guys got the paperwork?"

"Yes we do," said Beth, handing him a file folder.

As he examined the papers he said, "The boss is having a little shindig next week. At Chickie and Pete's."

"I love Chickie and Pete's," I said. "Especially the crab fries."

"Potatoes." R.T. snorted. "It's like mainlining sugar. You know why everyone and his brother is so fat these days?"

"Potatoes?"

"There you go. Potatoes and high-fructose corn syrup. You want to know the most serious problem facing this country?"

"High-fructose corn syrup?"

"Now you're getting it. But the roast beef is good, so

long as you chuck the roll. Call the office and Shelly will send you each a special invitation. And as always, your donations will be greatly appreciated."

I gave Beth a sad nod and mouthed the words "special invitations." She mouthed back "donations." Politics in Philadelphia is like politics everywhere else, except for the crab fries.

"This all looks to be in order," said R.T. Still holding the file, he turned to face the squat, windowless white building at the edge of the parking lot. The building's sign rose above its roof like a great beacon to weary travelers. THE EAGER BEAVER. And beneath that, just so the weary traveler wouldn't confuse the premises with, say, a diner specializing in roadkill, were the words: GIRLS GIRLS GIRLS.

"You sure it's in there?" said R.T.

"So I heard."

"Where in there?"

"We'll find it," I said. "Beth, why don't you go around back with the truck. We'll go in the front."

Beth nodded, walked over to the tow truck, climbed in the passenger seat. The tow truck pulled out of the lot.

"All right, Buckaroo," said Deputy Sheriff R.T. Pritchett, again hitching up his pants, rising to his role in the morning's drama. "Let's saddle on up and rope this doggy."

It was a bright day, but you wouldn't know it from inside the Eager Beaver. The lights were low, the music loud, the joint was practically empty and it smelled like soiled socks. Three men sat scattered at the round tables, drinking beer, all three scruffy as tomcats and evidently well practiced at wasting their days. A girl, no better at hiding her boredom than her breasts, was dancing slowly atop the bar. She was pretty enough and was wearing little enough and her shoes were high enough and her breasts were certainly big enough, but with the emptiness of the place, the smell, the tired pall of smoke, the humid heat, with everything, the scene was about as sexy as a root canal.

R.T.'s uniform drew the attention of a squat hunched man with a battered fleshy face and false black hair, who slipped off the bar and waddled toward us. "Ain't no cover this afternoon, gentlemen. You want a table close to the action?"

"There's action?" I said. "Where?"

"We're looking for a Derek Manley," said R.T. "You seen him today?"

"Don't know him. But I'm just a greeter here. Greetings. You want me to shake your hand, I will. You want me to get you a seat close enough to Wanda over there what you can smell her, I can do that too."

"I can smell her from here," I said.

"If Mr. Manley's not around," said R.T., "we'll talk to Mr. Rothstein."

"Rothstein?" The greeter scratched his head. "Don't know him neither. Maybe he's coming in for lunch."

"Cut with the act," I said, "and tell him he has visitors."

"He ain't in," said the man. "He don't come in much no more, what with his tax problems."

"You mind if we go through there?" I said, pointing to an open doorway loosely shielded by a curtain of beads.

He held out his hand. "Patrons ain't allowed in the back."

"We're not patrons," said R.T., taking a paper out of the file, handing it to the greeter. "Step aside, pilgrim, we got a right to be here. We're looking for a 2002 Cadillac Eldorado."

The man laughed. "An Eldorado, huh? Well, if you want, you can look under them tables, behind the bar, wherever, but I don't see no Eldorado. Who did you say you was again?"

"I'm a lawyer," I said, pulling a card out of my pocket.

Without so much as a glance, he dropped it to the floor, ground it with his shoe.

"Nice manners," I said. "In Japan they'd behead you for that. Just be advised I represent Jacopo Financing, which is owed a hundred thousand dollars by Derek Manley."

"A hundred thousand dollars? That's a lot of money. And you think it's here? Hey, Wanda," he called out to the girl on the stage.

She was bending over now, bending away from us, her legs straight, hands on her ankles, jiggling. With her head upside down between her knees she screeched, "What do you want?"

"This guy's looking for some money. You got a hundred thousand dollars maybe stuffed in your top?"

Wanda straightened up, turned toward us, pulled her straps forward so she could look down. "I don't think so," she said, and then she lowered the straps so that her breasts tumbled out like two soft, red-eyed bunnies. "But my boyfriend says these are worth a million."

"Can we seize those, R.T.?" I said.

"Sorry, Victor," said R.T., shaking his head. "Appealing as it sounds, I don't reckon we can."

"That's a shame," I said. "According to Mr. Manley, he owns a third of this club."

"I ain't no corporate lawyer," said the greeter, "so I can't tell you who owns what. But there's no car and the club's worth squat. You ain't going to find a dime. Sorry, gentlemen, but it looks like you wasted your time."

Just then a dark-haired woman in a sheer robe and high heels stepped through the beaded curtain and came up to the greeter. With her hand on her hip and a strong accent she said, "We out of ice in back, Ike. Chou mind? And get the air conditioner fixed, why don't chou?" The woman looked at us, gave us a smile as quick as a wink, spun around and walked back through the beads.

The greeter raised his eyebrows at us. "Bunch of spoiled brats, all of them."

"Ike," I said. "She called you Ike."

"No she didn't," said the man.

"You're Ike Rothstein."

"No I'm not. I told you, I just work here."

"You know what the penalty is for lying to a public official?" said R.T.

"Is that what you are?" said Rothstein. "A public official? I thought you was one of the Village People. Why don't you both just park your asses here while I call my lawyer."

He turned and disappeared through the curtain.

R.T., standing beside me, looked around the empty, dreary club. "You sure the car's here?"

"My man says it's here, so it's here. Somewhere. Let's go in the back."

We headed toward the doorway where Rothstein had disappeared and pushed through the beaded curtain, walking smack into the woman with the sheer robe.

"What chou want?" she said.

"We're looking for a car."

"Not back here chou not. This is private. Does Ike know chou back here?"

"He told us to follow him."

"Cherk."

"Who, me?"

"Ike. He knows he's not supposed to send no one back here. There's rules. And what about the damn air conditioner. It's been broke for two week. You can't dance when it's hot like this. Everything, it rides up."

"Tell me about it. And the chafing."

"Chou got that right."

"Does a guy named Derek Manley, who owns part of the club, come here much?"

"Asshole."

"Who, me?"

"Him. Manley. Every time he walk by he think he entitled to squeeze."

"I guess he's a hands-on owner. I'm looking for his car."

"What are you, repo?"

"Of a sort."

"Well, if it's that asshole's car chou looking for, there's a bunch of locked up sheds in the back."

"Keys?"

"Hanging in the office."

"And the back door."

"Through the office."

"Thanks. You don't happen to be Esmerelda, do you?"

"That's me."

"The Brazilian Firecracker."

"Chou know my work?"

"Absolutely. By the way, nice shoes."

"Really?"

It didn't take long to find the office, a cheesy little place with thin wood paneling and a cat calendar. What kind of strip joint owner has a cat calendar hanging on his wall? Made me wonder what was hanging at the SPCA. Rothstein was on the phone and he stood up and waved his arms like a traffic cop when we entered, but we ignored him. I walked past Rothstein to the back door, popped a jumble of keys off a hook, tossed them once in my hand, and headed outside.

There was an alleyway behind the club with a bunch of sagging garage sheds on either side. Beth and the tow truck were there, waiting.

Rothstein followed us out. "I'm getting my lawyer on the phone," he said. "He's in a meeting right now."

"You owe him money, right?" I said.

"How'd you know?"

"And you got tax problems?"

"Well, yeah."

"Then take my word, it's going to be a long meeting."

I stepped to the shed closest to the club, fiddled with the keys, found one finally that fit, turned the lock. I reached down and pulled up the door: a bunch of old tables, a couple of sagging, stained couches, dented metal beer kegs, a pile of trashed speakers, mops. I didn't even want to imagine what the mops had mopped. I pulled the door closed.

I strode over to the shed next to the first and fiddled again with the keys. I reached down, pulled open the door: a busted-up motorcycle, cardboard boxes with water damage, four decrepit mattresses leaning one against the next. It was amazing how much junk people saved for that one time when they might just have four moldy guests who needed four moldy mattresses.

"The club rents these out," said Rothstein. "We only use the first one you opened. There's nothing in the rest but crap. It's a nation of crap. You're welcome to it, but it ain't what the paper says you can take and it ain't worth a hundred thousand dollars, no way no how. All together it ain't worth six bucks."

I turned another lock, reached down, pulled up another door: mannequins, naked mannequins piled high in the middle of the space, arms and legs in a strange geometric confusion like a plastic orgy without genitalia. And on the side, neatly stacked, dozens of boxes with advertising printed on their sides. I looked closer. VCRs. Camcorders. DVD players. Stereos. Computer monitors. Not so kosher, whatever it was, but not a clue who they belonged to and not a car. I yanked the door down. It slid closed with a roar.

I took two steps toward the next shed and stopped. Something Earl Dante had said sparked in my memory. Manley sent his trucks all over the northeast, said Dante, delivering to department stores. Department stores. And what do they have in department stores but mannequins and DVD players. It wouldn't be out of character for Derek to boost what he could from the shipments. I turned back and lifted that door once again.

There it was. Right there. What I hadn't noticed before. Behind the wild pile of plastic limbs was a black covering. The mannequins weren't just lying all over one another, they were lying atop something covered by the black tarp. I stepped forward, reached through legs and arms, past dazed faces and pointed toes, and grabbed hold of a piece of the thick black cloth. I yanked it aside.

A headlight.

"You'll hear about this," Rothstein said.

"I suppose I will."

"Derek won't be happy."

"I suppose he won't." I thumbed at the boxes. "Are these yours?"

Rothstein looked at the stacked boxes and his eyes blinked a bit as he did the calculation of how connected he wanted to be to a load of stolen electronics. "Never saw them before in my life," he said finally.

"Then we'll take them too, is that all right, R.T.?"

"It's your seizure," said R.T.

"Derek won't be happy," said Rothstein.

"I suppose not," I said. "The name's Victor Carl. Carl with a *C*. Derek will know how to get hold of me."

CHAPTER

24

Where sit the honorable justices of the Pennsylvania Supreme Court?

Any place they want to.

The Pennsylvania Supreme Court has a lovely chamber in the statehouse in Harrisburg, with fine leather chairs and murals on the walls and a great stained-glass dome, but who the hell wants to sit in Harrisburg? So there is a court-room in Philadelphia and a courtroom in Pittsburgh and satellite chambers in each of those cities, and the honorable justices of the Pennsylvania Supreme Court can pretty much work anyplace they choose. Which is why Justice Jackson Straczynski spent most of his time in his home-town of Philadelphia.

It's not a bad life, the State Supreme Court life, the pay is high, the perks many, and the justices get to wear those boss robes. A lot of lawyers have their eyes on that partic-ular prize and there is only one small requirement for get-ting your very own seat: enough votes. Aye, there's the rub. It takes not merit to rise to Pennsylvania's highest court, just politics.

What do you get when you mix justice and politics?

The Marx Brothers starring in *Duck Soup*.

I don't mean to paint the Pennsylvania Supreme Court as a bunch of vaudeville clowns honking horns and making wisecracks to Margaret Dumont, but then I don't have to, they do a good enough job themselves. And I'm even not talking here of their legal decisions, which are generally considered boneheaded at best and venal at worst. The court is infamous for charges of ethical violations, counter-charges of case fixing, vulgar insults hurled from justice to justice in the public press. One guy got impeached for sending his employees out to buy Valium and jockstraps. I'm not making this up. He used the subterfuge so his enemies wouldn't suspect he was crazy. They suspected him anyway when he wore the jockstrap on his head. No, the honorable justices of the Pennsylvania Supreme Court have not covered themselves with glory. All except for Justice Jackson Straczynski.

Justice Straczynski was the most respected jurist to ever sit on that court, a brilliant legal scholar who used economic theory to slice through the Gordian knots of the most difficult legal problems. His great legal treatise, *The Economic Laws of Constitutional Interpretation*, once a fixture only on the bookshelves of the most conservative law student and right wing legal activist, had become, with the rightward tilt of the U.S. Supreme Court, a staple desktop reference for every constitutional scholar in the country.

After a stint making policy at the Department of Justice for Ronald Reagan, and a period teaching law at the University of Pennsylvania, his alma mater, Straczynski was tapped by the Republican Party to run for the Pennsylvania Supreme Court. He wasn't much of a campaigner, his speaking style was likened to that of an aardvark on Quaaludes, but it just so happened that during the campaign he published a much-publicized article interpreting the Second Amendment to protect the unequivocal right to buy and bear anything with a trigger. Two things are wildly popular in the Commonwealth of Pennsylvania, guns and funnel cakes, both are tasty, both are deadly, but if the state's denizens had to pick one, well, you can't kill an eight-point buck with a funnel cake, now can you? Straczynski won his election in a walk and now he sat on the state's highest court, writing uncompromising decisions of uncompromised brilliance and waiting for that call from Washington. The pundits all said it was coming.

"So we agree, right, Kimberly," I said, as we sat side by side on the beige couch in the justice's wood-lined waiting room, "I'll do all the questioning, you'll just sit quiet and watch the show."

"Whatever."

Kimberly glanced at the stern-eyed secretary with the high gray hair manning the desk in the middle of the room. "But remember," Kimberly said in a hushed voice, "Mr. D definitely wants his name kept out of this."

"Mr. D?"

"Sure. He was very clear about it."

"Okay."

She sat for a moment, something obviously bothering her. "What if a question sort of pops out of my mouth on its own?"

"Gosh, I hope it doesn't. He might not want to tell us his favorite boy band."

"Excuse me?"

I looked her up and down. She was dressed like quite the career woman, so long as the career was taking place in the early 1960s, bright green faux-Chanel business suit, matching heels, and small clutch.

"You look like a bowl of Jell-O in that getup," I said.

"We're visiting a judge, right? This is my government outfit. Mint green, get it?"

She gave a little smile, but the way she bit her lower lip

with nervousness made me feel like a jerk. She had that way, did Kimberly.

"Okay," I said. "Ask what you want. But my advice would be to say as little as possible to this guy. He's not your usual drunken frat boy."

Just as I said that a tall man in a black suit came into the waiting room. "Mr. Carl, Ms. Blue," he said, his voice gilded with an Island lilt. "My name is Curtis Lobban," said the man. "I am Justice Straczynski's file clerk."

Curtis Lobban stood straight and tall, with the deep voice and dignified manner of a dignitary, his dark suit, broad shoulders, and the gray at his temples all added mightily to the effect. He held in himself the same hush of serious purpose that pervaded the entire suite of offices and he looked down at me with a gaze of thinly veiled contempt that made me feel every inch the two-bit hustler invading some grand temple of the law. I jumped to standing at the sight of him, fighting the urge to salute.

"Pleased to meet you, Curtis," I said. "We talked on the phone, I believe."

"Yes, we did," he said slowly.

I reached out a hand to shake, but Curtis Lobban, his face as somber as his outfit, refused the proffer. Pleased to meet me too, obviously.

"The justice, he is sorry to have kept you both waiting and is ready to see you now. Follow me, please."

He turned and led us out of the waiting area into a large library, its walls lined with huge sets of law books. State reporters, federal reporters, U.S. Supreme Court reporters, digests of all sorts. Two young lawyers, a man and a woman, were hard at work at a conference table, books piled around them, legal pads thick with notes. Gnawing at the pylons supporting the Bill of Rights like hungry termites, I figured. They both gave Kimberly a long look.

Kimberly always drew long looks, especially dressed in mint green, but the clerks barely noticed my presence, and why should they? Only the best and brightest clerked for Justice Jackson Straczynski, and I was neither. They only paid me enough notice to wonder what the hell I was doing there. What the hell indeed?

It's not so easy to get close to a Supreme Court justice, even a State Supreme Court justice, so I hadn't expected much when I called that morning before running off to seize Manley's Eldorado. I mentioned my name, I mentioned Tommy Greeley, I waited on the phone a bit. And then it was this Curtis Lobban who came on the line. "What is the purpose of the inquiry?" he asked in his deep somber voice. "It is personal and I can't say anymore," I said. "Hold on for a moment please," he said. I waited, and when he came back on the phone I was told, shockingly, that the justice would see me that very afternoon.

So here we were, Kimberly and I, passing by the serious young law clerks, headed for a visit with their august boss, Tommy Greeley's old college pal.

"Right through here," said Curtis Lobban, courteously holding open a door at the far end of the library. We stepped through the doorway and into a Moorish fantasy.

Most judges go for the tree and tome look for their offices, you know what I mean, dark wood paneling, bookshelves filled with thick legal texts, tree and tome, all designed to give the office a sheen of serious scholarship so often lacking in the robe's wearer. But Justice Straczynski's office was nothing of the kind. The walls were a rich red, pillars of golden fabric fell from iron pikes, the ceiling was patterned with octagonal indentations painted in a riot of colors. Ornate arches rose above each window, the arches covered with intricate paintings of vines and flowers, and the wooden floor was covered with piles of oriental carpets. Dark wooden furniture scattered across the room was accessorized with plush pillows, maroon and gold, intricate geometric shapes in the weave. The justice's desk was less a workplace than a fantastically carved piece of oriental sculpture straight from the Ottoman Empire. The whole place, scented lightly with sandalwood, was like the official chamber of a pasha's grand vizier.

The justice was hunched over at his desk, his back turned, on the phone, and so I took the opportunity to examine his strangely exotic office. I walked around, dazed by the beauty and strangeness of the room. There was no ego wall in the office, no pictures of the justice with presidents and senators and movie stars. But there was, carved into one corner, a series of shelves with ceremonial objects. Tiny Japanese statuettes carved of ivory and jade, fertility fetishes from India, masks from Africa. There was a frame made out of Mayan slate surrounding a picture of a very young woman taken from the neck up, a lovely woman with a heart-shaped face, downcast eyes, and shy smile, her shoulders bare, her head held in an overly dramatic pose. And something out of place among the splendors of the distant world, a garish and tall fencing trophy with a golden swordsman on top captured in the midst of a lunge.

"When was this?" said the justice, still on the phone. His voice was deep, sharp, and slow. Like, well, like an aardvark on Quaaludes. "And what did he take?"

Something moved beside me. I backed away. There was a long dark divan covered with pillows by the shelves and in the space beneath the divan crouched a cat, purely white. It stared at me for a long moment and then stepped arrogantly past me. In the darkness behind the first cat, two green eyes glittered.

"Yes. I see. I will do what I can. But you knew this could happen."

In front of his desk were two chairs with brilliant golden upholstery. I joined Kimberly standing behind them and waited.

"Be patient. I will talk to him and try to find out what is happening, but calm down. Getting so upset doesn't help anything."

He turned around, saw us, startled for a moment at the sight of Kimberly, and then smoothed the features of his face back to his basic bland. He motioned us to sit in the chairs and we did. He was a thin, elegant man, wearing his suit coat even in his office. His hair was blond and wispy, his face was round and youthful, though slightly askew.

"I know you're angry and scared," he said, still on the phone. "So am I. But we have to deal with this the right way. Now I have some people in my office. Yes. Of course. I'll talk to you later. Don't do anything hasty that you will later regret. Yes. Bye now."

He hung up the phone and gave us an awkward, almost embarrassed smile, as if he had been caught at something. "My mother," he said. "She's been complaining of dizziness so she went to the doctor. Now she's complaining about all the tests the doctor has taken and about his communication skills. And when he tells her she is perfectly healthy she'll be complaining about that too."

"This office is like, oh my God," said Kimberly.

"My wife designed it." He raised his brows, the time-honored dismissal of a wife's eccentricities. "I gave her carte blanche and as usual she exceeded her limit. I believe I recognize you, Mr. Carl. Have you been before the Court?"

"I've never had the honor, no. But some of my cases have been notorious. Maybe you've seen me on the local news."

"I don't watch television," he said. "Do you perhaps have artistic talent?"

"None," I said, cheerfully. "Not a lick. I am as artistic as a brick."

"That's a relief. My wife seems to collect artists. I am inundated with artists. So we haven't met?"

"Not that I recall."

"Just as well. And you, Miss Blue"—he paused and examined her closely for a moment—"are you a lawyer too?"

"No. Please. I'm a vice president."

"Really? Excellent. Is there perhaps a school for vice presidents at the University of Pennsylvania? I didn't know. Did you get a graduate degree in vice presidenting?"

"Not really. They just sort of hired me."

"Who hired you?"

Kimberly didn't answer.

"What's the matter, Miss Blue? You're suddenly silent."

Just then the white cat jumped atop an ash can and then the desk. It strolled across the desktop and dropped into the justice's lap. The justice curled one of his arms around it and bowed his neck as he stroked its head. The cat stretched its back and gave me a victorious sneer.

"Did you eat Miss Blue's tongue, Marshall," he said to the cat. "Naughty boy. Give it back." He laughed a high, ugly laugh.

Kimberly blushed. I wondered how he had known she had gone to Penn.

"Miss Blue works for a client, which wishes to remain anonymous at this point," I said.

"Of course it does," said the justice. "Do you like cats, Mr. Carl?"

"Not especially."

"You're a dog person then."

"I prefer fish. With a beurre blanc and a glass of Chablis."

He glanced up at me in disapproval and then back to his

cat. "I like cats. I like their softness, their independence. Their discretion. I like that they don't crap all over the place. Shall we now discuss the weather, or maybe sports? Do you want to discuss baseball, Mr. Carl?"

"Let's assume that the formalities have been completed," I said.

"Grand." He turned his attention from the cat and stared at me for a long moment. "On the phone you mentioned Tommy Greeley."

"Yes," I said. "Right. I did. I'm trying to learn what I can about what happened to him twenty years ago. I was told that you were his closest friend in both college and law school."

"We were friends, yes."

"Close friends?"

"For a time. We were on the fencing team together. But eventually we drifted apart. We had different interests."

"Such as?"

"I'm curious from where this interest in Tommy Greeley arrives. Tell me, Miss Blue, why does your employer care about ancient history?"

"It's kind of a long story," said Kimberly.

"I have time. I like stories."

He scratched the cat's neck for a long moment and then pushed it off his lap. The cat jumped down and stalked back to the divan. The justice arched his hands on the desk, leaned forward.

"No story, Miss Blue? What a shame. I took the liberty of looking you up in Martindale-Hubble, Mr. Carl. And I asked around. I hope you don't mind. It's not often I get a query about Tommy Greeley. You do criminal work, isn't that right?"

"Primarily."

"And you have no obvious political affiliations."

"Not anymore. I used to take it more seriously but then I stopped seeing the humor in the jokes that kept getting elected."

"Including me?"

"I wouldn't presume—"

"But you just did. So, if this isn't a cause of the heart, then you are a hired gun, isn't that right, Mr. Carl?"

"That's what a lawyer is, Mr. Justice."

"And so who has done the hiring? Which organization has asked you to dig into my past."

"Excuse me?"

"Oh, let's treat it like a game. Let me guess. Is it the ACLU? Or is it perhaps the AFL-CIO? Or maybe the NAACP? What about the ADL? That might be up your alley. Or the AARP? Greenpeace? The Sierra Club? Have you gone to work for the UFW or the Teamsters? Public Citizen? Common Cause? Corporate Watch? The National Gay and Lesbian Task Force? Americans United for Affirmative Action? Or maybe the harridans at NOW? Is that it, Miss Blue, are you an aspiring Gloria Steinem? Which of the instruments of the left have hired you as their Torquemada, Mr. Carl?"

"I think you have a wrong—"

"Isn't it a little unseemly to wallow in the mire of the distant past in order to scuttle a nomination while the nine Justices in Washington are still hale and hearty?"

"I have no intention of—"

"You should be made aware, Mr. Carl, that I will not sit idly by while you attempt to ruin my reputation. I am not without means. The great right wing conspiracy almost took down a president. Think of what it can do to a milquetoast like you."

"You are under a misapprehension, Mr. Justice."

He tilted his head, surprised, I think, at the amusement

that I let twist the edges of my mouth. "Then educate me, Mr. Carl."

"This might shock you, Mr. Justice, but I don't give a whit about your chances to rise to the U.S. Supreme Court. I'm like the rest of America, more concerned with my own bowel movements than the lofty progress of your career. But I had hoped you'd be able to tell me about Tommy Greeley's college life, his other friends, his girlfriend. I had hoped you'd be able to help me figure out what happened to him in the end. In fact, being a friend, I expected you'd be anxious to help. But we come here in good faith and suddenly you give us the third degree and start laying on threats. Now is that polite, Mr. Justice?"

"What do you want?"

"I want to know who set up Tommy Greeley's murder?"

"We don't know Tommy was murdered," said the justice. "He only disappeared. He might have run away."

"He was murdered."

"Have they found his body?"

"No."

"Then how are you so sure?"

"One of the killers told me."

"Jesus, God. Who?"

"He's dead also, Mr. Justice, his throat slashed and his body dumped beside a shipping container on one of the piers along the riverfront."

The justice's face tightened and grew more lopsided. "When was this?"

"A few weeks ago."

"Why?"

"The police don't yet know. It could be anything. But twenty years ago he had been hired to beat up Tommy Greeley. He got carried away. That's why Tommy disappeared. The man with the slit throat was a client of mine;

I'm now representing his mother in a wrongful death action. To that end, I'm trying to learn who hired him to beat up your friend Tommy Greeley in the first place."

The justice stood from his desk, placed his arms behind his back, and strolled around me toward the shelves above the divan. He reached for the fencing trophy, held it with one hand as he tested the tip of the statuette's foil with his thumb.

"Do you remember a nominee to the court named Douglas Ginsburg," he said. "A stellar judge, nominated by Reagan. Reports came out that, while a professor at Harvard, he was at parties where marihuana was smoked. Can you imagine parties at Harvard where marihuana wasn't smoked in those days? Still, it was enough to scuttle his nomination."

"And that's the danger for you represented by Tommy Greeley?"

"He was my friend. He was a drug dealer. It won't take much for the Neanderthals on the left, sitting back stoned on their couches, to make their insinuations."

Even as he said it I thought of an organization the justice missed in his litany of opponents, TPAC, the Telushkin Political Action Committee, membership one. I could see him now, Jeffrey Telushkin, sitting on his chair, clapping his hands with glee as I sat here asking Jackson Straczynski about his former friend, now dead, who might be used to sully his reputation and sink his chance for the big seat. The image turned my stomach.

"I really am not here to hurt you or your chances, Mr. Justice. I just want to learn what you can tell me about Tommy."

"I entered college in the seventies," he said, without the venom his voice had carried before. "Drugs were everywhere, at every party, in every dormitory hallway. It was impossible to avoid, and many had no desire to avoid it. Tommy Greeley was one of those. We both went out for the fencing team. I liked him from the first. He was smart, rebellious, entrepreneurial, an innovative young man and a brilliant fencer. We both started with the sport at Penn, were well behind the rest who had fenced in prep school, but Tommy was a natural. Other than fencing, I was interested in art, literature, culture. I was something of an aesthete. Dorian Gray. An embarrassment now, but the way it was. Tommy, other than fencing, was like the rest of my generation, interested only in getting high and getting laid. I told you we had divergent interests. That was where we diverged."

"You didn't use drugs at all?" said Kimberly.

"What's next, Miss Blue, boxers or briefs? Let's just say it is an improper question and leave it at that. I won't answer it here, or in the Senate if I get the opportunity. But I will tell you this. I had a younger brother named Benjamin who lost his way. Speed turned him crazy, truly, and his craziness got him killed. I saw first hand with my brother a drug's insidious power to destroy."

"When did Tommy start selling?" I said.

"Early on. At first it was only marihuana, just enough to keep himself supplied. Then he fell into a crowd that was selling more and, with his entrepreneurial bent, he quickly took it over. He teamed up with a man, short and thick with a scarred face—Prod I think his name was, Cooper Prod— and together they began selling far beyond the confines of the university. This was now his junior year or so. I met my wife at about the same time, fell deeply in love, moved off campus to live with her. Eventually, even before I graduated, we married. But Tommy had found something perfectly suited to his talents. And even as he ran his enterprise, he still received excellent grades, enough to get him into law school. Later, during law school, I heard he had moved up to cocaine. Less product, more profit. There were even a few law students who had gone in with him. But by then I had pretty much cut him out of my life, for understandable reasons. Occasionally we would have dinner, the four of us, talk about law school, our futures. But he never mentioned his business and I never let him. He knew what was happening to my brother, knew how I felt about it. That was it, the extent of our relationship."

"You said the four of us."

"My wife and I. Tommy and his girlfriend, Sylvia. Sylvia Steinberg."

"Was Tommy seeing anyone other than this Sylvia?"

"Why?"

"The police report on the missing persons complaint filed by Mrs. Greeley seemed to indicate that he and Ms. Steinberg had broken up."

"All I knew for certain was Sylvia. But it was a difficult time. There was an FBI investigation, there were indictments. It was a huge scandal at the law school. The people he was working with, they all went to jail. When he disappeared we figured he had run away from everything."

"Do you have any idea why anyone might have wanted Tommy hurt or killed?"

He put the fencing trophy back on the shelf but didn't turn around to face us. And as he spoke the following words, his sharp voice grew sharper and his tall elegant frame seemed to contract upon itself, to deform itself, to hunch itself into a taut knot.

"The truth is, he was dealing with dangerous people, Mr. Carl. Maybe he didn't know how dangerous. He was greedy, he always wanted more. He had made hundreds of thousands of dollars selling his poison, he had a beautiful girlfriend, he had the whole world at his feet, but it wasn't enough. Tommy Greeley was hungry, ravenous, he wanted everything he could lay his grasping little hands upon and finally he took too much and paid the price."

"Too much of what?" I said.

But before he could answer the door burst open and a green-eyed woman stepped into the office, stuck out her hip, flung her arms up to the sky like a showgirl jumping out of a cake. She was tall and slim, energetic, she was dressed like a gypsy with hoop earrings and a bandanna over her hair. Red gloves came down to her elbows, her frilly skirt came down to her ankles. In one raised hand was a bottle of champagne, in the other were two champagne flutes.

"Darling," she said. "I have wondrous news. We simply must celebrate."

I recognized her. She was the woman with the shy smile whose picture was in the slate frame, older now by a couple decades, but still her smile was bright, her face was all glittering angles, her eyes so glowed with vivacity and spirit it was as if she vibrated with some fierce energy. The proprietary way she stood in the doorway, the way she perfectly matched the exotic decor, stated without a doubt that she was the justice's wife. But as he turned to her, still in that strange hunched posture, as he turned to gaze, startled, at his wife, his face held not the arrogance it had showed to us, or the bored, overfamiliar visage of the long married. No, as if one of the masks on his shelf had been pulled from his features to show the reality behind, his face was seething with emotion. There was passion, there was fascination and fear and disgust. And most of all there was love, pure and painful, innocent and imprisoning, a love that was strangely sad, perversely lonely, and absolutely abject.

His expression recovered quickly, the mask was replaced, the swirl of emotions that had flooded his features for a brief second disappeared as suddenly as it had come. And it was only later that I began to wonder if maybe, just maybe, in the powerful stream of emotions that hunched the justice's posture and distorted his features, there lay not just a glimpse into the painful depths of a troubled marriage but also the seeds of a motive that might have cost Tommy Greeley and, yes, Joey Parma their lives.

CHAPTER

25

Whatever waters I had expected to roil by my visit to a State Supreme Court justice, they didn't take long to splash back into my face.

"That judge's wife was so hitting on you, V," said Kimberly, as we walked back to my office after our meeting with the justice.

"Don't be ridiculous."

"Oh, please. The way she was going, 'Victor, Victor, darling,' the way she insisted you stay for champagne, the way she laughed uproariously at all your jokes."

"They were good jokes," I said.

"Lame, V. They were tripping over their crutches. But she was laughing and fawning all over you like you were some Chippendale. And you were all, 'Oh, Mrs. Straczynski' this and 'Oh, Mrs. Straczynski' that and she was all, 'Call me Alura, darling.' It was a brutal display, V. Really. I was embarrassed for you."

Kimberly was right that Alura Straczynski had been inappropriately flirtatious with me, but she was wrong that I had liked it. It more than made me wildly uncomfortable, it gave me the skives. The judge's clerk, Curtis Lobban, had been invited to join the little party and he had stood in the corner the whole time, staring at me with his piercing gaze of flat contempt. And worse, as the justice's wife leaned toward me and touched her throat, the justice himself was watching, carefully, with utter control, his face again a mask without an ounce of emotion.

"But did you believe what he told us?" she said.

"Yes, about not being part of the drug business, at least. His ambitions, even then, were too large to risk on something as stupid as dealing cocaine, no matter how lucrative, and the FBI was never able to link him to the organization. But I sensed that his connection to Tommy had been stronger than he let on and that there was some unfinished business."

"About what?"

"That's the question, isn't it?"

"Well, he was lying about one thing," said Kimberly.

"Really?"

"He said he didn't watch television."

"Maybe he doesn't."

"Oh yes, he does," she said. "He went all Evita on us when he said it, like he was better than the rest of the world because he didn't vegetate in front of the tube. But he watches, when the wife's away playing her games, he watches, yes he does. And the bad stuff too."

Just then we turned the corner and saw the suit. He was standing at the front door to my building, just under the big sign of the shoe. The man had a name, but the name wasn't important, just the suit and the haircut and the way he pushed himself off the wall when he saw me, the way he flashed his credentials with a flip of the wrist.

"I'm supposed to walk you to the District Attorney's office, Mr. Carl," he said.

"What if I'm busy?"

"I was told you're not that busy."

"What if I refused, sat right down on the sidewalk, and sang 'Freebird' at the top of my lungs?"

"Then I'd have to have you arrested, Mr. Carl."

"On what charge?"

"Singing Lynyrd Skynyrd without a shred of talent."

"Fair enough. Should I bring a toothbrush?"

"Prudence might suggest so," he said.

"Let's leave her the hell out of it, shall we?"

"Are you finished trying to be clever, Mr. Carl?"

"Trying, huh? They hire you right out of law school?"

"Yes, they did."

"Where'd you go?"

"Harvard."

"Three years of Harvard and this is what they have you doing?"

"I'm so proud I could burst."

"Okay, I'm yours. Lead on Macduff."

"The name's Berenson."

"And don't you forget it," I said, even as I gave Kimberly a shrug and then let Berenson lead me back the way I had come, back to a dressing down at the DA's office, where I'd be lucky if I was left, by the end of it, with even my boxers.

CHAPTER

26

The nine blocks between my shabby office and the District Attorney's shabby offices were familiar ones. I had made that walk hundreds of times, knew every storefront deli between here and there, so the suit hadn't been sent to make sure I didn't get lost. And he hadn't been sent to make sure I showed, a polite phone call would have done as much. I'm a polite guy, you're polite with me, I'm polite with you, everything can be oh so polite. And that was the point, I understood perfectly, of the suit.

The DA's offices were in an old YMCA, and I could still smell the sweat oozing out of the finely carved wood in the lobby. The suit used his magnetic card to open the glass door, signed me in, slapped a visitor sticker on my lapel, took me into the elevator, led me down the hallway of the seventh floor. He walked past the secretary, sitting at her station, and opened the door for me. I stopped at the secretary's desk.

"Hello, Debbie," I said.

"Hello, Mr. Carl."

"Have you done something different with your hair?"

"Yes, as a matter of fact."

"It is very becoming," I said.

"Thank you for noticing. That is so nice."

"See," I said to the suit still standing at the door. "I can be polite. I really can."

Funny, he didn't seem to care.

"Is that Carl I hear out there, Berenson?" came a weary voice from the other side of the door.

"Yes, sir," said the suit.

"Then will you politely ask that bastard to step inside and close the door behind him."

K. Lawrence Slocum, chief of the DA's homicide unit, was sitting at his desk, shirtsleeves rolled up to his forearms, his glasses off, his fingers rubbing at his eyes so insistently it was like he was rubbing at an instant play lottery card in search of a jackpot. No luck there, for when he stopped his rubbing, put his thick glasses back on, peered through the lenses and across his desktop, he was peering at me. K. Lawrence Slocum had broad shoulders, thick forearms, and a grizzled jaw. He was a sweetheart, really, so long as you didn't cross him. But just now, he stared at me like I was something odoriferous he had just scraped off his shoe.

"Do you know why I asked you here this evening, Carl?" said Slocum.

It wasn't so hard to figure out, actually, what with the timing of the summons. And it wasn't so hard to figure out, what with Detective McDeiss standing in the corner of the office, leaning against a bookcase, his arms crossed, trying mightily to suppress a grin. Still, I saw no reason to make it easy on him.

"Dinner and a show?" I said.

Slocum sighed. "Oh man," he said, and then rubbed his hand across his mouth.

"Is it cold out there?" said McDeiss from the corner.

"Where?"

"Out there, where you're standing, in the middle of the

lake, with the wind howling and you precariously perched on that razor-thin sheet of ice. Is it cold? Because if it isn't cold yet, it is going to be."

"I just asked a few questions."

"He is a Supreme Court justice," said Slocum, his voice slow and soft and yet stiff as steel. "He is no friend of criminals, which means he is our friend indeed, and he has a power that extends beyond his docket. So when he calls the DA and drops a load on her, she needs to know it is being taken care of. Which means she drops the load on me. And now I am covered with it and frankly, Carl, it stinks."

"Lysol," I said. "It works wonders."

"He is a Supreme Court justice."

"I made an appointment. He agreed to see me. I didn't stalk him, though, to be honest, I am not above stalking."

"Whatever the basis of your relationship with the justice, it is now at an end. You are not to bother him again—or his wife. I asked you here this evening to make sure you understand what I have just said. Do you understand?"

"Oh, I'm sorry, Comrade Prosecutor. I thought this was America."

"Do you hear that, Carl?" said McDeiss.

"What?"

"The ice beneath your feet starting to crack."

"Do you know an attorney named John Sebastian?" said Slocum.

"The lead singer for the Lovin' Spoonful?"

"The John Sebastian who is representing Derek Manley in a collection case in which you are representing a creditor named Jacopo Financing."

"Oh, that John Sebastian," I said, not liking the tack the conversation had suddenly taken.

"He filed a complaint against you with the Bar Association."

"He's a little oversensitive," I said.

"Claimed you asked a series of improper questions for an improper motive. He included as an exhibit the deposition you took of his client. It made for some quite interesting reading, especially the part at the end about the night twenty years ago on the waterfront. Mr. Sebastian didn't know where that information came from, but then again he wasn't privy to your conversation with Detective McDeiss at the scene of Joseph Parma's death. You know, Carl, don't you, that it is improper to use privileged information from one client for the benefit of another client."

"I can defend my conduct."

"It looks like you may just get that chance," said Slocum.

"Crack crack," said McDeiss.

"In addition to your violation of the precepts of the Bar Association, it appears you have been interfering with a homicide investigation. Obstruction of justice is a felony. It is hard to practice law from a jail cell."

"Oh please. What grounds are you inventing for that?"

"First, you're holding back," said McDeiss, "which pisses me off. Next, Derek Manley has disappeared. Since your improper deposition, he has vanished. Vamoosed. We have received phone logs from Parma's apartment which bring Manley into play. We wanted to ask him some questions, but you, apparently, scared him off."

"That's not obstruction of justice."

"It feels like an obstruction to me."

"Are you talking about your investigation or your bowel. Look, I'm representing Joey Parma's mother in a wrongful death case. As part of that representation, I am trying to find out who killed her son and it looks like you boys need all the help you can get. It's more than two weeks after the murder and what do you have? I'll tell you. *Bupkes.* You know what *bupkes* is?"

"Isn't that the cake with cinnamon and raisins?" said Slocum.

"That's babka," said McDeiss. "Very tasty."

"*Bupkes* is goat shit," I said.

"You guys eat that too?" said Slocum.

"We're making progress," said McDeiss. "We would be making more progress without your interference."

"My interference gave you the name Tommy Greeley. My interference gave you Teddy Big Tits."

"He admits he was owed," said McDeiss, "but he denies killing Joey."

"Well, that is a surprise. He denied a murder. You press him hard on that? And what about Bradley Babbage?"

McDeiss looked at Slocum, Slocum looked at McDeiss. "Who is Bradley Babbage?" said McDeiss.

"Babbage was the informant who finally took down Tommy Greeley's drug ring. Babbage was the guy who got away with no jail time and a bundle of money. And Babbage was the guy who died of mysterious causes in his swimming pool out in Gladwyne a week or so before Joey Parma had his throat sliced. Are we seeing a pattern here, gentlemen?"

Slocum looked again at McDeiss, McDeiss shrugged. It was nice to put them back on their heels for a moment, but it didn't last.

"You talk to Dante yet?" said Slocum.

"What?"

"Manley, in the deposition, mentioned Earl Dante," said Slocum. "I was just wondering if he got in touch with you yet."

"Dante?"

"He will. It is why Manley mentioned Dante in the deposition, to let you know he was being protected. You ignored his gentle warning. Dante now has to let you know that he knows you ignored it. Guys like Dante, they don't like to be ignored. It makes them look weak. He'll get in touch and we might be able to help you when he does."

"Thanks, but I can take care of myself."

"We are this close to taking Dante to a grand jury. This close. And he knows it. Things are starting to get dangerous. Dante is going to make everybody pick sides. You're either with him or with us. Being with us means you tell us when he gets in touch and anything he says to you. Anything, you understand? Being with us also means you do us small favors when we ask. Like agreeing to keep the hell away from Justice Straczynski and his wife from here on in."

"And if I don't?"

Slocum's voice had been soft and controlled, but now it stretched and filled with exasperation until it rose to shake the office.

"Oh just please shut up," he shouted. "Just shut the hell up."

He took off his glasses, began again rubbing his eyes, the muscles in his jaw throbbed. There was a long silence and then his voice, when it came, was as slow and soft as before.

"You cannot go tromping off and badgering a Supreme Court justice. You just can't, do you understand? He has more muscle than you can imagine. He'll squash you like the bug you're pretending to be. I'm trying to help you here, as a friend, and you're acting like a damn lawyer. Just promise me you'll stay away from him. Just promise me. Please."

"Okay."

Slocum took his hand from his eyes, stared at me without his glasses, his bare eyes seeming small and beady when not behind his thick lenses. "Is that all it took, just for me to yell?"

"Or maybe it was the 'please,' " I said.

"So you'll keep away from him, really?"

"Yes, really."

"And his wife."

"Yes, yes, yes, I'll stay away from him and his wife."

"I'll tell the DA. She'll be pleased."

"I'm so glad. Are we through? I have dinner plans."

"With that girl Swanson you been eating with lately?" said Slocum. "Or is tonight's date with Stouffer's."

"Tonight I'm guest of honor at a Banquet."

"Ah, the single life," said Slocum. "I remember it well." He put his glasses back on, leaned back in his chair, gave a nod to McDeiss.

"So, you looking for a date these days, Carl?" said McDeiss. "You in the market?"

"No."

"Searching for someone to share those long walks in the rain."

"Really, no."

"Because I know a someone who's available."

"I'm sure your wife's friends are very nice, Detective, but trust me when I say that I am not interested."

"Oh I think you will be, Carl. Listen close. Seven ninety-nine Wolf Street. Apartment Three B. The name is Beverly Rodgers. Got that? Just your type, a real piece of work."

"I'm a little busy."

"Oh, not too busy for Bev, I'll bet. Not for Bev. Everyone calls her Bev. And she's a honey, yes she is. You're lucky though to catch her now, see, because she's back on the market. It turns out her last boyfriend had his throat slashed down on the riverfront. Funny how that is. And she's not saying anything to the police, nothing, for some reason. But you ask me, Carl, odds are she knows something about it."

CHAPTER

27

I was thinking it through, what Slocum and McDeiss had just given to me, the lead I had been looking for, the name and address of Joey's girlfriend, when I reached Spruce Street and turned toward my building. Spruce is pretty and tree-lined, a street of quaint old town houses either refurbished spectacularly for the urban rich or chopped up into apartments for the urban not-so-rich. I was very much a not-so.

In the vestibule of my building, I leaned forward, opened the lock on my mailbox, reached in for its delightful little surprises, the magazines, the catalogs, the bills, the notices of unpaid invoices, the bills. As I grabbed the bundle and pulled it from the box, something heavy landed with a thud on my shoulder, blossoming into a flower of pain and driving me to my knees.

Something grabbed the back of my neck and slammed the top of my head into the metal wall of mailboxes and I felt less pain than I ought to have felt and the light dimmed almost to black, but only almost.

Something hit me hard in the stomach and the air vanished from my lungs. Whatever siren had begun to sound was silenced with the vanished air.

With all the fighting instincts of a pill bug, I fell onto

my side and curled into a ball and felt the pain swarm through my body.

A foot stepped onto my face and ground it into the hard tile floor before lifting and slamming onto my hip. Before I could raise my head to get a glimpse behind me, a hand pressed itself onto the side of my face, pushing so hard upon my nose I couldn't move my head either way. The breadth of my vision now encompassed only the line where the floor met the wall and two splayed fingers spreading across my face.

"You are trespassing," came a near indecipherable hiss in my ear. "Trespassing on property where you don't belong."

I tried to say something but the hand pressed harder on my face and my nose bent further sideways and a different voice said, "Don't speak until you are asked a question."

My eye closest to the floor began to burn. One of the fingers had a ring on it, I could see that, golden and thick.

"Who are you working for?" said the first voice, the whisper so soft I could barely make it out.

I tried to say something but the hand on my face gurgled the sound.

"Answer the question," said the second voice.

"I can't."

"Oh yes, you can," hissed the first voice. "Most assuredly. You've stepped into our territory now. The past is off limits to you. It belongs to us, you are not welcome here. Our possession of it is open, hostile, exclusive, continuous, adverse, do you understand? The signs are up, the fence is electrified, the dogs are loose and they are hungry. One more step inside and you won't survive."

"Someone's coming," said the second voice.

"Why do you care about what happened twenty years ago?"

The hand pressed down harder, my eye burned fiercer. "Answer the question," barked the second voice.

"Who are you working for?"

"We have to get out of here. Someone is coming."

"Who?"

"Now."

"Tell him we will find him," came the first voice, the speaker so close now I felt his breath on my ear. "And if you persist we will deal with you like we deal with all trespassers. This is your requisite warning. There won't be another."

The hand pressed harder on my face, the foot lifted from my hip and stomped hard onto the side of my stomach.

I contracted my body into an even tighter curl and stifled my groans and felt my stomach heave as footsteps poured out of the vestibule and I was left alone with the pain and the nausea and the spill of my mail all about me.

CHAPTER

28

    I was still on the vestibule floor when the Good Samaritans arrived. A man and a woman, they put their hands on me and raised me to a sitting position and inquired with calm voices as to my well-being.

"I've been better," I said.

They told me I was bleeding from my head.

"At least no place important," I said.

They asked me where I lived and I told them I lived in that very building and they offered to help me up the stairs so I could call the police and I told them I didn't need any help but they insisted, like Good Samaritans will. I thanked them and let them scoop up my mail and let them hold on to my arms as I struggled to my feet and let them steady me as we climbed up the stairs to my apartment.

I dropped my jacket onto the floor and loosened my tie and stumbled into the bathroom to take a look at myself. The hair above my forehead was matted with blood, a trickle had slid down my temple, smeared into my right eye, dropped onto my white shirt. I rolled up my shirt-sleeves, washed my face and hair clean. The water swirling down the drain was a sweet rosy pink.

When I came back to the living room the Good Samaritans were still there. They bade me sit upon the couch and I sat. The woman offered me a towel filled with ice cubes

from my freezer and I took it and placed it upon the wound
on the top of my head.

"Dude, let us look at the cut," said the man, his voice
hoarse and hearty.

I lifted the ice as the woman stepped toward me. She
leaned into me, separated my hair with her fingers, bent
forward to peer closely at the wound. She smelled of
vanilla and spice, her gauzy shirt brushed my cheek.

"Nothing too serious," she said. "You'll live. What happened?"

"Just a mugging. They wanted my wallet. The money I
didn't mind, but I'm partial to the photograph on my license. It makes me look dangerously deranged, which is
helpful in my racket. Did you see them?"

"Only from behind," said the man. "They were running
away. Two dudes. One older, the other taller."

"Do you want us to call the police for you, Victor?" said
the woman.

My chin lifted, my eyes opened wide. "How do you
know my name?"

"From your mail," said the man, quickly.

"How did you happen to be at my apartment building?"

"We were just walking," said the man.

"We're only trying to help," said the woman. "Do you
want us to call the police and report what happened?"

Through the fear and pain and sudden paranoia that had
enveloped me, I peered more carefully at the two Samaritans standing in my apartment. The man was stocky,
bearded, dressed for a motorcycle rally with a T-shirt,
boots, denim vest. He wore a ponytail and was as hyperac-
tive as a teenager, but the gray in his beard and lines
around his pale blue eyes put him in his forties.

The woman was tall and thin, with long straight hair
and bell-bottom jeans. She was older than me, but not by

much. To get a sense of the state of my condition you need only know that just then was the first time I noticed how startlingly beautiful she was, with a narrow face and big brown Asian eyes that held a lovely sadness. It was a strange sight, the two of them, the woman, who could have been a model, and the motorcycle man, utter strangers, dressed as if the eighties and nineties had never happened, standing in my apartment, standing over me as I slumped on the couch, and it sent my already jagged nerves into a jig.

I looked at them for a moment longer and tried to think things through and failed. My head ached, my ribs hurt, I still felt pressure on my nose, yet even as I struggled through the pain to make sense of everything that had happened that night, one thing became clear, one thing shone with absolute certainty.

"No," I said, finally. "Don't call the police. It was just a spoiled mugging. They got nothing, so there's nothing the police can do. But thank you for helping. I don't know how long I would have lay there if you hadn't come along."

"We were glad we could help," said the woman. "Do you want something to drink?"

"Yeah, sure. That would be great. There are beers in the fridge. Why don't you take out three?"

"Dude," said the man.

His name was Lonnie. Her name was Chelsea. He fixed motorcycles in a small shop he owned in Queens Village. She worked in an insurance office. They were just old friends, out for a walk, and I liked them, I liked them both. Lonnie was jittery and funny and his eyes were bright. Chelsea was like an ocean of calm, sitting lovely and straight in her chair, her long legs together, her hands in her lap. When I told them I was a lawyer they groaned good-naturedly, but she started asking me questions about her landlord. And then, watching them carefully, and without mentioning any names, I told them about what happened to Joey Cheaps and about the deposition of Derek Manley and about the crime that was committed twenty years ago. I told it well, used my jury skills to keep it dramatic, stretched it out, watched the reactions. Lonnie leaned forward as I did the telling, his knee bouncing. Chelsea kept glancing at Lonnie.

"So that wasn't just a mugging, was it?" said Chelsea.

"No."

"What did they want?"

"To scare me off, to stop me from looking into the past. They said I was trespassing, as if the past is a piece of land governed by the laws of property."

"So what's it all about?" said Lonnie. "You got any idea?"

"Some," I said. "I asked some questions of an important man today and that seemed to get a lot of people rattled."

"Who was he?" said Chelsea.

I looked into her pretty eyes, saw there a curiosity that was more than idle.

"He's a State Supreme Court justice," I said. "A long time ago one of his friends was the head of a huge cocaine ring. The ring was busted by the FBI and the friend disappeared. I think the ring, the friend, the long-ago crime, the murder on the riverfront, I think everything is related."

"What are you going to do?" said Chelsea. "Are you going to stop asking questions like they told you?"

"What do you think I should do?"

"I don't know," she said. "We have a friend who lives in New Mexico and has become kind of a spiritual mentor. He always says that the past can be a pretty dangerous place."

"And, Dude, think about it," said Lonnie. "You could be

getting into something way way over your head. You could be stepping into a serious firestorm. If two dudes came up to me and started playing handball with my head, I'd be doing more than wondering what the hell I was getting myself into. I'd be thinking it might be a good time to check out the Baja for a while, work on my tan."

"That's a bit extreme, don't you think? I'm sure nothing I'm involved with is as dangerous as a tan."

Chelsea flicked her hair and laughed.

"If you want, some of my customers are definite muscle heads," said Lonnie. "You need any backup, give me a call." He reached into his vest, pulled out a card. THE CHOP SHOP. LONNIE CHAMBERS, PROPRIETOR. *WE FIX EVERYTHING SO LONG AS IT'S A HARLEY.*

"No need to turn a little collection case into Altamonte," I said, "but I appreciate the gesture. I appreciate everything."

That was the cue, I suppose. Lonnie stood and then Chelsea stood and then I stood, towel still on my head, the water from the ice now dripping down my temple in a steady stream and onto my bloodied shirt.

At the door I shook Lonnie's hand, hard, rough, and then Chelsea's hand. She smiled at me and her eyes lit and she squeezed my hand, softly but still hard enough to convey a message of sorts.

"Thank you for everything," I said.

"It wasn't nothing," said Lonnie.

"Oh yes, it was. I'd like to show my appreciation." Chelsea smiled at me and I felt it in my chest. "How about if you let me buy you both a drink in gratitude. There's a place in Lonnie's neighborhood. You guys know the Continental?"

"Not my usual hangout," he said.

"Mine neither, that's what will make it fun. Say tomorrow night? Nine?"

"I don't know," said Lonnie, but then Chelsea spoke up.

"That would be great. Really. We'll both be there."

"Terrific," I said. "See you then."

I stood at the door and watched them go down the stairs and listened for the front door to open and close and then I went inside and peered out the window and watched as they made their way, side by side but not holding hands, definitely not holding hands, east on Spruce, back to the section of the city where they lived, with all its bars and restaurants, far from this mainly residential edge of center city.

As soon as they left my sight I put down the bloody towel, picked up the phone, and dialed.

"Telushkin here," said the voice on the other end.

"Mr. Telushkin, this is Victor Carl."

"Oh, Victor, yes. I'm so glad you called. How are things going? Have you checked out that lead I gave you?"

"I called about something else," I said quickly, not wanting to discuss with Telushkin my meeting with the justice. "Was there anyone in Tommy Greeley's crew named Lonnie Chambers, or was there a woman named Chelsea?"

"Let me think, let me think. Oh yes, of course. There was a man named Chambers, I think they called him Lonnie. He was a mule, mostly, and a debt collector when that was needed."

"Was he indicted?"

"Oh yes, convicted too. Conspiracy. Drug trafficking. I think there was a racketeering count along for good measure. Ten years, but he wasn't a kingpin and so was eligible for parole and time off for good behavior. He'd be out by now."

"And the girl?"

"I remember her, remember her quite vividly," he said.

"Her name was Chelsea Cartland. She helped with the money, helped break down the big shipments, added the cutting agent, bagged it into salable quantities for the customers. She pled guilty, received only sixteen months. A slap on the wrist, really, nothing more. But she was very pretty, very young, and the judge seemed smitten with her."

I could understand that, how a judge could be smitten with a woman like Chelsea, I could understand it completely.

It was starting to come clear, the crimes of the past that were visiting themselves upon the present. Amidst the warning from Dante and the violent threats from the thugs that night, and the gentle caution issued by my Good Samaritans, who had come into my life, I now was sure, to deliver their message just as clearly as had the goons who had come before them, it was all starting to come clear. A drug conspiracy awash with money. A friendship turned bitter. A lovely sad-eyed woman with a perfect body. A small-time loser who fell into something from which he never recovered. And between everything was a single link holding it all together, a link that could provide some of the answers if I could squeeze it just enough.

Derek Manley.

I had seized from him already a car, a stack of stolen electronics, and I had my man out searching for more. He wasn't going to like that, no he was not. And I had the feeling, yes I did, that it would not be long before Derek Manley got hold of me.

Unfortunately I was right.

CHAPTER

29

"What the hell you want from me, Vic?"

"How about," I struggled to gasp out, "you letting go of my crotch."

"Not until we get this straight," said Derek Manley, his angry face an inch from mine, his foul breath warm on my cheek, one huge hand grabbing hold of my lapels, forcing my chest up against a brick wall, the other, well, you ever see the back of a garbage truck close down on a sack of trash? "Tell it to me, Vic. What the hell you want?"

"To sing bass again?"

"You a singer?"

"No."

"Then that makes you a smart-ass. You a smart-ass, Vic?"

"Yes."

"I don't like smart-asses."

"Please."

"You ain't so funny now."

"No."

"Shut up."

"Okay."

"You got a red face, you know that. You must got some Irish blood in you. You got some Irish blood in you, Vic?"

"My grandmother."

"She was Irish?"

"Ukrainian."

"I don't get it."

"Let go and I'll explain."

"I don't want no explanation. I want you to stop your squeezing."

"Me?"

"You're killing me, you son of a bitch."

"Me?"

"You."

"Let go."

"You let go."

"You."

"You."

"Please."

"Fuck." Manley's face twisted in some sort of fearful rage and he let out a bellow that deafened me with its frustration.

In response, I let out a scream of my own, filled with pain and fear.

And so there we were, in that dank and stinking alley, face-to-face, screaming and bellowing like a couple of wild apes.

Then he let go.

I fell onto the wet cracked cement like a limp bag of mush, pulled my knees to my chest. My hands covered my crotch as I tried to catch my breath amid the sickeningly thick snakes of pain twisting through me. I felt like throwing up, I felt like crapping, I felt like checking to see if my soldiers had survived the battle.

Manley himself, seemingly exhausted by his rage, slid down against the wall until he was sitting beside me.

I manfully tried to stop my sobbing.

He shook his head, ran his fingers through his crew cut, let out a whoosh of breath.

If someone had looked in at that very moment, they might have misconstrued.

"Yo, Vic," he said softly, "you want a cigarette?"

"I'm having a hard enough time right now breathing without one, thank you."

"Funny how that works, ain't it?" he said as he shook out a cig.

"Yeah. Funny."

"They wouldn't seem to be connected to the lungs."

"They're connected to everything."

He flicked open a lighter, spun the wheel, leaned over to light his cigarette. "I guess I got a little carried away."

"A little."

"But you have no idea how I'm getting squeezed here."

"I think I have an inkling," I said.

"No hard feelings?"

"Screw yourself."

"Fuck it, then. So sue me."

"Don't worry. I will."

"Yeah, well, stand in line. Twenty years busting my gut and I got nothing to show but debts I'll never pay, a company that's owned by the bank, a pint-sized mobster chewing on my butt, and a girlfriend what won't even let me pinch her tits no more because I can't no longer take her out in the style to which she's grown accustomed, even though it was me what accustomed her to it in the first place. And it ain't like they're the greatest tits in the world neither. But a man likes to get in a pinch or two, you know? Oh, Jesus, ain't life a poke in the gut? This ain't the way I planned it all when I was starting out, I'll tell you. I had different ideas than this. But the thing is, Vic, the thing is, and I know'd this from the start, I ain't all that smart. That's the problem right there. I just was never smart enough."

The snakes slowed their twisting and the pain eased just a bit. I carefully pushed myself up until I too was sitting, right beside Manley. His legs were stretched straight ahead of him, his basketball-sized belly was flopped on his lap, and he was sweating. He wiped his forehead with the back of his hand, coughed, inhaled.

"I'm too old for this," he said.

"We got the Eldorado."

"Rothstein told me. And my piece of the club, whatever that's worth."

"Not much, I figure."

"Tell me about it. Most expensive hand job in the history of the world. What else you looking for?"

"Whatever you got."

"Why?

"We'll stop if you give us a name."

"Whose?"

"The guy who hired you to rough up that guy with the suitcase twenty years ago."

He laughed lightly, blew out a thin stream of smoke. "You're a stupid son of a bitch. You don't understand what the hell you're messing with."

"Why don't you tell me, then?"

"Take everything I got. It don't make no difference. I can't give you what you want. Take my balls. Go ahead. What with my new situation, they're not doing me no good no more. Take them."

"No, thank you."

"It don't matter. I can't give you what you want."

"Why?"

" 'Cause I give you that, I'm dead." Manley shook his head, stubbed out his cigarette. "It's complicated. You know I got a son. Stashed away some place in Jersey. Hidden from everyone. Whatever I'm into, it don't affect him.

Except that I'm his sole support. I fall behind in my payments, the little bugger's begging in the street. And he's got this problem with his eyes. And he don't breathe so good. That's the only thing I keep up, even before the girlfriend who ain't letting me near her tits no more. The support and the insurance, in case something happens to me. And I'm good as gone, already. No place left to go. I knew it, soon as you asked them questions in that deposition. I been hiding out ever since, but it's closing in on me, I can feel it. Why are you being such a prick, anyway?"

"I'm a lawyer. I get paid to be a prick."

"It's nice for you that you found your calling. But what are you really in this for? I mean really. And it's not the money, 'cause I ain't got none."

"Joey," I said.

"Cheaps?"

"Yeah."

"Really?"

"Yeah."

"What a putz."

"Me?"

"No, Joey."

I didn't say anything.

"We was kids together, Joey and me. You think he was a putz as an adult, you should a seen him when he was seventeen. You want to know the only reason I ran with Joey when we was kids? His mom. You went over to that house, you ate like a god."

"Her veal."

"Forget about it. The best. And it's not like she skimps on the servings either. She the one gave you that picture?"

"Yeah."

"Joey Cheaps."

"Why'd you take him along on the waterfront thing?"

"I started out by doing some small things for the boys, when Bruno was still in charge and things they made sense. Small things, you understand, nothing major. And Joey was always begging me for a chance to do something, anything, like he always did. Then when Bruno was whacked and the Scarfo craziness started, I wanted nothing more to do with them, none of them. So I got the job, the trucking job. And then this thing came along, right out of the blue, and I needed help with it, but the guy what set it up didn't want to get the boys involved, and I understood that. Once they're involved, Jesus, you know. So I thought Joey, he could be my help."

"This wasn't mob work?"

"No. Something else. Something for a friend."

"And it turned bad."

"Yeah." He rubbed his hand again through his hair.

"If you can't tell me who hired you, can you tell me what happened to the suitcase?"

"The suitcase. Now that's a story. Wouldn't mind having that back, it would solve a lot."

"What happened to it?"

"Who knows? Gone, I guess. Look, Vic, you're all right. You do what you got to do, that's up to you, but Joey, what you were saying in that deposition thing about me. You're off base. I didn't whack him."

"Who did?"

"Beats me. But you find out who it was, you give me the name, that's all you got to do, and I'll take care of it."

"You want to help me, Derek, you tell me who hired you twenty years ago."

"I can't. Leastwise not now. Maybe if things change. But I'll tell you this, it wasn't him who did Joey. That I can promise. It wasn't him."

"You're sure?"

"Yeah, I'm sure. He's dead, for a long time now."

"Dead?" That didn't make sense. Too many people still cared too much for the guy who set up Tommy Greeley to be long dead.

"So, Victor," said Manley, "now, you gonna leave me alone?"

"No."

"I ought to wring your frigging neck."

"Next time," I said, "that would be preferable."

"Yeah," he said with an appreciative chuckle. "I bet."

"So what are you going to do?"

"I don't know. It don't look like there is nothing I can do. But I got to find something, some way to get out of this, don't I? Take the pressure off, take care of my kid in Jersey. You know, in a life turned to shit, he's the only bright spot. I need to take care of him. Leastwise, I got the insurance, right?"

"Health insurance?"

"You are a smart-ass." He reached out a hand and I shook it. Then he pressed himself to standing. "Take care of yourself, Vic. Be careful, right? Don't expect you'll be seeing my mug again."

"You're not going to . . ."

"I got to do something, don't I?"

"You're really not going to . . ."

"Desperate situation, desperate measures." He laughed lightly, leaned out of the alley and scanned the street beyond.

I felt sorry for him just then, as sorry as you could possibly feel for a man who had just placed your balls in a vise and twisted the handle. But as he looked both ways and then hitched up his pants, shot his cuffs, slid out of the alley like a boy sneaking out of trouble, he didn't seem so formidable, or so rotten. All his life he had tried to short the system, and though he had a bit of a run, nothing had worked out in the end like he had hoped, starting with a rough-up that had turned into a murder, and now here he was more than twenty years later with nothing left but his sad resignation and his failures. And the only answer he could fathom was a life insurance policy with his son as beneficiary.

I wondered if maybe, like with Joey, what had happened two decades ago at the waterfront had ruined Derek Manley too. That strange traumatic event was like a Charybdis whose dark swirl sucked in and destroyed everyone who ventured too close to it, starting with Tommy Greeley and moving outward. And I was getting closer, not close enough yet to glimpse the root of that swirl of destruction, but close enough to feel its pull. And it felt to me, just then, that it was Tommy Greeley himself who was pushing me into its nihilistic grasp.

CHAPTER
30

I limped into the hospital to visit my father, leaning precipitously, my face as green as Seussian eggs. I put on a smile as I struggled through the lobby. What Manley had done to me was bad enough, I didn't need some overeager first-year resident to code me right then and there. *But he looked like he was having an attack.* And I did, I had no doubt. Every step was a new little agony, and Manley's gift was just the capper on the beating I had taken the night before. This case was getting less and less fun by the hour.

"Oh, Mr. Carl," said the nurse at the desk in front of the fourth-floor elevators. "Before you go in to your father, Dr. Hellmann would like to talk to you."

Well, that made me feel a whole lot better.

"We're concerned about your father's condition, Victor," she said, her sincere face showing sincere concern, her eyes staring at the chart she held before her like a shield. "We've tried two different courses of antibiotics, but his infection is not reacting as we had hoped. Apparently he has a stubbornly virulent strain."

"It's my father," I said. "I could have told you that from the start."

"I like your father."

I was taken aback. "You do?"

"He's crusty, sure, but sort of soft inside."

"You're talking about my father and not a baguette?"

"I think he's sort of sweet. What happened to your forehead?"

"A golfing accident," I said as I smoothed my hair over the cut.

She tilted her head, examined me for a moment as if I were some obscure abstract sculpture that made not a whit of sense, and then shook her head. "If there's no improvement in your father's condition we're going to try a new antibiotic, Primaxin, which has more universal coverage. The pulmonary specialist has told us this drug has gotten good results in similar cases, but we can't be certain this will work either."

"Is there anything I should be doing? Anyplace I should play the squeaking wheel to make sure something gets done?"

"We're doing everything we can. Really. And"—she smiled—"I've made sure everyone knows that the patient's son is a lawyer."

"Does that help?"

"It's like a plate of tofu."

"It sticks in your throat and makes you gag?"

"No, Victor. It might not help, but it can't hurt."

"I heard that line differently."

"I had a good time the other night."

"So did I," I lied. Oh, stop it, you would too.

"You haven't called back."

"Work has gotten pretty intense."

"Looks like it, from the way you're standing."

"I had a run in with an angry debtor."

"I thought the reason you didn't call back was my cats. I got the sense maybe you weren't a cat person."

"I'm not, actually." Think, think. "It turns out I'm allergic."

"Really?"

No. "Yes."

"That's too bad. They're so cute. They have pills for that, you know."

"Isn't it hard to get their little mouths open?"

"Is that a joke?"

"No."

"Okay." She stretched the word out, widened her eyes, made me feel every inch the fool. "If it doesn't get better soon, Victor, you should know that we're going to have to take more drastic action."

"You're talking about my father now, not the cats."

"Right. That's what I wanted to tell you. He's having a harder time breathing, his respiratory rate is above where we'd like to see it, and there is only so much oxygen we're able to put through the nasal canula. We might have to put him on a mask and, if things get any worse, a ventilator. Try to keep him from talking too much, or getting upset, okay?"

"I'll try."

"Good." She wrinkled her nose at me and then walked off. I watched her as she leaned over the nurses' station to drop off the chart, her back arched, her left leg held straight out, the toe of her white sneaker pointed. I supposed they taught ballet out there in Ohio, taught it with much sincerity.

My father was sleeping fitfully when I entered his room, his mouth open, his breaths short and wet, his hand looking like a dead bony carp as it lay atop his sheet with its pulse oxymeter clip in place. His oxygen level was eighty-six, his respiratory rate was twenty-three, his heart rate was still over a hundred. All bad signs. I sat next to his bed, checked my watch, decided not to awaken him. Dr. Mayonnaise had told me to keep him from talking too much or getting upset and both had been occurring with regularity during my visits as he continued to tell to me, with a peculiar urgency, the story of his long-lost love. Maybe tonight he'd sleep through the hour of my stay, give us both a rest.

No such luck.

He awoke slowly and then started when he saw me, as if I were some emissary from a darker world come to claim him.

"Are you ready?" he croaked.

I put my hand on his shoulder, shook him lightly. "Dad. Shhhh. The doctor wants you to stay quiet tonight."

"The red door."

"Please, Dad, don't talk. Not tonight. How do you feel?"

"Like crap."

"Okay. Let's just be quiet then tonight. Just tonight."

He reached out and grabbed my wrist, his big hand weaker than I ever remembered it. "I have to tell you. I have to."

"Why, Dad? Why do you have to tell me?"

"You need to know. Before I die."

"You're not dying."

"Who are you kidding?"

Who indeed?

"Listen," he said. "Shut up and listen."

He was shaking my wrist now, the tape holding the IV line in his vein was coming loose. I pried his fingers from my wrist, patted his gnarled, veiny hand, rested it again on his chest. For some reason he wanted me to have this story, to own it, to carry it with me, always, to be able to take it out and refer to it like a big golden watch in my vest pocket. For some reason.

"Okay, Dad," I said. "Go ahead."

He coughed, fought to regain his breath, calmed himself enough so he could speak. "The red door," he said.

The red door.

It glows like a warning, across the street from where my father now stands in the shadows with his love. The sky is pitch, the moon has set, the city is quiet. They are in that soft, dead moment between night and morning when even insomniacs have drifted off to an uneasy sleep. No birds, no crickets, only the scritching claws of a city raccoon scrambling along a cement wall.

Do you have a key? says my father.

No.

Then how do we get inside?

There is an unlocked window, she says.

"And it was," said my father. "She knew. Unlocked."

Around the back, a window to a little-used mud room off the town house's back alley. As he climbs after her through the window, my father doesn't ask how she knows the window is unlocked, doesn't ask how it became unlocked in the first place, doesn't ask how the key to the locked mud room's door became taped beneath a storage shelf holding sacks of salt, thick woolen gloves, cans of antifreeze.

This way, she says as she quietly clicks open the lock to the mud room's door and he follows her inside.

They pass through a room, dark and warm, the kitchen—he can tell from the gleaming counters, the shining metal ovens. Then through another room, past a long dining table with chairs. Soft light is gathered up like a bouquet of color by a crystal chandelier, large enough for a hotel ballroom. She steps soundlessly across thick rugs and he follows, trying to step just as soundlessly but failing, banging into chairs, rubbing against a wall. They pass into a center hallway with a sconce lighted through the night. The hallway is papered with red velvet medallions, the floors are covered by a thick, deep blue rug. There is a wide stairway leading to the left and the great red door to the right.

He pulls her close. Where are your things? he whispers.

This way, she says.

Not up the stairs?

This way, she says, as she grabs his arm and tugs him forward, through the wide center hall, into a cavernous room. There is a light on in this room too, one dim lamp lit, and he can see the rich oriental rugs, the plush formal furniture, the piano gleaming, the great marble fireplace, its shiny brass andirons standing tall like sentries. Hanging from the walls are great classical paintings in thick golden frames, works like those hanging in the art museum sitting high on the hill above the bending river, each canvas huge, each painting covered with naked women, reclining or frolicking or, in the largest painting of all, fighting against the brutal intentions of their armed captors.

Where are your things? he asks again, this time more urgently.

In here, she says softly and then leads him, strangely, toward a wall. She places a hand on the wall, a panel slides.

"A hidden door," said my father. "She pulled me through."

She pulls him through the opening and closes the door behind them. Blackness, a darkness darker than night, darker than sleep, darker than death. He can hear a deep throbbing, like the beating heart of that very house, as if it were alive, as if it sensed their presence. Doubts assail him, he shouldn't be here, they shouldn't be here, in this house, this hidden room, this darkness. Something here will take her away from him, he feels it, knows it. All he wants is her, forever, and this house is a threat. He wants to grab her, to pull her away from the palpable evil pressing against his flesh. The vision remains of the naked women in that one painting succumbing to the force of men in armor. He wants to grab her and pull her away but she grabs him first, in the darkness, and places her hand at the back of his neck, and pulls his head down and kisses him with a passion that stuns, that leaves his knees weak and his certainty dulled.

Tell me you love me, she says.

I love you, he says.

I'll never leave you, Jesse.

Promise me, he says.

I promise.

Whatever happens.

Whatever. I promise.

I love you.

Yes, she says.

And then she flicks on the light.

My father gasped as he remembered, coughed, fought to find again his breath. "Treasure," he managed to get out. "A room filled with treasure."

The room is small, windowless, paneled in wood, with two plush leather chairs, a golden throw folded on the arm of each. The chairs flank a narrow table with a magnifying glass and a lamp on its surface. Wooden shelves cover three of the room's walls and every shelf is filled with treasure. Ancient books, small gold statues, gilt chests, intricately carved ivory, figurines of bright green jade. The wall without shelves has a perfectly lit single painting in a golden frame, a small highly detailed portrait of a monk in brown robes on his knees, praying with reverence in a rock-strewn landscape. My father is dazzled by the wealth in this small room, more wealth than he had ever before imagined could exist in one man's house. Some of the intricate boxes are open. Strings of pearls, coiled each atop the other, spill out of one. Another is filled with silver broaches covered with gems. There are rows of leather albums, their bindings embossed with the names of countries. France. Germany. U.S. Pre-1840. He spins around helplessly at the sight, dazed, and then he moves his gaze from this obscenity of treasure to the girl who has brought him here, the girl in the pleated skirt, his girl, his love.

Her chin is raised, her hands are shaking.

Where is your stuff? he asks.

Here, she says.

Where? he asks.

Look around.

This isn't yours.

She turns to stare at him, her eyes fierce, rapacious, the eyes of a canine protecting a bone.

He owes me, she says.

She steps toward one of the walls of shelves, takes down a large wooden box, its top precisely ingrained with stones and pearls in the shape of a kneeling Atlas, hoisting on his shoulder a great globe. She places the box on the table, turns on the lamp.

His coin collection, she says, her eyes widening with wonder.

She lifts the top. The interior of the box is divided into a series of equally sized squares and the squares are filled with small, flat velvet sacks, each with its own drawstring. Her hands shaking, she grabs one of the velvet sacks out of the box. She struggles in her haste to loosen its drawstring and pull out a coin. Her hands fumble the sack. It falls on the table with a muffled crack. She picks it up again, succeeds in loosening the drawstring, drops the naked coin into her hand, a golden coin with Lady Liberty holding a torch carved into its surface, the coin's bright skin glinting under the harsh light of the lamp, the hard yellow light reflecting like a knife's edge of gold in his lover's eyes.

"And then the wall," said my father, struggling now to get the words out. "A doorway of shelves. It swings. Swings open. And the old man. In the opening. The hidden doorway. The old man. Darkness behind him. Darkness streaming in behind him. And he's smiling. The eyes of a fox. Smiling. The old bastard. At his little treasures. At the coins. At the gold. At her."

Back from the hospital in the few moments before I had to leave to meet Lonnie and Chelsea, I found myself standing in front of the photographs pinned to my wall. There was something about my father's story that seemed to resonate in the mosaic of limbs and breasts, of bones and curves and flesh. For the first time I found the array of photographs frightening.

It was the lack of a face in the photographs, the missing lens through which we view another's humanity. Lies, despair, love, secrets, lust, all of it is found in the one part of this woman at which I couldn't gaze. I had liked that missing ingredient before, it had allowed me to imagine, to match the perfection of the captured body with my own inventions for her eyes, her cheeks, her nose, her mouth. It had made the pictures all the more alluring, all the more seductive. But right now, I was still suffused with the memory of my father's old lover standing in that hidden room, leaning over that open treasure box, the glint of gold in her eyes. The recesses of her soul were becoming ever darker and more mysterious to the man who had lay naked with her not a few hours before, and that was what I found frightening.

I wondered again who she was, this woman, whose objective beauty was pinned to my wall. And now I found myself wondering what were the desires, the demons, what were the secrets she kept from the lover who was standing behind the camera, capturing his obsession with obsessive care. It wasn't just my father's past that was coming alive for me these difficult days, it was Tommy Greeley's past too. And if there was an entwining of the two, it was happening here, only here, in the murky confines of my own rattled consciousness. Could one story, as it was being revealed to me by my dying father, incident by startling incident, help me fathom the other? I didn't know, but I did know that my own obsession with the photographs seemed to grow as my father's story deepened and darkened, my obsession with the dark limbs, the smooth skin, the missing lens.

I took a step back from the photographs so that the whole array became visible at once. The legs, the torso, the sweet thin arms, the neck. The beauty mark on the edge of the areola of the right breast.

And as I stared at the whole of it, once again the photographs all came together for me, once again all the varied parts of that miraculous body melded into one another and became as one, a vision standing out from the wall, separate now from the individual photographs that inspired it.

Except, this time, there was a difference.

This time I began to see a face, the mysterious missing face. The features weren't yet clear, the contours of her jaw, the shape of her eyes, it all wasn't yet clear, but it was slowly crystallizing for me. And damn if she wasn't starting to look like Chelsea.

CHAPTER

31

"**Back in the** day, Dude," said Lonnie Chambers, his eyes wide with excitement, "when the business was really churning, we had us some parties. Girls, booze, spreads to make a sheik sweat. Shrimp, you never saw so much shrimp. Piles. Mountains. Dude. And that was just the shrimp. You should have been there."

"Were you there?" I asked Chelsea.

Chelsea smiled, gave an expression of fake shock. "No girls allowed, at least no girlfriends allowed." She sipped her blue martini. "A regular boys' club."

We were at the bar of the Continental, a smoky, swanky restaurant carved out of an old chrome diner. I knew the old place, I had eaten there, and generally to see a diner tarted up as some swank joint for a swank crowd made me angry and sad, but this diner had actually been foul, nowhere near as swell as the diner that still parked across the street. And so, as much as it pains me to say it, the Continental, with its power crowd and neon lights, with its padded walls and skewered olive light fixtures and froufrou food was, actually, an improvement.

"The parties," said Lonnie, jabbing at me with his lit cigarette, his rough voice rising above the hum of the crowd, "they always started with the cars. Long black limos the twins, that ran the thing, they rented to pick us all up. Each one stocked with alcohol, some powder, and a girl. A sort of stewardess who would plump your pillow, get you comfy, pour your drink, unzip your fly."

"Lonnie."

"Victor here asked what it was like back in the day, so I'm just telling him. Drinks, drugs, a long-legged girl with a mouth like a washing machine. And that was just the car. We had it going, Dude. And the chicks at home, they never knew a thing about it."

"Don't be stupid, Lonnie," Chelsea said, standing from her stool at the bar. "We knew everything."

"No way. No frigging way." He tilted his head. "How?"

She picked up her glass by the stem, stretched her lovely neck, drained the last of her martini, placed the glass back on the bar. "We paid one of the regular whores to tell us." She glanced at her watch. "I have to make a call."

Lonnie's forehead creased in puzzlement as she walked away from the bar, past the tables, toward the restrooms. She was tall and her back was straight when she walked, but, in the way she gripped her elbows as she moved, there was a sense of her holding herself together, and in her lovely eyes there had been the lovely sadness I had noted before. We both watched her go and then Lonnie shrugged, took a last drag of his cigarette, squashed it among the accordioned remnants of his priors.

"Could be. There wasn't much they wouldn't do for money." A hearty laugh. "Wasn't much at all. Dude, you really should have been there."

"Lonnie, what would I have been?" I said. "Ten maybe?"

"Hell, it's not like you needed a driver's license. What with the limos driving us down the Black Horse Pike. Others would fly in from all over the country, from Boston, from Miami, from Phoenix. All coming to the same place to celebrate. There'd be a reason, usually a bachelor party, but I'll tell you this, it was, all of it, just an excuse. Hell, a lot of these guys just got married so we could have the party. Wild times, man, wild. You want a bone?"

I declined. Lonnie shook another Camel unfiltered from his battered pack, lit it with a Harley-Davidson lighter. Lonnie smoked with the unconscious determination of an old lady playing the slots, one pull after another after another.

"The twins, they would put money in the casino cage for each of us, so as soon as we arrived we could stride onto the floor, tap into the account, and start throwing the dice. Some of the guys, they played blackjack, but I always liked the dice. It's quicker, Dude, if you know what I mean? I figure if I was going to win I was going to win, but if I was going to lose, fine, let's get it over with so we could get it on.

"Upstairs, the twins, what with all the money they was putting into the cages, would get comped a huge suite with all kinds of connecting doors. We called it the Elvis Suite. Fancy furniture, mirrored ceilings in the bedrooms, TV the size of a bull. There'd be about twenty of us up there, along with the food and the coke, 'ludes, dope, whatever, and anything we wanted to drink. And after all of us, we were jacked to the stars, the twins, they would stand up on a table with a bottle of champagne in each hand and make pep talks about the pots of money we were all going to make in the upcoming year. And then they would get to shaking the bottles with their thumbs over the tops and spraying us all. And we'd all start cheering and howling and barking like dogs. It would get louder, wilder, we'd be ripping our shirts off as we barked away. And then the girls would arrive.

"A dozen of them, really prime, you know what I mean. Not like the skanks for sale in Philly, no way. This was Atlantic City and the twins knew how to get the best. Dancing, stripteases, lesbian love, whatever game you was into. The music would be pumping, the girls would help themselves to the drugs, the clothes would come off, the shrimp would fly, things would spiral way out of control. And, Dude, it would go on and on and on. The secret was meth, a little meth you could go all night, and I used to score that myself for the boys. That was my special thing. And with enough drugs, after a while you wouldn't know who you were screwing and you wouldn't care. We would go on all night, dancing and screwing and getting high, until everything just collapsed like a burst balloon.

"In the mornings after, Dude, it was like a tornado had run through the place. Shrimp on the curtains, roast beef hanging from the chandelier, champagne sprayed over everything. Blood and semen, condoms on the ceiling. The guys would be asleep, sprawled under the table or half-on half-off the couch, pants down, drool and coleslaw falling from their mouths. And there was always a girl, picking her way among the fallen soldiers, looking for pieces of her clothing.

"I remember one of the twins taking me aside after one of them parties and saying, 'You know, Lonnie, we just want to give the boys a memory they'll have for the rest of their lives.' And they did, those sons of bitches." His eyeballs, red already, grew glassy with emotion. "And I miss it, all of it, every day. It was the time of my life, Dude. Yes it was."

"Then what happened?" I asked.

"Ah, you know," he said, wiping a hand over his eyes and squashing his cigarette flat. "It was business. Business goes bad, that's the truth of it."

"Who were the twins?"

"Just two guys ran the business I worked in then."

"Brothers?"

"Nah, just friends, They didn't either of them look anything alike, but they always said they was Fric and Frac."

"I'll get the next round."

"Not for me. I got to go. I got a meeting."

"Motorcycle business?"

"Something like that. It was good talking to you, Dude. I'm glad we set this up."

"So am I."

"You find anything more about that dude you told us about? What was his name? Tommy something."

"Tommy Greeley. Yeah, I did."

"Good. That's good. But be careful, Dude, it's a scary world out there."

He slapped me on the shoulder, slapped me so hard I almost fell off the stool. And then he left, just as Chelsea was walking back. They met away from the bar, talked, Lonnie turned his head to look my way as he said something, and then he was gone and Chelsea was walking toward me.

CHAPTER

32

She was stunning. I've said that already, haven't I? But it was especially so in that place, with its sharp-suited crowd of striving professionals, each wearing the latest fashions, the latest shoes, keeping their eyes ever on the prize. Chelsea was a complete contrast. She wore old jeans, a gauzy shirt, her hair wasn't permed or styled, it just fell straight, with a lovely sheen. She wasn't the latest anything, yet still, she had the freshest look in the place. Everything I suppose comes back again, or maybe some people never go out of style. And I didn't have to imagine the magnificent body beneath the clothes; I had the pictures, didn't I?

I caught the bartender's eye, ordered the blue curaçao martini for her, the usual sea breeze for me. Weren't we a festive pair?

"Lonnie tell you all the sordid details?" she said as she slid back onto the stool.

"The good old days."

"They weren't that good."

"Lonnie seemed to enjoy them," I said. "He couldn't stop laughing as he told me his stories."

"You could hear him all through the restaurant. A doctor in a back room thought he'd have to perform the Heimlich."

"You don't laugh much, I noticed."

"Not anymore."

"It wasn't as fun for you, the good old days?"

"No, it was more than fun. It was perfect, like we were blessed."

"You were young."

"We were young and pretty and rich. But sometimes endings matter, don't they? The difference between a comedy and a tragedy is the last page."

"So it didn't end well?" I said and she looked at me with a glint of disappointment in her eyes, disappointment not just then at her past, but at me for acting like I didn't know the answer. Because I knew the answer and she knew I knew the answer.

"We've been told we could talk to you," she said.

I lifted my head at that. "You've been told?"

"Well, you know, you've been asking around about the past. But it's not your past, is it?"

"I'm trespassing, is that it?"

"Sort of."

"So you had to get permission."

"Yes."

"From who?"

"He wants to know what you're really after."

"What does he think I'm after?"

"He asked around about you. Sent out his scouts. The word came back that all you care about is money."

"Is that the word?"

"Is it true?"

"I'm a professional. That's what it means to be a professional."

"So what he wants to know is, where's the money for you here?"

"Where does he think it is?"

"He has some ideas."

"Do they involve a missing suitcase?"

She picked up her martini, looked at its brilliant blue, took a sip. "I don't know why I drink this. I like the color, I suppose."

"And when you hold it like that, it makes you look like Judy Jetson."

"Is that good?"

"Oh sure. Judy Jetson is way hot. Or will be."

"I don't think it's only the money you're looking for."

"Maybe not. My client was murdered. I have to do something, even if it's just to ask as many questions as I can and piss some people off."

"How are you doing?"

I touched the cut on my forehead, thought about Manley's squeeze play. "Oh, I've hit the jackpot there, yes I have. But I especially love the way everyone's eyes flutter when I mention the suitcase."

"Did mine flutter?"

"A little. It was charming."

She laughed, tucked her chin into her shoulder.

"I suppose all the boys wanted to kiss you," I said.

"Enough."

"Lonnie?"

"I would hope so. We were married."

I jerked back at that. "Really? When?"

"Toward the end, but before everything collapsed."

I suddenly wondered why Tommy Greeley had naked pictures of a married woman in his pocket on the night he died.

"What happened to you and Lonnie?" I said.

"We were going downhill anyway, and then we drifted apart."

"Different interests?"

"More like different sentences. No hard feelings though. Still the best of friends." She took a sip of the martini. "I'm supposed to find out if you know where it is."

"And all this time I thought you were here because you liked me. If we decided to kiss, would you need permission for that too?"

"Yes."

"Can you get it?"

"Not on the first date."

"But this is the second date. The first date you pulled me bloodied and beaten off my vestibule floor."

"That was romantic, wasn't it?"

"You weren't just walking by, were you?"

"We were asked to say hello."

"Your friend is being right neighborly, sending out the welcome wagon."

"Are you complaining?"

"No. Not at all. I'm very grateful, actually. So the suitcase, who did it belong to?"

"The twins."

"Let me guess. Tommy Greeley was one, and the other, the guy who gave you permission to speak to me but not kiss me, is his old business partner, Cooper Prod."

"I called him just now. It's phone time at his penitentiary in New Mexico. He gives his regards."

"But not permission to kiss."

"No."

"He's the one who said that the past can be dangerous territory."

"Yes. And he wanted me to tell you that the only thing more dangerous than someone else's past is your own."

"Maybe, but I'm not getting beat up over my past. Tell me about the suitcase."

"It was all coming to an end, and everyone knew it. The

business had just happened, had grown beyond anyone's imaginings, and we hadn't really thought about it much except for some pathetic rationalizations. But right then we all knew it was coming to an end. There were searches, seizures, this creepy little FBI guy was going around asking everyone questions. You don't know what it's like when the law turns against you. It's on your mind every minute, the fear is constant. Every time the phone rings you cringe. Someone knocks on the door, you hide. It's like you're waiting to die. We didn't say anything, none of us, and for a moment it looked like we might work our way through it. And then we heard that sleaze-bucket Babbage had started talking to the grand jury. The twins knew it was the last chance for them to save what they could. Tommy said he had a contact with a boat who would take care of it."

"Who?"

"An old friend, he said. From out of state. So the twins got hold of everything that was lying around and put it in the suitcase."

"Just the odd scraps lying around? It doesn't sound like much."

"You don't understand, do you? How much business they were doing. How everything was in cash. How hard it is to do anything with cash, especially if you can't prove where you got it. When it comes in like it was coming in sometimes you just stuff it into drawers and deal with it later."

"And later had arrived. How much?"

"It seemed like more back then. It seemed like an impossible amount, now baseball players make ten times as much. Still."

I did the math. Alex Rodriguez gets twenty-five mil a year to play shortstop for Texas. A tenth of that, she said. My heart ticked a little faster.

"Who knew about the suitcase?" I said.

"The twins."

"Anyone else?"

"Lonnie."

"Why Lonnie?"

"He was the guard. That kind of delivery, there was always two. Cooper trusted Lonnie completely and he had the gun."

"So, Lonnie was the guard. What does he say happened?"

"He doesn't remember. One moment he was with Tommy and the suitcase, heading toward where Tommy was supposed to hand it over, and the next he was in the hospital with the back of his head split open. He lost so much blood there were doubts as to whether he would survive. Sixty-seven stitches. He was the last one of us ever to see Tommy or the suitcase."

"And now Cooper Prod wants it back."

"He's just curious. It's a loose end. He wants to tie up all his loose ends before he gets out."

"I'm sure he does," I said. "Who knows about it now? Other than Cooper and you and Lonnie and me and the guy from out of town who was supposed to pick it up, who knows about it?"

"A lot. Everyone. Right after the arrests came down, people started talking about it, the suitcase full of money. It was just a rumor, but a rumor people listened to."

"And where did the rumors say it ended up?"

"The bottom of the lake in Roosevelt Park. The top of a church steeple. In a secret space at the law school. Buried under a tree in the backyard of the apartment building where Tommy lived. There have been fools caught digging around that tree, but they've found nothing."

"The mysterious missing suitcase. What would you do if you found it?"

She looked at me as if I had just said something incomprehensible. "I'd give it to Cooper," she said. "It's his money."

"But he's in prison and the money was drug money."

"Why would I steal from a friend?"

"Why would you sell drugs?"

She turned her head quickly, as if she had been slapped, then took hold of her drink and swallowed the rest. The lemon twist sat forlornly at the edge of a spent blue pool. I motioned the bartender for another. We sat and waited as he filled the mixer with ice, added the gin, vermouth, and blue curaçao, shook it vigorously, bruising the hell out of the gin, and then poured it through the strainer into a fresh frosted glass.

"I guess I was out of line," I said.

"Yes, you were. But it's not like you think. It's nothing like you think. I skipped college to go out on my own, a small walk-up the size of a closet, waitressing. There was a guy with money and charm who showed interest in me and at that age, for me, that was enough. He was educated, arrogant, clever, and he had all these amazing friends. His world was magical and he invited me in."

"Tommy?"

"Yes. We were together before I married Lonnie. We took great vacations, we had great parties, we drove a great car, had this great place to live. We seemed blessed, that's all I can say."

"Tommy Fucking Greeley."

"It was the happiest time of my life."

"But the engine of it all was his drug business. Didn't that matter?"

"No, not really. It made it more exciting, sure. Getting a load in, doing the breaks, getting it sold, getting the money together for the next round, it was all part of it, but just a small part. Everything else was bigger. The whole society of it. And even when Tommy dropped me for someone else, for Sylvia, he was still sweet to me, allowed me to remain in his world. That's when I hooked up with Lonnie, as a way to stay connected. But it wasn't the drugs that kept me there, it was the excitement, the camaraderie, the lifestyle, the love."

"I can see that," I said. "Except when you get right down to it, the charm, the car, the vacations, the fawning friends, they were all about the money, weren't they?"

"I suppose."

"And the money, it was all about the drugs."

"It's not that simple."

"Sometimes it is."

"I have to go."

"Don't. At least finish your drink."

"Screw yourself."

"All righty," I said.

I watched her as she slipped off the stool without glancing my way and headed out the door, tall, slim, clutching at herself as she hurried away. I didn't chase after her. I wanted to, I wanted to so badly, to chase after her and grab her by the arms and apologize profusely and fall to my knees and abase myself before her, to do whatever I needed to do to get her to smile at me, to get her to let me get closer to that body, the images of which I had pinned with obsessive care to my bedroom wall and to the plane of my desire. But I didn't chase after her. I didn't. I turned back to the bar and finished my drink, paid my tab, took a taxi home.

My clothes smelled like they had been cured in some sort of barbecue pit. I could only imagine the state of Lonnie's lungs. I stripped and put everything, suit included, in the hamper and then showered to get the smell off my skin and out of my hair. Clean and bristly, towel around my neck, I stepped out of the bathroom. The bedroom was dark, but through the slats of my blinds the streetlights imprisoned the pictures pinned to my wall in bars of light. I stepped toward the wall. A leg was illuminated, a hand, a knee. I gently rubbed a finger across the smooth arch of a foot.

I had been flirting with her, all the time feeling some deeper connection grow. And then, and then, and then I had pushed her away, like I was Cagney with a grapefruit. I suppose I was tired of hearing how wonderful things had been twenty years ago, how wonderful had been the parties, the cars, the society of young and beautiful friends, the money, the very life, how wonderful had been Tommy Greeley. They were still in the middle of it, Lonnie and Chelsea, Cooper Prod, even Eddie Dean, who was somehow involved in it all, somehow, and I had just then a very strong idea how. They were all still living it as if it had all been so wonderful, as if it had all been so proper and so swell. A life distant yet still alive, a life that could never include me. I felt like I was back in high school, pushed to the side as the cool kids strode like kings through the hallway. The hell with them.

And yet here, on my wall, was part of it too. The pictures, the body, the emotions. Her neck. Her shoulder. The bend of her elbow. The curve of her wrist. Maybe it wasn't them, maybe it was me. Maybe I had pushed her away because I was afraid. Afraid of getting too close to this, of getting consumed, or maybe of being consumed with disappointment. Answer me this, when had reality ever lived up to fevered expectation? Barely touching the paper I traced the bulge of her calf, the curve of her knee, the smooth inside of her thigh.

The phone rang.

I spun around. I snapped the towel off my neck and tied it around my waist.

The phone rang.

I panicked for a second, thinking it must be her, it had to be her. What should I say? How could I apologize? What were the magic words? There were always magic words. *I'm a fool. Forgive me, please. You're so so special. You frightened me, that's what it was.* Or the old standby, *Did you know I can lick my eyebrow?*

The phone rang.

I stepped forward and picked it up.

"I found another one," came the voice.

"Excuse me?"

"A car, mate. Another of Manley's cars."

"Skink?"

"Who'd you think it was?"

"No one. Go on."

"A 1989 LeBaron convertible. Who came up with that name for a car, hey? LaIdiot? But there it is. A LeBaron convertible, a classic much in demand with collectors, sos I hear. But that don't matter none to you, does it? LePiece-of-crap, it's one of two registered to the girlfriend, but she drives the other one, a Lincoln. This one, we traced the pinks back to a dummy New Jersey corp. what's stock is registered to our boy. It's behind her apartment down in Germantown. A la-di-da place called the Alden Park."

"I suppose we should go after it."

"Suppose?"

"It's just that Manley looks like a beaten dog already."

"Some dogs you just can't beat enough."

"You're a card carrying member of PETA, I presume. I'll set up a date with R.T. in the sheriff's office."

"Do that, mate, afore it disappears on us. The thing about a car is it's a mobile asset, innit? Here one day, cruising west on Route 66 the next."

"I don't think this one's going anywhere."

"How's the job going?"

"Confusing," I said. "It's like I'm lost in a maze."

"Oh, a rat like you will find his way eventually, I got no doubt, long as there's cheese at the end. Anything more for me?"

"Yeah, there is." I rubbed my scalp with my fingernails, rubbed it so hard I could feel the burn. "I want someone followed. Very discreetly. No hint you're giving her the tail."

"A dame?"

"That's right. But it's real Mission Impossible stuff."

"I'm caught or captured, the secretary will be disavowing any knowledge of my knickers, is that it?"

"That's it."

"All right, Vic. It's good to know where I stand. Give it up."

"Her name's Straczynski," I said. "Alura Straczynski."

CHAPTER

33

Seven ninety-nine Wolf Street. Apartment Three B.

Beth and I stood in the hallway, at the door. We had debated for how to play it. Vacuum cleaner salespersons? City health inspectors? Homeland Security investigators checking out a suspicious neighbor? We came up with a bundle of bad possibilities, and then decided to play it straight, sort of.

"Hello," said Beth, when the door was cracked opened by a heavy woman in a great red-and-purple muumuu. "We're looking for Beverly Rodgers. Is this her residence?"

"Yes."

"Are you Ms. Rodgers?"

"No." The woman gathered up the collar of her housedress in a meaty hand. "I'm just a friend who helps take care of her. And you are?"

"We're lawyers," I said, handing my card through the narrow opening. "We need to talk to Ms. Rodgers about a matter of some urgency."

"How did you get through the security door?"

"A nice lady on her way out held it open for us."

"They're not supposed to do that. A letter has been sent to all the tenants." She leaned out the doorway, looked behind us into the hall. "You'll have to leave. Beverly can't be disturbed right now. She is ill."

"Nothing serious, I hope," said Beth.

"I'm afraid it is. She is a terribly ill woman and she has insisted that she have no visitors. But later, if she gains enough strength, perhaps she'll be able to give you a call."

"Like I already told you, we are here on a matter of some urgency," I said. "It involves a will. I believe she knew a Mr. Joseph Parma, now deceased?" I looked behind me and then lowered my voice. "I can't talk about it in the hallway, but it might be in her interest to see us immediately, before Mr. Parma's mother takes charge of the estate."

"I'm sorry. She can't be disturbed."

"Why don't you ask her. We'll wait out here while you do."

She squinted at us for a moment and then closed the door. We could hear the locks engage and then the groaning of the floorboards as she stepped away, toward some back room in the apartment

"It won't be long," I said, and it wasn't.

Muumuu lady gave us a quick, halfhearted smile when she opened the door again. "My name is Martha," she said. "I'm a friend of Bev's. I help take care of her."

"Are you here often?" I said.

"Every day."

"Paid?"

"I said I'm a friend."

"So you knew Mr. Parma."

"They come and go," said Martha. "Bev is feeling a little better and says she is able to see you. This way, please."

Martha led us through a fussily furnished living room, with chintz throws thrown over the chairs and strange erotic statues turned into lamps. The place smelled of stale perfume, of spilt whiskey, of Dorothy Parker. A box of candy, its top off, its small brown papers strewn and empty, sat on a coffee table between a fluffy couch and an old console television. A couple of framed art nouveau prints of dancing women were side-by-side on a wall. Erté? Ouch. In the corner sat a wheelchair.

"How long has Ms. Rodgers been ill?" I said.

"Oh years and years," said Martha. "She has a weak constitution."

"Don't we all," said Beth.

Beyond the living room was a dark hallway, an eat-in kitchen to the right, a bathroom to the left, the hallway leading to a closed white door.

"Wait a moment," said Martha as she opened the door and went through, shutting it behind her.

"Bev's an invalid?" said Beth, quietly.

"Joey Cheaps, humanitarian," I said. "Who knew?"

"All right, Mr. Carl," said Martha, opening again the door. "Bev will see you now." And then Martha opened the door wide and waved us in as if we were about to have an audience with the queen.

We stepped into a boudoir if ever there was one.

"You told Martha something about a will," said a brightly lit woman sitting high in the bed, pillows fluffed all about her as if she were held aloft on a cloud, her voice as sharp and as grating as a cat with its tail pinned beneath a tire.

Bev Rodgers was a honey, all right, just as McDeiss had described her. She had short, coiffed blond hair, a pretty round face, and she wore a dressing gown trimmed with white fluff. She could have been anywhere between thirty and fifty, it was hard to tell with all the makeup so brightly and thickly applied. She had a mole, either natural or painted, beside her small shapely mouth, and she had a lit cigarette in an actual cigarette holder that she held between two crimson-tipped fingers. She looked like the lead in a Busby Berkeley musical and her voice was impossible.

"I'm very interested in wills," she said. "I was hitched to one once, but that's a short story. It's Vic, isn't it?" she said to me, her bright lips quivering as if to hypnotize.

"Yes, it is," I said.

"Joey mentioned you. You're the spieler, right? The one who's been calling."

"That's right. Why didn't you return my calls?"

"I don't like the phone. Nothing good ever comes over the phone. And besides, I been ill." She put a hand onto her forehead. "Oh Joey, dear, sweet Joey. What happened is tragic. Getting greased like that. Just tragic. I'm still not over it." She took a drag from her cigarette holder, exhaled a thin plume of smoke. "Now, about the will. What did my little scrumpkins leave me?"

"Well, he didn't mention you by name, Ms. Rodgers—"

"Call me Bev, Vic. We're all chums here."

"Thank you, Bev. And this is my partner, Beth Derringer."

"Pleased to meet you, I'm sure," said Bev, never taking her eyes off me, obviously not finding the female of the species worth a quiver of the lips.

"Joey didn't mention you in the will by name, Bev, but he stated he wanted all his debts paid by the estate. And prior to his death he did mention you to me."

"Something flattering, I hope."

"Oh yes, yes indeed. In fact, he said he owed you much. And so I wondered if, by chance, what he owed you was money."

"And if he did?"

"Well, then, Bev, you might be in line for certain disbursements."

"Did you hear that, Martha. Disbursements. I like disbursements. Tell me, Vic. Did my scrumpkins have enough scratch to make these disbursements?"

"I think maybe yes," I said, "if we can make our claims before his mother grabs everything she can."

"Ah, the mother. I know all about her."

"You've met her?"

"Not personally, no. But Joey, he spilled enough about her. And I know, Vic, that Joey, my Joey, would want me to get what I am owed before that vulture of a mother gets her mitts on anything. We were very close, Joey and myself. He wanted to marry me, and let me tell you, if I had known what was going to happen I would have said yes, believe me."

"Oh I do, Bev. Yes I do. So you are owed money?"

"Of course." She reached down and fluffed a blanket. "We're talking about Joey."

"How much?"

"Hundreds. Thousands. More. I don't have an exact figure offhand."

"But you can get it for me."

"Sure."

"With proof."

"No problem. Proof. Of course I got proof. That kind of money, who wouldn't have proof. Proof." Pause. "What kind of proof?"

"Anything. Something written down would be best. Testimony would work."

"You mean all I got to do is say he owes me?"

"Maybe. Someone else would make it better. Someone like . . . Martha."

"She'll say whatever you need her to say, won't you, Martha?"

"I remember everything," said Martha. "To the penny."

"I bet you do," I said. "Good, now we've got something. Get me the detailed information as soon as you can and I'll see what we can do. I, of course, will require a small percentage to facilitate the disbursements."

Her head tilted up. "How small?"

"Forty percent."

"That's robbery. I won't stand for it. Fifteen."

"Thirty-five."

"Seventeen-fifty."

"Thirty's as low as I go."

"You're bleeding me, Vic. Sick as I am, you're killing me."

"I'm just a lawyer, trying to get by."

"Twenty-five."

"I can't."

"Maybe I'll find myself another spieler."

"That wouldn't be wise."

"Twenty-seven-fifty."

"Done," I said, and from the way she smiled at me, like she had just eaten my lunch, I knew that by letting her win the negotiation I had won her over.

"You know what Joey said about you, Vic?"

"What?"

"He said you was a sharp little number. I suppose that makes two of us." Her lips did that quiver thing again. It was quite a talent. She could have set up on a street corner, dropped a hat to the ground, quivered for quarters.

"There is one other matter we need to talk about," I said. "I spoke to Joey on the morning before he was killed and he said he was working on some big money deal. Said it was going to make him flush. If we could figure out what he was talking about it might significantly increase the amount available for disbursements."

"Joey always had some cook-up working," said Bev.

"But see, later that night he was at Jimmy T's, telling the same sort of story. And then, according to the bartender, he got a phone call from you and he left the place straight away."

"I only called to say I missed my little scrumpkins. To tell him to come home and take care of me."

"Did he?"

"No," she said, and then she used the fluff-tipped sleeve of her dressing gown to dab at her dry eyes. "I never seen him again."

"And you don't know the details of any deal he was working out."

"No. I don't." Dab, dab, dab. "Why?"

"Because, Bev. Being his attorney, whatever deal he was involved with, I could follow it through, if you understand what I am saying. I could follow it through on behalf of the estate and the people who Joey owed so much."

"Like myself, for instance," she said.

"Exactly."

"Interesting. In-ter-es-ting. But I got to talk to someone first before I can say a thing."

"Fair enough. You have my number."

"Yes I does. I'll be in touch, I'm sure."

"But time is of the essence if we're going to keep the money away from his mother."

"Oh I understand that, Vic, yes I do."

"Good. And your natural aversion to the telephone might now be most prudent. The police have been here, right?"

"So?"

"I have some sources on the inside and they tell me your phone is tapped."

"Stinking bluecoats," she said. "I thought something funny was going on. Someone keeps on calling and leaving no message."

"I guess that's it. It was a pleasure meeting you, Bev."

"Oh, I'm sure," said Bev as her phone rang. It rang again and then again. Neither Martha nor Bev made a move.

"You ought to answer that."

"Why?" said Bev.

"It could be something important?"

"Nah," she said. "It never is."

Outside the apartment building, Beth and I sat together in my car, down the road from the entrance.

"What a spider," said Beth.

"Arachnids might take offense," I said.

"And what was that thing she was doing with her lips?"

"It was like visual pheromones."

"Did it get you going?"

"No, but every cockroach in the city reared up on their hind legs. The more I learn about Joey's life, the more I shudder."

"How long are we going to wait?"

"It won't be long," I said, and it wasn't.

I had thought it would be Martha in the muumuu who would step out of the apartment building, look around nervously, and then head off to some rendezvous. I thought it had to be Martha, what with the wheelchair in the living room, the way Bev was propped up on her pillows, the way Martha served her like Bev was an immobile queen bee, her abdomen swollen with a thousand eggs. But it wasn't Martha who stepped out of the apartment building in her high heels, her black stockings, her tight blue dress, her hat, her veil, her cigarette holder.

"Quick recovery," said Beth.

"A miracle," I said. "I should open a revival tent."

We followed at a distance in the car as she moved down

and around the South Philly streets, as she sashayed here and there. And it wasn't a surprise, it wasn't a surprise at all, where she ended. When does a lady stop being a lady? When she turns into a bar.

The Seven Out.

I parked well past the entrance. "Wait here," I said. "I'll be right back."

I didn't want to go in if I could avoid it. I didn't want her to see me and realize I had been following her and that maybe everything I had said, about the will, about getting her disbursements from the estate, about her phone being tapped, all of it had been a steaming pile of humbug. I didn't want to go in and I didn't have to. There was a curtained window at the Seven Out, big enough to hold the neon beer signs that let you know the joint wasn't a juice bar. Beneath the flashing Budweiser sign and above the Coors Light sign was a small gap between the curtains.

I leaned forward, shielded my eyes from the neon, peered inside. There she was, seated in the back, hat still on, talking urgently with a man whom I had never seen before in the entirety of my life, but whom I could name without a doubt.

Teddy Big Tits.

And yes, yes they were.

CHAPTER

34

I had set up a date with R.T. at Alden Park, so we could lehaul away Manley's LeBaron, but before that little joyous prank I had something else that needed doing.

Philadelphia College of Art is pressed between the Franklin Institute, with its great silver ball of static electricity that stands hair on end, and the Pennsylvania Museum of Natural History, with its giant skeletal T-Rex, posed to pierce flesh and bone. The art students hanging outside PCA seemed to have cheerily passed through both hazards and decided they liked the look. I liked the look too—on them. They glanced warily my way as I passed by in my navy blue suit, heavy black wingtips, narrow red polyester tie. I suppose the art students in their black clothes, colored spiky hair, piercings, their tattooed necks and shaved eyebrows considered their garb as a wry comment on society's mores. Funny, about the professional clothes I wore I felt the very same way.

So here I was back at school, feeling out of place among the throng, off to see the dean. Some things never change.

"I don't believe I can help you, Mr. Carl," said Dean Sandhurst, a tall rawboned woman with bright eyes and big hands, whose jaw twitched as she spoke. Her crisp white shirt was open at the top and, though her gray hair was so

tightly bound it eased the deep lines around her eyes, a few
stray wisps were left free to soften the edges of her face.
"Our admissions policies here are very strict and our responsibility is to the whole student body. No personal ap-
peals, other than the usual letters of recommendation, are
generally allowed."

"I understand that, Dean."

"I only agreed to meet with you as a favor to Philip,
who helped me through a difficult time a few years ago."
A divorce case, Skink had said, the usual thing, you understand, Skink had said. I did. No one loves a PI more
than a woman in trouble. "My return of the favor only goes
as far as allowing this meeting. It won't affect the admissions decision."

"Of course it won't. And it shouldn't. I just hoped I'd be
able to ease any concerns you might have about an applicant and maybe request the decision, whether positive or
negative, be made sooner rather than later."

"When would you need to hear? February? March?"

"By early next week."

"Mr. Carl, that simply won't be possible. There is a
process that must be followed. There are committees. We
can't rush these things. What is so important that the applicant must hear by early next week?"

"That is when he is due to be sentenced in Common
Pleas Court by Judge Horace Wellman."

"Ah, I see. Yes. You're a lawyer, Mr. Carl."

"That I am."

"Philip didn't tell me."

"I find he often leaves out the best parts."

"And the applicant you want to discuss is a client."

"Yes, he is."

"Nice try, Mr. Carl, but I can't help you. This is an institution of higher learning. We are not a tool to be used by

sly lawyers for the reduction of criminal sentences. You will have to find some other angle to help your client."

"This is not an angle, Dean Sandhurst. I have too much respect for PCA and for my client, Rashard Porter, for that. I've been a lawyer for almost a decade, but this is the first time I've ever spoken up for a client to a college dean. Most of my clients have talents in areas I don't want to encourage. But Rashard Porter is a good kid, in bad circumstances, who happens to be a stellar artist. Partly I'm here, yes indeed, because I think an acceptance would help at his sentencing. But I'm also here because I believe the sentencing itself could help Rashard in the next crucial phase of his life. The criminal justice system doesn't only have to be a way to mete out jail time, it can also be the one time a kid in perilous circumstances gets a clear-eyed look at his situation and a meaningful plan to transcend it. For some it's drug rehab that's needed, for some it's psychiatric counseling."

"But we are not a drug rehabilitation facility, Mr. Carl, nor a psychiatric institution."

"Of course not. But if Rashard is accepted at PCA, I could have his attendance and performance here made an important condition of his probation. Nothing focuses the mind like a judge looking over your shoulder. Rashard needs a little discipline, most nineteen-year-old kids do, but maybe the criminal justice system, and his lawyer, and PCA might help counteract the other forces in his life and give him what he needs to pursue his destiny."

"So, it is up to us to save him, is that it?"

"Like I said, Rashard's a good kid. The trouble he is in is minor. There's a lot in his life pushing him in the wrong direction, but in the end, I have no doubt that Rashard will save himself, on his own, like each of us in the end is forced to do. But you, Mrs. Sandhurst, you might be able to save the artist. Give him the training he needs, the validation he craves, show him the opportunities he doesn't know are out there. He doesn't believe you can make a living at art. Prove to him he can."

"And what if he's not good enough?"

"Then don't waste his time."

Mrs. Sandhurst pursed her lips, leaned back in her chair, put a hand to her throat, spun back and forth. Her jaw twitched as if in memory of something. "How is Philip doing?" she said.

"Fine."

"Still worried about his cholesterol?"

"Always."

"He was a big help to me in a difficult time. And not just with his professional services." With a finger she slowly curled a stray wisp of hair. "He listened to me, he heard me, and he helped. He's a strange man, and not one to follow all the niceties, but his heart is gold. Very tender. Very empathic."

"A model for us all."

She startled for a moment, as if awaking from a reverie. "God, I hope not. But he does have a fine set of teeth. Rashard Porter, is that it?"

"Yes."

"His application is complete?"

"So the registrar has told me."

"I'll need to speak to him personally."

"I can have him here at an hour's notice."

"You understand, I can promise nothing. Everything must be decided in committee, and any decision will, of course, depend almost entirely on his portfolio."

"So I always assumed."

"We need to see more than just routine adolescent scribbles. You said he was an artist. Do you know much about art, Mr. Carl?"

"Some. Who's that guy? Say what? Say what?"

"Cézanne?"

"That's the one. I like him, and I'm also a sucker for pictures of dogs playing poker."

She laughed. "I've always liked them too. We have a committee meeting tomorrow night. I will consider discussing your situation with the committee. That's all I can promise."

"Thank you."

"Give my regards to Philip, please."

"Oh, I will."

"You slept with her, didn't you?" I said.

Skink, sitting beside me in the car at the Alden Park parking lot, across from a blue LeBaron convertible, crossed his arms and said, "Get your mind out of the gutter, why don't you?"

"You're the one always talking about his ethical responsibilities and then you go and pull something like that."

Skink merely looked away.

"Have you no shame?" I said. I was enjoying this.

"It ain't shame what I got. It's called discretion, mate. I don't talk about my personal life one way or the 'nother. When's your cowboy coming?"

"He's coming."

"You know, the car, it hasn't been moved since first time I spotted it."

"Really," I said, starting to wonder. "Has he visited the girlfriend during that time?"

"Not that I've seen. Our boy, he's disappeared."

I thought about the insurance and the kid in New Jersey and Manley's sad slump of resignation. I didn't want to tell Skink, but I suspected we'd never see Manley again. "We were talking," I said, to change the subject, "about the dean."

"There's nothing to talk about."

"I just want to get it straight."

"All right, this is the straight of it. She was sinking fast, her marriage on the rocks, the very idea of herself plummeting. It was a dangerous time, but she made the right move and gave me a call. She was shaking when she told me her situation. But I sensed the story right off and it didn't take long. Her husband was an artist too, an instructor at that very same joint. A remote-controlled camera set in a bust of some naked twist got me all I needed. Snap snap. Caught the arsehole cavorting, yes I did, with a model atop a table set with two apples, a book, an overturned jug. A real work of art, it was. I entitled it: Still Life with Two Cocks. A good patch of work if I say so myself. She was a nice lady and she got herself out of a bad situation, and she gained a new understanding of her own needs in the process."

"You sound like Dr. Phil."

"Yeah, well, in a way we's in the same business, ain't we? Helping our clients confront the truth. Only difference is I do it with pictures. So I was glad to be able to help. And the penthouse apartment on Rittenhouse Square she got in the settlement after showing my work of art at the deposition, well that didn't hurt any neither."

"Such a sweet story."

"I do my best."

"So you slept with her, didn't you?"

Before he could respond, my phone rang. It was Ellie, my secretary, informing me that one R.T. Pritchett from the sheriff's office was on the phone. I asked her to put him through to my cell.

"Where the hell are you?" I said.

"Something came up," said R.T., his voice strangely empty of its western twang. "I'm gonna be late."

"How late?"

"You got a calendar?"

"Come on, R.T. What's going on up there?"

"We're busy."

"Not that busy."

"You don't understand."

"What don't I understand? That your boss needs to unload a few more bushels of crab fries and he's putting another hand in my pocket? There's only so many crab fries a man can eat."

"It's got nothing to do with that."

"Really? Then why don't you tell me the hell what it has got to do with."

"We're just busy, is all. The word's come down. We're simply too busy at the moment to help out when it comes to you."

"Me?"

"You."

"What did I do?"

"You tell me, Victor. You must have pissed off someone, someone the size of a gorilla. The squeeze has been put on my boss and so the squeeze has been put on me and so I got no choice but to squeeze you out."

"No choice?"

"None."

"After all we been through together?"

"Don't get weepy-eyed on me, Victor, it's the way it is."

"Anything I can do?"

"Not a thing, buckaroo."

"You're screwing me here, R.T."

"Someone's screwing you, Victor, that's for sure. I just hope you're enjoying it."

I hung up the phone, thought about it for a moment. "Let's go," I said finally.

"He ain't coming?" said Skink.

"Nope."

"He give a reason?"

"Someone is mad at me."

"Who?"

"I've got a pretty good idea."

"Someone heavy?"

"Morbidly obese, and mad enough that I'm not getting that car today. Or tomorrow. Or next week. Or next month. Which I figure is just as well."

"You want me to disable it so it don't go nowhere?"

"No. But I would like to know if he moves it."

"I could mark them tires, check on them every so often."

"Good."

"So who is it, Vic, the heavy out to shut you off? He high up politically?"

"Yeah."

"Councilman?"

"Higher."

"Mayor?"

"Higher."

"Jesus."

"Higher."

Skink laughed, a rough, sarcastic laugh, the laughter you loose at a clown in a barrel when he pratfalls.

"Yeah," I said.

CHAPTER

35

She was waiting for me in my office when I returned from my unsuccessful seizure of Manley's LeBaron. She had made herself at home, sitting in my chair, leaning over my desk, scribbling so intently in some notebook that she didn't notice me standing in my own door frame. I figured she'd show up, I just didn't figure it would be so soon.

Alura Straczynski.

I watched her for a moment. She was engrossed, totally, in her work, slim eyeglasses perched on her nose, bracelets jangling as her wrist moved swiftly across the page. She was dressed stylishly, if a little bit too, in a red silk shirt, a green bandanna around her neck, long golden earrings. There was in her manner and her seeming indifference to her surroundings the intensity of an artist at the easel and she nodded, yes, yes, yes, as if each word was a dab of paint on a brilliant canvas. The tension in the edges of her mouth as her pen flew and the bangles jangled was surprisingly sexy. A woman at work, Rosie the Riveter.

She glanced up, over the top of her glasses, and spied me spying. "So," she said as she put down her pen, closed the notebook, took off her glasses. "You've returned. From some great legal victory, I hope."

"Nothing so dashing," I said. "Something about a car."

"But still it went well, I am sure."

"Not really."

"You don't mind my using your desk, do you? Your secretary said you would only be a moment."

"And she brought you in here?"

"She asked me to wait in the waiting room, but really. What's the point in that? The seats are uncomfortable and your magazines are months old. Just sitting there made my teeth ache. When she stepped out for a moment I stepped in here."

"You weren't snooping around, were you?"

"What do you take me for? Of course I was. But too bad for me, I found nothing of a compromising nature. I suppose you don't compromise, do you, Victor?"

"Not really," I said.

"I couldn't help but admire your decor."

"I did it myself."

"Obviously. The folders on the floor, the mismatched chairs, the lovely scuff marks on the thrillingly beige walls. It must be reassuring for your clients to know you don't waste their money on interior design. You can tell a lot about a man from his office. I read yours as a little rundown, a little shady, a lot desperate, but with a tinge of strained heroism. I especially like the picture of the soldier on the wall."

"Ulysses S. Grant."

"Marvelous touch, that. Standing before his tent with that pose of calm ferocity. Why him?"

"Because he was pretty much a total failure well into middle age until the war came and he found his place and became the greatest military leader in the country's history."

"So there's still hope for you, is that it? Tell me about the dented file cabinet."

"A couple of new-age enforcers tried to enlighten my soul and scare me off a case at the same time."

"Did your soul enlighten?"

"No."

"Did you scare?"

"Absolutely. I scare quite easily."

"Do I scare you?"

"Your husband does."

"Jackson? I didn't know he was such a brute. But what about me? Don't I scare you even a little?"

"Sure, if you want."

"Oh, I want. It's late, I'm thirsty. Let's go get a drink."

"Do you think it appropriate for a married woman to have a drink with a man she hardly knows?"

"God, I hope not. Where would the fun be in that?" She stood, put her notebook into her purse. "Let's go, yes? I know just the place. And we have so much to talk about, don't we?"

I thought about my promise to Slocum, but I had promised not to bother her and here she was, obviously bothering me. So this situation could surely be distinguished from my promise and I could go and have that drink with her and still be keeping my word, couldn't I? Believe it or not, we actually do learn to think like this in law school.

CHAPTER

36

Alura Straczynski's arm clasped firmly in mine, she led me along the city streets, chatting gaily all the while. She was, I had to admit, engaging company. She pointed out passersby she found to be amusing, she window-shopped, asking my advice about that outfit, that painting, that vase, she responded to my occasional quip with a gratifying trill of soft laughter. There was an excitement about her, an electric current that seemed to transfer from her arm to mine. She exuded a sort of joy, as if this walk with me through the city streets, this day of hers, this very life was all she could ever have wanted.

"I have a secret to tell you," she said, leaning her head close to mine as we walked.

"Go ahead."

"I think I'm being followed."

I jerked around to see what I could see and spied nothing.

"Don't look, you silly. You'll tip him off. But I've noticed him. A greasy little man in a hat."

"Maybe your husband is worried about your going off to have drinks with strange men."

"Why would he be worried about that?"

"That's the way men are."

"Some men, I suppose."

We ended up at the bar of a little steak house I had never noticed before. It was one of those places that seemed to have slipped through time unscathed and walking into it was like walking into a different decade. Dark walls, leather booths, thick slabs of beef, ashtrays on every table. The man behind the bar in a red plaid vest had the open, sad face of an old-time baseball player.

"Mrs. S.," he said in a thick nasally voice when we sat on the red-leather stools. "Terrific as always to see you."

"Rocco, this is Victor," she said. "Victor and I are in desperate need of a drink. I'll have the usual. What will it be for you, Victor?"

"Do you make a sea breeze?" I said.

Rocco looked at me like I had spit on the bar.

I got the message. This was a serious place for serious drinking, a leftover from an era when the cocktail hour was a sacred thing, when a man was defined by his drink and no man wanted to be defined by something as sweet and inconsequential as a sea breeze. Kids in short pants with ball gloves sticking out of their pockets drank soda pop, men drank like men.

"What's she having?" I said, nodding at my companion.

"A manhattan."

"What's that?"

"Whiskey, bitters, sweet vermouth."

"And a cherry," said Alura Straczynski. "Mustn't forget the cherry."

"No, Mrs. S.," said Rocco. "I wouldn't forget your cherry."

I tried to think of a blue-blooded drinking drink that would satisfy Rocco's demanding standards. Martini? Too unoriginal. A Brazilian sidecar? Nah. Grasshopper? Rocco would throw me out of the place.

"I'll have an old-fashioned," I said.

"Very good," said Rocco, bowing slightly before sliding off to make our drinks.

"Nice choice," she said.

"I don't even know what's in it."

"Alcohol," she said. "And some other stuff. But Rocco makes his old-fashioned the old-fashioned way with only enough water to dissolve the sugar, and one slice of orange. No cherry for you, poor dear. Cigarette?"

"Don't smoke."

"Of course you don't." She pulled a cigarette from a silver case, tapped it on the metal, lit it. The smoke came out slowly from her mouth, rising like a soft veil. Behind the screen of smoke her features softened and she seemed suddenly younger. "You want to know why I like this place? Because when I light a cigarette here I don't get stared at like I am a leper. The only drawback is that whenever I enter I get the uncontrollable urge to buy myself a mink stole."

"I must have passed this place a hundred times without ever going inside."

"Exactly. I have a studio nearby, a place where I can work without interruption. A room of my own, as Virginia Woolf would have it. I've seen your office, you must come up and visit mine sometime."

"Where is it?"

"Oh, a smart cracker like you will have no trouble finding it if you decide you want to visit." She stared at me for a moment, her mouth twisting as if appraising a horse. I was almost expecting her to pinch up my lip and check my teeth. "Tell me about your life, Victor Carl. Is it perfect and exciting?"

"Hardly."

"What is it missing?"

"Perfection and excitement. Isn't this a little personal?"

"I hope so. We need to get to know each other."

"Need?"

"Yes. Isn't that what life should be, Victor? A series of desperate urgencies where everything seems to hang in the balance. Isn't anything less just a tepid excuse for not doing enough?"

"When I have a desperate urgency, I try to find the men's room."

Just then Rocco returned with our drinks. My old-fashioned sat in front of me, squat and bright. I took a sip. Wowza. Stronger than my usual. Rocco winked at me and ambled off to the end of the bar.

"What do you want out of life, Victor?"

"Isn't this way too personal?"

"Do you want to, instead, talk about the weather?" She roughed up her voice and gave it a cornpone accent. *"Oh, it's a hot one today. Yes it is."*

"People talk about the weather precisely to avoid talking about their lives."

"That's my point. Come now, Victor. Don't disappoint me. I could tell you were different from the first moment I spied you. What do you want out of life?"

"Nice day today, isn't it?"

"I'll tell if you'll tell."

I squinted and thought about it and grew curious myself. "Go ahead."

"I've known what I wanted from the dawning of my adolescence. I was a peculiar little girl, running home after school to spend my afternoons alone in my room, dancing by myself, or reading and writing, waiting for something better, something pure to take over my life. Can you see me there, Victor, in my room, pining? And slowly that something I was waiting for came and saved me, a decision that would guide every step of my life."

"To become a meteorologist?"

"Listen closely, Victor. This is important. I decided I would become an artist, I would become Matisse, a fantastic colorist, but with a great difference. Instead of splattering my art on a rough piece of canvas, I would live it. My life is my art, Victor. And I insist that it shimmer like a dream, that every moment be filled with glorious color. I never wanted to merely see beauty in a painting or read of it in a book, I wanted to drink it, breathe it, become it."

"How's that working out for you?"

"Surprisingly well. Rocco, darling, another round, please."

I looked at my drink, still half remaining. I narrowed my eyes and took a gulp. There was something strange in what she had just told me. This wasn't offhand, none of this was offhand, the meeting, the drinks, the questions about life.

"And this is all related to Tommy Greeley how?"

"Ah, the blunt simplicity of a simple man."

The drinks came. I snatched down the rest of my first drink, felt my head wiggle just a bit, started on the second. It didn't seem quite as strong, which was the first sign that it was way too strong for me. Alura Straczynski lit herself another cigarette, inhaled.

"My husband was very agitated after your meeting," she said.

"I'm sorry to hear that."

"No you're not. It is what you wanted, to upset him. And you succeeded. My husband had a very complicated relationship with Tommy. They were like estranged brothers. There was love, there were secrets, there was deep-seated rivalry. But in the end it was the drugs that separated them. My husband couldn't abide them."

"How about you? Could you abide them?"

"Drugs? Oh, Victor, haven't you listened? Drugs were never a part of my life, or my husband's after we met. That isn't shimmering brilliance, that is stupidity. Any idiot can paint his life in Technicolor with drugs, at least for a short time. A few ounces of that, a few tabs of this. But where is the art in that?"

"So Tommy wasn't your dealer?"

"No. Really now, Victor. How did you ever get that idea?"

"Something in the way your husband looked at you. Like he wanted to protect you from the past."

"Ah, yes. See, I was right about you. My husband, Victor, is more than a mere spectator to my life. He is a collaborator. When we first met we were like two shy flowers, waiting for the sun to open our blooms. We found our sun in what we created together. We would spend nights writing in our journals, not saying a word and yet so totally connected. He would read what he had written and I would read what I had written and it would be the same. Not the words, Victor, but the emotion, the intensity, the yearning. We were everything, one to the other. We still are, but it is different now. We are no longer so connected. He finds his art in the law, his little theories that so excite the men in suits, and that allows me the freedom to search for my own."

"Was Tommy part of that search?"

"Tommy Greeley was a worm. Pure and simple. Now worms have their uses, don't they? They aerate the soil. They help us catch fish." She thought for a moment, she bit the corner of her lip. "But still they are worms."

"I don't understand."

"Oh, Victor. What is there to understand? I've heard you described as a worm too. And yet I find there's something about you. A spark I'd like to explore."

I tapped my stomach with the side of my fist. "Just a touch of gas."

Her light line of laughter. "Maybe that is it."

"So who is it that described me as a worm? Your husband?"

"That would be tattling. But you can tell me something. Who is it who is so interested in our worm Tommy Greeley?"

"Me."

"Yes, you, for whatever reasons. Probably because you are paid. That is what I've heard about you, Victor. Money, money, money. But if that were true there would be Rockefeller on your wall and not Grant. But someone else cares too, yes?" Her eyes brightened as if she was eager to gain a salacious piece of gossip. "Who is so interested in our friend Tommy? Who?"

I took a sip of my drink.

"You refuse to tell me?" she said.

"I am nothing if not circumspect."

"Of course you are, you're Jewish."

"That's actually almost funny."

"Tell me about the girl. Kimberly, was it?"

"That's right. Kimberly Blue."

"Such a pretty girl. She works for you?"

"No."

"She sleeps with you?"

"Stop."

"Oh, I can see the answer in your eyes. Pity for you. So, then, she works for or sleeps with the man who is interested in Tommy, yes? Victor?"

"Did your husband send you to ask me all these questions?"

"My husband doesn't send me."

"Too bad."

"Don't be clever, Victor. Clever is like a sports car with a leaking gasket. It only takes you so far and then, well. But you"—she cupped her hand and placed it on my cheek and my jaw tingled—"you could go so far, if only you wanted. I'd like you to do me a favor, Victor. Do you think you could?"

"It depends on what it is."

"It always does. This is small. I am looking for some notebooks. Four to be exact. They have been missing for a long time and it is as if, without them, I am missing a limb. I am in the midst of a great endeavor, the endeavor of my life, really, and to complete my task I need those notebooks."

"Why would I be in a position to find them?"

"I sense things, it is my gift, and I sense you will. In your travels. And I'd like you to return them to me. Will you? Please?"

"Sure, if I find them."

"And only to me."

"Ahh, you mean not leave them for you at your husband's office."

"Who could ever imagine you were such a quick study? Good, that is settled. Now, Victor, it is your turn."

"My turn?"

"We had a deal. I'd tell if you tell. So tell me, Victor, what is it that you really want from life?"

I thought about it for a moment. It was a hard question, harder still when you weren't sure why it was being asked. I drained the rest of my drink and snapped my head at the burn of it and tried to come up with an answer and failed and realized that was what I wanted after all.

"Answers," I said after a long hesitation.

She leaned toward me. "To what questions?"

"It varies from day to day. Some days I want to know

the purpose of existence. Some days I want to know why it seems everyone else is happier than am I. Some days I wonder why God doesn't seem to go very far out of his way to help those who need it. And some days, most days, I simply want to know why my laundry place keeps using starch on my boxer shorts."

"Victor."

"Every week I say, 'No starch, no starch,' and the lady, she nods yes, yes like she understands, but she doesn't understand. Why doesn't she understand? It's a mystery all right."

"So what's today's great philosophical question, Victor? What is the answer you are looking for today?"

"Today's question? Today I want to know what the hell happened to Tommy Greeley and why."

She turned her bright green eyes away from me and bowed her head. There was a puddle of condensation on the bar. She moved her finger across it, her bright red nail leaving a strange trail, up, down, swooping around like a pen on a page. Her expression took on the same serious cast it had taken when she was writing at my desk. I moved my gaze away from her face toward those strange squiggles she was leaving in the damp. I tried to follow the movements of her finger, tried to decipher the strange glyphs she was forming, as if they had great meaning, as if maybe all the answers I had said I was searching for could be found right there.

And as we both stared down at the bar the edges of our foreheads touched.

"I get the feeling, Victor," said Alura Straczynski, her voice soft, her breath warm, "that you are going to be fatal."

CHAPTER

37

I was drunk and I was horny and I thought it more than passing strange, considering what a bad combination those two are, how often they pop up together. Pop up, get it? I did, and I thought it hilarious. I repeated it out loud as I staggered toward my apartment, "Pop up. Pop up," accompanied by my demented laughter. They say your judgment is the first to go but I'd say it is your sense of humor.

I was laughing at my little pun but all the while, through my drunken fog, I was trying to figure out what I had just been through with Alura Straczynski. It appeared for some reason she wanted to learn of Eddie Dean's identity. And it appeared she wanted to tell me, she was desperate to tell me, of her peculiar artistic goal of turning her life into a shimmering dream. And it appeared she thought I had something of hers, her notebooks. And finally it appeared, yes it did, that most of all what she wanted was to slip into my sheets.

I am not one who thinks that deep down everyone wants to screw my ears off. You know the type who do, those square-jawed boys who see in every glance, every smile, every nonhostile gesture an invitation. I am not that guy, I'm neither handsome enough nor smooth enough to be that guy, and my chest isn't hairy enough to be a proper setting for the obligatory gold medallion. Yet, even as she told me of those marvelous early moments with her husband, I had the strange sense that Alura Straczynski was angling to create her own marvelous moments with me. It was in the way she held her head, the way she smiled at me, the way she put her hand on my cheek. And once, when she was whispering in my ear, some funny secret about a man at the other end of the bar, something seemed to catch on my lobe. Was it her teeth? Wowza. Mrs. Justice Jackson Straczynski. When I realized what was going on I couldn't get out of there fast enough. Two, three more drinks, tops, just to be polite, and then I was out of there, yes I was. Out of there.

So I was on my way home, drunk, because Rocco knew how to mix a drink, and horny, because, no matter how much I didn't didn't didn't want to sleep with Alura Straczynski, there still is some strange connection between the ear and the prick so that when the first is turtle-snapped the second stands at attention. I wondered just then if it worked the other way around. *Did a bee sting your ear, or are you just glad to see me?* I was in a primed state of mind, yes I was, and the images that were floating in my mind just then had nothing to do with Alura Straczynski and everything to do with the photographs pinned to my wall, the legs, arms, breasts, thighs, the lithe lines of desire. Whose desire? Tommy Greeley's desire? My desire? Was there a difference right then worth noting? Oh yes, I was in quite a riled state, when I turned onto my street and approached my building and saw her on the front stoop, sitting there, waiting, for me.

She didn't rise when she saw me, she stayed there sitting on the steps as I approached, but she smiled, yes she did, and it whooshed through me and set me to tingling like a blast of radiation pure.

"You look like a mess," said Chelsea when I sat beside her.

"I've been working."

"At what?"

"Good question. Can I ask you something?"

"I suppose," she said, warily.

"Does my ear look swollen?"

She leaned close and examined first one ear and then the other. It was as if I could feel her gaze on my skin, warm, probing.

"Not really. Why?"

"Just wondering."

"I wanted to apologize for storming out like I did the other night."

"I wanted to apologize too."

"No, it was me. You were right. Even after all these years, I'm only starting to understand what exactly we were doing."

"And what was that?"

"Screwing up."

She was still leaning close and I leaned closer and then I kissed her softly on her lips. It was something I had wanted to do from the first time I saw her, and was angling to do during our date at the Continental, and now, filled with the false courage of half a dozen old-fashioneds, and spurred by the desire somehow coaxed out of me by Alura Straczynski but not aimed at Alura Straczynski, a more generalized desire that latched onto anything nearby—small dogs shuddered citywide—I up and did it. I leaned close and gently swept away the long black hair that fell in front of her cheek and I kissed her. I kissed her. And . . . And . . . And nothing. She didn't pull away, but she didn't respond either, she just let me, just let me kiss her. And when I stopped for a moment and pulled back to gauge the effect of my lips on her, she looked at me with a strangely blank expression and continued speaking as if nothing, absolutely nothing, had occurred.

"Sometimes I try to assign blame for what happened to us, to me," she said. "I blame the strange little agent from the FBI who started knocking it down, the people working with us who made the mistakes that got us noticed in the first place, the creepy money guy who testified against us. I want to blame everyone and everything when what I should be blaming is myself, for getting involved with it all in the first place."

I leaned in and kissed her again and it was exactly the same, like she was letting me, sure, but what she was really doing was waiting until I stopped so she could go on talking. And even so, I must say, she was delicious. There was something fruity and clean on her lips. I licked them softly, just rubbed the tip of my tongue over the tender ridges. Yes. Fruity, like she had just eaten a bowl of ripe cherries. I pulled back again and tilted my head at her.

"So what I wanted to say was that I am sorry about the way I acted. I'm sorry I left you in a huff like that."

"What is a huff, do you know?" I said.

"No."

"Is it a type of cat?"

"Maybe," she said, with a quick laugh.

"I just kissed you."

"I know. But I was apologizing and I wanted you to know that I am trying to be sorry for what I did."

"For storming out of the bar."

"Not just that. I want you to know that I am also trying to be sorry for what I was doing back then, for the drugs and the money and the stupidity and the belief that we were blessed when we were really only criminals. For the whole time I was involved with Tommy Greeley."

"You paid your price."

"But not in the heart. You see, not that. Not yet. But I'm working on it. Cooper's been helping me."

"Cooper Prod?"

"Yes. But it's not easy. Like he always says, the more we learn about the past, the less we will ever understand."

"He seems pretty evolved for a jailbird, Cooper does."

"He is. And he's very interested in you. He wants you to know that, and that he will help however he can."

"Is that why you came over, to deliver his message?"

"One reason, yes."

"How sweet."

"I could have called."

"Okay."

"There's something else I wanted to tell you. Something I thought I ought to make clear. I might have given you the wrong impression about something."

I kissed her again. This time I kissed a little harder and this time I could feel something give in her, and her head leaned back and her mouth parted slightly and her hand lifted gently to rest on my throat. And then with that hand she pushed me away.

"I need to tell you this."

"All right," I said, not really listening, just wanting to kiss her again.

"It's about Tommy and me and Lonnie."

"All right," I said, but even as I said it the fruity taste of her lips worked upon my mind like a drug and I tried again to kiss her. But this time, with that hand curled at my throat, she kept me away.

"No," she said. "Listen. I told you the thing with Lonnie and me—"

"The marriage you mean."

"Yes, the marriage. My marriage." She took her hand from my throat, rubbed her two hands together, as if cleansing them under a spigot. "I told you it was after my relationship with Tommy. But it wasn't, not really. Cooper said I should tell you everything and so I need to tell you this. Tommy and I were together sometimes even after I was married to Lonnie. It was just something we did, but we did it."

"I knew that."

"How?"

"I just did."

"But—"

I put my finger on her lips to quiet her and then I thought of something. I thought of something and I took my finger away and I kissed her, kissed her quick and rubbed my tongue again gently on her lips and then I pulled back and gazed into her sweet brown eyes.

"Did Lonnie know?"

"About Tommy and me?"

"Yes," I said. "About it continuing after you married him."

She turned away from me. "He found out."

"How?"

"I don't know. I wasn't trying hard to hide it. I think he suspected something and then followed me."

"How did Lonnie take it?"

"How do you think he took it?"

"Not well. That's how I would take it if my wife betrayed me with my boss. Not well at all."

"Maybe I should go."

"No, don't. Please."

"This whole thing, just talking about it has got me . . ."

"It's okay, Chelsea. It's over. All of it. Everything that happened was a long time ago. It's over."

She turned to me, her eyes glistening. "But it's not, is it?"

She wanted some assurance, but all the assurances I had were false. She was right. It wasn't over. Not all of it, not any of it. I had nothing I could say to her so instead I leaned forward and gently kissed a tear welling in one of her eyes and then kissed her cheek and her jaw and then again her sweet lips. And this time she kissed me back, as if she was suddenly relieved of a burdensome secret and was able, now, to respond, finally, to my touch. She placed her hand gently on the back of my neck and pulled me closer and kissed me. And it was lovely and soft and somehow as sad as her eyes and as we kissed I felt the alcohol in my blood start to boil.

And then I saw something approach us from the left, just the shape of something, of a man, of a man in black leather. I guiltily jerked my head away from her, certain I had been caught. Caught? Caught at what? Adultery? No. Who was married? Caught by whom? By whom else? By Lonnie Chambers. And for some reason it scared the hell out of me.

But it wasn't Lonnie, it was some guy with glasses, his black leather jacket butter soft and draped loosely over his narrow shoulders, leading a little white dog on a leash. The spurt of anxiety disappeared. The man smiled at us wanly, the white dog came close, sniffed my legs, my crotch, gave me a worried glance, and then hurried away.

"Let's go upstairs," I said, and we did, and what followed was the usual thing, you know how it goes, tender kisses, soft caresses, frantic unbuttoning, unbelting, long, languorous licks of the neck, the collarbone, the soft mounds rising above the black frill of lingerie, the reaching hand, the fumbled clasp, the bra falling away leaving breasts like the motherland itself, glorious and free—all followed by the inevitable howling bout of outright humiliation.

everyone? I'd let it all pass, all the confusion, if only
I could keep alive the kind of life that somehow seemed
just then the key, but even so, they were falling away, honestly,
truth, all my enthusiasms, each sliding, and I couldn't help
stop it, let the shudder leaving me, I was
aware.

CHAPTER

38

I was lying in my bed, alone, my head
turned toward the photographs pinned to my wall, my
mind not quite pinned to anything at all, but instead floating free with thoughts puzzled, prurient, and strangely
paranoid, when the doorbell rang.

I wasn't just then in the mood to receive visitors. I still
was half drunk, half dressed, half erect, fully confused, and
mortified. Let's just say it hadn't gone as well as I had
dreamed with Chelsea.

I rolled out of bed, made my way stiffly to the living
room, grunted a "What?" into the intercom.

"Is that you, Victor?"

"Yeah."

"Were you sleeping?"

"No."

"Do you have, like, a minute?"

"Yeah."

"Well?"

"Well what?"

"You're not going to invite me up?"

"Who is this?"

"Helloo? Jammy, V, who do you think?"

"I should have known," I said, and I should have, since
every sentence ended with a question mark. I looked

around at my apartment in disgust, figured it didn't matter, and then buzzed her in.

I took off my suit pants, slipped on a pair of jeans, a white T-shirt. I closed the bedroom door firmly behind me and started cleaning up the living room, putting the cushions back onto the couch, dropping the half-empty beer bottles into the blue recycling bin, tossing into the hall closet the clothes I had stripped off with hopeful abandon just a few dozen minutes before—my suit jacket, my tie and shirt, my belt.

I gave the living room a quick appraisal and, just as the first knock at my door came, I spotted something. Black and thin, like an accusing finger reaching over the edge of the couch.

I stepped over to it. It was a thin black strap. I lifted it up and with it came the whole of a lovely black bra. She had forgotten it, or couldn't find it, when she dressed to leave. Taking it off had been the highlight of my day, my year, and yet that very act had sabotaged everything.

I had led Chelsea up the stairs by her hand. She was strangely passive, it was like when we first kissed on the stoop, like she was allowing me this. Normally that would have stopped me, I don't like to be allowed to do anything, but in my current state, still brazened by alcohol, still sexually charged, still in thrall to the pictures of the younger Chelsea pinned to my wall, I didn't care that she was merely allowing me. Merely allowing me was enough.

I led her up the stairs, led her into my apartment, kissed her hard and long, led her to the couch. That led, of course, to the aforementioned tender kisses, the aforementioned soft caresses. I moved my hand through her long black hair like I would move it through a basin of water and then I brought the hair to my face and smelled its freshness, its organic herbalness. I closed my eyes and I saw her body, her younger body, naked, taut and lithe, I saw it as clearly as if the photographs were pinned beneath my eyes. And then I couldn't help myself even if I had wanted to. If you leave a greyhound on a metal run it will head off into a sprint with such abandon it will literally break its neck. The aforementioned frantic unbuttoning, unbelting, the aforementioned long, languorous licks of the neck and collarbone as I undraped the frilly white shirt from her shoulders. I bowed down to kiss the tops of her breasts, the same breasts from the pictures of which I had been staring at relentlessly ever since they came into my possession. I fumbled at the clasp behind her back, as I always fumbled at the clasp behind the back, and then the bra suddenly loosened and she herself raised her hands and pulled it over her shoulders and her breasts, her breasts came free.

And they were beautiful, gorgeous, ripe, perfect. And not the same. No, not the same. The nipples were smaller than those in the pictures, the areolae lighter. And yes, unblemished. Unblemished. Not the same at all. And something went out of me then, and everything sagged, my emotions, my hurry, my obsession, my lust. Everything sagged, yes everything did. And that had been the end of that. No lead in the pencil, no toothpaste in the tube. Time to hire the limo.

There was a second knock at the door. I searched quickly for someplace to hide the bra, jammed it under one of the cushions of the couch, and then let Kimberly Blue inside my apartment.

She sat down on the couch, right upon the cushion beneath which I had stashed the bra. She seemed troubled, did Kimberly, quiet, without her normal brassy confidence. I sat down across from her and tilted my head to get a good look at her.

"Nice place," she said, as she perused my digs with cautious eyes.

"No, it isn't."

"Well, it could be a dec setup if you would, like, decorate or, even better, clean."

"But that would be so out of character."

"Two words, V. Merry Maids. They come in, do a quality job, when you come home the place is good to go."

"How do you know so much about Merry Maids?"

"That was one of the primary employment opportunities I was looking at for after college."

"At the vice presidential level?"

"More like entry level."

"And then Eddie Dean came along."

"Yes," she said. "I don't know if you noticed, but we've been away."

"You and Eddie?"

"And Colfax, too. San Fran. The city of lights."

"I thought that was Paris."

"I don't know, San Fran was pretty bright. Mr. Dean had business out there he had to handle."

"And he took you along?"

"I think he likes having me around." She looked around nervously, bit into one of her cuticles. "Anything new on Tommy Greeley?"

"Just that he was sleeping with the wife of one of the guys he was selling drugs with."

"Who?"

"A guy named Lonnie Chambers."

"Did this Lonnie know Tommy was hooking up with his wife?"

"Yes."

"You think he was the one who set Tommy Greeley up?"

"I don't know."

"Pretty good reason, don't you think?"

"Maybe. You know I am always glad to see you, Kimberly—"

"Really?"

"Sure. But I'm a little tired right now. Why don't we meet up tomorrow afternoon at my office and we can go over everything then."

"I know where your office is, V. I could have gone there if I wanted to. I wanted to talk to you someplace not at the office."

"Oh?"

"Someplace private."

"Oh."

"I overheard something."

"Oh. I see." And I did. Kimberly was troubled, and there was something else I noticed now in her eyes that I hadn't noticed before. She was scared. I stood, went to the fridge, pulled out a Rolling Rock long neck, popped the top with an opener.

"How are you doing, Kimberly?" I said as I handed her the bottle.

"I'm not sleeping with him," said Kimberly.

"I believe you."

"He's yucky, you know what I mean? That face."

"I was wrong to even bring that up. I was a jerk to think it. And even so, it's none of my business. Whatever you do is none of my business, and I was wrong to imply what I was implying. But you should be careful around him, and especially around that creep Colfax."

"Oh, Colfax is all right. He's a sweetie."

"No he's not. Deep down I'm a sweetie, you just haven't seen it yet. But Colfax, deep down, is Jack the Ripper."

"What's really going on here, V? Do you have any idea?"

"Some, but not much. Why don't you tell me what you heard."

"It's nothing, really. Mr. Dean had a meeting with a couple of men and it got a little heated. I was in the other room so I couldn't be sure, but it sounded like one of the other men was pressuring Mr. Dean for some money and he was telling them to calm down, that he was on it, and that he'd have what he owed in a short time."

"So our Eddie Dean is not as rich as he lets on."

"He sounded scared, V. You know how he always has this droll, laconic thing going on? Well, here he sounded scared. And there was something else. He said he had a big deal going down in Philly and it was only a matter of time before he had the money. But V, all he does here is sit in the house building some wooden model of that ship of his, the one rusting down in the harbor? There is no big deal going down. The only place I can figure where he might be trying to get some money is from Derek Manley, but it sounded like he needed a brutal piece of change. Does Derek Manley have anything like that?"

"No."

"That's what I thought. Poodles. I'm going to lose my job, aren't I?"

"Is that all you're worried about, Kimberly? Your job?"

"Ayeah. Helloo. Remember Merry Maids? What do you think that would do to my nails? But that's not all. Am I, like, in trouble? Should I be scared?"

"Why ask me?"

"Because you know more than you let on. See, V, I know how much I don't know, I know how much I don't do. I'm the vice president of what? Of getting coffee and keeping the help in line? The job's a joke. But it pays. And I hope maybe it will lead to something better. I have skills, I could be good at something. Something. But this is where

I'm at now and I am asking you, should I be scared? Am I going to get in trouble? Should I stick it out and see where it goes or should I maybe hop a plane to Cancun."

"Tell me about how you got this job?" I said.

"The position was just posted on the job board, like hundreds of others."

"So why'd you apply to this one?"

"Well, it was, like, made for me, you know? They wanted a marketing major, which I was. They wanted someone who could speak Spanish, which I can."

"Really?"

"My dad was at the store all day, but he paid this nice old Mexican woman to look after me. I sort of picked it up."

"Does Spanish come in handy working for Jacopo?"

"Not yet."

"What else?"

"They wanted someone with experience designing ad campaigns for clothing lines."

"Let me guess. You happened to have had some experience in that very same field."

"My senior marketing project."

"But Jacopo doesn't sell clothes."

"No."

"Did you ever find out how many campuses they were recruiting on?"

"I think just Penn."

"I'm surprised they didn't require someone with red hair."

"Excuse me?"

"Just a story I read a long time ago. For some reason, Kimberly, Eddie Dean wanted you. Not someone like you, but you. The other interviews were a sham. They were just saying next, next, until you came in the door. But why, that's the question, isn't it?"

"Why do you think?"

"No idea. But they must need something you have, or something you know, or someone. There's a reason, and my guess is, Kimberly, when we figure that out we'll be ten steps closer to finding the truth behind this whole stinking mess."

"So what should I do, V?"

"Cancun is supposed to be nice this time of year, and if I thought you were in any real danger I'd tell you to stock up on Lomotil, lather on the sunscreen, and go. But Eddie Dean needs you. He's not going to hurt you. He's going to keep paying you an absurd sum to get his coffee until he decides it's time to tell you what he wants. And when he does Kimberly, do yourself a favor and give me a call."

After she left, I dropped back into my bed, turned my gaze upon the pictures on the wall, and tried to make some sense out of the night.

First there was Lonnie. I had been looking for someone with a motive to do Tommy Greeley harm and Chelsea had given him to me. Lonnie, who had found out about the continuing relations between his wife and Tommy Greeley. Lonnie had been watching over Tommy the night he was killed. It wouldn't take much for Lonnie to take himself out of the scene and leave Derek and Joey free to do their dark deed. He better than anyone knew what was in the suitcase, he surely would have known a place to hide it while he was in prison. And, best of all, if he had it, from the look of him he hadn't spent its contents, he had kept it hidden, where it waited still for someone sharp and resourceful enough to unearth it and make it his own. Lonnie Chambers, my oh my.

And then there was Eddie Dean. I had wondered what his angle was from the start, the childhood oath was too much to believe, and now I knew. He was seriously broke and in deep trouble. And how did he know about the suit-

case? Chelsea had clued me into that, I believed, at the
Continental. Tommy Greeley said he had a friend from out
of state who would launder and then stash the money for
him, an old friend, from out of state. Eddie Dean, I'd bet.
He had probably been there that night twenty years ago, on
a boat in the river, waiting, waiting for Tommy Greeley
and the suitcase full of cash. In fact he might even have
been close enough to hear Manley say, "Get him, Cheaps."
That explained how he knew Joey was involved, how he
got Derek Manley's name, and how he got mine. Now, desperate to pay back an impatient loan shark, he had used me
to find a murderer hiding a suitcase full of money that
could maybe save his life. Eddie Dean, that son of a bitch.

It was a neat theory about what had happened twenty
years ago and what was happening now, but it had holes.
Like who had killed Joey Parma? And what connection, if
any, did Justice Jackson Straczynski, or his wacko wife,
have to the disappearance? And what the hell was Kimberly Blue doing in the middle of everything? And what
about the pictures?

I stood up from the bed and walked over to the wall of
photographs, my photographs. They were once Tommy
Greeley's, created by him as a memorial to his desire, but
now were mine, along with the strange fascination they
carried like a virus. I rubbed a finger along a knee, a clavicle, the bumpy route of her vertebrae. It was almost as if I
could feel the bones beneath the soft taut skin of the photograph. If they weren't of Chelsea, then maybe they were
of the other woman in Tommy Greeley's life, his girlfriend,
that Sylvia Steinberg. I couldn't shake the sense that these
photographs had something to do with Tommy Greeley's
murder. I'd have to look her up, Sylvia, yes I would. Stop
over. Give her a look-see. Maybe I'd have better luck with
her than I had with Chelsea. Boy, I sure hoped so.

After it had become clear that nothing would happen that night between Chelsea and me, after I had seen her naked torso and realized the pictures were not of her and then had tried my best to keep it going, kissing her chest, her side, rubbing her thighs through her pants as I nuzzled her ear, after I had tried and failed, we lay together on the skewed cushions of my couch, both of us seemingly puzzled and tired but not particularly upset. She didn't tell me, "There are pills for that now," for which I was hugely grateful. And for my part, I didn't embarrass myself by telling her it never happens to me because it just had, hadn't it? Instead, quietly, I untangled myself from her limbs, opened the fridge, got us each a beer, watched as she sat upright on the couch and tugged her shirt over her shoulders and buttoned up.

She was lovely, so lovely, and just then I felt my erection stir because I was looking at her not as the woman in the pictures, an image which she couldn't live up to, but as a beautiful woman buttoning her shirt on my couch. Is there anything sexier than a beautiful woman buttoning her shirt on your couch? But then it was too late to make another play, the relief on her face was palpable, and I wondered just then why she had been willing in the first place and so when I handed over the beer I asked her.

"I don't know," she said. "Because you reminded me of him and with him I always just agreed. With him I was helpless to refuse."

"Who?"

"Tommy."

"I remind you of Tommy Greeley?"

"Oh, Victor, yes. Of course you do. The spitting image."

I blew wetly out my lips. "Maybe it's just because I've been asking questions about him."

"No, it's more. It's everything. You even look like him,

tall and lanky. His hair was longer but he had that same flat mouth, the same eyes with the touch of hurt in them, puppy-dog eyes. And he was both funny and serious and irreverent all at the same time, just like you. But it's something else. You carry the same sense of having been wronged a long time ago, of needing to overcome a disadvantaged start, a hunger to make something glorious of the future. And a crushing disappointment."

"Disappointment?"

"Oh yes."

"Disappointment with what?"

"With everything you each never had, and your failed search for the one thing that would make everything better."

"And what's that?"

"The one thing?"

"Yes."

"Oh, Victor," she said, standing now, placing her bottle on the coffee table. "You really do need to meet Cooper."

But it wasn't the enlightened Cooper Prod I ended up meeting the next afternoon, it was the freaking prince of darkness.

CHAPTER

39

"**They want to** build a mall here," said Earl Dante as we sat side-by-side on a bench at Penn's Landing overlooking the wide gray Delaware River. A stiff breeze blew in from the water, but Dante's waxy gray hair didn't budge. "And that of course is just what we need. More malls."

"Isn't this too public a place for a meeting?" I said.

"They have a photographer across from the restaurant where I eat. They have an unmarked sedan following my car. They are parked in front of my house, snapping photos of my wife. Public is all I have left."

"Where's the car now?"

"Wilmington. I took a Camry here. I cannot fully express the humiliation of being under constant surveillance, but that word comes close. Camry."

"What color?"

"Does it matter?"

"Just curious."

"Blue."

"And the interior?"

"Gray."

"Of course it is." I nodded at Leo in his green jacket a few yards down, leaning on the railing, eyes surveying the deserted strip of cement behind us. "Anyone else know we're here?"

"No. You called and said you had a question."

"Teddy Big Tits."

"Yes?"

"What, is he just fat or does he take some sort of injections? I mean there are porn stars who eye him with envy. We're talking triple D at least. How is this possible?"

"That is your question?"

"Inquiring minds."

"Theodore sucks the marrow from the bone of life."

"What does that mean?"

"It means he is fat."

"What's his racket?"

"He makes book, he lends money, he brokers deals. In this economy, we all must do what we can."

"Does he pimp?"

"Not precisely."

"Well, then, let's be precise."

"I told you to leave this be."

"You told me to stay away from Manley's company. I did. But I'm going to find out what happened to Joey."

"Loyalty or money?"

"Does it matter?"

"Then it must be money. Theodore has arrangements with certain ladies. Some of their suitors might be short of funds. They steer those suitors to Teddy. Teddy provides the funds at interest to the suitors and the ladies kick back some of the generous gifts to Theodore. Everybody wins."

"Except for Joey Parma."

"She's quite attractive in her way."

"Oh, she's a honey all right, that poor son of a bitch. What happens when someone can't pay his tab to Teddy?"

"Theodore has his ways."

"A slit throat?"

"More like a phone call to the wife. Or, in Joey's case, the mother, which was for him a far scarier prospect."

"And if the phone call doesn't work?"

"Then he talks to us and we earn our share. But we didn't earn it on Joey."

"And no chance Teddy did it on his own?"

"It is a nice suit I'm wearing, is it not? Specially made for me by a gentleman who flies in twice a year from Hong Kong. You couldn't tell just by looking at it how big the pockets are."

"And Teddy Big Tits is in your pocket. Okay, then maybe he didn't. So there is something you need to do. Before he was murdered, Joey had some sort of plan to pay off his debts. Teddy and sweet little Bev were in on it. I need you to find out for me what it was."

"I could ask."

"Thank you."

"But then you would have to do something for me."

"The hell with that. You owe this."

"I owe you?"

"You owe Joey. You should have been looking out for him. He grew up in your territory."

"He was a loser."

"He was a stand-up guy, at least in your world, and you let those two con artists take him for a ride while you sat back and took a cut. That wasn't right."

"He was born to lose."

"Anyone can take care of winners. Joey was looking for something more than he had, looking for love in the wrongest place imaginable, and you let those two pythons squeeze the life out of him. He was from the neighborhood, you should have been looking out for him. If you couldn't even do that, what good are you?"

He turned to me and smiled his scary little undertaker's smile. "No damn good," he said.

"They're going to take you down."

"They're going to try."

"You think you're different than Scarfo, than Stanfa, than Skinny Merlino. You'll be in jail with the rest of them."

"That's where you come in."

"What can I do about that? I am the least influential guy in this entire city."

"You'd be surprised, Victor. Derek Manley has gone missing."

"So he has."

"It is important I pass a word on to him."

"I think it's too late for that."

"It's never too late."

"What makes you think I'll ever see him again?"

"Because you have a knack for being in the wrong place at all the right times. If you see him I want you to pass on a word. Just one word. You will be doing both him and me a service."

"I'm not a messenger boy."

"That's right, you are lower than a messenger boy. You are a lawyer, a lawyer who has stepped over a line I had drawn. You are a liability. You are on borrowed time. Whatever jeopardy I am in, you are in deeper. One word, Victor. Magnolia. Do you think you can remember that?"

"I have to go."

"Magnolia."

I stood up from the bench. Leo pushed himself off the railing as if to intercept me, but Dante shook his head.

"I'll have a little talk with Teddy," he said. "You remember your word. We'll do fine."

"You should have taken care of him."

"I should have done a lot of things," he said. "I should have been a dancer."

"I understand they have wonderful programs in prison."

"Magnolia."

"I heard you," I said even as I was walking away.

It was always a dangerous thing to ask something of a man like Earl Dante, but Martha had called to say that Bev had no idea about Joey's pending deal, sorry, though an itemized list of what Joey owed to Bev would be sent to me shortly. It would be a breathtaking piece of fiction, no doubt, as epic as *Gone with the Wind* and nearly as long. Still, Joey had something going on and that something might have gotten him killed and it seemed only Dante had the wherewithal to get the answer. So I had called him and even as I had called him I knew that he would want something in return. You want a free favor, call a priest; guys like Dante always make you pay.

But I wouldn't have an opportunity to let slip Dante's word to Derek Manley. Manley had disappeared, just as Earl Dante had said, and I was pretty damn sure he wasn't ever going to be found. In that alley, after the big squeeze, he had as good as spelled it out for me: his hopeless financial and penal situation, the sickly son needing expensive care, the insurance policy that could take care of everything. A peculiar sort of heroism for a peculiar sort of man. So no, I wouldn't be passing Dante's word to Derek Manley, and so yes, Dante would be disappointed in me. Just add it to the list.

I was in the middle of something, of which I didn't have the first clue. I had gotten on the wrong side of a State Supreme Court justice, whose wife had developed an unhealthy interest in me. The guy who was supposed to pay my inflated bill was flat broke. Kimberly Blue was in some sort of trouble that I couldn't quite figure. My peter was petering. My cable was out. The next day I was due in Traffic Court to defend my license against a series of malicious attacks by the city's police force. My very existence was turning quickly to crap.

And to top it off, as my father fought for his life while struggling to tell me his sad lovesick tale, both his health, and his story, were about to take a serious turn for the worse.

CHAPTER
40

And then a doorway of shelves in that treasure room swings away, swings open. And there, in the opening, the hidden doorway, darkness streaming in from behind him, stands the old man. Tall, thin, his hair brushed back, his back only slightly bent by age, his eyebrows raised in mock surprise. And he's smiling, smiling with the eyes of a fox, smiling at all his little treasures, his golden statuettes, his jade fetishes, his pearls, his coins, her, smiling at her, my father's love, smiling at her as if she were merely another one of his trinkets that had only temporarily been misplaced.

He takes a step toward her and my father is at him like a panther, driven forward by his love and his rage. The old man's ropy neck is in my father's fist, the old man's crooked back is slammed so hard against the shelving that a crouching jade dragon is hurled to the ground and smashes in a dazzling blossom of green.

Don't touch her, my father growls.

I wouldn't dream of it, gasps the old man, his accent purebred Brahmin.

His sly smile, dropped only at the onset of the attack, returns. My father loosens his grip on the old man's neck.

I was merely admiring the coin, the old man says. A very rare twenty-dollar piece. Saint Gaudens. 1907. Ultra-high proof. The most beautiful American coin ever minted. Only twenty-four were struck, twenty remain in private hands. I own four. He looks beyond my father at the girl. You always had exquisite taste, he says.

I was well taught, she says.

Do you mind, the old man says to my father, tapping lightly on my father's wrist.

My father is puzzled at the calmness of the conversation. There is no shock on the old man's face at seeing the two of them in his treasure room, no threats of arrest from the old man, no howls of abuse from her. A brittle civility holds sway. He lets the old man go, steps back, slinks into the corner, subdued as much by the old man's accent as by the actual nature of the relationship playing out before him. Whatever has gone on in this house, he realizes, she has not told him the half of it. And whatever is to come, the old man's accent has marked with utter clarity their respective positions in the world, the old man's and my father's, has shown all the old man can offer to this girl and all that my father never could.

My father's voice as he recounted the scene to me was faint, barely discernible through the oxygen mask and beneath the rasp of his breath. His blood oxygen level couldn't fight its way above eighty-seven percent and his respiratory rate was in the mid-twenties. He was weaker than I had ever before seen him in his life. Nothing was working, the new drug wasn't working, death was coming, and he was struggling mightily to beat the scythe as he told me the story. He didn't have the strength to set the scene, to lay in all the details, so I was forced to do that for myself, but by now I had been so captured by the story, and by his burning desire to tell it, that it was not a burden to listen to his faint words and provide for myself the details of the conversation between the old man and the girl my father loved.

I knew you'd come back, the old man says.

Just for what I'm owed, she says.

And what do you believe is that, dear girl?

She gazes around the room, her eyes full of light. She scans past my father as if he were a ghost, while she takes in all the riches on the shelves. She looks down at the coin in her hand. She returns the coin to its small velvet sack, places the sack back in the box, closes the lid. Atlas with his burden stares balefully out at her.

Maybe just this, she says, placing her hand on the box. This should be enough.

I daresay it would, says the old man. That one coin is near priceless. The entire set is beyond imagining. More than one fortune has gone into acquiring what is in that box. Nora has asked for you. You didn't say good-bye.

How is she?

Her arthritis, well, you know. She hobbles through her day but is ever cheerful. She is making her famous duck tomorrow evening. Such an event, all the flame and pageantry. It was always your favorite. You must join us.

I can't, she says.

Just one last time. Please. For Nora's sake. To say good-bye.

She glances at my father. No, she says.

Her glance is quick, furtive, but the old man catches it with all its import. He turns to my father. So this is the one.

Yes, she says.

Our motorcycle man. Well, he certainly is big enough.

He loves me.

I don't doubt that. And you, my sweet. Do you love him back?

Her jaw rises, there is a quiver in her voice as she says, Yes. I do.

And that is why you can't share one last meal with me, one last evening to pass our good-byes, one last chance to share brandy by the fire, to kiss gently as the phonograph plays the Verdi you so much admire, to hold hands as we ascend together the stairs, one last time to spread the satin sheets on your soft featherbed.

Go to hell, she says.

My dear dear sweet. He mows lawns for a living.

Our love is enough.

Obviously not, or you wouldn't be here. But if that is what you want, then go. My blessing on you both, he says even as he steps forward to the table, grabs hold of the box of coins, snatches it away from her hand, and clutches it to his chest. Go, he says. But know that when you leave here, you leave with nothing. Let your lawn mower man take care of you from here on in. The two of you will be quite happy, I am sure, in your penniless love.

You owe me, she says.

Who owes whom? Go back to what you were when I found you, in your cheap clothes, chewing your gum, so very proud of your stenography.

She steps forward and slaps him.

And the old man laughs. He laughs, laughs his Brahmin laugh, his jaw tight, his laughter loud, mocking, carrying in it all the solid self-certainty of his class.

She hits him with the bottom of her fist, first the one then the other, she hits him on the shoulder, on the chest, she hits him again and again, hits him with all her fury, even as the old man continues his assaultive laughter.

It is then, only then, that my father feels able to intrude upon their scene. The same thing in the laughter that so in-furiates her sends a calm into my father. He knows where he belongs, he understands perfectly his place, finds a comfort in that knowledge that his son will never know. The truth is in the very Brahmin accent that intimidated him just a few moments before. Except he doesn't want anything that the world of this room, this house, this man has to offer. My father has already gotten all he ever wanted, his lover, his one true love. It was a mistake to come here, he knows, a mistake from the start. But he also knows, with a sense of relief, that it is over, that whatever she had come for is gone and it is now time to leave. He steps forward with his own calm, takes hold of her from the waist, pulls her back, away from the old man, who is now shielding himself with the box.

Let's go, says my father.

No, she says.

But he is pulling her away, away from the man, this room, this house. She is fighting him, fighting him and the old man both as he pulls her away, and then she slips out of his grasp.

She slips out of his grasp, grabs the box from the old man, swings it back, and slams it into the old man's head.

The old man falls to his knees.

She swings the box again, a corner plunges into his scalp, blood spurts. She swings the box again.

By the time my father is able to make sense of what he has seen, is able to gather his wits enough to grab her at the waist and pull her away, throw her to the other side of the room, the old man is sprawled dead on the floor, the bloodied box is lying by his side, and her skirt, her blouse, her hands are stained red with the old man's blood.

What have you done? he says, staring now at the devastation before him.

She rises from the floor, slowly, carefully, weaving back and forth as she rises, and when, finally, she is standing, she makes her way to her lover, my father, her lover.

I didn't mean to, she says. He drove me to it.

He steps away from her, backs away until his shoulders are against a wall and the corpse is between him and the girl, his love, the girl in the pleated skirt. But she steps up to the corpse of the old man until she is facing my father, close to my father and she says, It will be all right, Jesse, won't it?

My father is paralyzed with loss as she reaches her bloodied hands to touch him, leaves a trail of blood on his arm, his shoulder, his collar. She places her hands at the back of his neck and stands on tiptoes and pulls him to her as she pulled him to her just moments before in the darkness.

We'll be forever together, like we said, Jesse, like we promised. Together forever, you and me, like you told me was all you ever wanted, like you made me promise.

And then she kisses him, while they stand over the old man's corpse, she promises my father everything he ever wanted just moments before, and she kisses him, and my father, God forgive him, kisses her back.

"Kissed," he said in the softest of whispers as I leaned so close the plastic of his mask brushed against my ear. "Kissed her back."

It would have been nicely symmetric if the poison of the story had its way with him right then, sent him into respiratory failure, clanging the alarms, bringing the army of doctors and nurses and technicians rushing to that room to battle for my father's life as I stood by and watched with a horrified silence. But it didn't right then, not right then. My father whispered, "Kissed her back," and then his eyes closed and he drifted off to some finer place. And his respiratory rate eased, and his heartbeat slowed, and somehow the level of the oxygen in his blood started to rise.

Eighty-eight percent. Eighty-nine percent. Ninety percent. I left my father in the hospital that night with a slight sense of hope that maybe the worst had been revealed and so the worst was behind him.

But it was a feint, hope with my father was always a feint, and the alarms were sounded not long after I stepped out the hospital's front door.

CHAPTER

41

Traffic Court. 'Nuff said.

"All rise."

About time.

We'd been waiting an hour for the judge to show his face, all of us assigned to Courtroom 16 in the large brick building on Spring Garden Street. We had stood in a line that stretched well out the door, we had raised our arms through the metal detectors, we had checked our cell phones at the information booth, we had clutched our summonses and found our courtrooms and taken our places on the hard black benches. We were there against our wills, we had better things to do, like root canal and the *Jenny Jones Show,* but there had been no choice for us, we were required by law to atone and atone we would, for against the traffic laws of the City of Philadelphia we all had sinned. We had driven with suspended licenses, we had driven without insurance, we had driven the wrong way down one-way streets, we had failed to yield, we had parked where we had no business parking, we had driven drunk, God forgive us, for MADD never would. We had run through red lights, we had run through stop signs, we had sped, yes we had, and it had felt good, shifting our gears as the tachometer flared and our hearts sang and our rate of speed flew above the legal limits. But believe us,

Judge, the cops were out to get us, the radar guns were off, we didn't do it, and we won't do it again. We were good drivers, all of us, despite what our records said, and we were willing to pay the fines, but please, Judge, please don't give us the points, not the points, please.

"All rise."

We rose as one.

The judge was a creased old man with a sun-lined face and yellow hair combed back over his skull. An unlit cigarette dangled from his lips. If you saw him on the street you'd feel sorry for him and offer to buy him coffee and an egg sandwich, but here, standing now behind the bench in his black robe, even unzipped as it was, you saw not the face of a homeless vagrant but instead the weathered face of justice. He sat. We sat. His name was Judge Geary, we all knew that because of the plaque on the edge of the bench that read JUDGE GEARY. He took a deep breath through the unlit cigarette, cocked his head like Dean Martin before a song, and said in his croak of a voice, "Let's go."

The gray-haired clerk took the first file off his pile, called out a name in a voice sharp and loud, walked the file to the judge, and Traffic Court began.

It didn't take much crushing insight to figure out how Traffic Court worked in Philadelphia. The first names called were all of defendants represented by counsel. The judge would read the offense and shake his head with dismay. The lawyer would say a few rote words in defense. The judge would reduce the fine, order no points be given, admonish counsel to explain to the client what he had done wrong so he wouldn't do it again. It seemed, in those first few cases, that the judge was in a fine mood at this session and lenience would hold sway. We, all of us, sitting on our benches with our summonses in our laps and our licenses on the line, we, all of us, felt the stirrings of relief. And then the first case was called without representation of a lawyer and things suddenly turned.

"What were you doing going the wrong way down Locust Street?" said the judge.

"I was on my way to the doctor," said the defendant.

"Answer the question," barked the clerk.

"I didn't know—"

"Pay the fine, full points, court costs. Next."

"But Judge—"

"Next."

"Move along," said the clerk before he called the next name.

"You know you can't drive without insurance, don't you?" said the judge to the next defendant.

"I couldn't get it. No one would give it and I had to get to work. I got a kid—"

"But you can't drive without insurance. Here you are running stop signs without insurance. What would have happened to the pedestrian you might have hit?"

"I didn't hit no—"

"Answer the question."

"I slowed down at the stop sign, I did. The cop was—"

"Give me your license, Ms. Jenkins. Give it right up. You'll get it back in six months."

"But Judge, I got to—"

"Take the bus. Pay the two hundred, three points, license suspended, and not to be returned without proof of insurance. Next."

"But Judge—"

"Move along," said the clerk.

And on it went. And on.

It was a killing field in there, all manner of defenses shot down by old Judge Geary in the rigid pursuit of fines and points and the gleeful seizure of licenses. Except for those represented by counsel. Because, for some reason, the mere fact of having counsel by your side severely ameliorated the harshness of justice, and not just any counsel, but lawyers who make their living in Traffic Court, lawyers whose practice depends on the kindness of judges, elected judges, judges who must raise money every five years as they run for reelection.

Sniff sniff. What's that I smell? Crab fries?

Well, all right, that was the way the game was played. And no, in all my life I had never donated a cent to the campaigns of those noble public servants running for a position on Traffic Court. But still, I was wondering why the clerk hadn't yet called my name. Before court began I had identified myself as a lawyer, and he had pulled aside my file. In every courtroom in the land where the public stands before a judge, lawyers go first. It wasn't courtesy, it was custom, and yet here I was, still waiting.

I drew the clerk's attention. He was an older man, with big shoes, a tight smile, and a face full of secrets. His silver hair was shiny with grease and pulled straight back like the grill of a sleek old Caddie. He wore his navy blazer with the medallion of the Philadelphia Traffic Court at his breast and a thick ring on his pinkie.

I raised a finger, looked at my watch.

He nodded and called another name not my own.

There wasn't much more I could do. I sat slumped on the lawyers' bench in the well, watching the ruthless enforcement of the traffic laws in case after case after case, wondering if ever I would be called, when the back doors of the courtroom swung open and two uniformed cops, with guns on their hips, stepped into the courtroom.

I sat up straight, passed my gaze over those still waiting for their hearings. Uh oh, I thought, someone is not getting off with merely a fine and points. Someone is in serious trouble. And then the clerk, in a clear, hard voice, called out, "Victor Carl."

I stood, moved to the bench, glanced behind me at the cops, standing like sentries in the aisle.

The clerk handed the file to the judge, whispered something in his ear, the judge's eyes snapped up to take in the suddenly more interesting sight of me. The clerk slinked back from the bench and took his place beside me as the judge made a quick examination of my file.

"It appears you were in quite a hurry, Mr. Carl?"

"Your Honor, I am sorry to say that the police officer was entirely overzealous that morning and I don't understand how he could have thought to—"

"You weren't on Second Street?"

"I was, Your Honor, and there is a stop sign there, true, but—"

"You mean to tell me you came to a full and complete stop as per the traffic laws of the Commonwealth of Pennsylvania?"

"Your Honor, it was early and the street was empty and—"

"Answer the question," barked the clerk, and there was something in the tenor of his voice that tolled familiar. I turned and stared at the scowl on his face.

"I assume that means no, Mr. Carl," said the judge. "And this other ticket, this red light you ran on Washington?"

"I was committed to the intersection, Your Honor."

"Commitment. I love to see commitment in young people today. Some are committed to helping their fellow man, some are committed to saving the whales. You, I suppose, are committed to the intersection. What does that entail, exactly? Do you freshen up the paint, scrub the lights, pick up trash? And we haven't even gotten to the speeding charge yet."

"It was a short stretch of road and I have an expert who is familiar with police radar technology and is prepared to testify that there was not enough time for the officer to get a fair and accurate reading. Your Honor, I am prepared to contest all these charges, to appeal and force the various police officers to defend their own outrageous conduct. I am prepared to expend the police department's and this court's valuable time to exonerate myself and protect my record. But I am willing, sir, to give up that right, for a reasonable reduction in the fine and no points, which I think is only fair."

"We aim to be fair here at Traffic Court, Counselor."

"I know you do, sir."

"Well then, this is how we see fair," said the judge. "Full fine plus two hundred dollars. Full points. Court costs. If you mean to take this to a higher court, Mr. Carl, I mean to give you something to take with you."

I was stunned. I had been on the wrong side of a judge more times than I could count, but this was different, this fusillade from Judge Geary. This seemed personal. I stared at him, he glared back. This seemed personal, for a reason I couldn't fathom. I had never seen the guy before this morning, never even knew of his existence, and here he was slamming me like I was some sort of serial sniper.

I stared for a moment longer and then calmed myself. There must be an explanation. He didn't like my manner, he didn't like my tie. It happens. Even I didn't like my tie. Let it go, I told myself, don't say something you'll regret. I pursed my lips, bit my cheek until it bled, and then said, simply, in a voice studiously devoid of sarcasm, "Thank you, Your Honor."

I glanced at the clerk, glanced down at the ring, glanced

up again at the name tag. Geoffrey O'Brien. I'd have to look into him. I started to turn around to leave when the judge said, "Not so fast, Mr. Carl."

I turned again to face the judge.

"Mr. Carl, have you ever been to Lackawanna County?"

"Excuse me?"

"Lackawanna County."

"Sir?"

"It's a simple query. Have you ever been to Lackawanna County?"

"What does that have to do with my driving?"

"Answer the question," barked Clerk O'Brien.

"Do I know you?" I said to the clerk. "You seem awfully damn familiar."

"Watch your language, boy," said the judge. "I'm talking the towns of Jessup, Olyphant, Dickson City, Scranton. Lackawanna County. Have you ever been?"

"I suppose so," I said. "Scranton's right up the northeast extension of the Turnpike."

"Yes it is," said the judge. "How about Chinchilla?"

"The rodent?"

"The town."

"What's going on?"

"I have here in your file a bench warrant issued against you by the District Court of Chinchilla, Pennsylvania, located in the Forty-fifth Judicial District, Lackawanna County, that requires me to immediately place you into custody."

"Are you serious?"

"As a swollen prostate."

"You can't be serious."

"Step back, Mr. Carl," said the judge.

"Step back," ordered Clerk O'Brien.

Before I could even try to follow their directives, I felt two clamps fasten themselves, one to each of my arms. I

instinctively pulled away, to no avail. I spun my head as far
as it would go. The two cops. With their jaws jutting out.
The two cops. They had come into the courtroom for me.
Of course they had.

"This is all a mistake," I said.

"That may be," said the judge, "but we'll have to sort it
all out later."

"Arms behind your back, please," said one of the cops.

"Are you kidding me?"

"Do I look like a kidder," said the cop, his face as solid
and blank as a brick wall.

The judge stared at me with hard eyes as I was cuffed,
as if I had broken into his house and raped his daughter.
Somehow this had become personal between him and me
and I didn't know how, I didn't understand how. And then
I realized it wasn't personal, at least not between him and
me. It wasn't old Judge Geary who had turned on me like
a snarling raccoon. It was something far more dangerous.
The law itself, for some reason, had turned against me.
First I had been dragged into the District Attorney's office
like a common miscreant and then the sheriff had refused
to aid my collections and now a bench warrant had been issued against my person and I was going directly to jail.

"This is outrageous," I said. "This is patently unconsti-
tutional."

"File your writs, Mr. Carl," said the judge.

"Oh, I will, you can bet on it."

"And we'll get to them in due course," said the judge,
writing something brusquely on my file as the cuffs bit into
my wrists and the police officers led me away to a door at
the side of the well.

The judge slammed the file shut, handed it to the clerk,
and, just as I was being pushed through the door, said,
"Next case."

Another hesitant defendant came forward, head bowed, license held precariously in his trembling hand.

"You've been a naughty boy, Mr. Dayanim," said the judge.

The door closed behind me.

Traffic Court.

CHAPTER

42

I sat in the dinky little lockup at Traffic Court, leaning forward on the metal bench, my elbows on my knees, my head in my hands, contemplating the sorriness of my sorry life, when I looked up and was blinded by a great flash of light. Satori? No. Slocum.

"I hope you don't mind," said ADA Slocum, indicating the instant camera in his hand. "I just wanted to remember this moment, to savor it on those long cold nights when true justice seems elusive."

I stood quickly, grabbed hold of my beltless pants to keep them up. "Are you here to spring me?"

"Your partner called," he said. "I was in the middle of lunch with McDeiss. It's not a pretty sight."

"I've seen the lions being fed at the zoo, I get the idea. Are you here to spring me?"

"It pains me to say this, Carl, but yes. I am here to facilitate your release."

"Good. I've got someplace I need to be."

"Something pleasant, I hope."

"Just a woman."

"Nice looking?"

"She was." Pause. "So?"

"It appears," said Slocum slowly, "a bench warrant was

issued early this year in Lackawanna County against a Vincent Carillo, a resident of the City of Philadelphia."

"Ah," I said. "That explains everything. A perfectly honest mistake, because my name is neither Vincent nor Carillo and so, of course, I was cuffed in public and taken into custody and made to sit in this stinking cell for three stinking hours."

"There's no reason to raise your voice like that."

"Get me the hell out of here."

"They're finishing the paperwork. A few more minutes."

We stood there for a moment on either side of the bars, quiet, as if nothing more needed to be said. I gave in first. "So why did they put me in here if the name on the warrant wasn't mine?"

"There seems to have been an entry error on the computer," he said.

"Just so happens to have been an entry error with my name on it."

"Just so happens."

"No idea how?"

"None."

"Well, I have some."

"I told you not to mess with him."

"Son of a bitch."

"Did you keep away from him like you promised?"

"Yes I did."

"And his wife?"

"I tried."

"Tried?"

"She came to me."

"Uh huh."

"Is that a crime?"

He looked at me for a moment through the bars. "Evidently."

"He's up to his neck in something."

"Your horseshit is what he's up to his neck in."

"There's a clerk here who is involved somehow too. I think he beat me up and threatened me right after you called me into your office."

"You didn't tell me about being beaten up."

"Do you want to hear about all my problems? Do you want to hear about my father, my love life, the way Comcast unfairly cut off my cable?"

"No cable?"

"Don't get me started."

"You said you *think* he beat you up?"

"It was in my vestibule. I was facedown on the floor. I didn't catch a face, but I recognized the voice. His name's O'Brien. Geoffrey O'Brien. You might want to see if there is any connection between him and our friend."

"I might want to," said Slocum, "and then I might not want to get anywhere near your problems." He tilted his head and looked behind me. There were four other men in the cell, a varied assortment ranging from well dressed to not, all in deeper trouble than they ever expected when they stepped through the Traffic Court metal detectors. "You drum up any business?"

"I was improperly placed into custody and my good name was slandered in public by some crackpot judge maliciously executing a mistakenly entered bench warrant that was not so mistakenly entered. I don't need to drum up any business," I said. "I'll be too busy representing myself the next few months to take on any new clients."

Just then a cop came to the cell with a clipboard and the thick manila envelope into which I had deposited my keys, my belt, my wallet and watch. He unlocked the barred door, slid it open, called out my name as if I were in a crowd twenty feet away.

"Yes," I said.

"Mr. Carl, you're free to go."

As I stepped through the door, one of the men behind me said, "I'll call you when I can, Mr. Carl. My mom will get that retainer to you like you told me. Maybe you can pop me out quick as you popped out you self."

"Me too," said another one.

I turned toward them. "That will be fine, gentlemen. You all have my number, right?"

They each waved a small business card.

"Good luck, then. I look forward to hearing from you."

Slocum shook his head as he walked with me down the hall away from the cell.

"My prison posse," I said.

Slocum just kept shaking his head.

"What?" I said.

CHAPTER

43

I stood at the door of the small Mount Airy house and straightened my tie, licked my teeth, shined my wingtips on the back of my calves. I felt like I should have brought along a bouquet of red roses and a box of chocolates.

Sylvia Steinberg.

She was Tommy Greeley's girlfriend before his murder, she was Tommy Greeley's lover for who knows how long. If it wasn't Chelsea in the photographs then it had to be her. The long taut body, the smooth skin, the dark hair.

Sylvia Steinberg.

I had thought it would be a difficult feat of detection to find her after all these years, probably living in a different city, probably living under a different name, probably living the suburban dream and wanting nothing to do with her misspent past when she was the girlfriend of a cocaine kingpin. But sometimes fact-finding is ludicrously easy, all it takes is an attempt. Sylvia Steinberg was listed under her own name in the Philadelphia telephone directory, with a Mount Airy address. Mount Airy, where all the hippies who had congregated on South Street in the sixties had settled into their middle age, wearing their Birkenstocks, sitting on their porches, chewing their granola, passing back and forth their recipes for tofu turkey.

"Who?" had said Sylvia Steinberg on the phone. "You

want to talk about Tommy? Why? I suppose. You know where I live? That's right. Tomorrow at two. Come about then, why don't you?"

And about then I had come, down to a quiet leafy street, a small green house with a great sycamore in front, a neat lawn, a dainty porch, a door behind which stood a month's worth of erotic fantasies. I took a breath, calmed myself, knocked. Waited for the door to open, smiled when it did, identified myself, stepped inside as the door closed behind me.

When I left that little house in Mount Airy and started driving back to Center City, I was horrified and excited too. On the plus side, I finally knew who the woman was in the photographs, finally had a face with which to grace the perfect body. On the other side, I didn't like who it turned out to be, not at all, and yet my hormones were splashing, yes they were, and I could feel the arousal in my gut.

"I loved Tommy Greeley, I suppose," had said Sylvia Steinberg. "At least I thought I did."

We were sitting across from each other at her kitchen table when she said this. A coffeemaker burbled on the countertop, a small plate of Oreos was set between us. And she was talking about Tommy.

"What happened between you two?" I said.

"Do you know the Yeats line? 'Things fall apart, the center cannot hold.' Well, the center couldn't hold and so it fell apart."

"I don't understand."

"You can only hide from the truth so long."

"You're talking about the drugs?"

"I should think that was part of it too. I didn't know about his business when we first got involved and I never approved when I learned the truth. In fact, I refused to do

drugs myself. A few hits and all the fears I was trying not
to deal with would just flood over me. But still, I thought
we could just get married, move to the suburbs, have kids,
everything would be settled. As if I could separate the life
I imagined from his rotten business, even if it was the business that would buy the house, the cars, the private schools.
Can you spell schizophrenia, Victor? Two separate worlds,
which collapsed into each other when that FBI agent
started nosing around like a rabbit, sniffing here, sniffing
there. But by then, we were already crashing." She
laughed. "Tommy never knew what he was getting into
when he made his little suggestion."

The coffeemaker quieted, Sylvia pushed herself off the
table, ambled over to the counter.

She had been a very pretty woman in her youth, you
could tell by her lovely face, her dark hair, her smooth soft
skin. As she was talking to me, I was examining her closely,
trying to see in her the woman of the photographs. It was
hard, but I could envision it, yes I could, so long as I imagined that thin lithe body had been swallowed whole by another. If Sylvia was that woman, she weighed about a
hundred pounds more than she had twenty years before. I
couldn't help but do the math. Twenty years, one hundred
pounds, five pounds per year at 3,500 calories per pound.
That would be a mere 50 excess calories a day: three ounces
of Coca-Cola, four ounces of beer, or a single Oreo.

"Here we go," she said, bringing over two mugs and the
pot. "How do you take your coffee?"

"Straight."

"Puts hair on your chest that way, I suppose."

"I sure could use it."

She poured, fixed up her mug with milk and sugar, sat
down, took a pensive sip.

"You mentioned a suggestion," I said.

"So I did," she said, and as she smiled at the remembrance she popped an Oreo into her mouth.

Tommy Greeley, that scamp, that . . . that scamp. As I drove along the nicely serpentine Lincoln Drive, I couldn't help but admire his gumption. A suggestion, Sylvia called it, slurring the g's and overemphasizing the middle syllable just enough to indicate what the suggestion might have entailed. *Oh come on. Let's just try it. Open your horizons. It could be fun. You never know.* No, you never do. The logic of it is inescapable, at least to the male of the species. I mean if two breasts to suckle and fondle, to rub your face between are the great obsession of the young, four would be the grand salami of boyhood dreams, right? Four legs to caress, four lips to kiss, two belly buttons to lick clean, two tongues to suck their way across your flesh, four hands to explore, to massage, to tickle and pinch and grab. And the scent of it all, oh my, no thin solo but a veritable symphony. Tommy Greeley, that dog, that scamp.

Of course sometimes things don't work out quite how you had planned.

"He brought her over," said Sylvia. "A very pretty girl, quiet, strangely passive, besotted, it seemed, with Tommy. I had seen her before, knew who she was, had always thought her pretty. But this night she sort of glowed. Tommy opened a bottle of wine. We drank and talked and laughed, a sort of forced laughter. There were candles, if I remember, and incense. I felt like I was twelve again. Tommy was very charming, ever the ringleader. And I couldn't take my eyes off the girl. She was so, so pretty. In the candlelight. We finished up one bottle, were on to the next, and I was feeling it, the alcohol, the tension, the expectation. And then he put his arm around me and kissed me. Right in front of her. A long passionate kiss. And I was embarrassed. I could feel the blood rising through my face, the prickly sensation, which was unusual for me, for I was not the blushing type. Then he took my hand. And we stood. And he led me through the hallway to the bedroom, his arm around my shoulders, like he was ushering me into a whole new world. And I looked back. And she was following, through the dark hall. She was holding a candle and following us, the candlelight dancing across her features, following us like a ghost."

"And?"

"Well, yes, and. Definitely and."

She laughed, a rich, good-natured laugh and I couldn't help but laugh with her.

"I don't think Tommy enjoyed it as much as he had hoped," she said. "Oh, he made all the required gestures and sound effects, yes, snorting and neighing, a veritable barnyard of sounds, but eventually there was a touch of petulance to it all. He wasn't at the center anymore, you see, he was simply one bend on a triangle, and felt maybe like a child who suddenly discovers that everyone in the world isn't dancing to his tune, that there are other tunes being played."

"And for you?" I asked.

She didn't answer right off, but then she didn't have to. There was a footstep at the entranceway, the scrape of a key, the front door being opened, and then it all became clear as rain.

She had said she didn't like smoking reefer, that after a few hits all the fears she was trying not to deal with would flood over her. And later, she had hoped her hoped-for marriage to Tommy Greeley would settle things. But some things are not so easily settled, and some fears are not so easily outrun. Especially when the fear is of the truth and the hard uncertain future that its acknowledgment would demand. I could imagine Sylvia Steinberg wrestling with her demon, chaining it tight, stuffing it into a dark corner to keep it quiet, glimpsing its face only in restless dreams or flights of drug-induced paranoia, winning the struggle, winning, until her lover comes up with a suggestion. A suggestion. *Oh come on. Let's just try it. Open your horizons. It could be fun. You never know.* And there is alcohol. And there is candlelight. And there is a pretty girl along for the ride. And when the demon finally breaks free, smashing out of its chains with a startling ferocity, it is different than she ever expected. Bright not dark, soft not hard, warm not cold, and its embrace is not one of despair but of acceptance and ease that settles over the soul like a mother's sweet breath.

The front door opened, the bustle of domesticity, the soft yapping cry of a baby, and then a woman came into the kitchen. She was tall, blond, with a thin, pretty face and a baby held at her hip. She leaned over and gave Sylvia a long kiss on the lips.

Sylvia made the introductions. I was Victor Carl, the lawyer asking about Tommy Greeley. The blond woman, whose nose wrinkled with distaste at Tommy's name, was Louise. The baby, their baby, was Donna.

"Isn't she cute?" said Sylvia. "Isn't she just the cutest?"

"Yes she is," I said, thinking it true so long as they kept the slobbering little bundle away from my suit.

"She's been fussy," said Louise.

"She's just hungry," said Sylvia, reaching out for the baby. "Aren't you, sweetie pie. You're just hungry, yes you are. But not for long. You don't mind, do you, Victor?" she said as she unbuttoned her shirt.

"Not at all."

The shirt opened, Sylvia flopped out her right breast. I got a good look before the baby latched on and began moving her tiny jaw in time with her desperate swallows.

"Is Sylvia being helpful, Mr. Carl?" said Louise.

"Very."

"What is this all about?"

"I'm trying to find out why Tommy Greeley disappeared."

"It will come to you, I'm sure," said Louise. "It's not so hard to figure out. I'm taking a bath."

"Nice meeting you," I said to her back as she walked out of the kitchen.

"What did she mean?" I asked Sylvia.

"She doesn't think much of Tommy. The drug dealing, the parties in Atlantic City, the way he cheated on everyone. From all she's heard she assumes he was asking for it a hundred different ways. But she never met him. There was a sweetness there, and an energy, and a brash confidence that was infectious. He seemed freer than other people."

"Who was the girl?" I said. "The girl with the candle."

"One of the people in Tommy's other life. Her name was Chelsea. Ah, Chelsea. So pretty. I have to admit I fancied myself in love with her. I followed her around like a puppy for a while, which is sort of usual when you break through. Nothing came of it, of course, just a few nights without Tommy, which were very nice, lovely, yes, but nothing more. It would still be a number of years before I was ready to handle something serious."

"Like Louise."

"Yes, or like a few before her. But with Chelsea, a strange thing happened. Right in the middle of it, a man came to my apartment, rough-looking, with all this hair, his beard, wild eyes. He came to tell me, and this is what was so peculiar, he came to tell me that Tommy was cheating on me. Cheating on me with his wife. He wanted me to get all angry and to do something about it. But it turned out he was married to Chelsea. Which put me in a funny situation, since I had been with her too and wanted, desperately, to be with her again. The man seemed upset at my failure to react, when what I was really trying to do was hide my reaction at learning that my Chelsea was married to him."

"Was he angry?"

"Oh yes. Quite. It was frightening, really. I tried to tell him he needn't worry about Tommy, that Tommy was already infatuated with someone else, but he wouldn't listen. Left very agitated."

I leaned forward. "Who?"

"The man? I think his name was Donnie. Could that be it? I'm not sure."

"No. Who was Tommy infatuated with?"

She pulled the baby from her breast, laid the infant on her lap as she placed her right breast back in her shirt and pulled out the left. By then I wasn't so interested in the sight, by then I had seen what I needed to see, her right areola without a blemish or mark of any kind, to know that Sylvia Steinberg was not the woman in Tommy Greeley's photographs. So who was? It seemed she was ready to give me the answer.

When the baby was happily sucking at the left breast, the baby's jaw now moving more for comfort than hunger, Sylvia said, "I don't know. By then we weren't confiding in each other."

"So how did you know there was someone?"

"We were still pretending to be together—it was easier not to talk about the things we were going through with each other, easier to playact, you see—but I could tell. He was distant, distracted, he took a lot of showers, and then he picked up a new hobby which was so unlike him."

"A new hobby?" I said.

"Tommy was never one for introspection, so his new little pastime was very surprising."

"What was his new hobby?" I said.

And then she told me, and that's when I knew.

Lincoln Drive emptied onto Kelley Drive, which swept along with the Schuylkill River until it raced past the great brown art museum, sitting high and imperious, and spilled into the Benjamin Franklin Parkway. The afternoon was getting late, rush hour was on, but I was driving against the main flow of traffic, slipping into the city, so the drive wasn't an ordeal. Just a little stop and go, just enough time for me to put it all together. And I was, yes indeed, putting it all together. The luminous Chelsea. The furious Lonnie. The mysterious love interest that had given Tommy Greeley his new hobby. Somewhere in that matrix lay the root cause of Tommy Greeley's murder twenty years before, and most likely the killer of Joey Parma. Wasn't it exactly Joey's luck to somehow fall into the middle of that crew? And at the epicenter of it all, I could tell now with utter certainty, was the woman in the photographs, my photographs, that woman.

I found a place to park with time on the meter. How lucky was that? Half an hour, I wouldn't need much more, a couple quarters doubled it, and then I was on my way. I knew where she was, she had said a smart cracker like me could find it, and I was and I did. Skink had given me the address, an old rehabbed factory building, Skink had given me the security code to the front door, a pair of binoculars was all it took, he said, to snag that. No need to use the intercom, 53351 and I was in. Up the threadbare stairs, one flight, two flights, there was only one door on the third floor, large, metal, rusted around the edges and at the seams, the entrance to an old sweatshop of some sort. I gave it a bang.

"What was his new hobby," I had asked. I thought it would be photography, I had the damn photographs, it had to be photography, but that wasn't what Sylvia was referring to.

"What was his new hobby?"

"He started keeping a journal," she said. "A diary. Wouldn't let me peek, it was all very serious, very secret, but I could see him working all through the night, scribbling away, scribbling, scribbling. 'What are you doing all that for?' I asked him once. And what he said I thought was so terribly pretentious, so unlike him, that I knew it had come from someone else."

"What did he say?"

"Only this. He said, 'I'm turning my life into art.' "

I knocked again.

Footsteps. The door creaked open wide and there it was, smiling at me, the face I had been wondering about from the first time I had spied her naked body on those photographs.

"Come in, please. I've been expecting you for some time now."

Oh, I bet she had.

CHAPTER

44

Above her writing desk, framed and written out in fine calligraphy, was a peculiar quotation that I remember for its apt strangeness. There was much to see in the huge studio loft of Alura Straczynski, fine paintings on the walls, photographs, colorful scarves tacked to the plaster as if billowing in the wind. There was a couch and a chair and a huge four-poster bed that sat in the center as if an altar to some great pagan entity. The ceiling was open and rough, with a web of pipes and wires over the beams and large gas heaters yawning down. The floor was apparently the same wide and scarred old wood that had been there when the building had been raised a century before. A scent of musk and flowers and exotic incense permeated the space, a scent that was both warm and intensely feminine. And there were the books, journals in all shapes and sizes, arranged neatly in a great mahogany bookcase standing up by the desk. They sat on their shelves like the collected ledgers of a venerable corporation, so many of them that it almost seemed the purpose of that space was to create and to house and to protect them. But it was the quotation that struck me most forcibly, a quotation from a man with whom I often could identify, another urban Jew suffering an intense bout of dislocation, Franz Kafka:

You do not need to leave your room. Remain sitting at
your table and listen. Do not even listen, simply wait.
Do not even wait, be quite still and solitary. The world
will freely offer itself to you to be unmasked, it has no
choice, it will roll in ecstasy at your feet.

And now, here I was.

Alura Straczynski, lover of Tommy Greeley and subject
of his most ardent photographs, stood pensively by the
door as I examined her loft. She wore a lose peasant shirt
unbuttoned at the top, a long gauzy skirt, her hands were
clasped one in the other, her arms held before her like a V.
There was something of a dancer's grace in the way she
held herself back, tensed with anticipation. I couldn't help
but examine her closely, more closely than I ever had before, trying to see in her something of the woman in the
photographs. Her thin arms, the long legs I could glimpse
beneath her diaphanous skirt.

She caught me staring and smiled and there was something about the smile I didn't like.

I turned away and examined again the large open space.
There was a small kitchenette in one corner, a door leading
to a bathroom in another, and by the window stood the tall
writing desk with the framed quotation above it. No chair
or stool squatted before it, just the desk, its upper surface
about chest high and tilted slightly back, a heavy journal
open atop it, a fountain pen and a pair of glasses resting
atop the journal.

I noticed a framed photograph on the wall near the desk
that looked familiar. I stepped toward it. A young Alura
Straczynski, taken from the neck up, her shoulders bare,
her head held at a dramatic angle. Where had I seen this
photograph before? Yes, in the Mayan slate frame in Jackson Straczynski's office. But there was something else that

tolled familiar in the shot. The texture of her skin, the blank backdrop, the angle of the capture, the way the camera seemed to caress her features. I hadn't noticed it when I had spotted it before but now it seemed obvious.

"Tommy Greeley took this," I said.

"Why do you think so?"

"I've seen other examples of his work."

"Have you indeed?" That damn smile again, as if she knew exactly what I had pinned to my bedroom wall.

"What is this?" I said, looking around.

"This is my studio."

"And what do you do here?"

"Whatever I choose," she said. "This is my sacred place. Sometimes I dance naked. Sometimes I paint."

"Naked?" I said, staring once again at her. Her smile seemed strangely knowing.

"If I choose," she said. "But most importantly, I write. My journals. Recording my life with complete honesty is what I consider my most important work."

"Life into art."

"Yes, like we talked about. But it is more than just the glistening surface, Victor, though I want the surface to glisten. No, I have to admit to a grander ambition. I want to travel deeper, into the murky realms that have always seemed to defy exploration, into the very heart of what it means to be a woman. Some spend years in analysis to peer there. I have spent a lifetime with my journals, recording and rerecording, sifting, analyzing, distilling. Searching for that one unmentionable truth at the very bottom."

"The last thing," I said.

"If that's how you want to put it. And my studio is the tool I use to get there, so to speak. The ax for the frozen sea within. I sit here and the world comes to me, just as you have, dear Victor, and whatever happens in this loft is my raw material."

"I don't understand."

"Come over here and I'll show you," she said.

She moved toward the tall writing desk, almost glided there, and I followed, as if impelled by some unknown spell. She put on her glasses, took up the pen, a fine fountain pen with a golden nib.

"Stand closer," she said, and I did, until I could feel the heat off her shoulders, smell the fresh scent of her dark hair. Standing beside her as I was, I could lean forward and peer over her shoulder onto the pages of the journal. She dashed the pen in the air twice, put the date and time into the journal, and began to write in a careful and lovely script.

Victor Carl has come to visit. He is wearing his suit, his hideous red tie,

"Hey," I said. "What's wrong with my tie."

"Shhhh," she said. "Just read."

his thick black shoes. They are the shoes of a schoolmaster, or a parish priest, that is why I like them. They fit him so well: sturdy, earnest, plain, a little grubby. His shoes, in fact, are a main component of his charm. He seems angry that I have been holding back secrets. But of course I have been holding back secrets. What is a secret if not something wonderfully dreadful that is held back? But he has secrets too, this Victor Carl. He looks at me as if he is unable to force himself to look away. He looks at me, as if he were looking through me, or at least through the surface of me. Is he trying to see my soul, or something less metaphysical? The way he stares at me has created an electric tension that I find delicious. Is that

*what this is all about, our need for others in our
lives, not for comfort but for the tension in the real
that mirrors our own inner conflicts?*

"What are you doing?" I said.

"I am writing as truthfully as I can," she said. "I seem
always to be more honest on the page than I ever can be
with the spoken word. The barriers are lowered when I
write. You want the honest truth, don't you?"

"Yes."

"Then read," she said.

*He asks what am I doing. I am transferring the mo-
ment into something concrete. Like a photograph
captures light, I am capturing all the flitting moths
that normally pass through our brains and disappear
into the smoke of the past, all the sensations, emotions, ideas. Here, in my words, they are caught,
mounted on the pages as if with pins through their
wings. Later I will elucidate what I have written, re-
vise, analyze, relive again what is happening here
and now, the familiar and yet unique frisson when
two separate individuals first start rubbing up
against each other.*

"This is too weird," I said.

*"This is too weird," he says. It makes him uncom-
fortable to look into the mind of another so closely. I
don't blame him. It is uncomfortable for me to see
my own thoughts and emotions, my own pallid yet
unquenched desires, my own mortal failings lying
naked on the page. For him it must be some exquisite
torture. But it is having another effect too. I feel him*

*over my shoulder. First he looks at the page, then at
the nape of my neck.*

"Stop it," I said. "I'm not," I said, even though I was,
even though I couldn't stop looking at both her neck and
her words, and I very much didn't want her to stop writing.
There was something drawing me out, her very presence so
close, the heat from her body, the words that seemed to cut
so close to her bone, my obsession with the photographs
from her youth that had captured me from the first.

*There is something in his so-called quest for the
truth about Tommy Greeley that I hadn't understood
before, but it came to me today in a thrilling burst of
insight. It was in the way he was staring at me. He
was like a man searching for a memory. On his tour
of the studio he stopped at one of Tommy's photographs, one of the series taken decades ago and described fully in the missing journals. He examined it
as if it were both familiar and strange to him. I don't
know yet if he has found the missing journals, but I
believe now he has seen the other photographs. He
has found at least part of my puzzle. And if he has
seen the photographs, I have no doubt but that he
would feel what Tommy was feeling, he would be
captured by the images the way Tommy was captured
by the flesh.*

*Yes, I am right. It is flowing from him, the mesmeriz-
ing fragrance of unwilling desire.*

*He is something of an empath, this Victor Carl, he
has a startling intuition. That is what I wrote about
him in my prior entries and I feel it even more*

*strongly now, that unique talent of his. In that way I
suppose we are something like twins. Can you imagine a blind man and blind woman reaching out their
fingers to touch each other's face, to explore and see,
to learn and capture and possess. That is what we
would be together. The promise is enough to send
shivers into my very core. I want to deliver myself to
him as if he were a knife cleaving me to my essence.*

*He is leaning over my shoulder, reading this, and I
feel the urge to turn my head. It wouldn't take much,
just the slightest turn, and then our lips would brush,
would touch, our lips would touch and another line
would be crossed. The lines were so impenetrable at
one time, like walls, before Tommy, but now, with
each line, I approach as if I am running downhill
and hurtle it with ease. And with each line crossed I
feel myself getting closer to the ultimate truth. For
where does truth lie if not in the shattering of boundaries? And I sense Victor Carl feels the same.*

*I can't stop myself, I won't stop myself, and neither
will he. I will turn my head, moisten my lips with my
tongue, brush my lips against his, bite his ear, his
neck, offer myself wholly and unstintingly to him and
let the explosion of passion and lust overwhelm us
both with its urgent miracle of discovery. Slowly I
turn, my lips are wet, and as if in a dream I reach for
his mouth with my . . .*

I pulled my attention from the drifting line of prose and
there she was, staring at me, her eyes soft, her lips red with
life, leaning toward me, into me, her hip on my hip, her
shoulder on my chest, her chin raised, her face so close to

my own that I could feel her halting breath as she waited for me to take her in my arms, to press my body into hers, to feel that urgent moment of discovery as I kiss her. As I kiss her. Kiss her. Her. Kiss her.

For the moment I wanted to, it was all I wanted to do. I saw not her but the photographs pinned to my wall, the lines, the hollows, the soft arcs of flesh, and all I wanted to do was kiss her and hold her and feel that body, whose every curve and blemish I knew, against my own.

But I didn't.

Because that moment flashed through me in the quick of a blink and suddenly the spell was broken. Who I saw before me was not the woman of the photographs, a woman who lived truly only in the fevered artistry of Tommy Greeley's eye, but Alura Straczynski. And Alura Straczynski was not that woman now, and had most likely not been that woman then, no matter that it was her arms, breasts, hips, hands in those photographs. The only truth in art is in the artist's soul. The subject, in the presence of the art, is always a lie.

So I didn't kiss her. So what I did instead was back away.

She stared at me for a moment, puzzlement at first creasing the moist expectation in her face and then she smiled with a peculiar amazement, like a scientist finding a strange and wondrous result in the most banal of places, Alexander Fleming examining his spoiled petri dish.

"Is that how you seduced Tommy Greeley?" I said. "With your journals."

"I didn't seduce Tommy," she said. "He seduced me."

"Where?"

"Here."

"As if the bed wasn't sign enough of your willingness?"

"There was no bed then. It was open space, with a mirror on the wall and a barre. I was then primarily a dancer. He was my husband's friend. We double-dated. Occasionally, on the walks to one restaurant or another, we would have a private talk. And then one night he quietly asked if he could come to my studio and watch me dance. I looked away, shyly, I was very shy in those days, but I whispered yes. And as I danced for him, I realized how much I liked being at the center of his attention. He read me poems, Byron—*'And the midnight moon is weaving her bright chain o'er the deep'*—and I danced to the rhythms of the verse, and it was strange and magical and I liked it in a way that shocked me. Then he said he wanted to photograph me. He said he admired my lines."

"That's a pretty good one right there."

"Yes, it is, isn't it? He photographed me dancing at first. In my leotards. My movements, my positions. And as the session wore on, I could feel his emotions veer out of his control, as if my very movements conjured up his desire. But then he had a different idea. At first I said no. Absolutely not. I was happily married, devoted to my husband, why would I allow that? But when I woke up in the middle of the night and tossed in my husband's arms, I imagined the emotions of it, the vulnerability of it, the thrilling sense of violation. I wrote and wrote, pages, whole sections, working it out in my journals, what it might mean, stepping over the boundaries, opening my life up to what? And then, after enough thought, I found I couldn't stop myself."

"Is that always your excuse?"

She laughed. "Of course you are right. Remember when I said I have a harder time being honest with the spoken word. The rationalizations slip in without my even realizing it. I didn't want to stop myself. He threw a carpet down on the floor and then a sheet over the carpet and he laid me down in various poses. The bright lights, the soft linen beneath me, the sound of his camera clicking and spinning, the movement of my naked body, his presence hovering above me with that hard black object and its single thrilling eye. The sex seemed an inconsequential step after opening myself to him that way."

"Did your husband know?"

"What happens here is private. That was our agreement from the start. I rented this studio before I ever met Jackson. This has always been a room of my own. So no, he has never been up here, has never known what has gone on here."

"Never?"

"Once, and not again. What happens here is completely separate from my marriage."

"Did anyone else know about you and Tommy?"

"I told no one. Tommy promised to tell no one too. In fact, I insisted he give me all the photographic prints that showed my face. No one was ever to know that we were together. Only one other man might have found out."

"Who?"

"Some ruffian, some bearded motorcycle maniac. He came up here one afternoon looking for Tommy, banging on the door. Yelling. Said he had followed Tommy. Said he had to talk. Called him a bastard. We stayed silent, didn't let him in no matter how long he banged. When he stopped, I watched through the window as he left the building. He looked up, spied me staring down at him."

"Lonnie."

"I never knew his name."

"He told your husband."

"He didn't know me, didn't know who I was."

"Don't be a fool. And the bed only came into the studio after Tommy?"

"Yes."

"So there were others."

"I don't go chasing. They simply appear. If I wait long enough the world appears. As did you. And sex is merely a tool, Victor. Like a chisel cutting through opaque stone. It is a method of exploration, nothing more."

"I'm sure that gives your husband great comfort as he lies alone in his bed at night."

"My husband has his own ambitions to keep him warm."

"How did it finish between you and Tommy?"

"I ended it."

"Why?"

"He wanted us to be together. He told me so. It was quite charming, and at first I was almost willing. He painted such a romantic picture and he could be very convincing. But I knew it would be wrong for me. I loved my husband and I suppose I was more interested in exploring my being than in being with Tommy."

"He took it well?"

"I don't know. Once I decided, I didn't see him again before he disappeared. Now if you don't mind, Victor, I have work to do."

"You going to write up our little moment?"

"Oh yes," she said. "It is not often I am face-to-face with such a perfect example of an emotionally stilted coward."

I let loose a burst of laughter. I couldn't help myself, I laughed and shook my head and headed toward her door. "Maybe you're right. I cheerfully admit to being both emotionally stilted and a coward. But not today."

"You'll find them for me, won't you?" she said.

"Your precious notebooks."

"Yes."

"Don't you have enough here to keep you busy?"

"The work continues. I am distilling a life, my life. Those months are precious, crucial, defining."

"Who killed Joey Parma?"

"Who is Joey Parma?"

"A loser of no apparent worth."

"Then why would I be concerned with him?"

"You wouldn't," I said. "If I find your precious notebooks I'll let you know."

"Thank you, Victor."

"Today it wasn't so much cowardice as good taste."

"With that tie, Victor? I hardly think so."

I laughed again as I closed the door behind me. Just then I felt like a cockroach in Teflon boots, climbing to freedom out of a sticky mess of a web even as the spider, with all her venom, looked on with helpless contempt.

But I didn't worry much about Alura Straczynski anymore. I had lost the fantasy of the pictures but I had gained another piece of the puzzle. She had brought me one step closer, so close I could feel the answer to it all coming upon me. I needed only to dot one more *i*, cross one more *t*, and the word "guilty" would be writ large upon the forehead of the man who had set up Tommy Greeley's death.

CHAPTER

45

"All rise."

Those damn words again. I should have been on my guard, but what could I have to fear here, in the Criminal Courts Building, standing before the august Philadelphia Court of Common Pleas?

Dour Clerk Templeton did the whole "Oyez! Oyez! Oyez!" thing as Judge Wellman stepped into the courtroom. That word never failed to crack me up, Oyez. Like two old crones discussing their ailments. *You think you have oyez? You don't know from oyez. Vayzmir, I have oyez.* I must have been finding it so amusing, and my work that day so routine, because it was only later that I registered the clerk's hard stare or the judge's dark countenance as he ascended to the bench.

"What do we have?" said the judge.

"Your Honor, we're here today for the sentencing of Rashard Porter," I said, as I put my hand on Rashard's shoulder. I had him dressed in gray pants, green crewneck sweater, blue oxford shirt. He looked as if he had walked off the set of *Ozzie and Harriet,* if black men had ever been allowed on the set of *Ozzie and Harriet.*

"Go ahead," said the judge.

"If you remember, Mr. Porter pled guilty to a drug misdemeanor, simple possession. Because of his prior record you asked for a presentencing report. Mr. Porter has taken three blood tests since the plea and all have turned up negative. He has cooperated fully with the presentencing officer and in that time has continued his fine attendance at his place of employment. If I may, I'd like to pass up to Your Honor a letter from Janice Hull, his supervisor at work, calling Mr. Porter an exemplary employee."

"Have you seen this letter, Miss Carter?"

"Yes, Judge. No objection."

I gave the letter to Clerk Templeton and continued.

"I also have another letter for Your Honor. I am pleased to announce that Rashard Porter has been accepted into the upcoming class at the Philadelphia College of Art. Mr. Porter is a fine artist who is hoping to make a career in the world of art and design. This is his acceptance letter from Dean Sandhurst, along with the terms of his financial aid."

"Have you seen this letter too, Miss Carter?"

"Yes, Judge. Again no objection."

"And you've checked that it's legitimate?"

"I spoke with Dean Sandhurst just yesterday. She was very impressed with the defendant's portfolio and his potential."

"Go on."

"Mr. Porter has pled guilty and admitted his mistake," I said. "He has lived up to all the expectations of this court since his plea. He understands the rare nature of the opportunity that has opened up for him at PCA and intends to make the most of it. He has pledged to continue to work diligently, Your Honor, and his mother is here to say that she will be sure to make him live up to that pledge. In short, Mr. Porter is a perfect candidate for probation, Your Honor, and that is what we are asking for here. We have no objection to having his continued enrollment at PCA be an element of that probation. This is a young man who has turned his life around and earned this opportunity. We ask the Court to allow him to pursue it."

"Miss Carter?"

"We have no objection to probation under the terms outlined by Mr. Carl."

"That's all you have to say, Miss Carter?"

"Yes, Your Honor."

"Mr. Porter. What about you? You are entitled to speak for yourself."

"I'm sorry for what I did," he said softly.

"Speak up," barked Clerk Templeton.

"I know I made a mistake," said Rashard, "and I won't do it again, I promise. My mum's here and I promised her too. I'm sorry I let her down. All she's done for me, I can't let her down again. I'm going to do my best at that art school, Judge. I never expected there was a college for drawing, but I'm excited at the chance. That's all."

I took hold of Rashard's arm, gave a squeeze to let him know he had done well.

"Yes, okay, I guess I have what I need," said the judge, and I was certain he did. It was why my pleading was muted, no reason to go overboard on the verbiage here. For Judge Wellman, this was not a difficult decision, not, in fact, a decision at all. The ADA and the defense had agreed on a course of action, the presentencing report had concurred, Rashard's acceptance by PCA had sealed the deal. This was a kid with a chance and no judge in the courthouse would take that away from him. I could have maybe even gotten the sentence suspended, without probation, but I thought it might be profitable for Rashard to have a probation officer reviewing his performance at school, just to be sure, and ADA Carter had been insistent.

The judge looked down at the letters in his hand, looked up at the ceiling, then at me with a troubling expression. It wasn't that he wasn't smiling, judges don't smile at sentencings, but there was something else there. Was I just imagining it, or was he looking at me as if I were the man in the dock?

For a moment he conferred with Clerk Templeton, who was giving me the eye as she spoke, and the judge nodded. And then he began.

"I'm not as impressed as you, Mr. Carl, by Mr. Porter's good behavior between his plea and his sentencing. He is not a fool, he knew what he had to do to have a chance here today. He goes to work on time and has you wile his acceptance into PCA, but all that does not obviate the facts in this case. Mr. Porter was in a stolen car. He had a significant amount of marihuana on the front seat of that car."

"He pled to a single misdemeanor," I said.

"I am allowed to look at the totality of circumstances."

"The only crime relevant here is simple possession."

"And he has a number of serious priors which trouble me greatly."

"That is why we asked for—"

"I've heard enough from you, Mr. Carl. It is my turn. Is there no one in this courtroom thinking of the law-abiding citizens of this city? Driving around in a stolen car, high on a schedule-one substance. Miss Carter, you should be ashamed, going along with Mr. Carl's recommendation. Mr. Porter was in jail once, he obviously didn't learn his lesson. I believe he needs a longer time to think it over."

"Your Honor, this—"

"Quiet, Counselor. You have done your client no favors during these proceedings. Your whole strategy was to attack the police here, to smear as racist an officer simply doing his job, an officer, I might add, of the same race as the defendant. I do not wish to paint your client with the foul brush you have used before this court but your actions leave me little choice. Mr. Porter, you have some lessons to learn. One, stay away from stolen cars. Two, stay away from illegal drugs. Three, stay away from lawyers like Mr. Carl."

"This is uncalled for—"

"Shut up, Mr. Carl. Mr. Porter is hereby sentenced to one year incarceration, no part of that to be suspended."

"Excuse me?"

"You heard right."

"Judge."

"Quiet, Mr. Carl."

"That is an entirely inappropriate sentence for—"

"He was found with an ounce and a quarter, Mr. Carl. That takes him out of the personal-use category."

"By five grams, Your Honor? An extra eleven months for five grams? That's outrageous."

"No, sir," he bellowed, his face swollen near to bursting, "it is you who are outrageous. One more word from you and I'll find you in contempt."

I stared in disbelief at Judge Wellman, his face dark with an inexplicable anger, his hands shaking on the bench. Rashard was standing next to me, looking at me, wondering what had just happened to him. From behind I heard a "Dear Lord," coming from Mrs. Porter. Clerk Templeton was staring at me with victory in her eyes. I looked around and tried to understand. A year? Rashard was going to jail for a year? What the hell was going on? This was wrong, dead wrong. Judges get it wrong, that is another of the three immutable laws of the legal profession, but this judge wasn't getting it wrong for the usual reasons, out of ignorance or sloth or plain prejudice. No, this judge was getting it wrong simply because I was on the side of the right. Here was my final proof that the law had turned against me, but not only me. The law had also turned against anyone in any way connected to me, and it was moving with an unimaginable fury.

"You want to find me in contempt, Judge," I said. "Don't bother looking too hard, I'm there already."

"Five hundred dollars, Mr. Carl. Anything else to say?"

"He got to you too, didn't he?"

"A thousand dollars."

"You're just a tool for that bastard."

"Fifteen hundred."

"Go to hell."

"Two thousand. Another word from you and you go to jail."

I was about to loose a stream of invective but I stopped. It would feel grand, but it wouldn't do any good, it wouldn't help my client. There was only one place I could go to help my client now, and jail wasn't it.

"Step back, Mr. Porter," said the judge. "Bailiff, please escort Mr. Porter out of the courtroom."

As the bailiff started to take hold of Rashard, I put my arm around his shoulder. "This won't stand," I said to him softly. "I'll get you out."

"Mr. Carl . . ." said Rashard. The promise of his future was leaking out of his eyes along with his tears of incomprehension. He had trusted me and now there was this.

"Rashard," I said. "Listen to me. This has nothing to do with you. I'll get you out soon, I promise."

The bailiff appeared, holding out his handcuffs.

I gave Rashard a smile and a nod and told him not to do anything to make it worse. Then I started packing up my briefcase.

"Going somewhere, Mr. Carl?" said the judge.

I didn't answer, I finished putting my papers in the briefcase, closed it with a click, turned to ADA Carter.

"This isn't right," I said to her.

"I don't know what happened," she said.

"I do," I said. "And it isn't right."

"Going somewhere, Mr. Carl?" said the judge again, this time as I was walking down the aisle toward the door. "We're not finished here," he called after me.

I stopped, turned. "Oh yes, we are," I said. "Now crawl back to your hole and get that bastard on the phone and tell him I'm on my way."

CHAPTER
46

After scowling at the security camera and being buzzed through the security doors, I barged into the justice's reception area loaded for bear. The closest thing I found was Curtis Lobban, the justice's clerk. He was waiting for me, standing tall and broad, his suit black, his shirt white, his muted tie tied tight. His huge hands, empty of files or books, hung ready at his sides. He stood there before me like the personification of somber power and I stopped my barging at the very sight of him.

"These chambers, they are off limits to the public," he said, his deep voice soft and yet all the more menacing for its tone.

"I'm not here as a member of the public," I said.

"But that's all you are," he said. "Λ insignificant man without a scintilla of importance. You are not welcome here. You will leave one way or the other. One way is preferable to you, I suppose, but as to me, I don't care. Just so you leave."

The justice's secretary was away from her desk, there was no one waiting in the waiting room. It was Curtis who had buzzed me through and now it was just me and him, and him took a step forward.

"You're going to throw me out bodily?"

"If I must."

"You and what army?"

He looked at me, big somber Curtis Lobban, he looked at my pencil neck, my flagpole arms, my fists like pale undersized fish. "Do everyone a favor, Mr. Carl, especially yourself. Go on away home and leave us be."

"Who are you talking for?"

"All of us, the justice, Mrs. Straczynski, my own wife."

"Your wife?"

His fists clenched. "Don't think I don't know about the man you sent around to spy on us."

"I didn't send anyone to spy on your wife."

"She is ill. You have disturbed her delicate equilibrium. This whole affair has left her distraught. Go away, Mr. Carl, leave us alone. Leave us in peace."

"I'm here to see the justice, Curtis."

"He doesn't want to see you."

"He'll see me."

"No, he won't. And you know how I know? Because I am his file clerk. He does nothing without my say so. If a file is pushed to the top of the list, action is taken immediately, a decision is made, an opinion is written, an appeal denied or granted. Life moves on either way because I said it should. And if a file is shuffled to the bottom of the pile, or is somehow for some reason mysteriously misplaced, then it is as if time itself has stopped its course. There is no yes, there is no no, there is nothing. And all the world waits. You see, Mr. Carl, I keep the files, create the schedule, man the doors. I decide who comes in and who stays out."

"So you're the gatekeeper of justice, is that it? The gray ferryman with glowing eyes?"

"Yes, that it is, exactly. You know who got it for me, this job? The Mrs."

"Alura?"

"She is something of a saint."

"She's a spider."

"Maybe that too. But you only know that part of her, not the other part."

"I know enough."

"You know nothing. Go away, Mr. Carl. Go away and stay away and maybe things will take care of themselves. But know this," he hissed, "you are trespassing and you've had your warning."

There it was, that same voice, the exact same words. He had hid his accent that night in the vestibule, but I could still tell. *You are not welcome here,* he had said. *You are trespassing,* he had said. And the word "scintilla," a legal term that rolled so easily off his tongue, sort of like the rules of adverse possession had rolled so easily off his tongue when his foot was on my face.

"So it was you," I said, "along with your buddy O'Brien."

"If you persist, I'll have you arrested."

"You can do better than that, Curtis," I said. "You already had me arrested, in Traffic Court, and still, here I am. I've been beaten, thrown in jail, cited for contempt, and now my client has ended up totally screwed by some Common Pleas hack. So what's next? What's your boss going to do to me now? Revoke my citizenship? Have me deported to Lithuania? What?"

"You do not understand."

"Enlighten me."

"He is an important man."

"No, he's not. He's a speck of dirt in the public eye."

His eyes opened wide, a smile appeared. "So, this is political after all."

"No, Curtis. It's not political, it's personal."

I started for the library.

He took a step in the same direction.

I stopped.

He stopped.

Then I was off, tearing to the entrance to the library, throwing open the door, sprinting toward the big oaken table, Curtis following close by my heels. A law clerk was sitting at the big table, looking up from her book, her jaw dropping at the sight of me rushing in and Curtis Lobban rushing after me.

When I reached the table I tossed an empty chair behind me. I heard a smack, something falling, a grunt, a curse.

The law clerk stood up and said something snooty. I tossed her chair too.

When I reached the end of the room, I flung open the justice's door. He was sitting at his desk, hunched over a document. The justice looked up just as Curtis Lobban reached me and flung his thick arm around my neck.

"Mr. Carl," said the justice as Curtis lifted me off the ground. "I didn't know you had an appointment."

I let out an unintelligible grunt.

"No appointment?" he said. "I suppose that explains Curtis's handling of the matter."

I let out an unintelligible bray.

"A grip like that, you know, can be fatal. There have been cases. You really should have made an appointment."

I let out an unintelligible bleat.

"I'll hold him for the police," said Curtis, starting to drag me away even as I flailed at his arm.

"No, let him go. Men like Mr. Carl are like the weather. You have no choice but to suffer through them until a strong enough wind comes to blow them away."

Curtis tightened his grip. My eyes bulged.

"Let him go," said the justice.

Curtis released me. I landed on two shaky legs and lurched this way and that, trying to catch my breath and my balance, staggering around like a drunken Groucho Marx.

"You can leave us, Curtis."

"But Mr. Justice, he—"

"It will be fine, Curtis. I think I can handle Mr. Carl myself."

Curtis Lobban glared at me for a moment and then spun around and left, heading to some far off room. The justice went back to his paperwork. I collapsed into one of the chairs before his ornate desk and rubbed my neck. It wasn't long before one of the lines on the phone lit. The justice turned his head to the lit line, then raised his eyes to see that I had seen it too.

"He's calling your wife," I said.

"Most likely," he said, just as the white cat leaped atop his desk. "She makes it a practice of being kept informed of my business."

"And you're kept informed of hers?"

"As much as I care to," he said, scratching the cat's back, "which isn't much. You don't have an appointment. I don't see lawyers without appointments."

"I came about Rashard Porter," I said.

"Porter?" said the justice. "Rashard Porter? I don't recognize the name."

"He's a client. He was sentenced this afternoon to a year in prison for a crime that warranted probation at worst."

"And you've come to see me about a case? How wonderfully improper. An ex-parte discussion with a sitting Supreme Court justice about an ongoing criminal case." The cat curled to sitting on the corner of the desk, the justice went back to his paperwork. "I suppose the Bar Association will have something to say about this."

"The DA and the presentencing officer in Mr. Porter's case all agreed that probation was the proper sentence.

He's a kid with a future. He was accepted into art school. Everything was set until the judge turned around and slammed him with a year."

"Then it appears you have grounds for your appeal. But until it reaches my level there is nothing I can do, and now, because of this meeting, I would have to recuse myself in any event. Is that all you came in here for, to ruin your career? Because trust me, Mr. Carl, when the Bar Association gets through with you, it will be ruined."

"He was sentenced to a year because I was his lawyer, and because the word is out that I am to get screwed at every turn."

"Really? That is troubling—for you. And who put out the word?"

"Don't play the ignorant puss with me."

"Oh, Mr. Carl. You've become paranoid."

"Maybe, but that doesn't mean you're not out to get me. After our first meeting you chewed out the District Attorney and I got hauled into the DA's office and had my ass chewed out in turn. And right after that you ordered the sheriff to stop helping my collection action against Derek Manley. Then you had my name incorrectly placed on a bench warrant from Lackawanna County that ended up sending me to jail. And now you unjustly screwed my client, Rashard Porter, to the wall."

"I did all this."

"Of course you did." Pause. "Didn't you?"

It wasn't any denial that caused my doubt, it was the evident pain on his face. As I went through the litany of indignities recently heaped upon me by the law, he seemed more and more in agony, as if a kidney stone was starting to move slowly and painfully through his system. And even as he spoke, it was as if the stone continued to move, push, chew its way through.

"Have you learned anything new about Tommy Greeley's disappearance?" he said.

"Worried?"

"Curious. About a lost friend."

"I've learned that just before his disappearance he was cheating on his girlfriend."

"Cheating on Sylvia?"

"That's right. With two different women, both married."

"Tommy was ever the dog, wasn't he?"

"One was a woman named Chelsea. Her husband, Lonnie, was pretty steamed about it. Did you ever meet him? Lonnie Chambers?"

"I don't think so."

"Owns a motorcycle shop in Queens Village."

"Doesn't ring a bell."

"And the other woman he was sleeping with was your wife."

The justice winced, but not from shock. He twisted around as if in utter pain, as if the kidney stone was continuing to grind its way. The white cat stood up, stared at me for a moment, then stepped over to rub its cheek on the back of the justice's neck.

"Where did you hear that?" the justice said.

"She told me."

"Of course she did."

"Are you all right, Mr. Justice?"

"I think you should go."

"My client. Rashard Porter."

"Who was the judge?"

"Wellman."

"Common Pleas?"

"That's right."

"I'll take a look."

"I want more than a look."

"We all want more than we can have. Good evening, Mr. Carl."

He turned around to face me, grimaced, pushed the cat off his desk even as he dismissed me with a wave. The cat stalked off. I waited for a bit and then stood, walked toward the entrance. But before I reached the door I stopped and turned around.

"Did you know about Tommy and your wife?"

"Does it matter?" he said without looking up.

"Yes, it does."

"I don't intrude on my wife's affairs."

"But maybe they intruded on their own. Lonnie Chambers. He came to you, didn't he?"

"I said I didn't recognize the name."

"Then we'll have to see if he recognizes yours."

"Good evening, Mr. Carl."

I stayed there for a moment more, watching him try to work. His head was down, his pen was moving, but the pain was still there, the stone was still working its brutal way through his system, and I sensed just then that it had been working its way through his system for many many years.

"Why do you stay with her?" I said.

He looked up, puzzled for a moment at the question, and then nodded his head. "You're not married, are you, Mr. Carl?" he said.

"No."

"Well, then, here's some advice from an old married man. Don't ever presume to understand what is happening between a husband and a wife. Nothing in this world appears more transparent, and yet is more inscrutable, than someone else's marriage."

CHAPTER

47

I didn't know I was in a race. If I had known I was in a race I wouldn't have gone back to the office after my meeting with the justice. I wouldn't have briefed Beth on what had happened to Rashard. I wouldn't have called Rashard's mother to tell her it was all being taken care of, that I had already taken her son's problem to the highest levels. If I had known time was of the essence I wouldn't have answered my mail and filled in my time sheets before showing up to ask my question. And that's all I had, one question, a single question, whose answer I already knew.

The sign of the Chop Shop consisted primarily of a huge Harley-Davidson logo, with the store's name in small block letters beneath the great orange shield. It was a storefront on a narrow road in a grimy commercial part of the city just a few blocks south of South Street. By the time I got there it was dark already and the stores on either side of it were closed for the night and the street was empty. I thought I might be too late, that Lonnie might be gone for the night, but through the bars protecting the plate-glass window I could see a dim light.

I pushed open the door. A cowbell jangled.

The narrow front of the store was a jumble of parts and

accessories, exhaust pipes, saddlebags, gas tanks, tires, a row of handlebars fastened to the wall. The counter was piled with old engine fittings, loose papers, greasy rags, but it wasn't the mess that struck me first when I entered, it was the reek, a strong and vile combination of ammonia and gasoline and the sharp acridity of methyl alcohol. It forced me to put a hand over my nose.

"Lonnie?" I called out. "Yo, Lonnie. You there?"

No answer.

I made my way around the counter, through a dark doorway into a large space, lit thinly by a soft glow emanating from the rear. The reek became stronger, like a noisome wall, and I gagged as I moved forward. In the shadows I could see parts of a grease-stained cement floor, cinder-block walls, workbenches, hulking motorcycles in various states of being ripped apart.

"Lonnie?"

No answer.

Beyond was a wide, closed door, which I assumed led to the alleyway in the back, through which the bikes were brought. He might be in the alley, I figured. I carefully made my way around the workshop and headed for the door. The foul stench grew stronger, thick and vile, overpowering, it burned my nose and throat, my eyes. I coughed and thought I heard another.

"Lonnie?"

I hurried my pace, tripped over something metal, headed for the alley and fresh air, and then, just as I reached for the door, I tripped over something else.

I stopped, turned to see what it was.

"My God."

A body, faceup, lying half in–half out of a small office beside the doorway to the alley, a body lit softly by a flicker of blue fire. I reached into the office, felt around for a switch.

"Oh my God."

It was Lonnie, of course it was Lonnie.

He was lying on the floor, between two workbenches. The benches were filled with beakers and burners and vials set up in the whole mad scientist configuration, flames shooting out here and there, and the smell in that room was murderous. Even as I fought to hold my breath, my skin itched and my eyes burned and the chemical reek was like a living thing fighting to keep me away.

I leaned over him. He was warm, still. His face was in a snarl, his hands were clenched, a wrench in one of them, and there was a small hole in his forehead. From the thick pool beneath his head I didn't need to imagine what the back looked like. I turned to the side and threw up.

And over the brutal sound of my retching I heard something in the shop, a piece of metal spinning across the floor.

I leaped up, turned back to the shop, saw a shadow flit out of the doorway. I ran toward it. I ran toward it and something jabbed into my thigh and I flipped over. I fell hard onto my shoulder just as something heavy and metallic crashed beside me and a burning ran up my leg.

I tried to push myself up but I couldn't, my leg was trapped by a fallen bike. I grabbed the edge of the seat, heaved, yanked my leg free, and started again toward the shadow, banging my hurt shoulder into the door. The pain spun me around and knocked me to my knees.

I grabbed hold of the doorjamb, pulled myself up, headed again through the dark passageway toward the front.

All I wanted was a glimpse, I didn't want to stop him, I

was willing to let him go, that fit my style, no heroics, let him go, absolutely, but I wanted a glimpse, I needed a glimpse.

I lunged for the door and pushed it open and as soon as I did the store behind me exploded.

CHAPTER

48

There is something perversely cheerful about a crime scene in the middle of the night, the pulsating red and blue lights, the great beams of white, the strobes of—aw, the hell with it.

There was nothing cheerful about what was happening outside the Chop Shop as it burned to the ground along with the two stores on either side of it. The fire trucks came with remarkable speed and the firefighters moved with the calm alacrity of men and women used to holding back the thin yet lethal edge of entropy, but there was not much they could do, what with all the accelerants, both legal and illegal, in Lonnie's shop feeding the ferocity of the fire. It was Lonnie who had supplied meth to the gang twenty years ago, Lonnie with the wild burning eyes, and I supposed he had gotten back into the business.

Coughing all the while, I told a fire captain everything of what I had seen inside and he told me I should tell it to the fire investigators. I told the fire investigators everything of what I had seen inside and they told me to tell it again to the uniformed police. I told one of the uniformed police everything of what I had seen inside and she told me to wait for the police detectives to arrive.

"Get McDeiss," I said.

She raised an eyebrow at me.

"Tell him Victor Carl is the witness. He'll show."

I stood off to the side, my arms tight around my chest, waiting for the detectives. And then at the edge of the crowd I saw her, staring at the scene with wet eyes, her pretty face drained of all emotion except pain. Chelsea. I walked over to her, lifted the yellow tape. When one of the uniforms started giving me a hassle I just stared at him for a moment and he backed off. I brought Chelsea away from the crowd, to a spot where the fire's heat could still be felt.

"They said someone was dead," she said.

"Yes."

"Is it . . ."

"Yes," I said, reaching out and pulling her toward me, holding her as she cried.

"Damn him," she said, her tears hitting now the street. "Damn him."

"Who?"

"I told him to stop. I told him it was crazy dangerous. But he missed it. All this talk about the old days. His time in the center of it was coming back to him and he couldn't help himself. But it's like Cooper says, the old road always ends in despair."

"But it wasn't just a fire, Chelsea."

She pulled away, looked up at me.

"He was murdered," I said.

"No. It can't be."

"I found his body. Before the fire. He was shot."

"Stop."

"Any idea who?"

"No."

"Any enemies?"

"No. No." She turned toward the burning building, watched as the fire succumbed to the torrents of water. "Everyone loved him. He was just a kid. An old kid. He never grew up. But there was something rich about him, as if the current of life moved raw through his body. People felt more alive just being near him."

"And he loved you."

"Yes."

"Always and forever."

She bowed her head. "Yes."

"It was in his eyes every time he looked at you."

"Victor, what am I going to do?"

"What does Cooper say? He seems to have the answer to everything."

"You know what he says, Victor? He says the living go on dying, only the dead will rise unchanged."

"What does that mean?"

"I don't know, but right now I hope it's true."

Chelsea and I were still standing together some twenty minutes later when Detective McDeiss, wearing his black porkpie hat, ducked beneath the yellow tape, accompanied by our good friend K. Lawrence Slocum. By then the blaze was under control, the crowd had lessened, the street was strewn with water and debris, the air foul with the burning.

"Everywhere you show up is a party, Carl," said McDeiss, shaking his head as he scanned the desolation, acting as if I was the root cause of the current tragedy. "We ought to put a bell around your neck."

I introduced the detective and Slocum to Chelsea, told them she was the dead man's ex-wife. McDeiss asked a few questions and then led her to another officer.

"The detective will take her home after he gets a full statement," said McDeiss after he returned.

"Thank you."

"I suppose she'll have to identify him."

"I don't think there'll be much to identify."

"Probably not," said McDeiss.

"All right," said Slocum. "What happened?"

"I've told it three times already."

"Tell it again," he said, and so I did, everything from the moment I stepped into the shop until it blew up behind me.

"You see who it was who was running?" said McDeiss.

"No. As soon as I opened the door the place exploded and I was kissing pavement. It was all I could do to get to the other side of the street and away from the flames. By the time I remembered to look around there was nothing."

"Did you call nine-one-one?"

"With my cell."

Slocum was shaking his head at the ruined buildings, the singed facades of brick, the devoured roofs with just parts of the skeletal structure still poking through.

"You sure he was shot?" said McDeiss.

"Pretty sure. I didn't have time for an autopsy."

"Maybe he just was overcome by the fumes and fell. Dangerous thing cooking up crank."

"It looked like he was shot."

"Any idea of the caliber?"

"Look, I'm not Charlton Heston, all right. Only thing I know about guns is that when I see one I cringe and say, 'No, please, don't shoot.' "

Slocum rubbed his hand with his mouth. "Okay, Carl," he said. "I'm afraid to ask but I'm going to anyway. Who was he, this Lonnie Chambers?"

"Twenty years ago," I said, "he was in Tommy Greeley's drug ring."

Slocum rubbed his mouth again. McDeiss turned around and kicked the curb and then hopped around in pain.

"Here's the story," I said. "Twenty years ago Tommy Greeley was sleeping with Lonnie Chambers's wife. Lonnie didn't like that. Lonnie went to Tommy's girlfriend to tell her about it, but she didn't react like he had hoped. She had her own issues to deal with. So Lonnie started following Tommy to find who else he might be screwing and he did, yes he did."

"Who?" said Slocum.

"Who do you think?"

"Jesus Christ, Carl. Didn't we talk about this?"

"She came to me."

"And what about him? Have you been a good boy?"

"Until today."

"Carl."

"A client who should be in art school was stepped back into prison as a way for that bastard to get back at me. The client's a good kid and he's going to jail just so that bastard can make his point."

"You're exaggerating."

"Really? Talk to the ADA, Melissa Carter, see what she has to say. She was as shocked at the sentence as I was. And remember I told you I was beat up and threatened in my vestibule. I'm certain it was his file clerk, a man named Curtis Lobban, who did the beating and the threatening."

"You said you didn't see a face."

"I recognized his voice."

"That will sure convince a jury. You promised you'd stay away from them."

"She's a vampire," I said, "and he's a murderer."

"He's a Supreme Court justice."

"And a murderer."

"You don't know."

"It's pretty clear to me."

"You sure this Lonnie found out about the two of them?"

"She told me so yesterday."

"You sure he told the justice about it?"

"Pretty sure. It seems like he was looking for someone to tell. I was going to ask Lonnie about it just to be certain. That's why I was here. But I mentioned Lonnie to the justice today. I even told him where the shop was." As it dawned on me, I spun around in frustration. "I led the bastard right to him."

"So you're not sure that Lonnie told the justice back then."

"Not absolutely, no. But that's exactly why he killed Lonnie and set the place on fire. That's exactly why he killed Joey, because Joey could have traced back the killing of Tommy Greeley to him. He's covering his tracks. And that's how I ended up in jail when you bailed me out, because of him. He's doing what he can to discredit and discourage me because I am on to him."

"Or maybe it was simply an entry error."

"You don't believe that. You *don't* believe that."

"And maybe this Lonnie was killed by someone not so happy about a competitor cooking up methamphetamine and selling it on his turf. Perhaps one of the local motorcycle gangs who run the business up and down the East Coast."

"You're looking to look the other way."

"It's a tough business he was in," said Slocum.

"How does Babbage fit into your theory?" said McDeiss. "Why would the justice care about Babbage?"

"Maybe Babbage knew something to connect Straczynski to the drug ring. Or maybe Babbage's death was just a heart attack."

"Montgomery County coroner, when I asked him, seemed to think it was exactly that," said McDeiss. "Acute myocardial infarction. Only when I looked at the report something seemed a little off. Some missing hair off the back part of his scalp."

"Oh?"

"Torn out."

"It's him, I'm telling you."

"It sounds personal," said Slocum.

"He killed one client. Stepped back another into an unjust sentence. He sent his clerk out to beat me up. He threw me in jail. And now he almost incinerated me. Yeah. It's personal."

"How's your dad?" said Slocum.

"Not good," I said, "and getting worse," and as I said it a wave of hopelessness washed over me. It started with my thinking about my father, who was indeed getting worse, every day, every hour, and there was nothing I could do about it, but it wasn't just my father. I was up against a man whose power was beyond my comprehension, who could throw me in jail, ruin my clients, kill my friends with impunity. I was up against a man who could destroy me absolutely, if he wanted, and he apparently wanted. And the two men in the city's employ that I admired most, that I had trusted could help me, were turning their backs on what I was sure was the truth. And there was nothing, nothing I could do about it. Nothing.

"He's going to get away with it," I said, my voice flat with despondency.

"Why don't you go clean up and then visit your father in the hospital," said Slocum.

"It's past visiting hours."

"Go on home then, Victor. Get some rest."

"You aren't going to do anything. He's too powerful."

"Get some rest," said Slocum.

"You're terrified of him."

"By the way," said Slocum. "You'll find out tomorrow. The Bar Association has started proceedings against you on the Derek Manley thing. They're going to try to pull your ticket."

"It's him. Don't you see? Don't you?"

"Go home and get some rest, Victor. We'll be in touch. Just go home."

I went home.

I left Slocum and McDeiss huddled on the sodden, scarred street and went home. My suit stank of smoke and chemicals, was ripped at the knee and the shoulder, a total goner, as were my shirt and socks, all of it smelling as if I had been dancing like a medicine man in the middle of a campfire. Only my tie came through unscathed. But I didn't undress as soon as I came home, didn't strip and shower and scrub the stench of the black night off my skin and out of my hair. Instead, I went straight to the photographs pinned to my wall and began, one by one, to rip them down.

They repulsed me, now that I knew how they were taken and whom they were of. One by one I ripped them down and let them drop like dead leaves onto the floor. One by one. But then I stopped.

It was the despair that was driving me, I realized, not the photographs. There was still something clean about them, something of the ideal in them. They had captured not Alura Straczynski, in all her vainglory, but instead the dreams and hopes of Tommy Greeley. I could imagine him, atop his collapsing drug enterprise, the dogged Telushkin sniffing here, sniffing there, getting closer to closing it down and putting him in jail. But there, in that spider's web of a studio, behind the barrier of a camera, Tommy Greeley maybe thought he spied something true and pure, something that might be able to save his life. And he captured it. Snap snap. And it was still alive, on my wall. And even if it had proved a pathetic illusion, there it was, the thing he prayed would transform his life. On my wall.

My father had felt the same way as Tommy Greeley, I was sure, about the love of his life, his Angel. And though that vision had proven just as illusory, just having it was more than I had ever given him credit for. My father. It was all almost enough to give me some hope.

But only almost. Because I knew the truth of it, the truth behind everything. That our certainties are all false, our dreams are all lies, our loves will always betray us.

The living go on dying, only the dead will rise unchanged.

Maybe he was right, Cooper Prod, meditating on the sins of his past in his prison ashram. Maybe the only hope for life was death.

It was too late to visit, but I called the fourth-floor nurses' desk anyway, just to find out how he was doing, my father, how he was doing.

Not so well.

CHAPTER

49

"Victor?"

I looked up. Dr. Mayonnaise was in the room. Her head was tilted funny, as if once again, when she looked at me, she was seeing an art work that made no sense. This time a Magritte painting perhaps.

"Hi," I said.

"Are you okay?"

"Sure," I said.

"Is there anything I can get you?"

"No, I'm fine."

"What happened to your forehead?"

"A pigeon I kicked flew up and punched me in the head."

"While you were playing golf?"

"How did you know?"

"You want me to look at it?"

"No."

"We're doing everything we can."

"I know you are."

"It's still too early to tell whether the Primaxin is working. Sometimes the lag between first administering the drug and seeing a definite result can be seventy-two hours."

"Okay."

"I know it looks bad, Victor, but in these cases it's the best thing for him. His heart rate is down, his oxygen level up."

"That's good," I said.

"Indicators are promising."

"I can tell," I said, as I looked over at my father.

He was out, more unconscious than asleep, which I suppose was a good thing, considering there was a blue tube snaking down his throat. The respirator bellows were drawing and blowing at a steady clip, the heart monitor was letting out a steady bleep. He was being kept alive by a machine while they waited to determine that the latest antibiotic also was having no effect on the disease that plagued him. They were stumped, the doctors, stumped by my father, which put them in the same uncertain place I had stood toward him for the entirety of my life. I wasn't sure of the reasons for my own bewilderment, Freud would have a better theory for that than I could ever come up with, but I knew why the doctors were confused. They thought they were fighting a mere microbe, but what they were up against was far more virulent. The thing destroying my father piece by piece was his past.

"I'll inform you if there's any change," she said.

"Thank you."

"Let me get you some Kleenex."

"I'm okay, really,"

"Your tie's getting wet."

"Don't worry," I said. "It's indestructible."

"Handy."

"Can you do one thing for me, Karen?"

"What, Victor?"

"Can you save his life? Please."

She looked stricken.

"Can you? Please? Save his life?"

"Let me get you the Kleenex," she said.

"Okay," I said. I felt sorry for her, just then, Dr. Mayonnaise from Ohio. It was going to be a long career, fetching Kleenex and going around saying things like *Indicators are promising.* I used to jealous of doctors, the money they made, the status of their little degrees, the way everyone bowed and scraped in their presence and made it a point to use the honorific before their names, as if it were a sign of higher nobility. *Excuse me, Lord Wentworth, I'll have a table for you in a few minutes, but first I have to take care of Dr. Finster. He's a gastroenterologist, you know.* I used to be jealous of doctors, but not anymore. Dr. Mayonnaise was welcome to it, the money included. Before her time was up she'd earn it.

I sat alone in the room with just my father and my hopelessness for a long time. It was surprisingly peaceful there, with the predictable rhythm of the bellows. Resignation is a very peaceful emotion. I was through, I told myself, it was over. Joey Parma had given me a murder and now I was giving it back, along with his own. It was too hard, I didn't have enough fight in me. The bastard behind everything had the law on his side and he had won. Maybe I'd be able to save my career, maybe my life would return to where it was before McDeiss called me to the crime scene, maybe I'd finally get my cable back. It was funny how comforting maybe had become. And as I made that decision to give up, finally, my body unclenched and I caught myself once and then twice, my chin falling, my eyes drifting shut before they snapped open in panic. And then I didn't catch myself, I let myself slide into sleep, beside my father, with the soft rhythm of the bellows.

A nurse shook me awake.

"I'm sorry," I said as I jerked to a stiff position. "I know I shouldn't. I'm sorry."

"It's okay, Mr. Carl. You're allowed to sleep. That's not why I woke you. You have a visitor."

"I'm not a patient," I said.

"Not yet," she said, with a maternal smile. "But none the less, someone is here to see you. But he's not allowed in the room."

"Okay."

"You'll have to go out to see him."

"Okay," I said and I did. And he was waiting for me, leaning at the nurses' desk, hat in hand, chatting away, making the cute night nurse blush.

Skink.

CHAPTER

50

"**I knew a** girl once, name of Gwendolyn," said Skink. "Gwendolyn, not Gwen. She wasn't one of them thin twigs everyone goes for now. Gwendolyn had breasts like great piles of pudding, they was. I used to love my pudding. Tapioca. With the whip cream. Not no more though, on account of the cholesterol. But Gwendolyn was a lovely girl, nice feet she had, and we had us a lovely time. This was when I was living in Fresno. The girls there they didn't put on no airs. Of course what kind of airs was you going to put on in Fresno? Still. Gwendolyn."

Skink and I were in the hospital cafeteria. I had bought a coffee, an egg salad on white, and a bag of potato chips for my dinner. I brought half the limp sandwich up to my mouth and Skink stared at it as if it were some exotic island grub I was sticking into my craw.

"What?" I said.

"Why don't you just inject a pound of lard into your veins and get it over with?"

I took a bite of the sandwich and, with my mouth still full, I said, "Get on with it, Phil. Why are you telling me about lost loves?"

"Just shut up and listen. So one night I put on the Old Spice, grease back the hair, stuff a handkerchief in the suit pocket, and I'm ready for a night. I picks up my Gwendolyn, takes her to this frilly grease trough, what with candles and a violin. Dinner and a show and the show, it's going to be back at her place. So I'm laying on the sweet talk, laying it on so thick my tie is curling, when she ups and says, 'Philip, we need to talk.' "

"You don't have to go any farther." I opened up the bag of chips, offered it to Skink. "You want?"

"Don't be daft. So that's the last of her, I figure. She's a good-enough sport to give me a final plow for old time's sake, but that's the end. No more pudding for Mr. Skink. The last I figure I'd ever see of lovely Gwendolyn. But I was wrong, wasn't I? The next night, who's knocking at my door?"

"Gwendolyn?"

"Just wanting to see how I was doing. I'm doing fine, I says. Good, she says. You want to catch a movie? I thought we broke up, I says. We did, she says. So what's with the movie? I says. We can still be friends, she says. I wasn't in it for the friendship, I says. Oh, Philip, she says. Go put on a jacket. And damn if I didn't. You see what I'm getting at here, Victor?"

"Not quite."

"I began seeing more of Gwendolyn after we split up than I ever did when we was parallel parking. Every night she's stopping over or calling on the phone to check on me, make sure I was up and chirpy. One night I even found myself out drinking with Gwendolyn and her flock, some girls what made Gwendolyn look like a queen by comparison and a few other Joes what she also was at one time doing the boink but were now strictly friends. A little too pathetic there, don't you think? That was it for me. Bye-bye Gwendolyn, bye-bye Fresno. She's married now with a couple boys in the army, but Gwendolyn, she's still sending me Christmas cards. You see there, Victor, some girls, they ain't as interested in the bouncing as they are in the collecting."

"Okay. So?"

"Your Alura Straczynski, she's like my Gwendolyn, she is. A collector."

I stopped eating my sandwich, narrowed my eyes. "What do you mean?"

He took out his notebook, licked his thumb. "You'll be getting a full report, all names and numbers, along with my invoice. But I thought you might be wanting a preliminary idea of what I found. Every night she's Mrs. Straczynski, out with her husband, doing the rounds, like the perfect little helpmeet. But each morning she's up and out at the crack. Has got her errands to run, doesn't she? Busy girl."

"Go ahead."

"There's a bloke in a nursing home. He ain't much for conversation, never says a thing, had some sort of attack that left him like an eggplant, but she's there every day, visiting, reading to him. There's a panhandler on the street, his spot is Sixteenth and Locust, and she drops him a sandwich every day, and a kind word to boot. There's a print shop she has some sort of interest in, not a copy machine place, but a real honest-to-god print shop where they got this huge old press and they hand sew the books they prints up. She stops in every now and then, helping out the staff, sometimes coming out with her hands black with ink. And there's an invalid woman she pays call on every other afternoon or so and stays a bit. I was wondering about that so I knocked on the door, tried to sell the lady some knives."

"How'd you do?"

"No sale. Even though it is guaranteed to be the best knife you've ever used or your money back. Cutco. I keep a sample case in my car for when I need to go knocking on a door. Tools of the trade, so to speak. Sometimes I even get an order. Every dollar helps. But even without the sale it was a profitable visit. Because there she was, your Alura Straczynski, cooking up something in the kitchen."

"Are you sure? This doesn't sound like her."

"You ain't getting it, are you. It wasn't no charity work. It's like she has all these different family members what she collected. See what I mean?"

"Okay," I said, and then a thought struck about the invalid woman who had refused to buy the knives. *She is ill,* had said the justice's file clerk about his wife. *You have disturbed her delicate equilibrium.* "What was her name, the woman Mrs. Straczynski was caring for."

"Lobban," he said. "Matilda Lobban."

"Surprise, surprise. What else did you find?"

"Something good. Something you'll love. There was meetings and visitors to that studio place of hers. Usually men, but some women too. You was one of the visitors, drinking with her at that bar she's always at, she likes a drink she does, and then just the other day you going up to her studio."

"Business," I said, picking up the other half of the sandwich, taking a bite.

"Sure it was. I ain't here to judge." He gave a judgmental wink. "But there was others too. Somes I didn't recognize. But one I did, one I couldn't help but."

"Who?"

"And it wasn't just one time neither, him climbing up the stairs to that place of hers in the old factory building."

"Let's go, Phil. Just tell me who."

"But it must not have been going on too long, this one, or I'd a seen it before, wouldn't I?"

It was in the way he smiled his gap-toothed smile, it was in the way his eyes laughed. I saw his grinning little mug and the idea, crazy as it seemed, started forming. I put down what was left of the sandwich.

"No," I said.

"Oh yes."

"You're shitting me."

"Am I?"

"Don't."

"And it's almost sweet in its way, innit it?"

"Stop."

"Like a little family reunion. The way your Alura Straczynski, she's been spending quality time with your—"

"Frigging Eddie Dean," I said.

It didn't hit me right off, the possibility.

I tried to figure it, how Alura Straczynski and Eddie Dean might have gotten together. Even though I had decided to give up the chase, I couldn't help but try to figure it, yet nothing made any sense. A chance meeting on the street? At the same table at some fund-raiser for that rusting old liner he seemed to care so much about? Mutual friends? Kimberly? And I tried to make sense of the way the justice reacted when I told him all that had happened to me. He was my main suspect, absolutely, but he twisted around in a strange pain as if it were all being done to him as much as to me. Nothing but puzzles.

You work with puzzles long enough, your brain gets fried, and everything that had happened the last couple days had given me a pretty good head start. So after Skink left I went back up to sit a bit with my father and tried to think it through and failed. My mind, overworked and congenitally underpowered, went blank. Went blank. I simply sat there and watched my father and read the ever-changing lines of data on the monitors and listened to the sad iambic song of the respirator, in out, in out.

And then it came, as if sailing in from a place of great distance, it came, the possibility, first a dot and then a fly and then it grew and swelled until suddenly it burst out of the unconscious and shattered the bland quiet of my conscious mind. And with the quiet was shattered my hopeless resignation too.

"Oh my God," I said out loud.

I used my father's phone to make the call, and the party I called was Kimberly Blue.

"We're taking a trip," I said. "Tomorrow morning. Early. I'll pick you up outside your apartment, let's say at seven. No, not Eddie Dean's house, your apartment. I don't want your boss to know what we're doing. Trust me, all right. Just tell him you'll be busy with a friend or something and then I'll pick you up. You said you had some questions, right? I think I know where to find the answers, just so long as you let me do the talking. Maybe one night. Just south of Boston. The Shoe City of the World, remember? A little town called Brockton."

CHAPTER

51

A great Russian writer once wrote that happy families are all alike, while each unhappy family is unhappy in its own way. Like all oft-quoted lines from bona fide geniuses, it remains a truism beyond question—and yet from the moment I first read that famous first line I had my doubts. Raised, as I was, in an unhappy family that shattered apart before I was out of the single digits, I always believed the exotic and differentiated lives were lived on the other side of the dividing line between happy and not. The happy families I knew seemed to burst with possibilities; the permutations of their varied interests and eccentricities, the diversity of their achievements, the myriad of strange traditions and customs culled from their everyday happiness seemed unending. The life of our unhappy family was stunted and dark by comparison and the families of other kids in similarly unhappy situations had that same dark and stunted quality. The spur for the unhappiness might well have been vastly different in each case, but there seemed inevitably to be alcohol and bitterness about the past somewhere in the equation and it all combined into a palpable atmosphere of failure. You could sense it the moment you walked in the door. It made your scalp tingle.

I found myself on familiar terrain in the Greeley house

on Moraine Street in Brockton, Massachusetts. The glorious stone houses on Moraine, north of West Elm, were still standing as described by Eddie Dean, but the Greeleys no longer lived way up there. They had moved to a section of Moraine south of West Elm, a less prosperous section crowded with sagging old Capes and dark little cottages desperately needing their sidings painted and their lawns mowed. Something fierce and unyielding as time itself had batted the Greeleys down to the lower rungs of Brockton's class ladder.

"Nothing was ever good enough for my baby," croaked Mrs. Greeley in her harsh smoker's voice, sitting back on her couch, legs crossed, arms crossed, lit cigarette pointing up, its smoke rising mercilessly to the ceiling.

How is one to take such a line? Nothing was ever good enough for my baby because he was the light of my life, the seed of my soul, my very heart? Or, nothing was ever good enough for my baby because he was a greedy little bastard who always wanted more more more? It seemed Mrs. Greeley had intended to say the former, but her posture, the rasp of her voice, the upward curl of her upper lip betrayed her.

"Nothing was ever good enough for my baby," said Mrs. Greeley and I felt her resentment like a twitch in my back.

What was it that got to me, because being in the Greeley house surely got to me. Was it the fine furnishings with sags in the seats and grease stains on the armrests, with rings like trophies on the wooden surfaces, furnishings that bespoke with utter clarity of a fall from grace? Was it the fine layer of dust over everything that declared the Greeleys had given up even the appearance of trying? Or was it the woman sitting across from me with arms crossed and legs crossed, wishing we would just stop talking about her missing son and go away so she could have another drink? Oh yes, I could sense it in her, the crushing need for a drink, a need that was no doubt far more her lifelong companion than her husband. It was in the way she held her head so carefully, as if at the wrong angle it might slip off, the way her eyes slid from left to right, the way she made my scalp tingle. I could read the signs, my mother had taught me well.

"I did everything I could for him," said Mrs. Greeley. She was a tall, thin woman, dressed in slacks and a silk shirt. She had a face like a desiccated apple and her voice had a Katharine Hepburn shake to it. The cigarette was held in front of her so that the smoke acted as a gauzy shield. "I tried so hard. And for him to just disappear like he did, it broke my heart." She took a moment to draw a bit more nicotine from her cigarette and to dwell a bit longer in her past. Her face twisted for a moment into a cast of pure bitterness, and then she brightened falsely. "Do either of you have children?"

"Not yet," I said, shaking my head.

"And you, such a lovely young girl. Are you married?"

"No," said Kimberly.

"Heavens, what are you waiting for? But then you won't yet understand about children. They can be so hard to handle when they need so much. Tommy didn't just want, he needed, if you understand."

"Tell us about his childhood," I said. "Was it a happy one?"

"Oh my, yes. As happy as it could be, considering. Mr. Greeley suffered along with most of the town at the economic downturn. We had to sacrifice more than you could imagine to send Tommy to Cardinal Spellman. We gave up the club, then the house. When we moved here, I was in tears, but Mr. Greeley simply said, 'Shut up, it's still

Moraine.' But Cardinal Spellman was a fine school, far better than Brockton High with its element. You said you were a lawyer, Mr. Carl?"

"That's right."

"Tommy was studying to be a lawyer. At the University of Pennsylvania. Is that where you went?"

"I didn't get in there."

"How sad for you. But only the best for Tommy, we used to say. Tommy would have ended on the Supreme Court, or in the Senate, he had that way about him. I suppose such promise is always more difficult to handle, but I did what I could with him. Made my sacrifices."

The word "sacrifices" was said softly, but still it screeched in my ears. I pictured little Tommy Greeley sitting on his living room floor, watching his mother, her grip tight on her glass, as she berated him over and again about all her sacrifices.

"Did he have many friends?" I asked.

"Oh my, yes. He was very popular at Cardinal Spellman. And that friend of his at Penn, Jackson somebody, with the Polish name. They were very close. Jackson. Never Jack. But we didn't meet too many of his college friends. He was forever visiting with their families on holidays. We hoped, always, that he would come home but I understood. The invitations were just so inviting. And there was the girlfriend."

"Sylvia Steinberg?"

"That's it, yes. Steinberg. For that he went to the Ivy League?"

I swallowed and let that pass.

"How about here, in Brockton," said Kimberly. "Anyone he chilled with when home for a visit?"

"Chilled, like in a freezer?"

"Anyone here he kept in touch with," I said.

"Jimmy Sullivan. That's one friendship I tried to break up when they were still in middle school."

"Why?"

"Oh, the Sullivan boy might have been quite the little celebrity—I think that was what attracted Tommy to him in the first place—but he was always in and out of trouble and he loved nothing better than dragging Tommy along with him."

"Is he still around?"

"He works at a sub shop on the north side, I think. Which just goes to show, doesn't it?" She gave me the address.

I glanced at Kimberly and then said, "What about Eddie Dean?"

"Who?"

"A friend of Tommy's when they were young?"

"I don't recognize that name. But it's so hard to keep them all straight."

"It would have been when they were still just tykes," said Kimberly.

"There was a little blond boy he played with, a sweet boy, quiet, followed Tommy around like a puppy, but he moved. To California, I think. You said you had some news about my son?"

"Yes," I said. "I wanted you to know that the police have reopened the investigation into Tommy's disappearance. I received information of a confidential nature that has caused them to take another look."

Her face startled smooth. "Can you tell me what you learned?"

"No, I'm sorry," I said. "It is privileged."

"He's my son."

"I know that Mrs. Greeley and I'm sorry. But anything you can add might be very helpful to the reopened investigation."

"I told the police what I knew then, which was very little. Just that he hadn't called in so long and wasn't answering his phone. He was very busy in Philadelphia, didn't have much time for us. But I understood, a mother understands these things. Law school was very trying. He was working so hard. It took all his time and concentration to be at the top of his class."

"Who told you he was at the top of his class?"

"Tommy did, of course. Tommy was always at the top of his class."

"Okay," I said. "And you knew nothing about any business ventures he was in?"

"Not really, but he was doing quite well. He always had a nice car, nice clothes. He said he had made money in something to do with publishing."

"Do you have any idea what happened to your son, Mrs. Greeley?"

"Of course I do. He died," she said. "What else could have happened? He's dead. My son is dead. Dead." Her voice drifted off as she said the last word, and as her voice drifted so did her gaze, toward the small dining area. "Mr. Greeley went down there looking for him. Didn't find a sign one way or another, but twenty years of nothing is proof enough."

"I suppose so," I said. "So after his disappearance you never heard from him in any way?"

"No," she said. "Never." But even as she said it her eyes slid again toward the dining area. It was a small dingy alcove, overwhelmed by a dark table, high-backed chairs, a large dark sideboard with a china hutch above it. The hutch doors were ornately carved, with glass panels to show off the dishes. But there weren't dishes in there, there was something else I couldn't quite make out.

"Is Mr. Greeley around, we'd like to talk to him too?"

"He's at the golf course." Her nose twitched. "The city course. Every day," she said with a hard smile.

"Is he a good golfer?" said Kimberly, with a bounce of solicitous excitement in her voice.

"No," she said.

"You don't happen to have a picture of Tommy, do you?" I said. "Something we could take with us?"

"I might," she said, smashing out her cigarette and standing unsteadily. "In the other room. I'll be right back."

As soon as she left, I stood and meandered over to the dining area, right to that china hutch. I took a quick look around and then opened the doors.

"My God," I said softly.

There were bottles, the shelves were filled with them, a score of bottles, all clear, all still sealed, all filled with their magic elixir. Gin. Gordon's Gin. Same brand, stockpiled over the years, you could tell from the varied rates of yellowing on the seals. So much alcohol. Saved up for a rainy day, no doubt. Wouldn't want to go an hour without. I bet there were bottles stashed all over that house, in the kitchen cabinets, beneath the sink in the bathroom, under the bed, because you never know. And as we talked about Tommy, his mother couldn't keep her eyes from those bottles, waiting for us to leave so she could slit open a seal, unscrew a top, pour herself a stiff dose of amnesia. It was all too pathetic to bear.

When Mrs. Greeley returned with a photograph, I was again sitting beside Kimberly.

"This is from his college graduation," she said as she handed it to us. "I expect it will do."

Tommy Greeley, as his mother surely wanted to remember him, handsome and tall in his graduation robe, a mop of black hair falling from his mortarboard and almost cutting off his eyes. And a smirk that was particularly fulsome. There was an insinuation in that smirk, that this was just the beginning. It wasn't the kind of smile a politician gives, a false, toothy, trustworthy smile, it was something else. *Look what I scored,* it said, his smirk, *look what I pulled off. Aren't I something, a geeky Irish boy from the wrong side of Moraine, with a brutal father and bitter drunk of a mother, graduating from Penn, off to Penn Law School, with a million-dollar business on the side? Aren't I the damnedest thing?*

"It's fine," I said, standing, anxious to be gone from that house, that woman. "Thank you for your time, Mrs. Greeley. We'll be back in touch if there is any more news."

"Can I ask something?" said Kimberly.

Mrs. Greeley said, "Of course you can, dear, such a pretty girl. Such lovely skin. I had lovely skin as a girl too. But then you get old and you dry out. Think of an orange squeezed of all its juice. That's what a husband and a child will do to you. You'll see, my pretty. So, dear, ask your question."

"Now think first, before you answer, because this is, like, not a true-false, okay? If your son was an animal, which animal would he be?"

I sighed loudly. "Kimberly," I said.

"I saw it on TV."

"I'm sorry for the disturbance, Mrs. Greeley. Thank you for your time. Let's go, Kimberly." I was in the process of leading her out of the house when Mrs. Greeley spoke.

"He would be a polar bear, dear."

"Excuse me?" said Kimberly.

"He would be a polar bear," said Mrs. Greeley, "because he was always hungry and he roared when he wasn't happy and he could be very very cold."

52

"**I was just** trying to ask a question," said Kimberly, arms crossed and sulking as we drove through the streets of Brockton, "and you go tripping all over me like I'm telling a dick joke in front of the queen."

"I thought we discussed this on the plane," I said. "I would ask the questions. I have much more experience at this. Years in law school, in the courtroom, investigating my cases. That's why I get paid."

"You asked me along."

"Yes, but just to observe. I mean really, what kind of experience do you have? Asking questions at sorority rushes?"

"Rush can be brutal, V." She made a show of looking me up and down. "You'd last about a minute and a half."

"That long? But then I don't dress like a stewardess."

"You like it?" she said, her hand flying to her hat. She was wearing a sky blue suit with sharp blue pumps and a blue peaked cap. She looked as tasty as a cupcake with extra frosting, an adolescent fantasy come to life.

"Very becoming," I said, "though I'm not sure becoming to what."

"Becoming to a vice president," she said, "and it was a quality question."

"It was a touchy-feely piece of Baba Wawa nonsense," I said.

"Maybe I'm a touchy-feely Baba Wawa kind of girl, whatever the hell a Baba Wawa is. Is that, like, from *Star Wars*?"

"Who, the bounty hunter?"

"No, the big hairy thing."

"Chewbacca?"

"I always thought he was sexy."

"You're kidding me, right?"

"Give him a razor he'd be pimpin'."

"But he doesn't talk, all he does is grunt."

"A boy who knows he's got nothing to say. Very rare. And you have to admit, the polar bear answer was interesting."

"The only thing I found interesting," I said, "was how Tommy Greeley survived in that house as long as he did."

"I thought Mrs. Greeley was sweet. A little sad, sure. She still misses her son."

"She was a harridan, Kimberly. Wasn't it obvious? She was one of those women who numb their bitter resentment with alcohol and make everyone close to them pay for all the lives they failed to lead, all the goals they failed to achieve. She's a cold-blooded killer."

"You sound like you have issues, V."

"I know the type," I said, and as I said it I remembered those gin bottles, lined up like doomed soldiers standing at attention in their ranks. But something bugged me about those bottles, something different from the bouquets of glass I used to find around the house when my mother still lived at home.

"Is that it?" Kimberly said, pointing out her window.

My mind snapped back to the present. I looked down at the scrap of paper, looked up at a forlorn little storefront. "That's it." I managed to find a parking spot not too far off. "Now let me handle this, all right?"

"Suit yourself, V."

"What's this V stuff, anyway?"

"Like the president is W? You're V."

"And what are you?"

"I'm all that, V," she said as she checked her lipstick in the mirror, "that's what I am."

Butch's Sub Shop was a narrow little deli, with a brown linoleum floor and a few tables set out between the meat counter on one side and the tall glass-doored soda coolers on the other. At the register, a sharp-eyed older woman sat heavily on a stool, smoking a cigarette, gasping audibly for breath as she rang up a little girl and her ice pop. Other than the girl, the place was empty. Wiping down the deli counter was a burly dark-haired man with a mustache and a Red Sox baseball cap and above him a sign indicating all the varied sandwiches you could order so long as the sandwich you ordered was a sub.

"What can I get you guys?" said the man in a rough, Boston accent, his gaze taking in all of Kimberly.

"Are you Jimmy Sullivan?"

He turned his head and stared.

"You mind if we ask a few questions?"

His gaze slid to the woman at the register. "I'm working."

"It won't take long."

"I've got work to do. What's this about?"

"Tommy Greeley."

Something passed over his face just then, a cloud of dark emotion, and then it flitted off and his eyes darted to the right, toward the back of the store, as if he were debating whether or not to run for it.

"What about him?" he said, finally. "He disappeared, must have been like twenty years ago."

"We know. We have some questions about that."

"And so you come to me?"

"You're an old friend."

"Was." He went back to his wiping, leaning into it now, pressing hard with the rag as if to wipe away a stubborn stain, and then he stopped, let out a breath, deflated. "Hey, Connie," he called to the woman at the register. "I need a talk to these people for a moment."

The woman at the counter looked us over, coughed, and then nodded. Jimmy Sullivan waved us to a table. He swung his chair around and sat straddling the back, his arms crossed across the top rail, his chin buried in his arms.

"What are you guys, cops?" he asked.

"Do we look like cops?" said Kimberly.

"No, but you don't look like arm breakers neither."

"I should hope not." Kimberly thumbed at me. "He thinks I look like a stewardess."

"Maybe," said Jimmy Sullivan.

"I'm a lawyer, Mr. Sullivan," I said. "From Philadelphia."

"That explains it then."

"Explains what?"

"The way my skin crawled when you walked in."

Kimberly laughed a flirty little laugh and batted her eyes. I was almost embarrassed for her, but Sullivan didn't seem to react.

"So why are you guys asking about Tommy Greeley?"

"We're looking into Mr. Greeley's disappearance," I said. "Trying to learn what happened to him."

"A little late, isn't it?"

"Better late than never. We thought we'd start with his childhood and we learned that you were an important part of it."

"I knew him, so?"

"When was this?"

"We met in middle school, and then we was friends at Spellman."

"What was he like?"

"I don't know. He was just Tommy."

"Mrs. Greeley seemed to imply you were a bad influence on him."

His dark eyes darkened at that. "Is that what she said? She's something, isn't she, that Mrs. Greedy. How's she doing, the old bat?"

"Still alive," I said.

"Pickled, I'd bet. So that's what this is all about. You want to hear about my bad influence. All right." He took a deep breath, as if he were about to recite a poem in front of the class. "Tommy was a prince. I was the bad kid he hung around with. All princes have a bad kid they hang around with, don't they? It's like a rule. Didn't Shakespeare write about that? I was the one always getting in trouble between the two of us, so of course I was the bad influence. How's that? Is that what you wanted?"

"You have me confused with a guidance counselor," I said.

Sullivan lifted his chin, narrowed his eyes.

"I don't really care about the sad-sack story of your life, Jimmy boy. All I want to know is what happened to Tommy."

"When he went off to college, we lost touch. Who did you say you was working for again?"

"I didn't."

"Yeah, didn't think so. Look, what are you really after here? Why don't you just tell me, get it over with."

"Did you know he was selling drugs? Did you know he was indicted?"

"I'd heard something," he said slowly.

"When was the last time you heard from him?"

"I don't know. Before he disappeared."

"Do you have any idea what happened to him?"

"None."

"You weren't involved in his going missing, were you, Jimmy?"

"Is that what you think?"

"I don't know, that's why I'm asking."

He bit his lip for a moment, glanced at the old woman behind the counter who was giving him the eye. "Look. I might have been a bad influence, like old Mrs. Greeley said. But we was friends, Tommy and me. And like I said, he survived my bad influence. Maybe you should start wondering which of his high-class Ivy League friends he didn't survive." Sullivan pushed himself up from the chair. "I got to get back to work before breathless takes a bite out of my ass. Do yourselves a favor and go back to Philadelphia. I got nothing for you, understand? There's nothing here. Nothing."

He spread his arms wide and faced his palms to the ceiling, as if to emphasize the nothing, nothing in his hands, nothing up his sleeves. When he turned and made his way back to the counter he limped a bit and I noticed only then that one of his legs was shorter than the other.

When we stepped outside of the sub shop, Kimberly glanced back, through the front window, into the store. "He's scared of something, isn't he?" she said.

"Is he?"

"He was, like, all over me with his eyes before you mentioned Tommy Greeley's name. After that I was buzz kill."

"Maybe you're not his type."

"I'm his type, V. But I gave him my best little head-flick laugh and he barely glanced my way. Even my stewardess line didn't raise an eyebrow. One thing I learned is, guys, they go crazy at the idea of a stewardess. It's like genetic or something. Built into the chromosomes. Maybe there's some zygote in pumps and a smart blue jacket offering headphones and a Coke to the sperm as they freestyle their way up to the egg, maybe that's what does it. The stew could be a fifty-two-year-old grandma with bunions and still these boneheads are panting at the thought. But not this guy. The topic of Tommy Greeley scared him too much to even think about getting jiggy with me. Whatever it is, it's got him freaked."

"You think he was involved somehow in what was going down?" I watched Jimmy Sullivan as he went back to wiping the counter, glancing up now and then, squinting worriedly at us through the plate window.

"I don't know, but he sure is scared about something," said Kimberly. "And sad too. This Sullivan, he plays the Boston trash role, but he reads his Shakespeare, doesn't he? *King Henry IV Part One,* starring Tommy Greeley as Prince Hal and Jimmy Sullivan as Falstaff."

"I get all those Henrys confused," I said, squinting at her. "Wasn't the eighth guy the fat one with all the wives."

"Ah, yaah. Read a book, why don't you?"

I began to think about what she was saying, about how Jimmy had reacted. Mrs. Greeley had said he was a celebrity of sorts, but something had certainly come along to spoil everything. Now he was scared, absolutely, and sad, for some reason, and it seemed just then that Tommy Greeley was the cause of both. How could that be, twenty years gone by?

"Hey, you don't have to look at me like that," said Kimberly, misconstruing my thoughts. "I took a course or two in college, you know. I put in my time at the library."

"That's good to know, Kimberly, because I'm going to

drop you off at the public library before I go visit Mr. Greeley."

"Why the library?"

"I think we need to do a little research on our dear friend Jimmy Sullivan."

CHAPTER

53

A few years back, for the first time, they played golf's U.S. Open at a municipal course, picking a track out on Long Island, Bethpage Black. It's safe to say that D. W. Field Golf Course, the Brockton, Massachusetts, municipal course, Dee Dubs to the locals, is not next on the list. A flat nondescript layout with an old brown clubhouse and hot dog grill, Dee Dubs sat across from a mini mall sporting a pizza parlor and a kick-boxing joint. To most golfers it might look like a scraggly pasture with some flags stuck in the ground to let the cows know where to pee, but to its denizens it was as good as Pebble Beach, only better, because it was built without Pebble Beach's large and unsightly water hazard and the greens fees were about four bills cheaper.

I stood on the far side of the eighteenth green, just in front of the clubhouse, and watched the foursomes make their way up the fairway. I was looking for a man in a blue windbreaker, yanking his clubs along in a hand cart, most likely somewhere in the rough by the trees on the right side of the fairway. The way the old men on the practice green put it, Buck Greeley was so conservative he only played the right side of the course. I understood that to mean that Buck Greeley was such a stubborn old man that he refused to admit he had a slice.

I spotted him climbing up the right side, bent, without a hat, jerking the cart angrily behind him as he walked away from his playing partners and made his way toward the trees where his banana tee shot had landed. He grabbed an iron from his bag, looked up, glared at a couple of kids lugging their bags from the parking lot to the clubhouse, along a path that cut smack across the eighteenth fairway.

"Get the hell out of our way," he called out.

The kids maintained their placid pace. "We see you," one called back.

"You might see us but you're still lallygagging like a bunch of Nancies."

"You reach us, old man, and we'll scatter."

Greeley grunted, took a vicious swipe with his iron, watched as the ball emerged from the turf a low flash of white before smacking straight into the branches of a small maple and falling like a shot bird, forty yards short of the path.

The kids laughed and high fived.

Greeley replaced his iron, dragged his cart forward, until he was in position to take another angry swipe, and sent the ball smartly into a sand trap.

Two slashes later he was on the green. Two stabs with his putter left him three feet from the pin, a putt which he conceded to himself. A quadruple bogey, eight by my count, although who was counting, certainly not Greeley. I couldn't hear the conversation off the green but I could imagine it.

"What did you get there, Buck?"

"Five."

Men work their entire lives, salting away what they can in their IRAs, all the time dreaming of retirement so they can spend their sunset years on the links. They might as well just save up for dental surgery.

"Mr. Greeley? Do you have a minute?"

He was leaning over, lugging his cart behind him, his scalp, beneath his wispy white hair, red with exertion and sun. A surprisingly short man, heavy in the legs and chest. He lifted his face, a flat pug face, and took in my suit, my tie, my black shoes. "What do you want?" he barked.

"I'd like to talk."

"About what?"

"About your son, Tommy."

"Oh my God," he said, the hostility suddenly melting into something else. "Did they find him?"

I stared into his now wide eyes and was taken aback by what I saw, the pain, the fear, the loss, the hope, the hope. Whatever wound the disappearance of his son had burned into him, it had not yet healed, not yet completely covered over with scab and scar. I felt, just then, like I had stepped inside a stranger's house, pushed open the bedroom door, trespassed upon a scene of utter privacy.

"No, sir," I said. "I'm sorry, no."

His face closed again, just that quickly. "Then what the hell do you want?"

"I just want to talk. About your son. If you have the time."

"Of course I have the time. What the hell else do I have but time? But I need to eat first. Eighteen holes, taking as many whacks as I do, burns everything I got these days."

We took a table in the back corner of the clubhouse grill, a small dark room with white plastic chairs and green oilcloth covering the tables. The room was filled with old men, playing cards or staring at the Golf Channel on the television bracketed above the front door. The old men gave me the eye as I passed through, not many suits in the Dee Dubs clubhouse, I suppose. At the grill I bought two hot dogs and two Cokes.

"What do you like on your dog?" I asked him.

"Lobster," he said, "and hold the wiener. But if they don't have lobster, then onions and mustard."

I put both hot dogs in front of him. He tore into one with his big false teeth, devoured it, took up the next. The whole time he was looking at me from under his brow without saying anything, sizing me up. Halfway through his second dog, he nodded. "Go ahead," he said.

I told him I was a lawyer, which drew a wince, told him I had received information about the disappearance of his son from a client and was trying to figure out exactly what had happened. I said I had some leads and thought I had a chance to solve it once and for all.

"Why?" he said. "What's it matter now?"

"If it mattered then," I said, "it matters now."

"I don't know anything."

"Just tell me about him. Who were his friends? What did you know of his life at Penn?"

"Nothing," said Greeley.

I stared at him for a moment, during which he failed to elaborate, and then I said softly, "He was your son."

"What does that matter?" he said. "We didn't talk. All this talk about talk. Everything's a talk show now. Look at that, on the Golf Channel even. Talk talk talk. Has any society talked more and said less. We didn't talk, Tommy and me. The thing I respected most about him was he didn't tell me anything. A man's got to take care of his own damn business. A son shouldn't have to listen to his father talk about old girlfriends, about struggling to make a living, how everything turns to shit because he's white and Irish and didn't go to Harvard and the liberals say he's not deserving enough. A son shouldn't be burdened with that. And a father shouldn't be burdened with his son's struggle to pass algebra or get between some girl's legs or a prank gone bad. That's nothing a father should know about. We kept our own damn business. We didn't talk."

"What was he like?"

"Tommy? Cocksure, arrogant. Like me when I was younger. He had his own things going on and sometimes they blew up in his face. But he was always one for slipping out of trouble. And in those days I was around to bail him out, wasn't I? Though he was doing all right for himself in the end. Ivy League college and then a top-ten law school. Pretty damn all right. I thought things might be working out for him after everything."

"Everything?"

"Nothing. What do you want from me?"

"Your wife said you went down to Philadelphia looking for him when he came up missing."

"The police down there said there was nothing they could do. What the hell does that mean? A boy is missing and there is nothing they can do? They didn't give a damn. But he was my son. So I went down, asked questions. Fat good that did me. What was there to see? Nothing. And the rest were lies, all lies."

"What kind of lies?"

"About his business. Lies from people who were jealous that he was making money, making something of himself."

"About the drugs."

"Shut your yap." He looked around, lowered his voice. "You don't need to bring those lies up here."

"Okay, you're right. I'm sorry."

"There's nothing really to say, is there? He was here and then he wasn't. Pfft. That's the way it is with things. Money. Love. Youth. It's here and then it's gone. Look at me. But you don't think it will be that way with a son."

It was there again, that same thing I had glimpsed before, that private pain, which made me feel cheap as I spied it. What the hell was I doing, ripping open wounds I thought I was trying to salve?

"You never heard from him after the disappearance?"

"Course not. But that didn't stop that queer little FBI Nancy from coming up here every other month or so asking his questions."

"Telushkin?"

"Smoking his pipe, checking our mail. But there was nothing to find and eventually he disappeared too. That's the one thing right in the world. You wait long enough everyone disappears. Except my wife. But you met her, didn't you?"

"Yes I did."

Henry Greeley laughed, stuck the rest of the second dog into his mouth, and stood. I stood with him.

"I'm going to practice," he said. "I was making like a lawn mower on those greens. Putt, putt, putt, putt. Golf. Thing is, I never much liked golf. I played just to join that fancy club and when that went to crap I quit. Always seemed stupid to me. But what else am I going to do now, stay all day in that house? With her? Are you insane?"

"How's your game?"

"Shit. I thought I'd be better by now. But that's the lie that everyone believes. They go through life getting worse at everything but they think golf is different. They think, play more, score lower. But after ten years of retirement I still slice like a butcher."

I walked out of the grill room with him, shook his hand, watched as he wheeled his pull cart around the clubhouse toward the flat practice green between the clubhouse and the street. I tried to see in him the massive and stern Buck Greeley of Eddie Dean's story, but all I saw was an old man crushed small by the disappointments of his life. Except something didn't seem right. I couldn't put my finger iust yet, but something didn't seem quite right.

I crossed my arms, leaned against the side of the club-house, watched as Mr. Greeley sent his practice balls skittering across the green with derisive swats of his putter. *He was always one for slipping out of trouble* he had said of his son. *He was here and then he wasn't. Pfft.* And there was that strange greeting when I first mentioned Tommy Greeley's name. *Did they find him?* Him. Not his body, not his bones—him.

Maybe I was overreaching, maybe I was trying to force fit what I was seeing to the new possibility that had opened in my consciousness the night before while I sat beside my dying father, but still, these things Mr. Greeley said seemed to add up to something.

And then there were those bottles of gin in Mrs. Greeley's china hutch. Something about them was simply wrong. She was a drinker, Eddie Dean had said she was and Jimmy Sullivan had said she was, pickled was the term he used, and I could see it in her face. But then what was it with those bottles? I remember the bottles I found scattered in the drawers of my mother's sewing table, the table she never sewed upon. Open the drawer and there they were, bottles and bottles, empty bottles, until she got it together enough to throw them out, and start collecting the empty bottles once again. And that was it right there. When I found my mother's bottles they were always empty. She could never keep them full for long. So how was it that Mrs. Greeley had all those bottles still untouched. Apparently of differing ages, some there for years, decades even, and all of them full. As if kept for some reason other than the alcohol.

It wouldn't have come to me, it couldn't have come to me except that I had been feeling strangely connected to the doomed Tommy Greeley. He had been a poor kid fighting to make good, a tall lanky irreverent kid trying to charm and wile his way to success, the only child of alcohol and bitterness seeking to transcend the limitations of his parents' failures, and with all of that I could identify. And Chelsea had said we were so alike. And then there was the way Mrs. Greeley made my scalp itch, like only my mother could.

I never understood the first thing about my mother. Bear with me here, this has relevance here. I never understood the roots of my mother's toxic bitterness, never understood how she ended up married to my father, how she found herself in the sad fading suburb of Hollywood, Pennsylvania, with a husband she didn't love and a son who wouldn't stop crying. I never understood what my mother was trying so desperately to drown with her drinking. In fact, the only thing about her life that I could possibly understand was that she left it. I couldn't help but believe that my failure to understand my mother constituted a sucking wound, a whirlpool of ignorance that devoured much of the possibility from my life. How could I not trace my financial and romantic failures, both of them legion, to this primal failure? And how could I not therefore turn the bitterness I contracted from my mother like a disease back at her with a horrifying intensity?

I was engaged once for a short time until my fiancée ended it just before the wedding—not much to say, there was a urologist involved, which pretty much says it all— and for the longest time thereafter I drifted through life as if a spineless jellyfish adrift in a sea of bitterness. It was coming upon my mother's birthday. I was shopping for a suitable present. The usual places. Strawbridge's. Wanamaker's. The State Store on Chestnut Street. I found myself holding a bottle of vodka, my mother's spirit of choice. Nothing fancy. White Tower Vodka, I think it was, a house brand if ever there was one. And I weighed it in my hand

with all its awful implications. It was what she always
wanted, it was the only thing she really needed, it meant
more to her than I ever could. White Tower Vodka. And I
couldn't deny the pleasure I felt as I pictured her face when
she opened the gift, part greedy delight, part horror. Yes,
Mom, that much I do understand about you. Drink up.

But whatever level of bitterness I had fallen into, even
in that bleak year, it hadn't been deep enough. I sent a scarf
that year, nothing the next: better silence than what I had
been considering. Yet I had held the bottle in my hand, I
had felt its weight, I had thought it would make a jimmy of
a gift. I was close.

I watched Mr. Greeley chase the chimera of a holed putt
across the flat practice green at Dee Dubs for a long time
as I tried to put it together, tried to figure it out. Then I
pushed myself off the wall and headed toward him to ask
one question more.

A line of cars was stopped at a traffic light close to the
green. A kid in one of the cars yelled out "Fore." Someone
on the practice green yelled back "Five." Mr. Greeley
shook his head before standing up straight and watching
me approach. His eyes narrowed when he saw my face.

"I thought we were done," he barked.

"Just one more question."

"I'm putting here."

"Is that what you call it? Just tell me this, Mr. Greeley.
When do they come? I'm talking of the bottles of gin, the
ones your wife keeps in the china hutch. Her birthday? Her
anniversary? When?"

He stared at me and then stared over my shoulder and then
glanced around as if he was under an intense surveillance.

"Get the hell out of here," he said lowly.

"Twenty years worth of gifts, twenty bottles of gin.
When do they come?"

"What do you know about anything, you little bastard?"

"I know enough to stir things up. I know enough to ask everyone here if they knew what your successful son was up to before he disappeared. I could ask the neighbors too. I could spend days and days asking questions."   .

"This is none of your damn business."

"When do they come, Mr. Greeley?"

He stared at me for a long moment and I could see just then, beneath the old man's veneer, the ferocious Buck Greeley of Eddie Dean's story. He would have scared me then, thirty years ago, but it wasn't thirty years ago and he didn't scare me a whit and, when he saw that, something went out of him.

"Christmas, all right?" he said, softly.

"Okay," I said.

He glanced around once more. "Now get the hell out of here and leave us alone."

I felt bad about the whole thing, about the wound I had opened, so I did as he said and started walking away, and then I thought of something else. I stopped and turned around.

"Mr. Greeley," I said. The old man stared at me with a fierce hatred. "Was your son allergic to peanuts?"

"No," he said, a glint of triumph in his eye.

"You sure?"

"Sure I'm sure. Check the records. He wasn't allergic to nothing."

"Okay."

"Nothing but fish."

It was a warm day, the sun was shining, yet as I walked away from the putting green and then across the eighteenth fairway toward the parking lot, I couldn't suppress a shiver. It wasn't proof, there was nothing substantial I could take to Slocum or McDeiss, but, son of a bitch, just then I felt for a moment as if I were in the middle of an old George Romero movie, where the dead had come ravenously to life.

It scared the hell out of me, all of it, yes it did, and that was still a few hours before the big silver gun was pointed straight at my chest.

54

"We just want to talk, Sully," I said in the kitchen of his apartment, the bottom floor of a shabby three-decker in a part of Brockton called the Lithuanian Village, my hands raised, standing between Kimberly Blue and the revolver James Sullivan held in his right hand and aimed at my heart.

I wasn't standing between Kimberly and the gun out of any chivalric impulse, she was just better at ducking behind me than I was at ducking behind her. For a moment, as we jockeyed for position away from the gun, we were like a pair of vaudevillians trying to get the other to go first through the booby-trapped door. After you, no, after you, no, I insist, no, age before beauty, no, pearls before swine, no. We jockeyed and jostled as Jimmy Sullivan looked on with confusion, until our positions settled with me in front. "We just have a few more questions," I said after my last attempt to gain some cover was parried by the surprisingly quick Kimberly Blue.

It was what she had found at the library, on the microfilm machine, reviewing past issues of the *Brockton Enterprise*, that had sent us back to Sullivan. "He was a basketball star at Cardinal Spellman," she told me. "There's dozens of articles about him from junior high on. He broke all his school's scoring records, was the top

prospect in the whole area. The headlines were all, SULLY
LEADS SPELLMAN OVER FATHER RYAN, or SULLIVAN HITS 37 AS
SPELLMAN ROLLS. There were articles talking about his
being heavily recruited at U. Mass and some of the big-ten
schools. Iowa. Illinois. All the I states. But that was before."

"Before what?"

"Before the accident," she said, handing me a photostat.

And that was what we had come to Jimmy Sullivan's
house to ask about, the accident. But he wasn't happy to
talk to us, not happy at all. Maybe what cued me to that
was the fierce fear in his herky-jerky eyes when he saw us
at the door of his apartment. Or maybe it was the way his
mouth twitched when he asked what the hell we wanted, or
the jut of his jaw as we told him. Maybe it was all those
subtle signs, but what cinched it was the not so subtle sight
of the gun.

"I don't have what you're looking for," said Sully.

"Then why are you pulling a gun on two unarmed
strangers?" I said. "Why do your eyes wheel with terror
whenever the name of an old friend, twenty years gone,
gets mentioned."

"I told you to go on home."

"We're not here to hurt you. Whatever you're afraid of,
it is not us."

"I got enough troubles without the ones you're bringing."

"We only want to hear about Tommy."

"I'm done talking."

"People are dying in Philadelphia over this story."

"Shut up."

"Three deaths already, three people somehow connected to Tommy Greeley. In just the last few weeks."

"You're bullshitting."

"See this scrape on my head. I was there when the last one was killed. His building blew up with him inside. I almost caught it too. And I wasn't part of what went down twenty years ago." I stopped, watched as the fear flooded his eyes. "But you were, weren't you?"

"Shut up."

"It's coming to a head, Jimmy. Whatever has been festering beneath the surface for twenty years has erupted. And it's not going to stop at the Philly city limits."

"What do you want from me?"

"Just the truth, Jimmy. About you and Tommy."

"Get the hell out of here," he said. "Please," but as he made that final plea he backed away from us and the gun dropped to his side. I heard Kimberly release a breath from behind me.

"Put it away, Sully," I said. "We're not the ones you're afraid of. Put the gun away and we'll go out and have ourselves a couple of beers and we'll talk. And you might be surprised, whatever has got you so spooked, I think we can help."

He ended up taking us to a jauntily named joint called Café Lithuanian Village, a boxy place with opaque glass blocks for windows and a handwritten sign outside that said all you needed to know about the place. DOORS WILL BE LOCKED AT 1:00 AM. YOU MUST BE IN BY THEN. NO EXCEPTIONS. Whatever the law said about closing time, drinking at the Lit was an all-night affair. The place had a pool table, shuffle bowling, a little Budweiser fixture where the Clydesdales went round and round, and its very own weather system. Cloudy today, cloudy tomorrow, one hundred percent chance of clouds for years on end. Everything in the place had marinated in nicotine for decades.

"So what do you think of the Lit?" Sullivan said when we were finally seated, three abreast, at the U-shaped bar.

"It's brown," I said.

"It is that."

A squat man behind the bar, in a black LIT MOB T-shirt, gave Kimberly a long look and a martini, gave Jimmy and me each a bottle of Bud. I put a twenty on the bar. He took my money, dropped a pile of lesser bills in front of me. I took a long pull.

"We used to come to this place as kids," said Jimmy, looking down at his beer as he spoke, his voice flat. "Fifteen we were getting served. Six-ouncers for twenty cents. The Lit. Just down the bar there'd be a cop in uniform getting his belts in. We'd nod to each other. I won't bust you if you don't bust me. Brockton, man. What a place to be from. You're way too pretty for this place."

"Thank you," I said.

"Not you."

"Me?" said Kimberly. "Don't you think my eyes are too close together?"

Without raising his head or looking at her he said, "No."

"And my mouth's a little too small?"

"Too small for what?"

"I don't know. Just too small."

"No, it's not too small. You're goddamn perfect."

"I didn't think you noticed me at all."

"I've got a pulse, don't I? If there was any traffic in the place you'd stop it."

"That's so sweet," said Kimberly, beaming. "You are so sweet. Didn't I tell you he was sweet, Victor?"

"Sweet," I said.

"What is it you guys really want?"

"We just want to hear about you and Tommy," I said. "Why don't we start with the accident that gave you your limp."

He lifted his head. "What do you know about that?"

"Just what we read in the *Brockton Enterprise.* Prep star arrested at hospital. The only question I have is whose idea was it in the first place, yours or Tommy's?"

He sat for a moment, took a drink from his beer. "His," he said finally. "I can truthfully say every bad idea I ever had in my entire life was his."

CHAPTER

55

"Tommy told me it was easy money. We cased it one night, the next we got high and went out to do it. Drove the van up, snapped the chain, opened the gate, went right in. Stealing those motorcycles was the simplest thing."

"Why would you put yourselves at such risk?" Kimberly asked. "Tommy was headed to an Ivy League school, you were bound for glory on the basketball court. You guys had everything going for you."

"That was the point. It wasn't the first job we ever did, the bike thing, believe me. But everyone wanted something from us. He was his mother's prince, I was, like, the coach's dream on the basketball court. But we also smoked pot, screwed all the loose girls we could find, stole stuff. It was a way of keeping a part of ourselves for ourselves. And then we stole the bikes.

"We used a board as a ramp, loaded the van. One bike fell off the ramp, dented the gas tank, made all kinds of racket. Scared me shitless, but Tommy just shrugged and took another one. Three bikes. All loaded up, we replaced the chain and were gone. Done. Except Tommy wanted to test the merchandise.

"We filled up a gas can at a station and drove out to D. W. Field Park, by Cocksucker Cove—named for obvious reasons—and took out two of the bikes. When we kicked them up, God, they were screaming. I showed him how they worked, this is the gearshift, the clutch, the gas, the break. He was still trying to figure it all out when I stomped into first and blasted out. It wasn't long before Tommy caught up. No helmets, no nothing, we just rode. The wind blasting our teeth. On a lark, we turned off the road and started riding on the golf course, across the fairways, tearing up the greens. Nothing felt better than tearing up them greens. Too bad it wasn't Thorny Lea.

"Next thing I know I see Tommy atop the big hill by the stone observation tower. I rode up after him and right away I knew what he had in mind. This was the sledding hill. He wanted to go down. Hell if I was going to let him go first. I shot past him and then I was flying. The path dived down and I did too. But when I landed I landed wrong. Put down my foot to catch my balance, my knee locked and that—and that was the end of the leg."

He lifted up his beer, looked into it as if looking for something he had misplaced long ago, took a long drink from the bottle. It was hard to watch, the way he drank, with his eyes closed, as if trying to pull something from the bottle.

"By the time Tommy came up to me I was screaming, the leg was flopping and bleeding. He did what he could, but what could he do? He tried to lift me up so I could walk, but I couldn't move. Bones were shattered, I was bleeding and in shock. So he took off his jacket and wrapped it around the leg and sped off with his bike.

"It took me about a minute before I realized, with this demented certainty, that he wasn't coming back. I was still high, and that's the way you think when you're high, but it was also Tommy, and I knew Tommy. He'd just leave, I figured, and hope the situation would go away. I screamed for help—nothing. The bugs started coming, crawling on my face and hands, lapping the blood. I tried to drag myself to help, but the bones were moving around in there. I was sure I was going to die, to bleed to death. And then something big and black flew down and settled beside me, its head bobbing like it was ready to tear me to pieces, like I was already dead. I laid back, gave the hell up.

"That's when Tommy showed up again, that son of a bitch. I was never so happy to see anyone in my life, ever. He showed. With his father, who Tommy hated. They made a stretcher out of something and carried me back along the path to a clearing where a car was parked. They put me in the backseat, still lying down. They drove me to the hospital. And as we're driving, they're talking to me about what I ought to do, Tommy and Tommy's dad. I'm passing out from the pain and they're talking like two lawyers. I should just say I fell at my house, they told me. I was a big basketball hero, they wouldn't do anything much to me. There was no reason to get everyone in trouble."

"So what did you do?" said Kimberly.

"What they said to do. He was my friend, squealing wasn't going to help my leg. And they were right. Cops found the crashed-up bike, the busted lock at the bike shop, figured out what had happened, and even so I only got six months' probation. Everyone figured it was a prank and that I had paid enough with the injury, which I suppose I had. My leg was so broken up I never played again. That was college for me. I just didn't have any interest after that."

"What about Tommy?"

"Nothing. He came to visit me in the hospital and slipped me a couple hundred, my share of the money for the two bikes he sold. I didn't see him much after that. He said it was safer if we didn't hang out together. Safer for him, he meant. He went off to his college in Philadelphia and that was it, the end of Tommy Greeley in my life."

"But it wasn't the end, was it?" I said.

"Sure it was."

"No," I said. "Not by a long shot."

"How do you know?"

"By the fear in your eyes."

He shrugged, finished off his beer.

"Go ahead, Jimmy," said Kimberly.

"All right. What the hell. This is now five, six years after. It took me a while to come to grips with everything, it took years. I was a mess, but then I got hold of myself. I got off the drugs, stopped smoking, I lost weight. I found a job working this giant copier at some big company, making nothing, ten grand a year, but it was something. I even got a girl, a nice girl that I knew from high school. I was making a life, not what it would have been before the accident, but a life. And then, out of the blue, Tommy calls.

"I been hearing about Tommy, his mother had been bragging, how he's now in law school, how he's doing so well, how he got involved in some business and was already making real money. Tommy was Mr. Success."

"How did that make you feel, hearing that?" said Kimberly.

"How the hell do you think? But I was dealing with it. And then Tommy calls. Says he's going to send something up. Something that will be worth my while. Along with some instructions. And he does. UPS. I sign for it. A big brown box."

"What was inside?" says Kimberly.

"You have to understand, I was getting things together. I was making a new life for myself. I was getting close to happy. There is something very soothing in diminished expectations."

"What was inside?"

"A small boom box, with a selection of tapes. I thought it was a strange gift. Why was he sending me this? But there wasn't tapes in the tapes. Instead there was newspaper balled up, and nestled in the newspaper were glass vials. I knew what was in them right away, and I could tell the weight too. He had sent me ounces. Eight of them. Half a pound. You know how much half a pound of coke was worth in those days? I did, I had bought enough grams in the bad times. I was never much for math but drugs sharpen your arithmetic, no doubt about it. Grams were 75 bucks a pop. Twenty-eight grams to an ounce, so an ounce was worth $2,100. Eight ounces was worth $16,800. And you know what I paid up front for it all? Nothing. Nothing.

"He sent up a letter with some names and his instructions. He told me how to prove up the quality with methanol and a spoon. And he told me how much to take out as my cut. He was setting me up in business. His business. Tommy Greeley thought he was doing me a favor. He was going to make me rich, the son of a bitch. There was a guy in a bar. The name was in the letter. He tested it and bought three. A few of the other names came through. One bought two. Two more bought one each. It was so damn easy."

"You said there were eight ounces," said Kimberly. "You only told us about seven."

"I had to test it, didn't I? And then I had to test it some more. I ended up doing the whole eighth myself. And with some of the cash I bought myself a new car. Why not, right? So what I sent down to Tommy wasn't as much as I was supposed to send. But he didn't seem to care. 'Don't worry about it,' he said, and he sent up more right away. Federal Express this time. Next thing you know I was in the business. But I was using now and, after my girl left because of the drugs, I was spending even more money trying to live the life, getting farther into debt. I owed him five, I owed him ten, fifteen. It didn't matter because he kept on sending stuff up. Eight ounces at a time. Then a pound. I had so much stuff I had to front people myself, and not everyone was paying everything they owed, so I grew deeper into Tommy's debt. Twenty. Twenty-five. I quit my real job. How could I spend nine to five making ten a year when I owed Tommy Greeley thirty thousand dollars?

"As the quantities grew, he started sending up a courier, a motorcycle guy, who would drop off the stuff and remind me, to the dollar, of how much I owed. Thirty-five. Forty. Where was I ever going to find that kind of money outside the business? I was trapped. But still, from Tommy, it was like, whenever. No pressure from him to pay what I owed. Until it was no longer whenever, until it was right fucking now."

"When was this?"

"Just before he disappeared. He phoned me late one night. He was at a pay phone, that's what he used for business, and he said he needed the money I owed. By then it was like seventy-five grand and there was no way. 'Don't say you can't,' he told me, 'after all I've done for you.' How could I respond to that? He told me to open an account and put all my cash in the bank. Then sell my car, my stereo, whatever I had, and put that in too. Get checks for everything so there won't be a trail. And then collect all the money I was owed. Hire a thug if I had to and collect it. Give a discount for checks and put everything in the bank. And when you've got everything, wire it to an account. He gave me the number. It was something offshore, I think. I thought of just stiffing him, wondered what he could do about it, but then I remembered the motorcycle guy. So I did as he said. I sold my car, moved the merchandise I had, collected what I could. It wasn't much. I ended up with about twenty-five thousand and I wired twenty of it to that account."

"You kept five for yourself?" said Kimberly.

"Yeah, I mean, yeah. And I'm glad I did. Because that was the end of the line. No more shipments, no more deals. I was left with the five thousand, sure, but no car, no job, and an addiction I couldn't afford to feed. I tried to keep the business going, tried to find a supplier, but what the hell did I know, really? I ended up going to Cambridge and working out a shipment from an undercover cop and that was the end of that. Seven years. A third off for good behavior, a third off for parole, but still."

"You ever talk to Tommy after that call?"

"No."

"Ever hear from him?"

"No." But when he said it his gaze slid down to the empty bottle of beer in his hands, and his knuckles were white.

The fear, where did that come from? I wondered, as I ordered us another round. The one thing I still couldn't quite figure was why he was so spooked at seeing us. Why had we frightened him so? Why had he thought it necessary to draw a gun? I thought back over it all and I remembered what he had said the first time he saw us. *You don't look like arm breakers,* he had said. And how he made sure to tell us there was nothing here for us. And how he said, when he saw us at his house, that he didn't have what we were looking for. What did he think we were looking for? And then it hit me.

Lawyers are, at heart, archaeologists. Our job is to excavate history, to burrow into the dirt and pull out our shards of evidence. With enough shards you can reconstruct the pot, with enough pots you can reconstruct the past. We send out our document requests like telegrams to the past; what we get back are boxes. And somewhere in those boxes lay the outlines of our most precious tool: the story. Some lawyers see the cardboard cubes being wheeled into their offices and they cringe at the thought of all that paper to review, but not me. For me, each box represents a square plot of land at an ancient site, something to be dug into, sifted, organized, reviewed. And believe me when I tell you this, there is always a box.

"Let's hear the rest," I said.

"I didn't leave anything out."

"Oh yes, you did. Tell us about the box."

He startled for a second. "How did you know?"

"It's my job to know."

"Fucking lawyers."

"Yes we are," I said.

"What did he send you, Sully?" said Kimberly.

He paused for a moment, looked at Kimberly's wide eyes and small mouth, took a sip of his fresh beer. "A big tool locker," he said finally. "Red and black. Padlocked shut."

"When?"

"After I wired the money. He told me to bury it somewhere. That someone would come looking for it someday and until then to just keep it safe."

"And you thought Kimberly and I were the someones he referred to?"

"Yes."

"But you were scared. You pulled a gun on us. You were frightened, so you didn't keep it safe, did you?"

He didn't answer.

I lowered my voice. "It's all right. What else could he have expected. You were strung out and broke and you thought there might be some drugs inside, didn't you?"

"If I was strong enough I wouldn't have been in that mess in the first place."

"So you opened it."

"Snapped the lock."

"What was inside?"

"Crap. Nothing. Books, pictures, crap."

"But it's not the crap that has you so scared, is it, Sully? What else was in the locker? Drugs?"

"No."

"Money?"

"Yeah."

"How much?"

"A hundred thou."

"That's a lot of money."

"Yeah."

"And you took it."

"I was going to put most of it back."

"But you didn't."

"What do you think?"

"I think you pissed it away."

"Yeah. Maybe I did. Some. Most. And the rest I gave to my new girlfriend to stash. For when I got out."

"And did she?"

"I don't know. That was the last I ever saw of her."

"Good choice."

"Well, you know, she seemed pretty reliable with money. She was a stripper."

"It's amazing how that works. And since then every stranger who stepped your way made you jumpy. Every stranger might be the stranger who would ask for the box, and open it up, and see what was missing, and look to get it back."

He drained his beer, his Adam's apple bobbing as he drank.

"In all those years, anyone ever come asking for it?" I said.

"No. Not until now."

"You mean us."

"Not just you."

Kimberly and I leaned forward and stared at him. "Go ahead, Sully," she said.

"I got a call, not too long ago. Just a call. A voice I didn't recognize. It asked about the package I was keeping safe. I said I don't know what he was talking about. It asked again, told me to think back twenty years. I said I didn't know what he was talking about. The voice told me to expect a visitor. That's all I heard, and then you guys showed up."

I looked at Kimberly, whose wide eyes were now wide with the big questions. Who had known? Who had called?

"The voice," I asked, all the while watching Kimberly's expression, "was it British?"

"Yeah," he said. "It was."

And Kimberly's pretty wide eyes widened even farther. "Colfax?" she said.

"Who?" said Jimmy.

"That's right," I said.

"How'd he know about it?" she said.

"Who?" said Jimmy.

"What did you do with the other crap in the toolbox?" I said.

"Left it there," said Jimmy.

"In the box?"

"Yeah."

"Where is it now?"

"Buried. I moved it to the basement of the place I live at now."

"Let's dig it up."

"No. They might come for it."

"Tell you what, Sully. I'll take it off your hands, which will be a relief for you. And I can work it so you never get that visitor you've been fearing."

"You're full of shit. You can't do that."

"I'm a lawyer," I said. "I can walk through walls."

"Now I know you're full of shit."

"Trust me."

He laughed a sad, rueful laugh. "Do I got any choice?"

"Let's go dig it up," I said.

And we did.

CHAPTER

56

Flying home to Philadelphia I was trying to read a play I had picked up in the airport bookstore, a thrilling tale of murder by poison, of ghostly apparitions, of madness and vengeance and the madness of revenge. I figured if Eddie Dean was reading *Hamlet,* I ought to brush up on it too. The misty night, the father's ghost, the poetry of death. It was more thrilling than I had remembered it, but even so I found it hard to keep my focus. I was reading *Hamlet,* yes, but what I was seeing in my mind's eye was the arrogant visage of Tommy Greeley, the smirk that seemed to say, *Aren't I something?* Oh yeah, he was something all right.

Whatever I had thought of Tommy Greeley before my trip to Brockton, however much I might have identified with him in his rebelliousness, his irreverence, his striving to rise above his family's dysfunction, my opinion had changed completely after hearing Jimmy Sullivan recite the sad story of his withered life, and the friend, who was no friend, who had done so much to destroy its promise. Some of what Tommy had done to him was done out of malevolence, I could feel that, maybe an unconscious jealousy of a friend who had already achieved success, but there was something else at work too, something almost worse. Carelessness. A carelessness, I supposed, that defined everything about Tommy Greeley's life. He had been careless about one friend's basketball career, careless about another friend's marriage, careless about all the lives he was destroying with his drugs as he built his fortune. Just utter carelessness with other human beings. And when his carelessness had put him in danger, he had found the most careless way out.

Kimberly Blue was seated next to me in the plane, absorbed in her own reading. We were on the early-morning flight. I was anxious to get back to the office, to do some work and send a query off to California before I visited my father that night. She had to hurry back and see a man about a boat.

"A boat?"

"Something for the boss. External relations. Just a party thing, he said."

"But he's out of money."

"There's always money for a boat, V."

So there we were, on the early flight home, our carry-ons stashed in the overhead compartment, along with the tool locker dug up from Jimmy Sullivan's basement the night before. I watched Kimberly concentrate on the volume on her lap and as I did there was something about her that reminded me of the photographs. The line of her neck as she bent toward the book, the shape of her hand, the wisp of hair that covered her ear. I knew it was a trick, a transference from one woman to another, and I knew why it was happening. But still, it had its effect, the similarities, and I felt a wave of emotion toward her, a strangely paternal emotion.

"How's the reading material?" I said.

Before she raised her head, she carefully put her finger on the page of the notebook on her lap, a notebook full of diary entries twenty years old that we had found in the locker.

"Gad, V. She can't even blow her nose without writing all about it. And she goes on and on about the sex, like no one's ever hooked up before. Talk about a slut. I've gotten to the part about the veil we found."

"Interesting?"

"Yuck."

"All right, I don't want to know."

"But between all the sex stuff, you can tell she really was struggling. Caught between two men, a husband she loves and a man with whom she is sexually obsessed. She hasn't decided yet what to do. It's like she has to work it out on the page first. Are you going to read it?"

"Absolutely not. I've had enough experience with her writing to last me."

"But see, V, I was right about her all along, wasn't I?"

Yes, the notebooks for which Alura Straczynski had been desperately searching, the missing pieces of her solipsistic opus, were in the locker, along with all kinds of other stuff of varying levels of interest for me—a college yearbook, a fencing trophy, a Leica camera, snapshots of friends, a financial ledger, the yucky silk veil, a book of selected poems by Lord Byron, and a how-to book, a cheap-looking paperback from a publishing company called Loompanics Unlimited.

I had taken a special interest in the snapshots. Barbecues, parties, days at the beach, a lot of good-looking young folk having a rich old time. Most of the people in the pictures I had never seen before, but I did recognize a few, absolutely. Lonnie, poor dead Lonnie, here much younger but still with the beard and the motorcycle style, gazing at Chelsea, lovely Chelsea, with her arm around a man I recognized from the photo Mrs. Greeley had given me. Was that the triangle that took Tommy down? Or was it the other triangle, the one Kimberly was reading about in the notebooks? There was also a picture of Sylvia Steinberg, young, thin, absolutely stunning, her gaze cast not at the camera or her boyfriend but at Chelsea. There was a stiff shot of Jackson Straczynski, posed and serious in a suit, his hair long, his tie thick. There was a strange man, short, dark, husky, whose image was ubiquitous in the photographs. His dark eyes burned at the camera even as his mouth attempted a smile. The other partner, Cooper Prod, I assumed. And in almost every shot, of course, there was Tommy Greeley himself, standing tall, smiling slyly, the life of the party. But the party was running out of time.

The objects in the tool locker spelled out with utter clarity the last desperate days of Tommy Greeley. His drug empire was collapsing, the dogged Telushkin was doggedly pursuing him, indictments were as certain as the sunrise. Tommy Greeley, in the midst of a torrid affair with his best friend's wife, had decided on a drastic course of action. That Loompanics book we found was entitled *How to Disappear and Never Be Found*, and for Tommy it had provided a blueprint. He would run away, run away with her, take what money he could and start a new life as someone else, still rich, but now out from under the shadow of his criminal past. *He was always one for slipping out of trouble,* had said his father. Chapter Four of *How to Disappear and Never Be Found:* "Creating a New Identity."

Eddie Dean.

That was the possibility that appeared to me from a great distance at my father's bedside. That was what my query to California was all about, to see if there ever was a real Eddie Dean and, if there was, to learn whether he had died an untimely death, leaving a birth certificate and Social Security number for an old friend to use in making his escape, just as explained in Chapter Four. But if that was the case, how had Tommy Greeley survived his encounter with Joey Cheaps? I had a theory about that too.

Oh, what I wouldn't give to be able to show Joey Parma or Derek Manley the picture I now had of Tommy Greeley. Joey Parma had told me he had killed the man with the suitcase and so I had assumed that he had killed Tommy Greeley. But what if it wasn't Tommy Greeley holding the suitcase. What if he had gotten wind of the betrayal and given the suitcase to someone else to hold, had set someone else up to take the beating? Maybe he had learned something that made him suspicious, maybe he had been hiding, using the other to make sure it was safe. How characteristic of our Tommy Greeley would that be?

There was no proof. He could have told his friend Eddie Dean about the locker sent up to Boston. The allergy to fish might be a coincidence. He could have arranged for his special gift to be sent to his mother every Christmas before his murder, the twenty bottles of gin representing the bitterness carried like a seething wound in his breast. There was no proof, but if Tommy was truly killed at the edge of the Delaware River, then who had been using Tommy Greeley's past to wreak his revenge?

"How did Colfax know about the stuff Tommy gave Jimmy?" said Kimberly.

"That's the question, isn't it?"

"Maybe it was just someone else with a British accent. There are a lot of those in the world."

"Do you really think that's it?"

"I don't know, V. I don't understand anything."

I hadn't told Kimberly about my suspicions. She was too close to Eddie Dean, she would tip my hand. I thought it better to get the proof from California first, and then let the police handle it, but still I had my concerns. "I want you to be careful, Kimberly. Very careful."

She turned to stare at me.

"Let's just assume," I said, "we don't know anything about anybody. It's safer that way. Have you thought any more on why you got this job?"

"Maybe they saw something in the interview."

"Maybe they did."

"I have talents."

"I'm not saying you're not qualified. Or that you're not doing a great job. And I'm not saying that if they were picking on looks alone you wouldn't have snagged it easy, being you are fabulous-looking, no doubt about it. But I want you to be careful."

"What do you think is going on?"

"I'm not sure. Not yet, at least, though soon I will be, you can count on it. But believe me when I tell you this, there is something not right going on and it is rooted in the past and it is going to end very very badly."

"So, V," said Kimberly, her eyes turning suddenly bright. "You really think I look fabulous?"

"Absolutely," I said, and her bright smile at my compliment was both touching and a little sad.

She went back to her reading and I began to think about her. Why again had she been hired? What did she know that Eddie Dean, a stranger with a mangled face who had the same allergy to fish as had Tommy Greeley, would find valuable? I looked at her again, saw again the same angles and lines of the pictures on my wall. She was reading Alura Straczynski's journal and so in my mind's eye she was somehow taking on Alura Straczynski's shape. Look at her, the way her neck stretched, look at the shape of her ear, look at her hand, sitting on the page, the way it curled, the length of its fingers, the shape of its thumb. I had seen it before, I had a picture of that very same hand.

"Oh God, how disgusting," said Kimberly. "TMI."

"Excuse me?"

"Really now, is this something the world needs to know? The sensation of it, the taste of it, the burning as it slid up her throat. Some things are best left unsaid, believe me. I mean, do we really need to know every last detail of this? Do we really care that she woke up that morning bowing and scraping to the porcelain god?"

CHAPTER 57

Coming home from Brockton, I shouldn't have been surprised, what with the specter of Tommy Greeley's resurrection still haunting me, to see my dying father come heartily back to life.

"Where you been?" he asked, sitting up in his bed, free of the respirator and mask, with only the small plastic canula feeding oxygen into his nose. "That doctor was looking for you."

"I was away, on business. What happened?"

"I don't know. It started working."

"The drug?"

"Yeah, the drug. That Primaxin thing. It finally kicked in. Working like a charm."

"Apparently so." I checked the monitors. Oxygen rate a robust ninety-four percent, respiratory rate a leisurely sixteen, heart rate down to well under a hundred. I took another look at his face to make sure I wasn't in the wrong room. No, it was him, my dad, who was stomping on death's welcome mat just two nights before, now looking surprisingly vigorous. And what was that right there, on his face? Oh my God, was that a hint of a smile?

"They took me off the respirator last night. Now if they take this pipe out of my prick I could walk out of here."

"What about the operation?"

"I thought you was here to cheer me up."

"You don't look like you need cheering up. Did they say anything about the operation?"

"Right after they're done with the drug. Sit down."

I pulled a chair over. He reached out, put a hand on my arm. I gave his paw a wary glance.

"How you doing?" he said.

"Fine," I said.

"Really. How's it going, son?"

"Fine."

"We don't talk enough."

"Yes, we do."

"No, we don't. Tell me about your life. Tell me about your hopes, your dreams, your aspirations."

I took his hand off my arm. "Hey, Dad, you're creeping me out."

"Am I?"

"You're kidding, right?"

"Am I?"

"Tell me you're kidding."

Something in my face must have been quite hysterical because he broke out into a wet bout of laughter.

"Okay," he said as his laughter dissolved into a fit of coughs. "Yeah, I'm kidding."

"It was just a joke?"

"Got ya, you little bastard."

I did a little shaky thing, like I was skived to the bone. "What the hell's gotten into you?"

"You know, life would be an all right thing if they could pull a plastic snake out of your throat every night."

"But just remember," I said, "no matter how good you feel right now, things will eventually turn to shit."

"I know it."

"That's just the way of it for us."

"You're preaching to the converted."

"Good. Just so long as we're clear."

"We are. So"—he again put his hand on my arm, gave me a wink—"how's the love life?"

"Stop it," I said, even as his laughter began again.

It only took the dinner tray to sour his mood. Salisbury steak, overcooked peas, something blue. He dropped his fork with disgust.

"I can't stand it in here no more," he said. "They should just sharpen their damn knives and get it over with."

"Don't worry, they will."

He let out a hearty curse. Now that was my dad.

"So what happened?" I said.

"I told you. The drug."

"No, with the girl. In that room. With the old guy."

"Curious, are you?"

"Yeah. You know. I've been thinking about it."

"So have I. For a lot longer than you."

"Okay. So what happened?"

"I told you," he said. "She kissed me. She put her hand on the back of my neck, pressed me toward her, and she kissed me. And, son of a bitch, I kissed her back."

He kisses her back. Her hand at the back of his neck, his eyes closed, the softness, the wetness, the warmth of her mouth. He lets the electricity slide through him, numb him, he loses himself in the moment and lets the moment expand until it stretches out in four dimensions and he is adrift in the sensation, no here nor there, no then, just now, just her, just the feel of her hand, the pressure of her lips, the silvery slickness of her tongue. Until she pulls away, and he opens his eyes, and he falls back into the bloody hell of that treasure room, with the old man dead at his feet.

He sees it all again, the confrontation, the box of coins

slamming into the old man's scalp, the old man dropping to the floor. My father is in a panic, his mind races out of control. What to do? Where to run? Who to tell?

What have you done? he says to her. What are we going to do?

But he slows down when he sees her pretty face, the sharp blue of her eyes, the calm of her features.

"It was like she was taking a walk in the park," he said. "It was like nothing had happened."

I know where the jewelry is, she says.

What are you talking about?

I know where everything is, she says.

Do you realize what you've done?

It was an accident, she says. You know that. Jesse, it was an accident.

They're going to catch us and kill us, he says.

No they won't.

They will.

They can't. We were never here. We have alibis.

Who?

Each other. Jesse. You and me. You promised we'd be together forever and now we will. Now we have no choice. Darling.

She steps toward him and he steps away. He stares at her, this woman, his love, this stranger. He stares at her even as she reaches out to him.

"It was like I never seen her before. 'Who are you?' I said to her."

Who are you? he says.

Jesse, she says, her eyes brightening. Listen to me. Pull yourself together. Jesse. Listen. I know where everything is.

I don't want anything from here, he says.

But of course you do, she says, reaching down to take

hold of the box of coins, which she clutches to her chest. We deserve this, she says. Still holding on to the box she reaches up and grabs a fistful of pearls. He owes us this. We can't begin with nothing.

Stop, he says.

We need this to get started with our lives. We can't begin with nothing.

No, he says.

I can't begin with nothing.

Don't, he says.

But she does. She pulls down more pearls, she grabs a handful of diamond-encrusted broaches, jade figurines, beautiful ivory carvings. Her arms are filled with the old man's treasures, all of it smeared now with the old man's blood.

Stop, he says. But she doesn't stop, and with each piece of treasure she pulls from the shelves it is as if she is yanking the dreams straight from his chest, handful by handful.

He finally stops her physically, takes control of himself and then control of her, grabs her by the shoulders, spins her around so she is facing him.

Stop, he says again. We can't take anything. We have to clean everything. Do you understand?

And maybe she does, or maybe she is just frightened by what she sees in my father's eyes, for her face turns as pale as the old man's and, still with all the treasures in her arms, she backs away.

He looks around, grabs a throw from off one of the chairs, begins wiping the room, cleaning what blood he can off the shelves, the chairs, the table. He takes the objects from her arms, one by one, wipes them, replaces them, one by one, while she looks on, quiet and pale, as if the shock of what she has done has finally hit her. He takes the objects from her one by one and she lets him.

But when he tries to take the box, she holds fast, clutches it to her chest and won't let go.

We need to leave, he says.

Okay.

We can take nothing, he says.

Okay.

Give me the box.

Okay, she says, but she won't let go, she holds tightly to the box, the very box with which she shattered three lives, and he doesn't have the heart to wrench this final scrap of wood from her grasp.

He takes a last look around, a last look at his dearest dreams lying shattered on the bloody floor, and switches off the light.

"We stepped outside the room," he said, "and closed the door behind us. I used the throw to wipe away our finger-prints as we went. We slipped out the mud room window, out into the night. And we went home."

Home, home to his one-room apartment in North Philadelphia, where just that morning he had felt the infi-nite promise of the future pour through him. He lies in his bed, with his love asleep by his side, her head resting on his chest, feeling the tickle of her hair as he prayed he would feel each night for the rest of his life. But now the room feels small, cramped, the walls are closing in on him.

She groggily opens her eyes, she smiles at him, that same lovely smile that just hours before had been able to light the darkest corners of his heart. Together forever, she says. Just like we promised. And then her eyes close and she falls back to sleep and in her slumber she looks so much like an angel, his Angel, that to look at her physically hurts.

"But the box," whispered my father, his eyes now closed, his voice faint. "The damn box."

It is still there, the wooden box with Atlas on the lid. It sits on the bureau, atop the bloody throw, the box glowing in the moonlight. And it is as if the box itself is sucking the promise from the room, and, along with the promise, the very air. The weight of her head on his chest is constricting his breathing. He's having a hard time breathing. He coughs, he fights for breath.

"Are you okay, Dad?" I said, as my father struggled to catch his breath.

He didn't answer, he was lost in the memory, his heart rate soared.

I shook him softly. "Dad?"

His eyes popped open. He startled at the sight of me. "What?"

"Dad? Should I get a nurse?"

"No," he said, coughing again. "I'm all right," he said, gasping still for breath.

"Dad?"

"I was just remembering," he said. "Remembering the way I felt that night in my room. The way I felt ever since."

"And how was that?"

"Like an animal," he said. "Like an animal caught in a trap. Waiting to be put out of my misery. Waiting for the blessing of a shot to the head."

58

A dark blue Taurus was parked outside the entrance to the hospital. As soon as I stepped through the hospital doors, the car's lights turned on and it started ominously toward me.

I backed away.

The car kept coming.

I thought of turning and running, of loosing a high-pitched squeal and then fleeing for my life, but I fought the urge. Whatever end fate had in store for me, I doubted it involved being run over by a Taurus. An Eldorado maybe, a Lincoln Town Car, even a Lumina, sure, but not a Taurus.

I stepped back. The car slid to a halt beside me, the front window hissed down.

Slocum.

"What happened to the Chevette?" I said.

"I'm a supervisor now, higher pay grade."

"K. Lawrence Slocum, living large in his Taurus."

"You want a ride home?"

"Not in a Taurus."

"Get in."

"My car's in the lot."

"Get in anyway. I'll bring you back after."

"After what?"

"Someone wants to see you. Get in," he said, and I did.

He drove north on Broad Street, away from Center City until he hit Roosevelt Boulevard and then headed toward the wilds of the Great Northeast.

K. Lawrence Slocum was one of those private men who never let you glimpse his inner life but, even so, you found yourself trusting him absolutely. You sensed in him a strict code of honor. Its terms weren't exactly clear to the outside world, they were of his own devising and remained locked away in some secret place, but to Slocum himself they were explicit and unyielding. He looked at you always as if he were judging you against his code, and under that gaze you couldn't help but feel that you were failing his test. Except every now and then he smiled at you, a broad comforting smile, and you sensed that maybe, just maybe, you stood on the right side of his line. And you knew, with complete certainty, that so long as you stayed on the right side of his line, he would move mountains for you.

"Who are we seeing again?" I said.

"You were right about Lonnie Chambers being shot. The coroner confirmed it. The methamphetamine task force is investigating. They've been hauling in Pagans and Hell's Angels from all over the city. They're not getting very far."

"They're searching in the wrong place."

"Well, you know. The light is better over there."

"What about Rashard Porter?"

"We're looking into it."

"I hope you're doing a damn sight more than looking into it."

"Remember the young pup that escorted you down to the office?"

"The suit with the attitude. What was his name, Bernstein?"

"Berenson. Well right now, right this instant, Berenson's enjoying the wonderful hospitality of Chinchilla, Pennsylvania, in Lackawanna County, reviewing their bench warrant procedures."

"I hear Chinchilla has a wonderful Harvard Club."

"You have something against Harvard?"

"Just the ivy-covered snots that go there."

"Really? You know many Harvard graduates?"

"No. But I can imagine."

"So it bothers you that graduates of Harvard Law are swooped up by the New York firms and given untold riches while you struggle to pay your bills?"

"Every minute of every day."

"You ought to let go of that."

"Why? If I have any power at all it derives from the keen edge of my bitterness. Give me all I want in this world and I would shrivel up and die, like a leech in salt."

"I see your point, at least the part about you being a leech."

"Where'd you go to law school, anyway?"

"Yale."

"Well, bully for you. Who are we seeing again?"

"It's a surprise," he said.

He turned left off the boulevard, headed through some hard city streets, and then, suddenly, the signs changed, the edges softened, the roads turned downright leafy. He had driven me into the suburbs. The suburbs? Why would a city ADA be taking me into the suburbs?

It didn't take much for me to lose my bearings as he weaved through a matrix of dark suburban streets. He was driving almost as if he were trying to confuse me.

"You know where we are?" he said.

"Not really."

"Good answer."

He coursed along a dark narrow road that had no street

sign and then turned into a lot in front of a small row of
town houses. Slocum parked. We both stepped out of the
car. The town houses were cheap, temporary, a place in-
habited by short-timers, by the recently divorced. There
was a stillness in the air, like nothing happened here, ever.
Slocum scanned the parking lot, half filled with cars but
empty of people, and then headed toward one of the town
houses. I followed.

The door was opened by a burly man in his shirtsleeves,
blue suit pants, heavy black shoes, tie still tight, and a hol-
ster strapped around his chest. He nodded at Slocum,
leaned out to make his own scan of the parking lot, and
then stepped aside to let us in.

"You're late," said the burly man.

"He stayed past visiting hours," said Slocum. "Probably
going room to room giving out his card."

The burly man laughed even as he took my arm and
spun me around.

"What the—"

"It's all right, Carl," said Slocum. "Let him check you."

I leaned against a closet as the man slid his hand up and
down my pant seams, up and down my sides, my back,
around my belt, all along my chest. When he was done he
tapped me on the shoulder. "You're all right."

A voice from another room. "Remember, he's a
lawyer."

"Right," said the burly man, who immediately began to
pat himself, looking worried, before he smiled with relief.
"No," he called back. "It's okay, my wallet's still here."

That got a nice laugh from the other room.

The burly man led me through the narrow entranceway
into a generically furnished two-story living room, where
a man and a woman were lounging. A basketball game was
on the television, the woman was staring at the screen of

her laptop, the remnants of a take-out Chinese meal was scattered across the glass-topped dining table.

"Uh oh," said the woman, still staring at the screen. "Trouble, serious trouble."

"What?" said the guy on the couch, not looking away from the ball game.

"This bastard's shooting."

"Better get on that."

"What's going on?" I said.

"Hearts," said the burly man, "on the Internet."

"No, here. What is going on here?"

"Baby-sitting," said Slocum.

"Who?"

"Yo, guys," came a voice from the second floor, a strangely familiar voice. "Is there anymore of that shrimp pong ping crap?" I looked up just as an overweight man in boxers and a T-shirt ambled out of his second-floor room, scratched his balls, leaned over the balcony railing. "And I could use another beer, too, while yous at it."

"Son of a bitch," I said. "Derek Manley."

"Hey, Victor. How's it hanging there, you little pistol?"

"Better than the last time I ran into you."

"Yeah, sorry about that," he said, but he chuckled as he said it.

"You're the one who wanted to see me?"

"Me and only me. I told 'em I needed a speak to a lawyer and the one I wanted to speak to was you."

"Really? I'm almost flattered. And who are these guys?" I said, indicating the two men and woman who were baby-sitting.

"U.S. marshals," said Slocum.

"Marshals?" I said. "Derek, I thought you were gonna kill yourself."

"Who, me? What, are you crazy? I just told you I was looking for a way out."

"And this is it?" I said.

"Yeah, how about them apples? I made like a Russian gymnast and flipped. Witness protection. Come on up, Victor, and bring some of that shrimp pong ping up with yous."

59

"How do you like this setup?" said Derek Manley as we sat alone in his bedroom. It was a large room, furnished with a bed, a desk, a set of easy chairs, and a big-screen television. Everything a man could want except a telephone and a key. The windows, I noticed, were bolted shut and covered with metal bars. "I got three squares, I got a maid comes in once a day to freshen up the joint, I got the frigging U.S. marshals guarding my ass, I got Direct TV with, like, a hundred and fifty channels and Cinemax and Showtime."

"HBO?" I said.

"*Sopranos,* baby." He gave me a thumbs-up and then leaned forward, pointed to a fixture in the ceiling. With a remote control he turned on the television to some all-news-all-the-time station, leaned close, and lowered his voice. "They're listening in so I gots to keep the TV on and my voice soft, but you want to know the truth, I get some of my best material for the feds from that show. Tony pots someone, the next day I tell it word for word to the guy asking the questions, only I put Philly names on it. It keeps them tapes rolling, that's for sure."

"Don't be stupid, Derek. You have to tell the truth or they'll spit you out."

"I'm just giving them that stuff to keep it interesting,

I'm giving them real stuff too. But in this place, it's like I'm that broad what was wearing all the hankies and telling them stories to that big fat guy, trying to keep him interested enough so he wouldn't whack her."

"Scheherazade?"

"Gesundheit. Point is, I gots to keep them interested. Which brings me to that thing with Joey and me down by the waterfront."

"Did you tell them about it?"

"Well, no, you see. All theys really interested in is the stuff I can give them on Dante. And who the hell wants to cop to a murder that no one knows shit about? But then this city DA got word that I had turned and he came over here with a copy of that deposition I gave to you, remember, that day you raked me over the frigging coals. He wanted to know the details. I told him I wanted to talk to a lawyer. When I said the word 'lawyer' he winced. When I gave him your name he had a conniption. It was quite a sight."

"Why me?"

"Because of Joey. Because you said you was trying to find out what happened to him. You still taking care of him, so I thought for sure you was the one. So, Victor, I got a question."

"Go ahead."

"This is lawyer-client, right?"

"Sure."

"Tell me about that statue of limitations."

"You know, you guys, if you're going to talk about the law at least get the words right. Statute of limitations, all right. Statute. Say it after me. Statute."

"Eat me."

"Close enough. And the news is, Derek, there is no statute of limitations on murder."

"Crap. This could throw off the whole deal. When I told

them what I would tell them there wasn't anything about no murder."

"Let me show you something." I reached into my jacket pocket, pulled out the photograph that Mrs. Greeley had given me, the photograph of her son, Tommy, with that smirk on his face. I handed it over to Derek. "Was that the guy with the suitcase?"

He looked at it, squinted his eyes, turned his head to take it in sideways. "It was a long time ago."

"Was that the guy?"

"It's hard to be sure, you know."

"Was that the guy, Derek?"

"The prick with the suitcase? Yeah."

"You sure?"

"Pretty sure."

I took the picture back, thought a bit. "Tell me what happened that night?"

"It was like you said. Joey got a little overenthusiastic with the baseball bat. Got him in the face. The guy went down. Boom."

"Dead?"

"Sure."

"You check his pulse?"

"I seen enough fish in the tank to know dead. He wasn't moving."

"Did you check his pulse?"

"No."

"Put a mirror to his mouth to see if it fogged?"

"He wasn't moving."

"Did you have a stethoscope?"

"It was a rough-up, not a checkup."

"You ever see a live possum?"

"No."

"It's because they play dead."

"What the fuck you talking about, Victor? I never seen a dead one neither."

"What did you do to the body?"

"We kicked it into the river."

"Did you wrap it in chains? Did you weight it down with blocks. Did you stuff the body into a canvas duffel? What?"

"I told you, we kicked it into the river."

"Just kicked it into the river."

"Yeah. What's wrong with that?"

"Your hit man technique stinks."

"We was young."

"You were stupid."

"Go to hell."

"You stupid son of a bitch, you stupid stupid son of a bitch."

"Victor, why are yous coming down on me like this?"

"If you and Joey are going to spend your lives cursed because of a murder, you might as well make sure you commit it proper."

"What are yous saying here?"

"Look, I think you're in the clear. I think what you did is well beyond the limitations period."

"But you said—"

"I know what I said. Give me a few days before you say anything to anyone, all right, and by then I'll know for sure. But you have to tell me something now. You have to tell me who it was who hired you to give that kid the rough-up in the park."

He leaned forward, looked around, lowered his voice even more, so it was barely audible over the continuing screed of the television news. "All right. You sure you want to know?"

"Spill."

"It was Deep End Benny."

I just stared.

"Remember that picture you showed me in that deposition, the three altar boys? Joey, me, and some other guy? Well, the other guy was Deep End Benny. It was the three of us growing up, except Benny, he was a vicious little snipe, off the deep end, which was how he got his name. And that was before he got into crank. He hired us."

"Where's Benny now?"

"Dead. He built up a rep and started working for the boys. But he was too crazy even for them, too crazy for Scarfo. You had to be son of a bitch crazy to be too crazy for Scarfo. Shot through the head, tossed off a bridge, run over by a truck. They wasn't taking no chances with Benny."

"So why were you scared to tell me if he was dead?"

"Because Dante knew. He was still just a pawn boy then, Dante, standing like a nothing behind the counter in his shop, but he found out."

"How?"

"Joey pulled a watch off the dead guy's wrist. When he pawned it, Dante asked his questions. Joey didn't know enough to say nothing. That was how Dante made his way to the top. He knew everything what was happening in the whole of South Philly because of who was pawning what."

"But why would Dante still care if Benny was dead? I'm missing something here."

"You ain't so swift, is you, Victor? It wasn't important right off, but Dante, he stored it away until it became something that he could use. And he's been waiting, patiently, for a time to use it. Deep End Benny, he had a big brother, a wimp what meant nothing to nobody except to Benny when we was growing up, or even later, when this whole thing went down. But eventually, Benny's brother, he made good, damn good. And when the time comes, Dante is going to take the info and turn it into a free pass out of whatever trouble he gets into with the law. See, here's the thing. Our boy, our friend, the guy what Joey and me, we was altar boys with, it was Deep End Benny Straczynski."

60

It was all coming into focus, what had happened twenty years ago and what was happening now, it was all coming into focus. The only question was what to do about it.

"I can't tell you," I said as Slocum and I drove back toward the hospital, where my car was parked. "We were lawyer-client."

"Did he pay you?"

"I'm treating it as privileged. But he'll tell you everything as soon as he can. I made sure of that. Do you have a meeting set up?"

"The feds are guarding their time like a jealous lover. But, day after tomorrow, McDeiss and I have been given a couple of hours to question him about twenty years ago."

"Good. That should give me enough time to find out what I need to find out." My query had been sent to California, but no telling how long before I heard back, and I had a quicker way of finding out the truth. "Make sure you ask him in detail about what actually happened to the body. And make sure you ask him who it was who hired him."

"Interesting?"

"Oh, yes."

"Will I want to hear the answer."

"Oh, no."

"Damn it. I got a big enough headache as it is. Did anything else happen up there? Did you say anything to get him upset?"

"Me?"

"Yeah, you. He looked a little peaked when he came down the stairs."

"Did he?"

"Oh, yes."

And Slocum was right, he did. Derek Manley was positively pale when he followed me down the stairs, his eyes bulging, his hand shaking ever so slightly. It was like I had passed him a virulent flu with the utterance of one simple word.

I had thought long and hard about whether I should pass that word along. I didn't want to do Dante's bidding, and I considered telling Slocum about what Dante had asked me to pass along before I climbed those stairs, but in the end I decided to handle it as I handled it. Whatever game Derek Manley was playing, he thought he could see all the angles. Dante was using me to tell him that there were angles he hadn't anticipated, dangers he hadn't sidestepped. It wasn't up to me or Slocum or the feds to decide what risks Manley was willing to take. Derek Manley was a big boy, he was making the decisions, he should know the price he would have to pay, what precautions he would have to take. So after he had told me all I needed to know, and I told him what I thought had happened that night twenty years ago, I also told him I had a message from a friend, and I leaned over and placed my lips to his ear and whispered the single word.

His face, when he heard that word, was like a time-lapse film of the wilting of a flower, an ugly bulbous flower, true, but still a flower, losing its bloom in the blink of an eye.

"Magnolia."

It took me a while to figure it out. Was it code? Was there a particular tree? Was it the name of one of Manley's strippers? *Gentlemen, get ready to open your hearts and wallets for the jolt from Georgia, a walking heart attack who puts the hospital in Southern hospitality, the one, the only, Magnolia DeLight.* It took me a while to figure it out, but I did, finally. And Manley himself had given me the clue. For Dante, in a desperate situation, would have threatened Manley at his softest point. And the only soft point Manley appeared to have was a son, in troubled health, stashed away somewhere in New Jersey. All it took was a quick look at the atlas and there it was, between Barrington and Somerdale, between Kirkwood and Runnymede, the little hamlet of Magnolia, New Jersey. Dante was threatening Manley's boy, and he was using me to do it. But you tell me if Manley didn't deserve to know.

"Where are you heading now?" said Slocum as he dropped me off in front of the hospital's parking garage.

"Home. To sleep. Perchance to dream."

"You sure?"

"I could use some."

"Look, Carl, I respect that you promised Manley not to tell us what he told you. I don't know if privilege is really attached, and we could probably get a judge to force it out of you except that we'll hear it from the horse's mouth soon enough. But whatever he told you, if it really did have something to do with that fire the other night, you should let McDeiss and me take care of it."

"Fair enough," I said. "You're the pros."

"Yes, we are."

"And I'm basically a coward."

"That's one of the things I most admire about you."

"Much appreciation," I said, "though you shouldn't

slight my ignorance. That deserves your admiration too. Along with my general lack of physical prowess."

"Not to mention you're as ugly as the wrong end of a dead dog."

"Thank you for that."

"So you're going to go home now, right?"

"Right."

"To sleep?"

"Heaven knows I need it."

"Good. I'll be in touch."

I watched as the Taurus drove away, then wandered around the parking garage looking for my car, which didn't bother me much since I decided I would wait a bit before I drove out anyway, just to make sure Slocum was gone. While I waited I called a number Derek had given me, 609 area code, and gave the woman on the other end of the phone a message I didn't understand: "That time on the way to the beach, it's that time again." Then I called Beth. There was no answer so I left a message on her machine, saying I had news, big news, and I would tell her everything tomorrow morning at Lonnie Chambers's funeral.

Slowly I backed out of my space, followed the painted arrows down the ramps, paid my fee, all the time checking my rearview mirror. I kept checking it even as I pulled out of the lot, turned right and then left and then right and then left again, driving through the narrow North Philly streets as if through a maze, making sure I wasn't followed. Satisfied, I headed south, not up Broad, where I would be expected to drive, but up Nineteenth, again checking behind me. I would go home to get some sleep some time that night, just as I had told Slocum, but not just yet. I had someplace first to visit. See, it was all coming into focus, and it was focusing on one man. Up Nineteenth, across the Benjamin Franklin Parkway. Around

Rittenhouse Square, and then again up Nineteenth until I found a parking spot.

"What the 'ell do you want?" came the familiar voice over the intercom speaker.

"I'm here to see Mr. Dean."

"Mr. Dean has retired for the night."

"Tell him I'm here. Tell him I've got a question for him."

"You've got a question? That's a surprise, isn't it? Solicitors are always full of questions. Like a cow is full of shit."

"Tell him I'm here."

"Ever seen a slaughtered cow split right down the gut. The shit slides right out onto the ground. I wonder if it's like that with solicitors, slit their bellies and the questions come sliding out, slapping down on the floor, along with their intestines, small and large."

"Thank you for that image. You should write children's books."

"You've got a question. I've got your answer right here. Bugger off."

I rang the bell again.

"You didn't 'ear me?"

"Oh I heard you. Tell your boss I'm here."

"Climb into your bung hole and get lost."

"Do we have to keep doing this? Isn't it getting tedious, this little give and take? Because in the end you're just a servant boy, working for the boss. So be a good little servant boy and let your boss know I'm here."

"I already said he's asleep."

"Or maybe he's standing right behind you, whispering in your ear. Either way, I think he'll want to see me. Tell him I'm here. Tell him I have a question. About the Dane."

CHAPTER

61

"Hamlet?" said Eddie Dean from the doorway.

I was in the parlor once again, with the red walls, the grand piano, the paintings of horses, the model ship, farther along in construction than before, but still incomplete. I was standing by the shelves of books, holding the volume of Shakespeare's tragedies, opened to *Hamlet*. I looked up to see Eddie Dean, in his paisley dressing gown, with his dead face, his ascot, his cigarette and long blond hair, looking like a ludicrous mannequin from a long-gone age. He belonged on that dead ship he was so concerned about, I thought. They both were ghosts.

Behind him stood the glowering Colfax.

"You told us *Hamlet* was a great favorite of yours," I said. "I've been reading it myself and I find I have a question."

"This late at night?"

"Literature doesn't keep banker's hours, does it? I have a question and I thought you'd be the perfect person to ask."

"I'm no expert," he said, a false modesty stretching his voice.

"Don't slight yourself."

Maybe my voice was a bit harsh, because Eddie Dean's

chin rose for a moment before he turned and nodded at Colfax. Colfax stepped inside the room and closed the door behind him. Dean walked toward me. "Fire away, then, Victor. What part of the play can I elucidate for you?"

"See, here's my problem," I said. "I've read it over a couple times now and each time I can't help wondering why it is that Hamlet dithers so."

"It is part of his nature. A fatal flaw so to speak. It is simply what Hamlet is."

"A dithering fool?"

"Not a fool. But a man, perhaps, who is unable to act with great force because his mind goes off in too many directions."

"When it should be focused on the one."

"Precisely."

"Revenge," I said.

"Yes, well, remember, Victor, it is, at heart, a simple revenge play after all."

"And Shakespeare was such a simple writer." I looked down at the book, carefully turned a page. "So you believe Hamlet is right to seek a bloody revenge against his uncle, the king?"

"The king killed Hamlet's father, he married Hamlet's mother, he usurped Hamlet's crown and wealth. What else is to be done?"

"Ergo murder."

"I believe in the law it is called justifiable homicide."

"No, it's not," I said. "Revenge is not a legal justification for anything. A man named Lonnie Chambers was killed a few nights ago. His funeral is early tomorrow morning. It turns out he was an old friend of Tommy Greeley's."

I looked carefully at Eddie Dean's face. It was a mask, frozen, inscrutable, hideous. "I didn't know."

"This Lonnie Chambers might also have betrayed Tommy. Lonnie was supposed to guard his old friend the night Tommy was killed. He obviously failed, but maybe by design. He was upset that Tommy was sleeping with his wife."

"Very interesting, Victor."

"Except you knew that last part already, because I told it all to your vice president of external affairs."

"Did you?"

"There's a famous line in the play that troubles me, when the ghost of Hamlet's father says—where is it?" I paged back through the play, being careful to touch only the gold gilt on the edge of the pages. "Yes, here. The ghost says, *'Murder most foul as in the best it is.'* Even assuming that murder for revenge is the best kind of murder, it still is characterized, even by the ghost who is urging it, as being most foul."

"Obviously he's not referring to the killing of his own killer."

"Obviously?"

"Maybe you should go home and read it again."

"I returned my copy to the library. May I borrow this?"

He waved a hand dismissively. "Yes, yes, be my guest."

"Babbage. Ever hear of a man named Babbage?"

His frozen face didn't change, but he hesitated a moment before he said, "Cabbage?"

"Babbage."

"No. Can't say that I have."

"He was the man whose testimony drove a stake through the heart of Tommy Greeley's organization and would have put Tommy in jail. Babbage died just a few weeks ago. Heart attack."

"Pity."

"Although," I said, tapping my head, "a clump of hair

was missing, so the heart attack might have happened while someone was in the process of interrogating him quite forcefully. Maybe the same way Joey Parma was interrogated quite forcefully."

"I hardly think so."

I nodded, stepped back and then forward again. "But why does he dither? I'm talking of Hamlet again. If killing the king is so obviously the right thing to do, why does he hesitate? There is a moment when he no longer has any doubts about what his uncle has done, and he spies the murderer kneeling, and he unsheathes his sword, but he can't bring himself to use it."

"Because the uncle was praying, Victor. You must not have read the text very carefully."

I started looking through the play, turning a page, scratching my head.

"Give the book to me," he said as he grabbed it away. He licked his thumb and paged through the volume until he found the scene he was looking for. He traced his finger down one page and then the opposite and then tapped the line in victory. "Yes, Hamlet doesn't want to kill his uncle when his uncle's thoughts are turned toward God. He says, *'A villain kills my father, and for that I, his sole son, do this same villain send to heaven?'* He decides to wait, so that he can catch him in a more compromising position and send him to hell. See?"

He turned the book toward me, pointed at the line. I took the book and started to read the section and then stopped. "Okay," I said. "I see." I laid the silk marker in the page and then closed the book. "Maybe you're right. Or maybe Hamlet is rationalizing because a part of him, the best part of him, doesn't want to do it at all, knows it is wrong, knows a bloody revenge can end only in his own physical and moral destruction."

"What is that, Victor, the Quaker interpretation?"

"Or the author's, because that's pretty much what happens to our hero. I mean, it's not a tragedy simply because Hamlet dies in the end, is it? Hamlet at one point describes himself as *'crawling between heaven and earth.'* It seems to me he's split, one side wants to kill, but the other side yearns for something better, finer, more spiritual, maybe more moral. I wonder if it is that split which causes his hesitation."

"The man killed his father, Victor. The killer deserved to die. What would you have him do?"

"Use the law, maybe."

"But the killer was king. The law wasn't available to Hamlet."

"Then let God and conscience take care of it."

"Which means doing nothing. Sometimes nothing is not an option. He had to do something. He had a duty to do something."

"Duty? And who imposed such a duty? A ghost, covered head to toe in armor."

"The ghost of his father."

"The ghost of a murderous pirate, of a criminal, the ghost of war, the ghost of violence. If Hamlet had a duty, it was to remain true to the best part of himself, the part that loved art, that loved Ophelia, that worshiped life, not death."

"You simply don't understand. You can't understand."

I stopped, stared. It was as if an emotion was struggling to form itself in the lifeless flesh of his face, something dark and bitter and wholly personal.

"Maybe you're right," I said. "Maybe I'll never understand the play the way you can. What happened to your face?"

His features smoothed back toward their bland frigidity,

as if what I had seen had been merely a phantom of emotion overlaid on lifeless wax, and he turned away slightly. "There was an accident."

"What kind of accident?"

"It is time for you to go."

"I don't know if you noticed, but I was out of town. Paid a visit to the Shoe City of the World. I visited Tommy Greeley's mother. Sad lady, but I did see something extraordinary. In her china hutch, saved as if they were presents from a god. Twenty bottles of gin. She gets one each year on Christmas."

"Charming."

"And I also visited an old friend of Tommy's, a man named Jimmy Sullivan. He gave me something he had been saving all these years."

Eddie Dean cocked his head slightly, as if waiting for some revelation.

"Some sort of tool chest that Tommy had given him to hold," I said.

"How intriguing. Maybe you should hand it over to me for safekeeping."

"It's pretty safe where it is. I know who betrayed Tommy Greeley."

"For certain?"

"For pretty damn certain."

"Tell me, Victor. Tell me who."

"Not yet," I said. "Not until I get the answers I'm looking for."

"What do you want?"

"I want to know who killed Joey Parma."

"That again. I can't help you. I don't know."

"Okay."

"Truly, I don't."

"Okay."

"What are you going to do?"

"I'm going to find out. So how do you think it turns out in the end? The play, I mean."

"Oh, pretty well, I would say. The father is avenged, the king is dead."

"Yes, but so is Hamlet, and his mother, and his love, and all that his father had won with blood on the battlefield is turned over once again to his enemies."

"A warning against indecision."

"Somehow I don't think so." I lifted the Shakespeare volume, said, "Thanks for the book," and then headed past him, along the long wall of bookshelves. As I passed a specific collection of volumes I stopped. I pulled one out, looked at it. It was part of a set, all in fine leather bindings, the collected works of Alexandre Dumas.

"By the way," I said, "the Dumas novel you loved as a child, the one that gave you the greatest reading experience of your life, that wasn't *The Three Musketeers,* was it?"

"No," said Eddie Dean.

"It didn't come to me until just now. The Count of Monte Cristo's faithful and devoted servant was named Jacopo, wasn't he?"

"If you say so."

I turned, faced him as I slid *The Count of Monte Cristo* back into its place. "See, here's the problem with using literature as a guide for life, Eddie. From everything I've learned about him, it's pretty clear that Tommy Greeley was not the innocent and noble-hearted Edmund Dantes. And Alura Straczynski, I can tell you with utter certainty, is not the fair and loyal Mercedes. And Hamlet, well, in the end what can you say except that our pal Hamlet, despite all his evident talents and depths, was a careless son of a bitch who royally screwed the pooch."

* * *

I banged on the door. It was late and he was most likely asleep and so I banged hard enough to shatter his slumber. Through the little glass peephole I saw a light switch on, then be blocked by a peering eye.

"Oh," said Jeffrey Telushkin when he finally opened the door. "It's you." He was wearing pajamas and a robe, his hair was mussed, his little beady eyes red beneath his round glasses. He wrapped his robe more tightly around himself. "Do you know what time it is?"

"Is it too late for a visit?" I said.

"What do you want?"

"A dance?"

"Are you serious?"

"No, just tired. Do you still have a contact in the FBI?"

"Maybe."

"A contact you trust, a contact who can move quickly on evidence you give to him."

His eyes narrowed behind his thick lenses and his lips curled in curiosity. "Yes, I do."

"Don't get too excited, we're not getting married here."

"What do you have?"

I handed him the leather-bound volume of Shakespeare's tragedies. He looked at it for a moment and started to open it.

"Don't," I said. "Treat it like you would a fragile piece of evidence. Put it in a bag and give it to your contact to take down to the lab. Have them check the inside for fingerprints, especially the pages where the silk marker sits. Then compare what they can lift to some old prints you might still have hanging around."

"Old prints?"

"You know."

His head jerked up. "Is he alive? Have you found him?"

"That's why I came here," I said. "For you to tell me.

The person whose prints are in the book is named Eddie Dean. He's living for the time being in a rented town house on the southwest corner of Rittenhouse Square."

"Does his reappearance have something to do with the eminent jurist whose relationship to these matters we discussed?"

"I don't want to talk about him."

"But his involvement could have far-reaching consequences. Any revelation would have national importance. It is most vital."

"Not to me. But if you're going to move on Eddie Dean, you better move fast."

He turned the book over in his hands, the eyes behind his thick glasses glistening now with excitement. "Don't worry about that. We'll be quick as snakes."

"I bet you will. Call me when it's done. But be warned. He has a goon with him, name of Colfax, so if you find a match, you might not want to show up alone."

CHAPTER

62

It was just after eleven when I finally got to the office after Lonnie Chambers's funeral, a faint dusting of Lonnie still on my shoulders. It had been an almost touching ceremony at the burned-out building that had once been Lonnie's shop, what with the howl of the motorcycles, the roar of the boom boxes, the belch of the beer cans in tribute before one of the motorheads had taken the urn with Lonnie's remains, opened the top, tossed it high into the air so that the metal dropped into the burned-out hulk of his shop and his ashes fell upon the mourners and the neighborhood where he had worked and died. And then had come the guitar. Soft chords, a simple progression, A to D to E to D back again to A, over and over again, played as slowly as a dirge, before a voice started and others joined, singing slowly and softly as if the most solemn hymn.

> *Wild thing,*
> *You make my heart sing,*
> *You make everything*
> *Groovy.*
> *Wild thing.*

I had stood off to the side for the whole event, conspicuous in my suit, and after the strains of "Wild Thing" disappeared, replaced by something loud and Metallica played from a boom box, I was about to turn and leave when I saw Chelsea come my way. She was crying and smiling at the same time.

"He loved that song," she said.

"How are you doing?"

"Better. Thank you. I still miss him, I think I'm going to miss him for the rest of my life. There's a hole in my heart."

"Is someone helping you deal with what happened?"

"I've been on the phone."

"I meant someone trained in grief counseling."

"Cooper's very advanced."

"He's a convicted felon, Chelsea."

"Which makes him a perfect adviser for me, right?"

I must have showed my chagrin at the loose remark because Chelsea, also a convicted felon, put a hand to my cheek.

"I'm going out there for a while," she said. "I'm leaving this afternoon. He's spent the last twenty years working through his past, the good and the bad, the mistakes, the waste. You know, he was planning to run away, they both were, he and Tommy. But Cooper in the end decided not to. He decided to face up to what he had done and suffer the consequences with the rest of us. And through it all he's been a rock. I think he can help me finally find some peace."

"Did he help Lonnie?"

"For a time, but in the end Lonnie didn't want to be helped. Did you think about what I said at the fire?"

"The dead rising?"

"Yes. Cooper thinks that's what's going on."

"So do I. If it's true, it's being taken care of while we speak."

"By who?"

"Remember a little FBI guy named Tclushkin?"

She wrinkled her nose with disgust and then turned toward the burned-out building. "You know when I was with Lonnie, I was never really with him. He wasn't the key to my past, and I couldn't see him as part of my future, and so I let the present slip away from us. When I think back, I think I failed him. I think I failed everyone. Myself too."

I thought of telling her it was all right, I thought of giving some false comfort, but the thing about Chelsea that I admired most of all was that she didn't want false comfort, she wasn't looking for an easy way out of her sadness. So I gave her a hug instead.

"Good luck," I said. "I hope your friend helps."

"You know what Cooper says? He says if you can't accept your past, understand it, even love it, if you can't do that, then you become its slave. You spend your life either running from it or toward it, but either way you are running."

Was there an answer in that? If there was I couldn't yet see it, all I could see was the sad woman beside me and the desolation behind me and in front of me a pack of frightened rabbits running for their lives.

Beth was supposed to have joined me at the funeral, but I didn't blame her for missing it. She had never met Lonnie and had apparently traded the funeral for another hour of sleep, but I was anxious to see her now. I had much to tell her, we had much to figure out together. Things were absolutely coming to a head. I was waiting still for word from Telushkin, but I wasn't holding my breath. The prints would confirm my suspicions and the FBI would pick up Dean and with him in jail I could start to tie that bastard to

Joey Parma's murder. I was counting on Beth and Phil Skink, what I considered my brain trust, to help me figure out how.

"She's not in yet," said Ellie, my secretary.

"Was she supposed to be in court today?"

"It's not on the schedule."

"Maybe something popped up. Why don't you call her cell and if that's not answering, call her home, see if she's sick."

"Will do, Mr. Carl. There's someone waiting for you in your office."

"Waiting for me? Who?"

"He didn't give his name."

"And you let him into my office?"

"You don't pay me enough to have tried to stop him."

I eyed my office door nervously. "What is he wearing, a suit?"

"A sport coat, a green sport coat. Bright, very bright. The jacket I mean."

"Ah, yes," I said. "I see. And I don't blame you."

I snatched my messages and mail from the plastic holders on Ellie's desk and headed into my office.

Leo, Dante's boy, was sitting behind my desk, his eyes scanning the walls, his thick fingers drumming on my desktop, leaving, I had no doubt, impressions in the wood.

"This place is a dump," he said.

"Maybe, but I call it home. You going to buy patches for that jacket?"

"I got three others just like it. The saleslady, she said the color matched my eyes."

"And now you want me to sue?"

"The boss, he wanted to know if you delivered his message."

"Tell him yes."

"He'll be pleased." He took an envelope out of his jacket pocket and handed it to me. "He asked me to deliver this personally. It is a certain number that a certain party was calling about a certain scam of his."

"How'd you guys get it?"

"We twisted a nipple, if you know what I mean."

"Teddy?"

"There you go."

"It must have hurt."

"You have any idea of where he is now?"

"Who, Teddy?"

"No, the other guy, the guy what you gave our message to."

"No, no idea."

"You sure?"

"Yes, I'm sure."

"Do yourself a favor, Victor. If you find out where he is, you let us know. We want to talk to him ourselves." He stood up, straightened his jacket, looked around. "You ought to spruce this place up a bit, Victor. A little color would do wonders."

"And I bet you have one in mind."

After Leo left, I ripped open the envelope. A single yellow sheet was inside and on the single yellow sheet was a single phone number, a number that looked vaguely familiar. The person on the other side of this line was the one Joey Parma had been looking to for money, enough money to pay off his debt to Teddy Big Tits and keep his girlfriend, the impossible Bev Rodgers, satisfied.

I picked up the phone, dialed it, and when I heard the greeting hung it up again. That fool, that stupid fool. This was the problem with taking up Joey Parma's cause. Every step you followed in his sad little life became ever more pathetic.

I closed my eyes and rubbed my face and tried to snap myself back into focus. There was work to be done, work I had been neglecting, a motion for a reduction in sentence to be filed for Rashard Porter, a response to the Bar Association's frivolous action against me, time sheets to fill out and bills to prepare, criminal opinions to review, cases that I had long been ignoring to stop ignoring. But I didn't do any of that. I went through my messages, tossed out anything not related to Joey Parma or Eddie Dean or Tommy Greeley—if it was important enough they'd call back—and ended up with two pink message slips in my hand.

"This is Victor Carl," I said into the phone. "Tell me the news."

"Where is he?"

"I told you. Did you take the book to the lab? Did they ID the prints?"

"Yes, yes. We did all that. Where is he?"

"Oh hell, Telushkin, did you lose him again?"

"Two hours ago a joint task force of police and FBI entered the town house rented by the Mr. Dean you mentioned to me. It was deserted, nobody home, no sign of habitation. Cleaned out."

"Of course it is," I said.

"Where is he?"

"I don't know. What took you so long? He was there when I handed you the book. I came right from his place."

"These things take time. They can't be rushed. All procedures must be followed, evidence gathered, warrants issued. We moved as fast as we could."

"Apparently not fast enough."

"They want you to come down to the federal building and give a full statement."

"I can't right now."

"I won't let him escape me this time. I won't."

"You already have, haven't you?"

Once again the fugitive had eluded his grasp. That was Telushkin's fate, to be skewered by Tommy Greeley. Now it was up to me, though I had suspected it would be up to me from the first, and I was clueless as to what to do. I knew who had set up Tommy Greeley—Jackson Straczynski, using his hood of a brother to beat up and rob the man who was screwing with his screwy wife—but I didn't know what to do with that knowledge. Whatever crime had been committed it was twenty years old and no murder had occurred and so the statute of limitations had long expired. Joey had been in the clear all along, that stupid son of a bitch, and Derek Manley now had nothing to fear, and neither did the justice. The only one who could still be prosecuted was the running man, Eddie Dean, Tommy Greeley, one and the same, whose indictment had stopped the limitations period from expiring, but he was back on the lam and I had no idea where to find him.

Maybe Kimberly could help. A boat, she had been off that very morning, she had said, to see a man about a boat. What did that mean? He hadn't left yet, of that I was pretty sure. He still had business here, he wouldn't leave without the suitcase or the stuff I had brought back from Brockton, or the money he thought was still hanging around. So I had some time, but whatever I did, I would have to do it quickly or he would be gone again, and with him would have fled my last best chance for learning what happened to Joey Parma. That's why I needed Beth and Skink, together, to talk through the options, to keep me from doing something stupid. On my own I am prone to stupidity, but Beth and Skink keep me sharp, keep me focused.

I looked at the second message, shook my head, dialed the phone.

"We need to talk," said Slocum.

"That's never a good sign," I said. "Does this mean you're breaking up with me?"

"We need to get together right away."

"I'm a bit busy now."

"What did you say to him last night?"

"To who? Derek?"

"The feds have been chewing my ass all morning. They want to know what you said to him. They want to know why after your visit last night he went ape shit. They want to know why he disappeared and where he went."

"Derek is missing?"

"Gone."

"What about the baby-sitters?"

"The bastard slipped out the window."

"There were bars."

"He had a screwdriver."

"Nice security."

"They were secured on the inside. He was the one that wanted protection. But for some reason, after your visit, he wanted out. They need to talk to you immediately at the federal building."

"I seem to be pretty popular down there right now. Tell them to wait."

"What's going on?"

"When I find out you'll be the first to know."

"By definition that's a lie."

"So it is."

"Carl, this isn't funny."

"I'll be in touch."

"Carl."

I hung up lightly, not angrily, so lightly Slocum was probably still calling out my name before he realized I wasn't there anymore. So Manley had slipped out the window. Maybe he knotted his sheets together, or maybe he leaped out onto a leafy bush, now a leafy dead bush. That must have been a sight, like a whale falling from an apple tree. What would Newton have made of that? I suppose Manley had some business to take care of and, after delivering his message to that 609 number, I had a pretty good idea of what it was. That was why Leo had come, not to give the envelope, but to enlist my aid in finding Derek. The feds weren't the only ones rushing around like Keystone Kops looking for him. Run, Derek, run, I thought, because they are all coming after you. But Manley, I figured, could take care of himself; I had other things to deal with.

I saw a light flash on my phone, Slocum phoning back to shout in my ear, I presumed. I didn't want to talk to him right now, I didn't want to be hauled down to the federal building and locked in a room with a hungry pack of U.S. marshals who had been embarrassed by a fleeing witness, with the FBI in the hallway waiting for their own crack at me. I didn't have time for that right now.

"I'm not in," I called out to my secretary.

She stepped into my office and closed the door.

"I can't find Ms. Derringer," she said. "Her cell phone doesn't answer and neither does her home phone. I left messages on both."

"Okay," I said. "Maybe she took a spa day."

"She never takes a spa day, Mr. Carl. And there's a call for you."

"I don't want to talk to Slocum."

"It's not Mr. Slocum. It's someone else. He said you'd want to talk to him. He had an accent."

"What kind of accent?"

"I don't know. Michael Caine? Like that."

I waited for Ellie to leave and close the door behind her before I picked up the phone.

" 'Ello, Victor," came Colfax's slow angry voice.

"What do you want?"

"I thought we'd 'ave ourselves a little chat."

"I don't want to chat with you."

"Not even if we talk about your pal Willie Shake? You're a grand one for talking about Willie Shake."

"What do you want?"

"Oh, don't be like that. It was quite a performance you put on last night. You would have made a fine little public school boy, staying up all night with the other lads, discussing Shakespeare in your common room as you buggered one another to the dawn. A regular Oscar Wilde."

"Go to hell."

"There's a bar, Fadó. On Locust. Do you know it?"

"I know it."

"Join me there in thirty minutes, why don't you?"

"Why don't I? Because you're an asshole and I've got nothing to say to you."

"But I've got lots to say to you. Fadó. 'Alf an 'our. You and me, we can chat about life, about long-dead playwrights, and about your partner."

"Beth?"

"You've got another partner we don't know about?"

"What about Beth?"

"Seen her lately?"

"What about Beth, you bastard?"

"Come alone, Victor, but do come."

CHAPTER

63

I could barely restrain my anger as I strode down Locust Street. I wanted to wring someone's neck, to twist my hands around someone's throat and squeeze until a head popped off. Whose head? It didn't quite matter, but I had my list and it started with Colfax, that cocky cockney bastard, and it included his very creepy boss, and there was Justice Jackson Straczynski and there was Alura Straczynski and there was Joey Parma for getting himself killed and getting me and Beth into this steaming pile of dung in the first place. They had already messed with my profession, my freedom, my finances, but when they messed with my partner, they had gone so far beyond the pale they were well nigh invisible. Oh yes, I wanted to wring a neck, a peck of necks, but I had to restrain myself. Anger wasn't what Beth needed. Cool calculation was what Beth needed, which was a problem, wasn't it, since in our partnership she was the cool calculating one.

I took a deep breath, tried to calm myself, pulled open the door and entered Fadó. A bit of the home sod it was, all carved mahogany and painted ceilings, with corned beef and cabbage on the menu, folk songs from the speakers, Guinness on tap. It was trying too hard, a theme park version of a Dublin pub, when all it really needed to be authentic enough was the Guinness on tap and a villainous Brit at the bar.

"Where is she?" I said in as low a voice as I could maintain.

"What, no pleasantries?" said Colfax, turning from his pint, already three quarters gone, and giving me a superior little sneer. His face was ruddy, his hair short, he was wearing a three-quarter-length black leather coat with its pockets bulging, and he seemed to be enjoying himself. "No 'How's it going?' No 'Fine day today, isn't it?' No 'Would you like another round, Mr. Colfax?' None of that, ay? Just right to the bone of it. 'Where is she?' "

"Where the fuck is she, you Euro slime?"

"Now that's a bit crude, and from a man who so reveres his Willie Shake. Sit down, 'ave a pint. Don't take it all so personal."

"But it is," I said through gritted teeth.

"Good. Because for me it's just business, and when it's business versus personal, well, the business always wins out, doesn't it? She's fine, Victor. A nice girl, that. Showed a fine respect for Mr. Beretta, and didn't give us a spot of trouble. Right now, I can assure you, she's being well cared for."

"How do I even know you have her?"

"Oh, you know."

"Prove it."

"Give her a call and find out. Call her right now, why don't you? On her cell."

I took out my phone, glared at him, found Beth on the auto dial, stepped away, and turned my back to Colfax as I waited for the call to go through.

And then I heard the most sickening sound. A phone, ringing, her phone ringing. But not just on my line. Slowly I turned.

Colfax grinned as he sat with the ringing phone in his hand. He opened it with a switch-blade flick of his wrist.

" 'Ello. Fancy 'earing from you. Yes it is a nice day, isn't it, Victor, you wanker."

I stared at him for a long moment, trying to figure out what to do, but there wasn't much choice, was there? If I jumped him, he would pummel me into applesauce. If I canceled the call and immediately called McDeiss, Colfax would leave and there'd be no telling what he and his boss would do. They wanted something and I had a pretty good idea what it was. Even so, I decided to let Colfax tell me. It would make him so happy, and I aimed to please.

"How's it going?" I said as I climbed onto the stool next to his. "Fine day today, isn't it? Would you like another round, Mr. Colfax?"

"Now you've got it," he said, closing the phone. "Now you understand the terms of the thing. Don't mind if I do."

I waved to the bartender. "Two Guinness," I said, "and make mine a light."

That always got a good laugh at an Irish pub.

"Can I ask a question," I said after the pints came.

"What's this one about, *Macbeth*?"

"Where do guys like Eddie Dean find guys like you? Do you advertise in the back of golf magazines? Gunsel for hire, not too bright but suitably nasty. Or is there a union shop where an employer comes in, says I need a hatchet boy to shine my wingtips for a couple months, and the guy behind the booth pulls out a card and calls your name."

"You really want to know?"

"Actually, yes."

"There's a pub in Southgate."

"That's it? The whole secret? A pub in Southgate?"

"That's it."

"What's it called, the Bloody Swordsman?

"The Prissy Miss."

"You're kidding. The Prissy Miss?"

"There you go."

"Ooh, sounds ferocious, the Prissy Miss."

"Go in and say that, Victor. The regulars will cut your tongue off and stick it up your nose. You'll be licking snot the rest of your natural-born life."

"And Eddie Dean came into the Prissy Miss?"

"Yes, 'e did."

"And hired you?"

"Yes, 'e did. 'E was looking for specific qualifications and I fit the bill."

"Murdering scum, was that it?"

"That was just the bonus for him, wasn't it?"

"He pay you yet?"

" 'Alf up front. Them's the terms."

"And you expect to get the rest with him busted flat?"

"That's where you come in."

"I see. Okay, go ahead. What does he want?"

He finished his first pint before he said, "These are the terms. He wants what it is you took up there in Massachusetts."

"I don't have everything he thinks I have. There was—"

"Oh, for Christ's sake, shut up already. We're not a debating society, understand? I'm not 'ere for excuses, just to give the terms. 'E wants all of it. It's up to you make sure all of it's there. But that's not the all of it. 'E also wants the suitcase."

"I never said I had that."

"But you know where it is, don't you?"

I pressed my lips together and said nothing.

"And 'e wants the sot that betrayed 'im twenty years ago. 'E wants the name."

"I can't do all this."

"And 'e wants it tomorrow."

"He's crazy."

"You've noticed that too, 'ave you? Well, them's the terms, Victor. It's all about terms. And them terms are non-negotiable."

"Does he want me to bring it all to the house?"

"No, after your visit last night 'e thought it prudent to move on out. Just bring it to me 'ere. Tomorrow, same time as this. But be certain, no police, no tails, just the materials. Them's the terms, and the terms is rock solid."

"I bring what he wants, then what happens?"

"When I get them and get away without any problem," he said, climbing off his stool, "your partner walks away with nothing but a story to tell 'er kids on long winter nights and we sail off into the sunrise."

He reached for his second pint, drained it, wiped the foam off his lip with his sleeve.

"Now be a good little servant boy and take care of this tab, won't you, Victor?"

"You didn't like that crack, I suppose."

"Fancy this, Vic, it didn't bother me none at all. See, I don't take it personally."

I didn't respond. He didn't care. He put his hands in the bulging pockets of his long black leather jacket, turned around, and headed out of the bar.

By the time I paid for the bill and left the bar, he was nowhere to be seen. I spun around in frustration on the street and as I spun my stomach fell with fear. What the hell did I expect? I went into Eddie Dean's house, let him know what I knew, let him know I was going to take him down. How could I not have expected the bastard to fight back? If I had talked it over with Beth first, she would have stopped me, she would have applied her cool calculation and found a better path. But now those paths were closed to me. Beth. Beth. What to do about Beth? It was too late to count on Telushkin and his FBI to handle it. Colfax had stated the terms with utter clarity, unless I could come up with a better plan I would have to come through. Somehow I would have to get that bastard what he wanted. And I knew how to start.

I took the yellow sheet out of my pocket, the one Dante's boy had given me, called the number written there. It rang for a moment, and then came the voice, a woman's voice, secretarial, the one with the high gray hair.

"Pennsylvania Supreme Court," she said. "Justice Straczynski's chambers. How can I help you?"

CHAPTER

64

He walked up the path with a slow, awkward gait, his head swiveling guiltily, his blue suit bunched around his hunched shoulders. It was Rittenhouse Square in the middle of a fine spring afternoon and the park was lousy with pretty girls and slackers and office workers taking in some sun and shoppers with their bags, resting before another bout of rabid acquisition. It was crowded, loud, urban—a perfect place for an anonymous meeting. Across the park, on the southwest corner, stood Eddie Dean's rented and now-deserted mansion, a touch that gave me a nice ironic jolt even if as yet it meant nothing to the man in the suit cautiously making his way to my bench. When the man spotted me, his head recoiled as if from some stark fulsome scent. I seem to get that a lot, but not often from a Supreme Court justice.

"Well?" he said, standing before me.

He was bent forward, his high forehead glistening with sweat, his thin blond hair disheveled, his fists balled with anxiety. I was leaning back on the bench, my arms spread leisurely on either side.

"Sit," I said.

"I don't have much time."

"Yes, you do," I said. "You have all day. Sit."

He sat at my command like a lapdog.

The hardest thing was getting him on the line. When I gave my name to the secretary she patched me right through to the vigilant and violent Clerk Lobban. No, said Curtis Lobban, the justice was not available. Why don't you tell me, said Curtis Lobban, the purpose of the call? Of course, said Curtis Lobban, whatever you say I will relay to the justice word for word. No, said Curtis Lobban, it is not possible for you to speak to him right now. There was again an ominous note in his voice that raised the hair on the back of my neck. This was not simply a gatekeeper, this Curtis Lobban, shuffling files and appointments, beating up trespassers, doing the bidding of a sitting jurist, this was something else, something fearsomely protective. I wasn't getting through, he wasn't letting me through, and I didn't quite know what to do until a voice broke into our conversation.

"I will speak to Mr. Carl," said the justice, harshly.

"Yes, sir," said Curtis Lobban.

"We need to meet," I said.

"When," said the justice.

"Now."

"That is impossible," said Curtis Lobban, still on the line. "There are appointments."

"Hang up the phone, Curtis," said the justice, "and cancel my appointments."

And now here he was, Jackson Straczynski, standing before me, fidgeting and wincing as if preparing to be beaten about the head. And now sitting down next to me, leaning forward, elbows on his knees, wringing his long pale hands as if he were auditioning for a role.

"I want to apologize, Mr. Carl," he said, speaking as if it were a struggle to get the words out. "After your last visit, I made the inquiries I told you I would make. Everything you said turned out to be true, and I am appalled."

"But of course you knew."

"No."

"About my being locked up at Traffic Court? About Rashard Porter."

"No, I did not."

"It was your doing. It had to be."

"But it wasn't."

"Then who could—"

I stopped in midsentence and thought it through. The secretive Clerk O'Brien in Traffic Court. The dour Clerk Templeton in Common Pleas Court. The fearsomely protective Clerk Lobban in the justice's own chambers.

"Son of a bitch."

"I fear," said the justice, "that one of my employees might have acted to safeguard my position well beyond his actual authority."

"A conspiracy of clerks."

"Clerk Lobban's loyalties run very deep, deeper than in a normal employee-employer relationship. He knows my wife, in fact it is she who hired him for me. His wife is ill and my wife helps in her care. It is very complicated."

"I can imagine."

"No," he said. "No, you can't."

"What kind of car does your clerk drive?"

"Something small, I think. Foreign."

"Toyota?"

"I suppose."

"Color?"

"I don't know. Look, I have spoken to Judge Wellman. He denied any pressure was brought to bear, but I have reason to believe a motion to vacate Mr. Porter's sentence would be well received."

"What about Lonnie?"

"I read about Mr. Chambers in the newspaper. Very distressing, and I know what you must think. But I never told Curtis anything about him. Our prior conversation remained absolutely private."

"And Joey Parma?"

"Who?"

"Joseph Parma. He called you a number of times."

"No. You must be mistaken. I never heard of Joseph Parma."

"He was a friend of your brother's."

"Benny?"

"Yes. An old friend."

"Benny did have a friend named Joey when he was younger. They were altar boys together. I think they called him Joey Cheaps."

"Bingo."

"But why was he trying to call me?"

"Because Joey was an idiot. And he had done something twenty years ago for your brother. And he thought he could turn what he did twenty years ago into cash today."

"And that was the client you were referring to, who had his throat slit."

"That's right."

"Mr. Carl. Oh God. Mr. Carl. I think I am going to be sick."

CHAPTER

65

"**If it had** been anyone else but Tommy," said Jackson Straczynski, still leaning forward on the bench, his stomach still riled, "I might have handled it differently. That's not an excuse. I have no excuse. But it may be an explanation. Have you ever had a friend to whom you feel very close and yet with whom you can't help but compete over every available scrap? That was the way it was with me and Tommy Greeley.

"I met him on the fencing team. I had thought fencing might be something interesting to learn, a good aristocratic sport. Yes, that was how I thought about things then, anything to wipe the South Philly out of me. Which is funny, when you think of it, because all the while I was working on my parries and feints and lunges with the purpose of rising in class, my younger brother, Benjamin, was building an entirely different reputation with a blade of his own. Tommy was new to the sport too, but from the first he dominated me on the piste, forcing me to break ground, scoring off me at will. And his smile, that little victorious smirk when he ripped off his mask, would eat like an acid at my bones.

"There were other arenas to compete in, of course, grades and girls being the most prominent. I studied more than Tommy and yet he was so damn quick his grades were the equal of mine, and with his smile and charm he got the best of the girls too. It wasn't long before every time I saw him smile I wanted to choke a goat. And yet, through circumstance and familiarity, we remained as friends. Maybe I wanted to keep him close as a sort of mirror. I knew I would be succeeding if I could best Tommy Greeley.

"My dream was to go to law school. Fair enough. Clarence Darrow, Thurgood Marshall, all the great liberal lawyers were my guides. I was still young, things have changed, but that was the dream. So I worked hard, kept my grades up. Tommy had no real dream, as I recall, except to get high and get laid, the great twining goals of our generation. Tommy was, undoubtedly, having more fun than I, but I could console myself with my future. That's where I would prevail over Tommy Greeley. It was one of the greatest days of my life when I got into Penn Law. It was also one of the most bitter, because an hour later I heard that Tommy Greeley had also been accepted.

"It was in law school that his little side business took off, that the marihuana he was selling for a nice profit turned into cocaine, which he was selling for an absurdly huge profit. He drove around campus in his sports car, he threw parties, found himself a series of gorgeous girlfriends, and all the while, through sheer brilliance, he kept his grades up. It would have killed me with jealousy, it would have devoured me, except I had found something else by then. I had found my wife.

"Love, sex, beauty, art, purpose. For me she was the repository of all that in my life. I suppose, Mr. Carl, therein lay the problem.

"Our first years together were an idyll, truly, a sweet and dreamy time of absorption in each other. It was all about devotion, communication, art. It was all about the journals. That was our evening activity, after I finished my law studies. We would sit together, at the kitchen table, translating our emotions, our experiences, our love into words so that we could make them hard and real and forever. She had been keeping journals since she was a child, they became a part of her, a necessary organ, like a lung, in which to breathe in her life. For her, nothing was real without them. And together, with our writing and our intimacy and our love, we created art. Love as art, Mr. Carl. Never was a drug so potent.

"Without it ever being stated, our roles in the relationship were agreed upon. I would be the lawyer, I would financially support us. And my wife Alura, she would be the artist. She was a dancer when I met her, but she wanted to explore other fields, every field, she wanted her whole life to be a work of art. She believed no endeavor could be more noble, and I agreed. Yes. I agreed. Together we would play these disparate parts in our singular endeavor. And so, slowly, I spent less time with the journals, more time at the law. She immersed herself in her art, I immersed myself in legal theory. And we were happy.

"Until that man with the beard and the motorcycle vest. He came to me, almost deranged, spouting off about how some bastard was sleeping with his wife, and that he was sleeping with my wife too. I couldn't believe it, I didn't believe it. Until he said that the bastard was Tommy Greeley. Tommy was a pig, I could believe anything of him. And Alura had been growing distant, things between us were changing. So I did something I had never done before, and have never done since, I staked out her studio and waited. And waited. And waited.

"And then I saw. Him. My mirror. Opening the door of my wife's building. Climbing the stairs to my wife's studio. Through the window I saw him reaching out his arms and embracing my wife's body. The pain I felt was so physical it felled me, it actually threw me to my knees. And behind my closed lids I could see his little victorious smirk, and I retched, right there on the sidewalk."

"What did you do about it?"

"I did the worst thing I could possibly think of doing. I told my little brother."

"What did you tell him?"

"Just what I heard, what I saw. I didn't tell him to do anything, but I told him, and I knew what he was. So when Tommy Greeley came up missing, I had little doubt what had happened."

"That's it?"

"Isn't that bad enough?"

"You didn't tell him where, when, what he'd be carrying?"

"What are you talking about?"

"There has to be more."

"I told my brother. My brother was a drug-crazed maniac. Tommy disappeared. What more is there? Later, in a panic, I went to him. I asked him if he had anything to do with Tommy's disappearance. And what he said, Benny, what he said was 'Don't worry about it. You just keep hitting them books.' He was always so protective, so proud, my little brother, and that's what he said. And he winked. And I knew.

"And what was it all for? Tommy Greeley was just the first. I confronted my wife about it. In her studio, and she was unapologetic, defiant even. 'What do you know of art?' she said. She accused me of giving up art for mammon. 'You made your choice, fine, but don't come in here and judge what I must do to fulfill my artistic destiny.' My wife was exploring the depths of her sexuality, the depths of what it meant to be a woman. And she told me it would continue and it was none of my business. That was the last time I ever entered her studio."

"So why do you stay with her?"

"Love, sex, beauty, art, purpose. Whatever she was, whatever she has become, she is a part of me I am unable to deny, the better part of me, Mr. Carl. I had aspirations to be an artist myself. Now I have Alura. I can't bear even the thought of losing her."

"And what about the baby she was carrying?"

"You know? How?"

"I can see your wife in her."

"She's quite beautiful, isn't she?"

"Yes, Kimberly is."

"I meant Alura."

"Okay."

"We couldn't keep it. She didn't want it. Whatever she is, Alura is not maternal. And how could I bear to raise this symbol of betrayal in my own house, to see her smile every day, the same smile of the man who humiliated me at every turn. When Alura came to me it was too late for an abortion. She had the child, we put it up for adoption, that was the end."

"But it wasn't the end, was it?"

"I couldn't leave it at that. I felt responsible for her. I helped support the family, I was able to arrange her acceptance into Penn, I paid her tuition. It was hard on a government salary to support Alura and the baby both, but I felt I owed that, at least, to the child of my wife and the man for whose death I was responsible."

There was sincerity to what the justice had just told me that I found striking, an utter honesty, and part of it was that his story made him out to be about the biggest weenie on the planet. I mean, here he was, tolerating a wife who felt totally free to sleep around and humiliate her husband all in the name of art. And at the first sign of trouble, instead of dealing with his wife himself, he went running to

his little brother, the same little brother that had undoubtedly protected his big brother's butt in the schoolyard. Yes,
if a statement against one's penal interest is considered reliable by the courts, what about a statement like the one the
justice had just given me, which you could say was baldly
against his penile interest. But it wasn't just that which
convinced me he was telling the truth. His story meshed
perfectly with everything else I had learned, and it pointed
perfectly at the person who had truly set up Tommy Greeley for his brutal encounter at the river's edge.

"You've been torturing yourself about this for twenty
years," I said.

"Of course I have. It has colored everything in my life,
including my political philosophy. Personal responsibility,
reverence for life, harsh enforcement of the criminal code.
Everything."

"But you weren't responsible," I said to the justice.

"Excuse me?"

"Responsible for Tommy's death. It wasn't you."

"Don't be a fool, Mr. Carl. What do you know of my
brother?"

"Enough. I know he hired the men who beat up Tommy
Greeley. But it wasn't you who put him up to it and told
him what he needed to know."

"I don't understand."

"And Tommy wasn't murdered that night."

"Mr. Carl . . ."

"Let's take a walk, you and I."

"To where?"

"To find a suitcase."

CHAPTER

66

He stood before the old rehabed factory building with a sense of reverence, a sense of awe, as if it were some shrine to a long-ago battle that ended badly. He shifted his weight uneasily, twisting his head from side to side. If it weren't for our suits, any cop walking by would have taken us for second-story men.

"This isn't right," he said.

"Sure it is."

"We can't just barge in."

"Sure we can."

"Mr. Carl, she is my wife."

"That's right. Your wife. That's what makes this perfectly legal."

He looked at the security box at the front door. "I don't know the code," he said, a note of relief in his voice. "If she doesn't answer we should go."

I tapped the numbers into the box: 53351. The front door clicked open.

"How did you—"

"Come on," I said, standing in the doorway, waiting for the justice to go through.

After he did, I turned around and scanned the street. I spied whom I was looking for standing in the doorway of a clothing store, on the opposite side, a few addresses down, standing as stiff as a mannequin with his dashing haberdashery. Skink. Our eyes met for a second, I gave him a quick nod, and then followed the justice up the threadbare stairs, one flight, two flights, to the large rusted metal door on the third floor.

The justice stood aside as I gave it a bang.

No answer.

"She's not in," he said.

There was a mat. I lifted it up. No key. There was a plant in the pot by the door, a large rock on the surface of the dirt. I lifted up the rock, turned it over in my hand. No hidden compartment, no key, just a rock. I lifted up the pot itself. No key. I ran my finger across the top of the door frame. No key.

"Where does she keep it?" I said.

"We can't just enter her space. This isn't right."

"She would have a spare so her visitors could have easy access. Where would she keep it?"

He turned. "I'm going."

I grabbed his arm. "No, you're not. Twenty years ago you stepped out of this room and a part of you was left behind. It's time to get it back, Mr. Justice."

"Don't be crude."

"Where is the key?"

He looked down at my hand on his arm and then at my face, and he must have seen something there, some desperation, because he backed away slightly.

"Something's going on, isn't it, Mr. Carl?"

"That's right."

"Something serious?"

"As melanoma."

"Is my wife involved?"

"Up to her neck."

He looked away for a moment, bobbed his head, and

then stepped over to the light fixture sticking out of the wall by the door. The glass covering the bulb was on a hinge. He opened it, reached in, took out the key, handed it to me.

Just like that we were in.

I didn't take a moment to gawk at the surroundings, I didn't take a moment to look at the furnishings, the alluring pictures of Alura Straczynski on the wall, the quote from Kafka, the great bed in the middle of the floor, I didn't take the time to wander around as if wandering through the source of some great mysterious power, I left that for the justice. Instead, I noticed the one crucial difference from my prior visit. The journals and notebooks that had before been on the great mahogany bookshelf were now arranged on the floor in great listing stacks, as if they were being inventoried, rearranged, readied for a move. And in one corner, still flat and folded, were heavy cardboard book boxes all in a pile.

So, someone was taking a trip. All the more reason to make my search, starting with the closets.

I searched through the clothes, the art and office supplies, the high shelves with their hat boxes, the low shelves with their shoes. As I was searching, the justice was running his hand over the tilting stacks of journals, as if amazed at the sheer amount of words, words, words. The hell with that, I was looking for something more substantial. I went through the drawers, the chests, I wasn't dainty about it either, no sir. Let's just say the lingerie was flying.

I wasn't finding it, but it was here, it had to be here. For Derek had been told by Benny Straczynski about a suitcase, and if Benny didn't learn about it from his brother then he must have learned about it from someone else, someone else who knew about the suitcase and Tommy's plans, perhaps the someone who was planning to run off with him and all that money. Maybe someone who was planning to run off and changed her mind and used her brother-in-law to get back what she had planned to run away with, the notebooks, the money, not to mention the photographs. Funny how it all came back to the photographs.

From the shelves of a linen closet I pulled down towels, sheets, cartons of cosmetics. I pulled books off the shelves to see what was behind. I kicked at walls to look for hidden spaces. I stood on a chair, jumped up to grab a rafter, pulled myself up to see what might be hidden in the overhead tangle of pipes and wires and wood. I was trying too hard, I was being too clever.

I found it under the bed.

An old, green, hard-sided Samsonite. As soon as I hoisted it onto the center of the mattress I knew something was wrong. It was light, way too light.

"Is that the suitcase you were talking about?" said the justice as he held one of the journals open in his hand.

"Who pays the rent on this place?"

"My wife."

"With what money?"

"After the incident with Tommy, she refused to take any money from me for the studio. She said she had an inheritance from her mother. She said she would provide for her own artistic endeavors. Something about Virginia Woolf."

"That's why it's so light."

"What is that suitcase? Who is it from?"

"It was the suitcase Tommy Greeley was carrying the night he disappeared."

I didn't think it was possible for the justice to grow any paler, but he did, he blanched, like a cauliflower in boiling water. But I'll give him this, Justice Straczynski, he didn't ask how it got there. The poor son of a bitch was quick enough to figure it out on his own.

I tried to open the suitcase, but it was locked. I went through smaller drawers looking for a key. Nothing. I didn't want to have to break the lock, I wanted it to look pristine, unchanged from that fateful night. I made a quick return to the closets, I pulled down the hat boxes, checked between and beneath the pillows.

I was making such a racket with my search that we didn't hear the front door opening, the footsteps upon the stairs, we didn't noticed the figure standing in the open doorway. Didn't notice her at all, until Alura Straczynski, holding her great swath of keys out in front of her, said,

"Looking for these?"

67

The justice, hunched over one of the journals, stared at his wife with the same exotic expression I had spied when I first visited his chambers, the admixture of passion and fascination, of fear and disgust and abject love, but there was something else, something that hadn't been there before but which came through with stunning purity: hate. With everything else now, there was hate on his face, and the strength of that emotion seemed to startle Alura Straczynski, though just for a moment, before she gained again her brilliant self-possession.

"What are you reading, dear? Anything interesting?"

"Not really," he said, closing the journal in his hand.

"Then put it down."

The justice trembled a bit, as if trying to gain control of his very muscles, and glanced my way before he carefully placed the journal atop one of the piles.

"Good," she said. "Now, tell me, why have you broken into my studio."

"I was just—"

"This is my private place, as private as my soul. You have no business meddling here. I made that clear many years ago."

The justice gestured to the suitcase on the bed. "Mr. Carl says this is Tommy Greeley's suitcase. Is he correct?"

"Our Mr. Carl is quite a pain in the ass, don't you think so, Jackson? I told you we had to watch out for him."

"How did you get Tommy's suitcase?"

"That is none of your business."

"What did you do, Alura?"

Her anger took control of her for a moment, anger at being forced to justify anything in her life, but then her gaze cast about the room and she took in the situation, my presence, the closets emptied, the clothes scattered about, her husband asking questions that he had never dared ask before. She stepped forward toward her husband, stepped forward until she was standing before him, only a pile of journals between them, standing before him like a penitent, and then she bowed her head so it touched his chest.

"Long ago I decided to stay with you, my love," she said.

There was a moment when it appeared he was going to reach out his arms and embrace her, accept her, tell her all was right. It was what he had always done, what he was about to do, but then something seized him, perhaps the anger, perhaps some sickness at the heart. He stepped back, away from her, leaving her standing there, head bowed, in the middle of the room, alone.

"What did you do?" he said softly.

"Tommy was about to be indicted. He was running away. There was a boat. He had a plan. He wanted me to meet him at the dock and leave with him."

"And you couldn't just have told him no."

"He was leaving. There were things he had possession of with which I couldn't let him leave."

"And so you brought in my brother."

"No, Jackson, dear. You brought in your brother. But when he came to me, angry as a beast over what he considered my betrayal of his precious brother, I told him the truth."

"The truth?"

"Yes, Jackson. You must believe. The truth. That I loved you. That I couldn't live without you. That I was staying, that it was over between Tommy and myself. But there were some precious things of mine that Tommy still possessed. They would be in a suitcase. And I told him where Tommy and his precious suitcase would be found."

"You let me think it was me. All this time."

"I let you think what you wanted to think. You wanted to bear the guilt, so be it. If it was to be borne, you were better able to handle the burden."

"You're a witch."

"Why such a frown, Jackson. I chose you. You should be grateful."

"You were all I ever wanted."

"I know, dear."

"And you're a witch," he said, and then he seemed to totter. He reached out his arm, braced himself on the writing desk, clutched his gut. The whole of his marriage was coming clear to him in a way I would never understand and it was enough to send his stomach reeling.

She rushed to him, reached out for him, pulled him close. "Jackson," she said as she held him. "Oh, Jackson, my darling, Jackson."

I stepped over to the charming scene and took hold of the keys she still held in her hand. She gave me a bitter glance before she released her grip. I went through them quickly and found the smallest ones. It only took me three tries to fit one neatly into the suitcase's lock. With a quick click I opened it, unlatched the latches, pulled up the top.

A few old shirts, old socks, a yellowed undershirt thrown into the suitcase with haste, and then, within the fabric, three bundles of cash. The bills were old, the denominations varied, the bills like the shirts packed up in haste. I went through them quickly. Twenty, thirty thousand maybe. I took the bundles out of the suitcase and showed them to her.

"Those are mine," she said, staring at me even as she clutched at her husband. "Put them back."

"I don't think so."

"How dare you?"

"I dare. How much was there when you first opened it up. Enough to pay for this room of your own for twenty years, along with the drinks, the clothes, the affairs, all the former lovers you continued to support. Lovers like Curtis Lobban."

"Remember what I said about being too clever, Victor? Give me the money."

"You stole enough," I said as I slipped the bills into my jacket pocket, along with the suitcase key.

She let go of her husband. "So now you're taking your cut, is that it?"

"Yes," I said. "That's it. But it wasn't the money you were really after that night, was it? That was just a lucky pull. You were looking for something else. Something that's been gone since then. Until now. The photographs."

"Yes."

"And your damn notebooks."

"You found them?"

"That's right," I said.

"You have my notebooks?"

"Yes," I said, but when I said it I noticed something muted in her reaction. Before, whenever she mentioned her missing notebooks her eyes had lit with excitement, and the need to seduce them from me. Now the excitement had been dimmed, the need weakened, as if she already knew that I had the notebooks, as if she already knew how she was going to get them.

"Your notebooks?" said Jackson Straczynski, standing straighter now. "You had my brother kill Tommy for the notebooks?"

"I foolishly gave some to Tommy for safekeeping. I didn't want you to find them. But then I realized without them there was a gap."

"They're just words."

"They are my life's work, Jackson. Don't minimize what you don't understand."

"So you used my brother to fill the gap."

"He wasn't supposed to kill him," she said.

"All for your precious notebooks."

"They are my life," she said. "You know that."

"Yes," he said. "I do."

He traced his fingers gently over the cover of one of the journals perched high on a pile. "Your journals," he said as he caressed another, gently touching the skin of the cover as one would touch a lover, brushing it with the tips of his fingers, stroking it with the softest touch. "Your precious journals."

And then he gave the pile a light shove.

The stack teetered for a moment, teetered, and then collapsed, the notebooks falling one upon another, some skidding across the floor, splayed open.

Alura Straczynski gasped, as if it was she who had been pushed to the floor.

He pushed another pile to the floor, and then a third.

"What are you doing?" she said.

He turned to stare at her as he gave another pile a quick kick, sending a stack of books sliding and then collapsing onto the floor, the volumes spreading open in the air, their pages flapping from the force. The sight of the books sprawling open was almost obscene.

Alura Straczynski rushed to her husband and called out

"Bastard," as she shoved him away from the journals. She fell to her knees, picking up the notebooks, her notebooks, and placing them carefully in her arms. She picked up as many as she could possibly hold and clutched them to her chest, rocking them almost as if she were easing their pain.

"They're a curse," he said.

"They're my life's purpose," she replied, without looking at him.

"They should be burned."

"Touch them again and I'll kill you," she said, her lack of affect positively chilling.

"Alura?"

"Don't," she said.

"Alura."

"Shut up," she said.

And he did, and they stayed there for a moment in the pathetic tableau, she mothering her journals as if they were a child, turning her back on the husband who loved her far too foolishly and far too well. And he, trying to explain himself to a woman who cared not a whit for anything but the jottings of an inner life that was warped by the very process of its saving. The unexamined life might not be worth living, but the examined life is pure murder.

"All right," I said, finally, "are you guys through with your marital drama here, because any more and, frankly, I'm going to puke all over the bed."

The justice stared at me for a moment and then at his wife, still kneeling with her journals, still holding them tight to her chest. Then he looked around at the whole of the studio, the scattered books, the photographs of his wife taken by her lover, the mess of clothes I had thrown about in my search, the great bed sitting like a lurid whale in the middle of the space, and on top of the bed, Tommy Greeley's suitcase. *This is my private place, as private as my*

soul, she had said. *You have no business meddling here.*
She was wrong about him having no business there, but it
seemed clear, as he looked around, that he couldn't bear to
stay there any longer.

"Don't worry, Mr. Carl," he said, his face twisted with
disgust. "I am finished here."

And then he walked out of the studio, passing by his
wife as if she were made of stone, slamming the door
closed behind him, the rusted metal banging shut with the
solid echo of a cell door.

Alura Straczynski seemed to slump at the sound, and
then, without looking my way, started placing her notebooks back in their stacks, checking each one for the date,
sorting and arranging. I looked again at the pile of folded
book cartons in the corner.

"Where is he?" I said.

"I don't know."

"Why don't I believe you?"

"Because you are a cynic, Mr. Carl, as well as a coward.
I want my notebooks."

"You've made that clear to me, and to him too, I'm sure.
Are you going to leave with him this time?"

"I'm a married woman, Mr. Carl."

"Not for long, I figure."

"Oh, I'm not so easily rid of."

"Sort of like syphilis. But still you are packing."

"I haven't yet decided my future path for certain."

"Can I ask you something? One thing that's still not
clear to me."

"Ask what you want."

"Were you the one who bashed Lonnie in the head that
night?"

"The motorcycle man? I only found out at the last moment that he would be guarding Tommy and the suitcase.

There was no telling what could have happened had he spotted Benjamin's men at the meeting place."

"So you cracked his head open."

"I was a switch hitter in softball."

"Oh, I bet you were." I closed the suitcase, pulled it off the bed. "Do you know where he is?"

"No."

"Do you want to tell me where you're meeting him?"

"No."

"He's a selfish psychopath out to further his own rotten ends."

"He always was."

"Okay, then," I said as I walked toward the door. "Just tell him if anything happens to my partner I'll never stop until I destroy him."

"That's between the two of you."

"No, it's not," I said. "You're smack in the middle of it and so I'm holding you responsible too. You know, I must say, Mrs. Straczynski, I look at you and I am stumped. I have no idea of what makes you tick."

"I'm a simple girl, Victor, with a simple view of the world. Everything on this earth exists only for the purpose of providing either for my pleasure or my art."

"Well," I said, "I guess that explains it."

68

I planned a quick visit to the hospital, just to say hello to my father, to spread some cheer, to banter like a bantamweight, and then I'd be free to finish my preparations. I had planned a quick visit, but Dr. Mayonnaise had different ideas. She was behind the desk at the nurses' station on the fourth floor and when she saw me leave the elevator she nearly jumped out of her chair.

"Victor, I'm so glad you're here. Have you spoken to your father? Have you heard the news?"

"No," I said. "News?"

"Good news," she said, her face bright, her blue eyes shining. "Great news." She stepped out from behind the desk, took hold of my arm, started leading me down the hall. "We've scheduled your father for tomorrow."

"Scheduled? You mean his release?"

"No, Victor. His operation."

"I thought his condition had to be stabilized first."

"But it has. His response to the Primaxin has been terrific. There's no reason to wait. And you'll be really happy to hear that a hole opened up in Dr. Goetze's schedule and she's agreed to do the operation."

"Dr. Goetze?"

"She's brilliant. Really. Amazing. The top pulmonary surgeon in the region. Your father's very lucky."

"Lucky lucky lucky." I glanced at the door to his room, partially opened. "Does he know yet?"

"Of course."

"Has he met Dr. Goetze?"

"Just this afternoon."

"And?"

"And what? Victor, trust me. If you need someone to surgically resect your lungs, you want it to be Dr. Goetze. She practically invented the procedure. The operation is scheduled for tomorrow morning. Your father is fasting now and we'll gently sedate him tonight so he gets a full night's rest. He'll spend the next couple days in intensive care and then, after a few more days of recovery, you can take him home."

"It all sounds so easy. So tell me, Karen, how did a hole open up in Dr. Goetze's schedule?"

She squeezed her lips together. "Oh, you know," she said. "Things happen."

"Yes, they do."

"Good luck, Victor. We're all very hopeful."

"I'm sure all indicators are promising."

My father was lying in his bed, his eyes closed tight, his arms placed at his sides. It was as if he was already in position for the coffin. I think all the death we see, all the funerals we attend, are in some ways practice for the day we bury our fathers. I should have been prepared, I should have been overprepared, but still, to see him there, lying peacefully, without his anger or bitterness, without his prickly personality, without everything that had made him my father, brought me to tears. I don't think I would have felt like that before he entered this hospital, before he started to tell me his story about the girl in the pleated skirt, but something had changed, something in me, and now grief at the possibility of losing him overwhelmed me.

I closed the door behind me, sat down by his bed, leaned my head back, tried to gain control of myself. That was when something started shaking in my pocket.

Yes, I know, no cell phones in hospitals, but I was in the middle of an emergency, dammit, and so I hadn't turned my phone off, just set it on vibrate. I grabbed it out of my jacket pocket and snapped it open.

"Is that you?"

"Yes, it's me," I said softly. "Where are you, Phil?"

"Still outside that damn studio. She went out for a bit of errands, had a drink at that bar of hers, and then went back to her building. You said she had a bed in there, right?"

"That's right."

"It looks like she might spend the night. How long you want me to stay out here."

"Until morning if you have to. If he shows up, call the FBI at the number I gave you. If she goes somewhere, follow and then call me. If we can take care of this tonight, that's what I want to do."

"All right, mate. It's your call."

"We have to find her, Phil."

"I know we do."

When he hung up I raised my chin and let out a great sigh of fear and frustration, and it was that sigh, I think, rather than my conversation, that woke my father, because when I looked down again there he was, eyes open, staring at me. It gave me a start, like a corpse coming to life, and I jumped a bit.

"You look like you seen a ghost," said my father.

"Well, you woke up," I said. "How are you doing?"

"Lousy. I'm hungry. Go get me a candy bar, why don't you?"

"You're not allowed to eat."

"The hell with their rules."

"You're having your operation tomorrow."

"The hell with their operation."

"Your operation. How do you feel about it?"

"All of a sudden you care about my feelings? Well, this is what I'm feeling, I'm feeling hunger."

"I heard the doctor came in and spoke to you."

"Yeah."

"What did you think?"

"Seems to know what goes where."

"So you're okay with the surgeon."

"One can kill me as well as the next."

"I thought you might, you know, not be thrilled that the surgeon is a woman."

He let out a bark. "For the whole of my life, women been slicing me up and taking out pieces. Why should this be any different?"

"Well," I said, patting his hand and starting to stand up. "You need your sleep."

"What, you in a hurry?"

"No."

"You look nervous, you got a date tonight?"

"No."

"With that doctor of yours?"

"We're just friends."

"So where are you off to?"

"I don't know yet."

"Then don't go so fast. I'm getting cut on tomorrow. Don't go."

"All right, Dad."

"All right, then."

"So maybe we can talk," I said.

"Don't get carried away."

"Why don't you tell me about your hopes, your dreams, your aspirations?"

"Screw off," said my father.

"Okay."

"You want to know, really?"

"Sure."

"They're the same they been every day of my life. To make it past tomorrow."

I sat and thought on that for a moment. "By that standard, at least," I said, "your life has been a roaring success."

He laughed at that, my dad, and I laughed with him. We laughed together, laughed at the strange and wondrous fact that he was still here, sitting with his son, with enough breath in his lungs to be able to laugh. In the middle of it I thought back and wondered when was the last time I laughed with my father. I couldn't remember. We never had anything to laugh at before, but now we did. He was still alive.

"So go on with the story," I said, when our laughter had subsided and his disposition returned to its natural state of grump.

"I told it," he said. "It's over."

"No, it isn't. You were there, in your apartment, with the girl's head on your chest and the box of coins sitting on the bureau. What happened the next morning?"

"She woke up," he said.

"Go on."

"She woke up, she stretched, she sat up in the bed."

She wakes up, she stretches, she sits up in the bed and the blanket falls off her chest and her shoulders are smooth, her breasts are free, her smile, when she spies him sitting in the chair across the room, is iridescent. And her eyes, her wide moist eyes are as innocent as the morning. She is the very vision of loveliness, she is the very vision of perfection, she is all he ever wanted. Yet as she wakes up and stretches and sits up, as the blanket falls to reveal her proud breasts, a shiver goes through him.

Come to bed, she says, her voice still slow with sleep.

No, he says.

Then let's go somewhere. Where do you want to go first, Jesse? Anywhere but here. New York. Chicago. Hollywood. Someplace we can be somebody.

We can't go anywhere, he says, his voice flat. There's a man dead. He is connected to you, and through you to me. If we leave they will know it was us.

But then let's buy something. We can sell one of the coins and buy something marvelous, something we could only dream about before.

We can't buy anything, he says. If we buy anything they will know it was us.

She pouts, sticks out her pretty lower lip, then bites it. Okay, she says. Maybe you're right, for now. But let's just look at what we have.

She climbs out of the bed, naked, her legs strong, her hips, the pillow of her belly, her breasts rising as she raises her arms over her head to stretch some more.

Let's just look at what we have and dream about the future, she says. Dream about all the things we'll buy. She moves about the apartment with the excitement of a schoolgirl, searching. Where are they, Jesse? she says. The coins. Where are they? And why are you dressed already?

I've been out, he says.

Where?

Just out.

And the coins. Where are the coins?

Gone.

What did you do? she says, her voice rising. What the hell did you do?

I buried them.

Dig them up.

I can't.

They're mine, she shrieks.

No, they're not. They're his. If they link them to us they will know what we did. If they link them to us we will go to jail. Separate jails.

You had no right.

It was the only thing to do, he says. The only way.

Where are they?

I don't know.

Dig them up.

I didn't make a map. They could be anywhere.

Without those coins you have nothing. You are nothing. You cut lawns for a living for God's sake.

There's no crime in that.

Get them back.

This is the only way, he says.

Where's the shovel?

Remember? Together forever?

Don't threaten me, you bastard. Where's the damn shovel?

They're gone.

Get them back. Get them back. Get them.

"What could I say?" said my father, in his hospital bed, the night before they were going to slice open his chest and hack out pieces of his lung. "What could I do? I turned away. Closed my eyes. And what did I see? You know what I saw. I saw her, but she wasn't naked, she wasn't standing over me, bent in anger, shouting at me, hitting me on the shoulders, the neck, the chest. I saw her, and she was dressed in white, and she was walking down South Street, her pleated skirt swaying with every step, walking down South Street, walking to me."

* * *

I stayed until they gave him the shot. He barely grimaced as the needle slipped into his flesh. I stayed until the shot took effect, and his eyes widened and then closed and the tremor in his hand eased and he was overtaken with blessed sleep. It was almost as good, that shot, as his Iron City, and after he fell asleep I stayed for a while longer. Visiting hours were long gone, but they didn't disturb us as I stayed with my sleeping father the night before the operation he would most likely not survive. It was coming to a head, the whole Gordian knot Joey Parma had laid at my feet, it would all come to a head very soon, but I waited a moment more as my father lay peacefully now in his bed, his arms once again at his sides. I waited with him as the hour grew late and the night deepened and quiet fell hard over that room.

My pocket started shaking, like an electric toothbrush gone off.

"She's on the move," said Skink. "Caught a cab. I'm following."

"Probably going home to patch things up with her husband."

"I don't think so, mate. She's headed in the wrong direction for that."

"Which direction?"

"East," he said. "Toward the river."

"Of course she is. All right, let me know."

I stood up and started pacing back and forth in the little room, pacing back and forth until I lost track of time. All I could think about was Beth, pulled out at gunpoint, Mr. Beretta that bastard Colfax had said, pulled out at gunpoint and taken somewhere, probably tied up, probably scared. She was tough, Beth, tougher than I ever could claim to be, but still she certainly was scared. And in danger. And all because I had taken this stupid case, I had decided to find out what happened to Joey Parma, I had started taking things personally. It was my fault, she was my responsibility.

The phone jazzed in my pocket.

"You won't believe this, mate. No, you will not."

"Go ahead."

"There's a big sign on Columbus Boulevard with the words 'Piers 82 to 84.' "

"Okay."

"I'll be there waiting for you."

"Good work, Phil. Give me twenty-five minutes."

I checked my watch. Five to ten. Twenty-five minutes. At this time of night, with traffic light, that would be plenty of time.

I stopped in front of my father, looked down upon his sleeping body. The breaths were ragged and shallow, his face was tense, almost flinching. I wondered at the dreams he was dreaming. They say as you face death your whole life passes before your eyes, but for his sake I hoped it wasn't true.

If you can't accept your past, had said Cooper Prod, *understand it, even love it, if you can't do that, then you become its slave. You spend your life either running from it or toward it, but either way you are running.* My father had spent the whole of his life running from his past, facing it only as he faced death. And then there was Tommy Greeley, the years he wasted dealing drugs, the years he wasted plotting his revenge, never understanding what he had done or what he was trying to do, just running, running. And then there was me, just as bad, just as much a runner, even though I wasn't ready to admit what it was that I was running from. We were all running, weren't we, my father, Tommy Greeley, myself. Maybe it was time to stop.

I leaned over, kissed my father's forehead as he lay sleeping in the bed.

"Good night, Dad," I said, softly.

I was wiping at a piece of dust that had fallen into my eye when I passed the waiting room on my way to the elevators. I spied a figure rising from a chair, walking toward me with untoward haste, and I heard my name called. I stopped, turned, ready for something awful to happen, expecting some goon. But who I saw, standing before me, was the Honorable Mr. Justice Jackson Straczynski.

CHAPTER

69

"What the hell are you doing here, Your Honor?" I said.

Justice Straczynski stood awkwardly before me, uneasy in my company, as if unsure of our positions one to the other. He was used to lawyers groveling for his favor, he was used to sitting on high. But now the roles were reversed, it was he who had come to me, and I knew far too much of what was far too personal for him to be comfortable in my presence. He stepped toward me, swiveled his head as if making sure he wasn't being overheard, and then said in a low voice, "Mr. Carl, I need to speak to you."

"How did you find me?"

"When I couldn't reach you at home or at your office I called Mr. Slocum. I said it was an emergency. He told me your father was in this hospital. How is he doing?"

"Not so well," I said. "You told Slocum it was an emergency?"

"That's right."

I shook my head. This was bad, a serious problem. Slocum wouldn't just put it to the side, he wasn't that kind of guy. As quick as the justice hung up he would be on the line to McDeiss. This was turning into a mess.

"I have to go," I said. I turned away from him and

started toward the elevator. He followed, speeding up so that he could walk beside me.

"I'm sorry about your father," he said.

"Mr. Justice," I said as I reached the elevators and pressed the down button. "I don't have time right now to chat."

"You mentioned something today about Tommy Greeley."

"Did I?"

"You said Tommy wasn't murdered that night twenty years ago. What did you mean by that?"

The elevator came. I stepped into it, turned around, pressed G and door close, door close, door close.

"Mr. Carl?"

"He wasn't killed," I said as the doors slowly shut in front of me.

The justice's long thin arm shot through just as the gap between the doors was about to disappear. The doors fell back and he stepped into the car with me.

"Mr. Carl," he said as the doors now closed behind the two of us. "I don't understand."

"Your brother only meant to rough him up. But the guys he used let it get out of control. They thought they had killed him, but they were mistaken."

"So what happened to him?"

"Can't we talk about this some other time."

"No, Mr. Carl. We can't."

"Well, we will have to, won't we?"

The doors opened into the lobby. I stepped through and started rushing toward the exit. The justice, studiously ignoring my hints, followed.

"My wife is missing, Mr. Carl."

"And that is a problem how?" I said as I stepped outside and headed toward the parking garage, the justice all the while close behind.

"Don't be unkind."

"Have you checked her studio?"

"Yes."

"Are her journals there?"

"Yes, but in boxes."

"She's not going anywhere without her journals." I turned around, he stopped in his tracks. "Look, Mr. Justice. Tomorrow night, one way or the other, it will all be over and we can talk about it then, but right now I don't have the time to discuss this."

"He's come back, hasn't he?"

"You'll have to excuse me. I have to go."

The garage was right behind me. I turned around, jogged into the entrance, took the stairs two at a time to my parking level and then found my car. I checked my watch. Two minutes to ten. Time to go, time to get out of here.

"You said he wasn't killed so he is most likely still alive," called out the justice as he ran out of the stairwell, his voice coming in spurts between his gulps for breath. "And with everything that has been happening it only makes sense that he has come back."

"I have to go," I said, putting the keys in the car, opening the door.

"He's come back for her."

He was standing now right behind my car. I couldn't pull out with him standing there.

"You have to let me go," I said.

"You're going to him now?"

"Yes."

"And she'll be there?"

"Yes."

"Then take me with you."

"Mr. Justice, he didn't come back for your wife. If anything, she's an afterthought. He came back for money he mistakenly thought he could recover here. And he came back for revenge."

"Take me with you, Mr. Carl."

"You don't want to find him, Mr. Justice, trust me." I checked my watch again. "I have to go."

"Not unless I come too."

He was standing behind my car. I couldn't pull out with him standing there unless I ran him over, not that it wasn't an attractive option. Still, I didn't think Slocum would be so thrilled, the flattened party being a sitting Supreme Court justice and all. I thought about what to do, glanced at my watch. Skink was waiting.

"Get in," I said.

CHAPTER

70

Before Justice Straczynski had a chance to snap shut his belt, I slapped into reverse, spun out of the spot, shifted into first and then second as I made my way for the exit. I slammed my brakes at the booth. The driver in front of me slowly searched her purse for the single coin that would give her exact change. I tapped the wheel impatiently. When my turn came I threw the card and a ten in the metal tray, told the man to keep the change, and was off. Up Broad Street, through the wilds of North Philly and then the northern stretches of Center City, past the Moorish-inspired synagogue, past the hideous State Office Building, past the tall white *Inquirer* Building, and then right around City Hall.

"Where are we going exactly?" said the justice.

"I want to show you something," I said.

I continued south and then cut over, heading east into Queens Village. At one point I pulled into a parking spot, turned out the lights, checked my rearview mirror. I didn't see anyone pull over behind me and, as the thin stream of traffic moved by, I didn't see anything suspicious flow past. Maybe I had been wrong about Slocum, maybe he had just passed on my whereabouts to the justice and left it at that. Sloppy sloppy sloppy; I'd give him an earful when this whole thing was over. Satisfied, I pulled out again and took a now familiar route that led me onto the street with the burned-out storefronts, the yellow tape still wrapped around the entrances, where I stopped the car.

"This was where Lonnie Chambers died," I said.

The justice's jaw tightened, but he didn't say anything.

"He was shot in the head and then his shop was burned around him so that his corpse was little more than a cinder. I just want you to know what we are dealing with, what kind of anger and rage and pent-up violence. He's a bitter man seeking a bitter revenge."

"I can handle Tommy."

"No, Mr. Justice, that's just it. You can't. He has no real beef with me, but he thinks he does with you. Why don't I let you out here?"

"My wife is with him."

"He's already killed at least two whom he thought betrayed him, including Lonnie. He thinks you betrayed him too."

"And you intend to tell him that it wasn't me."

"That's right."

"And so he'll know it was my wife. Do you realize what he might do to her, have you thought of that?"

I didn't respond because he was right.

"Let's just go, Mr. Carl," he said.

I gave him a long look. He was staring ahead, his face set with both fear and determination. The sight of him strangely calmed me. His motivations were obscure, the source of his loyalties was unfathomable, and yet there was in him an undeniable bravery that I found comforting. I am, by instinct, a loner, but I didn't mind just then having his bravery beside me.

The traffic on Columbus Boulevard, south of the movie theater and the strip joints and the Home Depot, was sparse. The road here was full of potholes, train tracks jogged between the lanes. When I saw what I was looking for, I did a U-turn across the tracks, across the northbound lanes, into a separate drive that serviced the piers in the day and was completely deserted at night. I drove down a bit until I reached the huge white sign Skink had mentioned and then pulled into a small parking area right beneath it. To our right was the pier where Joey Cheaps's body had been found. To our left was that big ghostly boat.

"Let's go," I said.

As the justice climbed out of the car, I went into the trunk and pulled out a large blue flashlight and the suitcase. The suitcase was heavier now than it had been when I had taken it from Alura Straczynski's studio. In addition to the old clothes that had been left there, I had filled it with everything that had been in the footlocker buried at Jimmy Sullivan's house, including Alura Straczynski's precious notebooks, and I had added the photographs, all of them taken down, finally, from my wall. I was bringing everything that had been demanded of me, everything except the money, but I was doing it at a time of my choosing.

Skink was waiting for us at the gate, but so well hidden in the shadows that if I hadn't been looking for him I would have missed him completely. I would have to ask him sometime how he did that.

I introduced Skink to the justice and then Skink pulled me aside, none too pleased at the company.

"What is he doing here?" he said in a low voice.

"He insisted on coming."

"Why didn't you just insist on saying no?"

"He didn't give me much of a choice, and he might be of use. His wife's in there, right?"

"That's right."

"I figure he deserves a chance to say good-bye."

"I don't know. It's hard to be stealthy with six shoes stomping."

"We'll be fine. We'll split up. Straczynski and I will keep the bastards occupied while you search for Beth. When you find her, call the number I gave you."

"All right."

"But not before. I don't want anything to endanger her, which also means no shooting."

"There won't be no shooting. I didn't even bring my gun."

"No gun?"

"Well, not the big one anyway."

"Is the gate locked?"

"Was."

The guard booth at the entrance was lit, but empty, and the chain-link gate, which had been fastened by a padlock, was open just enough for the three of us to slip through. Walking three abreast, Skink, me with the suitcase, and Mr. Justice Jackson Straczynski, we walked across the long wide pier, strewn with piles of scrap metal, walked past a long row of bright yellow school buses, walked toward the huge looming ocean liner moored to the side of the pier with great blue ropes.

"The SS *United States*," said Skink, when we stood in front of the massive boat. "Back in the day, it was something special, it was. Back in the day it was the fastest ship in the world."

And so it was, back in the day, though that day had long passed. What it was doing on some squalid Philadelphia pier I couldn't tell you, but there it was, the huge passenger liner, glowing dully in the dim city light. It was obviously once some great and gaudy ocean steamer, with its sleek dark body and two huge raked stacks, the red, white, and blue paint flaking as if from some foul disease. It floated high in the water, still proud and haughty even as it rusted away on the Philadelphia waterfront, a ruined relic of some bygone era, ready to be scrapped for steel to make refrigerators or Chevys. Its appearance there was so anachronistic and yet so perfectly apt it almost made me laugh. It was as if the past itself, in all its fetid glory, had floated up the Delaware to meet us.

"Up there," said Skink, pointing to a faint glow coming through a row of windows high on the ship's port side. "I scouted it some already. There's a crew entrance a little ways back toward the rear, one of the big doors is open, and a metal gangplank leads into it. Five steps up, careful and quiet over the metal and you're in. The door leads into one of the engine rooms. It's dark in there, use your light, and don't get spooked by the birds. We'll take a left and climb the narrow metal ladder that leads to one of the service decks. From there we continue on about a hundred yards to the forward stairs. It's about seven flights to reach them lights. If we're splitting up, I'll lead you to the stairway. Then you two will go first. I'll be your backup."

I looked up at the ship, that great ruined monster. Stepping inside would be like stepping inside history itself. And sitting in there, like some pasha sitting atop his silken tufts of bitterness, was that son of a bitch Tommy Greeley.

CHAPTER

71

It smelled of oiled metal, stale air, must, ammonia, rot, carpet glue and bird dung, old triumphs, faded hopes, dust and ruin; it smelled, in short, of the past.

Straczynski and I climbed slowly up the old wide stairway rising through the bow of the great ship. We moved as quietly as we could. It was as black as Tommy Greeley's heart inside that old boat and so the flashlight was our only guide, the beam intermittently catching glimpses of the companionway's railings, the raw perforated aluminum of the ceiling, the bare metal bulkheads yellow with primer, the long deserted passageways leading off to the various decks. The ship had been stripped of everything not integral to its structure, not a stick of furniture or piece of plaster remained, the cabin walls were now mere outlines of aluminum. We were climbing through a skeleton.

At each step I waved the beam to be sure it was clear and every now and then we stopped and listened for a sound, any sound. A few flights up we could see a faint glow of light slipping out from Tommy Greeley's hideaway. And at the bottom of the companionway, Skink was waiting, listening to us climb, listening to see if something went wrong, if someone stopped us, if disaster struck. So far disaster had patiently bided its time as we rose through the ship.

I halted; Straczynski stopped behind me. I could hear his breath, hear my heart. I put down the suitcase, bent low, concentrated the beam on something that had caught a razor's edge of light. It was a line, fishing line. I followed it with the beam, from where it was attached at one end of the stairway, across the entire step, to where it fell down into the well. What was it attached to? An explosive? A firearm?

Old strips of sheet metal.

A crude but effective alarm system. I turned to the justice and whispered, "Do you have a handkerchief?"

He reached into his inside jacket pocket, pulled one out. As carefully as I could, I tied the white cotton around the fishing line so that Skink would find it on his climb, and then carefully stepped over the line. Straczynski did the same and we moved on.

It was another flight and a half to the deck from where the soft light leaked into the stairwell. We climbed more slowly, more carefully than before. There was another line a little farther up and this time I had the justice give me his tie to wrap around it.

"Why don't you use your tie?" he whispered.

"Yours is silk," I said. "One drip of gravy and it's gone anyway. But polyester lasts forever."

We stopped at the landing with the soft leaking light. I turned off the flashlight, put down the suitcase. The suitcase had grown heavier as I climbed. I moved my arm back and forth to ease the strain. We were at a dimly lit hallway. A muffled voice could be heard, a bright light came through an open doorway about forty yards off.

I turned to Straczynski, raised an eyebrow. He nodded. I picked up the suitcase, started down the hallway, stepped as softly as I could. The voice grew louder, grew more distinct, snatches of words came clear.

". . . wouldn't fancy getting caught in between . . . quick stop in Freeport maybe . . . after George Town we could . . . a mate told me about this here Ambergis . . ."

I recognized Colfax's arrogant Cockney drawl, and I could tell what he was doing just by the gaps in the sound, the slowness of his voice. He was looking at a map, most likely tracing the possible routes with his finger, tossing out suggestions of where to go, where to hide. And I recognized the route too, a water route, which told me all I needed to know about their planned escape from the city. Kimberly had said she was going to buy a boat for her boss. Something comfortable, no doubt, maybe a sailboat or a small fishing vessel to take them down the coast, around Cuba, down to George Town, not the Georgetown in Washington, D.C., but the George Town in the Cayman Islands, where money travels when it wants to disappear.

We kept walking down the hall, closer and closer to the door with the light.

"What about Negril?" came a different voice, a woman's voice. "I've heard wonderful things about Negril."

A sharp breath from behind me, Justice Straczynski recognizing his wife's voice as she plotted her escape from him.

"Yes, maybe, why not?" said a third voice, with a sharp Brockton accent. "Why not Negril?"

Something grabbed my arm. I almost jumped up and shouted, but I didn't. I gained control, turned around, saw Straczynski with his eyes glistening. "That's Tommy," he said.

I nodded, looked down at my arm until he let go.

"Are you ready?" I said softly.

He waited for a moment, peered past me down the hallway as if he was peering into both his painful past and his uncertain future, and then nodded.

Slowly, silently we walked toward the open door. We had to be careful. I had wanted to surprise them, to catch them off guard, to learn what I could before they were aware of our presence and to give Skink the time he needed, but I didn't want to surprise them so much that Colfax started shooting before he realized who we were. So it wouldn't do to just appear at the doorway, no that wouldn't do. I would be polite, I would knock.

I rapped once, twice.

"Hello," I called out. "Anyone home? Victor Carl here, and I have a delivery."

72

There would be a sword fight, of course there would be a sword fight, how could there not? Isn't that how all great revenge stories end, with a sword fight, and wasn't Tommy Greeley aiming to make his revenge into a great story, casting himself in the leading role? So there would be the inevitable sword fight, yes, but before that stirring duel we had to deal with Colfax, who stepped out into the hallway, glowering, in his hand a gun, matte black with a wooden grip. Mr. Beretta, I assumed.

"What are you two doing 'ere?" he said.

"I didn't want to wait," I said and then jerked a thumb at the justice. "He came for his wife."

"You want 'er back?" he said, his voice wide with astonishment. "I figured you were the only one making out 'ere." He peered beyond us along the hallway and into the stairwell. "Who's with you?"

"No one. We came alone."

"You're not really that stupid, are you?"

"Yes," I said cheerfully. "Yes, I am."

Colfax glanced down at the suitcase, glanced over at Straczynski. "You brought everything?"

"Everything I have."

"Bring him in, Colfax," called Tommy Greeley from the lighted room. "Don't make us wait."

Colfax looked at us for a long moment, checked again the hallway, and then shook his gun at us, indicating we should step through the doorway.

It was a large stark room, divided by white stanchions, and well lit from spotlights hanging from overhead steel girders and hooked up to a large battery on a table. The room was stripped like the rest of the ship, but with some homey touches remaining. The floor was black, with a few scattered linoleum tiles, and there were the remnants of a curved, art deco bar, posts of bar stools lined before it, some of the seats still in place. Standing by the bar was Alura Straczynski; sitting on one of the remaining stools was Tommy Greeley. He was dressed all in white, white shirt, pants, bucks, like some wax model of Gatsby that had been left out in the sun. His shiny face was too immobile to show interest, but his eyes behind the lifeless flesh were focused intently on the justice. On the bar were charts and maps and, off a bit to the side, a large black cloth.

"Ah, Jackson, Jackson, Jackson," said Tommy. "You've gained some weight, I see."

"Hello, Tommy," said Justice Straczynski. "I thought you were dead."

"I was. And I suppose Victor's bringing you here means you were responsible. But after you killed me, as in all great stories, came the resurrection."

"You always did have delusions of grandeur."

"What are you doing here, Jackson?" said Alura Straczynski.

"I came to take you home."

"By the hair?"

"If necessary."

"Tell me, Jackson," said Tommy Greeley. "How do you like my ship? Quite a thing, yes? I've been on the committee to save this old relic for years. I've always been one to conserve the past. Sorry about the condition, but they found a bit of asbestos and were forced to strip it bare. This was the tourist-class lounge. I prefer first-class accommodations, but this room still has its original floor, the original bar. How did you find us?"

Colfax waved his gun at Alura. "They followed 'er."

"Ah, yes, of course. How careless of you, dear."

"I did everything exactly as you said," she complained. "I obeyed all your instructions. I checked repeatedly. There was no one."

"See, the problem with birds like you," said Colfax, "is you're oblivious to anyone but yourselves."

"Who are you again?"

"I'm the 'ired 'elp," said Colfax. "All right now. Enough of our tender reunion. Let's 'ave a look."

He grabbed the suitcase out of my hand and hoisted it onto the bar. Then, standing to the side, as if afraid of a booby trap, he opened the latch and lifted the top. With the point of his gun, he rummaged around.

"Let's see," he said. "Old clothes, looks like they could use a wash, with plenty of bleach, mind you. Some old notebooks."

"They're mine," said Alura Straczynski.

Colfax heard something in her voice, some sense of desperate longing. "Are they now? What's in them? Something valuable?"

"No," she said as she strode over and grabbed the four bound notebooks from the suitcase. "Nothing of value to anyone but me."

"Thank God you found them, Alura," said her husband. "Now your life is complete."

"Yes, Jackson. Now it is."

"Because we all know that life itself was never enough."

"What's this?" continued Colfax. "Photos. Snapshots and the like. 'Old on," he said, lifting an old envelope, the old law school envelope, taking out the stack of photographs, those photographs, my photographs, undoing the rubber band, pawing through them. "Racy little things, they are. Who's the juicy number?"

"I'll take those, thank you, Colfax," said Tommy Greeley.

With some unerring animal instinct, Colfax looked through the photographs and then turned to Mrs. Straczynski. "They're you, aren't they? Yes, they are. Well, I suppose, given enough time, even the tastiest plums turn into prunes."

"Who is this man, Tommy, and why is he here?"

"I'm the man who gets things done," Colfax said as he tossed the photographs to Tommy. "But I don't see no money. Where's the fucking money?"

"There is no money," I said.

"That's not possible," said Tommy Greeley.

"It's all gone," I said. "All of it. There's nothing."

Colfax stared at me for a moment, something dark and very personal rising in his features, and then he smacked me across the jaw with the point of his gun, smacked me across the jaw and sent me spinning to the floor. A line of pain shot from the edge of my jaw, through my teeth, into my stomach.

"Colfax, stop it," said Tommy.

"Shut up, you pompous fool," spit Colfax and Tommy seemed to shrink at the words. "I'm owed money. Where's my money?"

"Calm down," said Tommy, slowly. "It has to be somewhere. Let's start with the money from Brockton. Victor, there was money in the same place as the notebooks. What happened to it?"

"What do you think happened to it?" I said as I climbed

onto my hands and knees. I touched my jaw. It hurt like hell and felt misaligned. Blood came away in my hand and two of my teeth were loose. "You turned Sully into an addict with your Federal Express deliveries. He was using, going into debt, ever more desperate. And you trusted he wouldn't bust open a locker you asked him to keep safe? You trusted he wouldn't grab what money he found and suck it up his nose?"

"Bloody 'ell, you didn't tell me he was a frigging addict."

Tommy looked to the side, thought for a moment. "What about the money in this suitcase, the money stolen from me. Where is that?"

"Spent," I said, grabbing hold of one of the thin white columns, pulling myself to standing. "Gone. All of it."

"You spent my money, Jackson?"

"Guess again," I said. "You're asking the wrong—"

"Yes, I spent it," said Jackson Straczynski. "All of it."

"What are you—"

"Quiet, Mr. Carl," the justice said. "I gave it to charity, I gave it to the poor. I couldn't wait to get rid of it all. You should be glad, Tommy. You did some good in your miserable life after all."

"You always were jealous of me," said Tommy Greeley.

"I wasn't the one coveting your wife."

"Not just coveting."

"Everything was never enough for you, was it?"

"Don't lecture me about ambition."

"I haven't broken every law and commandment known to man."

"Oh, do you all smell that? The bright scent of pure self-righteousness. I didn't do anything anyone else didn't do, Jackson. The whole world was buying and selling.

There were a hundred operations on campus. I just did it better. That was my crime. I did everything better."

"Enough already," said Colfax. "Such a tender scene, old friends and all, but I frankly don't give a crap whose dick is bigger. And it's not like she cares none. All she cares about is 'er silly books."

It was true, Alura Straczynski was staring into her journals, her past lives, entranced by long-ago written words, long-ago described emotions, only dimly aware of what was going on around her. In the silence, she looked up, saw us all staring. "What?" she said.

"What indeed," said Colfax. "What the 'ell are we going to do about the money?"

"That's your business," I said. "I did my part, now I want Beth."

Tommy Greeley's neck bent in puzzlement. "Beth?" he said. "Your partner? What about her?"

I looked at Tommy and then back at Colfax, and then back at Tommy and then back at Colfax, and suddenly a whole new possibility arose. It was in the way Colfax spoke to his supposed boss, the way he had taken control of the present encounter. The way he held the gun. Colfax, that son of a bitch. From the start I had read the balance of power wrong.

"Colfax," I said. "You've been a bad boy."

"What did you do, Colfax?" said Tommy.

"The legal term is kidnapping," I said.

"Colfax, dammit. How could you do that without—"

"Don't start balking at my tactics now. If I left it to you, we would have been sleeping fast when the coppers stormed the house. 'Don't worry, Colfax, 'e doesn't know for certain.' 'Ell 'e don't, and 'e got your fingerprints on that book and next morning they come streaming in. I was promised another payment. Them was the terms. So don't go all surprised I had to take matters in my own hands. I got your suitcase here, didn't I? I got them journals. And even the bloke you wanted for that little sword fight of yours, he showed up. Everything you told me you wanted you've got. So, don't 'Colfax dammit' me."

"Sword fight?" said Straczynski.

I shook my head and it hurt, but I couldn't help but shake it, even with the pain in my jaw. "A sword fight," I said. "Of course there would be a sword fight. Now this is truly pathetic."

"Poetic, I thought," said Tommy Greeley as he walked over to the black covering at the end of the bar. He whisked it off, revealing two fencing swords.

"What are you doing?" said Straczynski.

"Take hold," said Tommy as he tossed a sword into the air toward the justice, who ducked and let it rattle at his feet. "Come come, man, you can do better than that?"

"You're not serious," said the justice.

"Of course he is," I said. "He wants to duel. He wants to stage some magnificent scene of derring-do, gaining his revenge at the end of some thrilling sword fight. He fancies himself another Edmund Dantes."

"You're insane," said the justice.

"Come on, sir."

"Says Hamlet to Laertes," I said.

Straczynski looked down at the blade at his feet. It was thin, about three feet long, with a shiny guard at the hilt and, at the point, a small round loop. The sword in Tommy's hand had the same loop.

"Pick up your saber," said Tommy. "That's what you preferred, right, Jackson? Sabers? The cutting blow. Twenty years I've been living with this. Twenty years."

"And what have you learned in twenty years?" I said.

"What great new insights in the human condition did you discover? Twenty years and the best you can come up with for transcending your miserable failed past is a stinking sword fight?"

"At least I'm being proactive."

"I'm not going to fight you, Tommy," said the justice.

Tommy took up a fencing position as best he could with his stiff left hand at his back hip, his right knee bent, his right foot facing forward, the sword held straight in front of him. He lunged and a loud SWAK rose as he slapped Straczynski on the biceps with the sword.

"They beat my face in with a baseball bat, did you know that?"

"I'm sorry."

"You're sorry? That makes it all better."

Another lunge. Another SWAK. This time against the left side of the justice's face. The justice cringed in pain and when he stood up straight again, a red line had appeared on his cheek. Blood dripped from the edge of the wound.

"They beat me senseless and bloody and when they were done they rolled me off the pier, so my corpse would float out to sea."

"I didn't want that to happen," said Straczynski.

Another lunge. SWAK. This time a backhanded blow against the justice's right shoulder.

"A barge dragged me out of the water."

"Stop this."

"I was unconscious," said Tommy. "Near death."

"Get hold of yourself," said Straczynski.

Another lunge, SWAK, this time a sharp downward flick of the wrist that slapped the sword against the justice's chest.

"All I had on me was my new ID. My old friend Eddie

Dean had died of leukemia while still in his teens. I was planning to use his name, his Social Security number in my new life. I had already obtained a Delaware driver's license in his name. So it was that when I woke up, Tommy Greeley was dead and Eddie Dean was on life support."

Tommy lunged again, trying to slap at the justice's right cheek, but this time the justice ducked low as the blade passed over him. When he stood again, the other sword was in his right hand, held off slightly to the side, the blade pointing up toward Tommy Greeley's eyes.

"*Passata soto,*" said Tommy with a nod. "Nice tierce position."

"It's coming back to me," said Straczynski.

"Let's see."

Tommy lunged, trying to slap down upon the justice's chest, but this time the justice, with a flick of his wrist, raised the blade into the air horizontally and parried the blow.

"Quinte," said Tommy. "Very good."

"You're not as fast as you used to be," said Straczynski.

"I never fully recovered from what you did to me. But I'm still fast enough."

Tommy Greeley lunged, Jackson Straczynski parried, and they went at it for a moment, two middle-aged men with swords in their hands, the ringing grate of steel on steel, the slap of their feet on the black linoleum, the clash of metal sabers one on the other. It would have been stirring, almost, if after their moment they both hadn't been leaning forward, hands on their thighs, gasping desperately for air.

"What," said Tommy Greeley between his fitful breaths, "no riposte?"

"I'm not," gasped the justice, "going to—fight you—Tommy."

"Of course—you are. That's why—you're here."

"No, it's not. I'm here—to take my wife—home."

"She's not going home."

"Yes, I am, Tommy," said Alura Straczynski, holding her notebooks tight to her chest.

"But you said—you loved me. You said you always would."

"I did, yes. And I suppose I do. But Jackson is a part of me. I can no sooner leave him as leave my heart, my lungs, my journals. I couldn't leave my life then, I can't do it now."

"And you would take her back, Jackson? Again?"

"Again and always," said the justice. "Without hesitation. Her life is my adventure."

"What does that mean?" said Tommy.

"She knows."

"Yes, I do," she said. "Let's go home, Jackson."

Tommy Greeley stared at her for a long moment, his waxy face betrayed by the emotions flitting through his eyes. He turned his face to his old friend Jackson Straczynski. He raised his sword high, prepared to give a brutal blow, when he stopped at the sound.

We all stopped at the sound. From out in the hallway. From down the stairwell. The sound of metal sheeting clanking loudly, the fishing lines strung across the stairs being tripped, first one, then the other.

Colfax raised his hand to quiet us, pulled back the slide on his Beretta, walked over to the door. With two hands on the gun, he leaned on the door frame and carefully aimed his gun at the edge of the stairway where I was certain, positive, that Phil Skink, who had obviously missed my signals, who had clumsily set off the alarms, where Phil Skink was about to appear. And I feared at that moment that Skink's life depended on me having to do something courageous, something athletic, which only meant that Phil Skink was in serious trouble because courageous and athletic was not me, really, honestly, not me at all.

73

"Helloo?" came a familiar voice from the hallway and with it I let out a breath of relief. "Helloo? Is, like, anyone home? For some reason I'm tripping all over these wires, like what is that all about? Wires? Helloo?"

"Bloody Kimberly," said Colfax. "Get in 'ere."

"'Sup with the gun, Colfax? Put that away before you hurt someone. What are you, shooting the rats? This place is a major creepazoid. Why can't you just stay in a hotel or something? I know, I know, the boss wanted to get the feel of the old ship, but really now. Puhleeze. Just know I'm not staying. Sooner I get off this old bucket the happier I'll be."

Kimberly Blue entered the room carrying a brown paper grocery bag. She was dressed down, blue jeans, a loose white shirt, and maybe that was why I thought there was something different about her. Something wary maybe, without her usual obliviousness, something sad yet determined. Different.

"Victor?" she said, still holding the bag. "What are you doing here? And Justice Straczynski and Mrs. Straczynski? And those swords? What, is it a party? You should have told me, I would have dressed. I have this really mad sailor's outfit. And instead of lunch meat I would have gotten something festive." She walked, seemingly unconcerned, to the bar, put down her bag. "Maybe a bottle of imported vodka and some hors d'oeuvres. I could go for some hors d'oeuvres, couldn't you? Those little quiches, with the spinach. Yah. No fish, of course, I learned my lesson, but how about crab puffs? Are crab puffs okay?" She looked at her boss, and then at me, took in the strange scene, the somber tone. "So, everyone," she said. "What's going on?"

"Did you see anyone outside the ship on your way up here?" said Colfax.

"Ah, no. Like, everyone's got someplace better to be than a rusting bucket sinking in the harbor. And I still don't know why I couldn't just put the supplies myself onto the little boat. I mean, I put them in the truck, I could certainly take them out and put them in the boat. I'd rather stay there than here any day. At least that boat has a bed. But Colfax is all, don't go on the boat. And I'm all, but where do I put them? And he's all, just leave them in the truck. And I'm all, but that's pretty stupid."

"Kimberly?" said Colfax.

"Yes?"

"Just shut up."

"Okay."

"Where's the boat?" I said.

"At the end of the pier," said Kimberly. "Maybe you didn't see it because it's hidden by the warehouse. For some reason that's where Colfax docked it."

"I said shut up," said Colfax.

"So that's where she is."

"Who?" said Kimberly.

"Beth. Colfax kidnapped her and put her on the boat."

Her eyes widened, her head came around and then again like an old-time comedian doing a perfect double take. "Excuse me."

"And the FBI is searching for your boss," I said.

"Why?"

"Because he's been a fugitive from justice for twenty years. Because he's really Tommy Greeley."

She took a step back and staggered onto a stool, looked over at Tommy, still standing with a sword in his hand.

He shrugged and smiled.

"And now," I continued, "he's trying to have a sword fight duel with a sitting Supreme Court justice, whose wife was planning to sail away with you guys to the Caribbean but has decided to stay. And everybody is looking for money that isn't there. That nails it pretty much, doesn't it? Except maybe for the murders."

"Murders?" said Tommy.

"Yes. Murders. I thought it was you who had done all the killing, I was certain it was you, following the path of betrayal, meting out your wild justice, but now I'm not so sure. Because the guy who committed the murders is the guy who's looking hardest for the money. And that doesn't seem to be you, does it? You're looking for something else."

"All I wanted was to get back what I lost."

"What was that?" said Straczynski.

"Everything you took away from me."

Tommy lunged, but meekly now, the lunge of a man too tired to really try. Straczynski parried with a flick of his wrist.

"You were going to jail," said the justice.

"I was going to freedom, but you took it all from me. My love, my life, my money. So that's what I was trying to get back, just that, yes. But I'm not a killer."

"No, you're not," I said. "And you know what convinced me? Something as small as a dime. The loop on the sabers. If you were out to kill your enemies, why would you leave the loop on your saber. Why wouldn't you file it off, sharpen the point, dip it in poison, stick it in your enemy's eye?"

"It wouldn't be sporting," said Tommy.

"No, it wouldn't. I thought it was you following the path of your betrayal, but it was someone else, following that same path for reasons of his own. Colfax," I said, "you've been a very bad boy."

"It was business, just that, you understand," said Colfax. "Nothing personal. But terms is terms and I need to be paid. I was just making a proposal to our friend Babbage, a little gentle persuasion, and next thing I know 'e's flopping around like a tuna on the deck. And that Lonnie, I was passed word 'e knew who 'ad taken the suitcase. I came in with questions, he came after me with a wrench. I didn't 'ave no choice. It was self-defense."

"You stupid son of a bitch," said Tommy.

"You owed me the payments. What did you expect me to do? Take you to court? I'm just satisfying the terms of my engagement. And don't you be all 'igh and mighty yourself, Victor. Nothing more bracing than a lecture on morals from a lawyer. It's like an hyena teaching the lion to tuck in his napkin. And even with all I done, I'm still owed my money and no one's going nowhere until we figure 'ow to take care of that."

A sound pierced his speech, a soft high-pitched sob, and then another, and another, each louder than the sob before it. It was Kimberly, on her stool, her face covered by one of her hands, crying.

"What's the matter with you?" said Colfax.

"This is the worst, just the biggest poodle," she said between her sobs. "This is so humiliating. I knew there was something wrong. I'm, like, the vice president, remember, the vice president of external relations, and still nobody tells me anything. I mean, I'm supposed to know things.

I'm an officer, dammit, and a shareholder too. I have rights. But you're running out of money and does anyone tell me? You're Eddie Dean and you're Tommy Greeley both and did you tell me? Colfax is running around killing half the world and do you tell me? No. Don't tell Kimberly anything. She's only good for making coffee, and I don't even make good coffee. And then you go kidnapping our lawyer, like that's okay too. It's a poodle, totally. This whole thing skinks."

"Skinks?" I said.

She looked at me and I saw it, right there, yes, in the knowing glint in her eye.

"Stinks," she said. "Whatever. You know what I'm going to do. I've been thinking about this for a long time and you know what I'm going to do?"

"Who the 'ell cares?" said Colfax. "We got—"

"Shut up, Colfax," said Kimberly, with steel in her voice, and Colfax shut up. "Mr. D, or G, or whatever. I'm, like, grateful and all for the opportunity, but I think I'm going to quit. This is all too much for me. I'm just a little girl from Bellmawr, New Jersey. I didn't know this was the way business was done. Really."

"Kimberly, dear," said Tommy. "I want to explain."

"I don't want an explanation. Thanks for everything, really, but I just want to quit. It's a matter of ethics or something like that."

"Kimberly."

"Besides, your last check bounced."

"Enough already," said Colfax. "I don't want to 'ear about who loves who, who's leaving who, I've had enough of your bleeding duel. What I want is my money."

"You heard Victor," said Tommy. "There is no money, I'm afraid. None. I was heavily invested. Playing the margins. You know how that goes. Poof. No money."

"Oh, there's always money, isn't there?" He pointed his gun at the justice. " 'E's got some, I know that. 'E took it from you, didn't 'e? But 'e didn't give it all away, no 'e did not. Probably put it in the bank for some rainy day. And right now it's pouring. So you're going to get it for me."

"Not a penny," said the justice.

"Don't be a stupid sot."

"Too late for that."

"It won't work, Colfax," I said. "It's over. The FBI's already on the way."

"You're lying."

"No, I'm not. Beth has already been rescued off that boat and the FBI is on the way, probably crawling all over the dock as we speak."

"It's good you don't play poker for a living, Victor."

"It's not a bluff."

"Look, I'm not kidding around 'ere." He turned his gun away from the justice, toward Alura Straczynski. "You, the prune, you're coming with me."

He grabbed her by the arm, pulled her close.

"Let go of me," she said. "Jackson, stop him."

He placed the gun against her cheek. " 'E ain't doing squat. I got the gun and I'm getting off this damn bucket. If Victor's on the up, you'll keep the coppers off and at the same time convince your loving 'usband to bring the money."

"Leave her be," said Straczynski.

"Sure I will," he said, "soon as I get my money."

There was a moment when Jackson glanced at Tommy and he glanced back, a moment when they were back to a pair of undergraduates, still young and full of possibilities, young men with swords in their hands.

Two quick lunges. *SWAK, SWAK.*

Colfax recoiled, lines of blood appeared on his face.

"Are you insane?" he said as he held Alura tighter to himself and pointed the gun at the two men.

SWAK, SWAK, and as quick as that the gun spun out of his hand, spun right to Kimberly, who gazed at it with curiosity for a moment and then picked it up as casually as if picking up a seashell at the shore.

"There you go, Kimberly," said Colfax, reaching out his hand, his hostage still in front of him. "Be a nice little quail and hand over the gun."

With a quick flick, she pointed the gun at him. It didn't quiver in her hand. Colfax saw something in her face and stepped back.

"You might want to go now, Mr. D," said Kimberly.

"Are they really coming?" said Tommy.

"For sure," she said. "It's my fault, I'm afraid. I wish now I had waited. They're probably already at the door. But you know the ship, you probably know another way off. You can always jump."

"Kimberly," I said. "What are you doing?"

She glanced at me, and as she did Colfax tossed Alura aside and lunged for the gun. Tommy slashed him in the leg, sending him sprawling. Jackson Straczynski put the button of his sword on Colfax's neck and pressed down.

"You better hurry," said Kimberly, the gun now pointing at Colfax's face.

"Kimberly?" I said.

"I know what I'm doing, V," she said and I could see in the squint of her eyes, the set of her mouth, that she did know what she was doing, exactly what she was doing.

"I thought you'd come with me," said Tommy.

"I can't, Mr. D. I already quit, remember?"

"Kimberly, there's something I need to tell you." He glanced at Alura. "There's something we need to tell you."

"No there isn't."

"You don't understand."

"Yes, she does," I said. "She understands everything."

He turned to me. "I was blaming you for all that went wrong, but I guess I should be thanking you instead."

"Don't."

"Okay. So I should just go."

"That's the best thing for everyone, Mr. D."

"Hey, Tommy," I said. "How about this Christmas, instead of sending another bottle to your mother, why don't you send roses?"

Just then we heard it, the jangle of sheet metal, something slamming to the ground, a bellow, a curse.

"Go," she said.

"What will I do? Where will I go?" he said.

"Figure it out," said Kimberly. "And this time, maybe, forgive a little."

He looked at her, his immobile face filled, for the first time I ever saw, with something close to emotion.

The sound of footsteps came clear, echoing, more than one set, more than two sets.

"Go," she said.

"Okay," he said. "Yes. But I'll be back," he said, and then, just like that, with surprising quickness, he was gone, sword and all, out the door, down the hall, into some other passage, away.

"Kimberly," I said.

"Shut up," she said. "Just shut up for once, all right, V?"

And I did, we all did, with Colfax on the ground and Kimberly holding the gun and Justice Jackson Straczynski now standing, with a sword in one hand and the other around his wife. We stayed there, quiet, as the footsteps thundered, as the thunder closed in, we stayed there, wordlessly, waiting for them to come.

CHAPTER

74

It was McDeiss who had tripped on the wire, who had banged his shin on the step, who had bellowed like a walrus and cursed like a sailor. And it was McDeiss who first limped into the room, his revolver drawn, followed by another detective, three uniforms, and an Assistant District Attorney, who seemed, for some reason I couldn't quite fathom, quite peeved at me.

"Where's Beth?" I said as soon as McDeiss entered the room.

"She's fine, she's being looked after outside."

"I'll be right back," I said, but before I could leave a uniform stood in the doorway, blocking my exit.

"No one, and I mean no one, leaves this room," said McDeiss in a voice loud enough to shake the hull of that old boat. "No one leaves until we figure out exactly what happened here. And that means you."

"Me," I said.

"Oh, yes," said Slocum.

So I stayed, and I gave my statement, and I answered questions, and all the while Slocum was staring at me with a visible malice in his eye.

"What's your beef?" I said to him, finally.

"You said you wouldn't do anything stupid," said Slocum.

"I can't help it, it's in my nature."

"I won't disagree. You could be the poster child for adult stupidity. Do you know how much danger you were in?"

"I didn't know you cared so deeply."

"Something happened to you, Carl, it wouldn't exactly ruin my day. But then you go dragging a Supreme Court justice into it and suddenly my day is looking decidedly worse."

"He dragged himself, Larry."

"Is that what he did?"

"After you told him where to find me."

"I knew I made a mistake as soon as I hung up the phone."

"But I have to admit, he did pretty well for himself," I said, nodding to the justice, who was standing in the corner with his wife, giving his statement to a detective. With every word his future was disintegrating—even if he had done nothing wrong his nomination to the highest court would be too controversial now—but he didn't seem to care. In fact, he seemed supremely happy, almost giddy, having come through an adventure with a sword in his hand, still in his incomprehensible marriage, but now, seemingly, relieved of the burdens of his ambition. He lifted his gaze and spotted me, gave me a smile, and I smiled back. I didn't envy him, his life, that wife, but it was his and it seemed to be exactly what he wanted.

McDeiss, with his notebook out, limped over to Slocum and me.

"Can I go now?" I said.

"Not yet," said McDeiss.

"I'd like to see my partner."

"I told you she's fine. But first we need to get some things clear." He pointed over to Colfax, on the ground, scowling, his hands cuffed behind him. "So what exactly are the charges to be filed against this Colfax?" said McDeiss. "I want to make sure we don't miss anything."

"The murder of Bradley Babbage," I said. "The murder of Lonnie Chambers. The kidnapping of Beth Derringer, along with various charges of arson and firearms violations."

"Is that all?"

I put a hand up to my jaw, still aching, blood still oozing from my gums. "You can add battery."

"What about the Parma murder?"

"He didn't kill Joey," I said. "Colfax pretty much admitted everything else he did, but he didn't say a thing about Joey."

"So who killed your boy?"

"Larry, did your man in Chinchilla ever track down that bogus bench warrant thing?"

"He traced it back to Justice Straczynski's chambers," said Slocum, "just like you suspected."

"But I was wrong about it being the justice who was behind it. His file clerk is named Lobban, Curtis Lobban. He owns a Toyota. You might want to check if it has a gray interior and, if it does, whether there are any traces of blood in the interior."

"A clerk?" said McDeiss.

"Not just a clerk. Lobban is connected to the justice's wife. They had an affair years ago. Alura Straczynski was now helping take care of Lobban's ill wife. It was almost like she had adopted the family. Joey was trying to blackmail the justice about something that happened twenty years ago at the waterfront. Lobban knew the justice would never submit to blackmail and would probably be forced to resign, so he made a call, arranged a meeting, picked Joey up, and slashed his throat. Then he dumped him right at the scene of the earlier crime. I don't know if it was a financial thing or just a brutal, misguided sense of loyalty, but it looks like he saw the threat to his boss and his former lover and eliminated it."

"What was Parma blackmailing the justice about?"

"You'll have to ask the justice. But whatever it was, it happened long ago and it is now well beyond the limitations period."

"Lucky him," said McDeiss.

"Not with that wife." I kicked at the floor. "I want to thank you both. The way you charged up here with guns drawn, all just to save little old me, brought a tear to my eye."

"It looks like you had things under control," said McDeiss.

"Looks like I did," I said, and then I gave one of Kimberly's encouraging punches. "But you guys get an A for effort."

It would have almost been a touching moment if they hadn't both been shaking their heads with disgust.

Just then a dark-suited force burst through the doorway, flashing badges, flashlights, barking out orders, taking control of the room. In the middle of the dark suits was the small round figure of Jeffrey Telushkin.

"Where is he?" said Telushkin. "Where is Greeley?"

"Gone," I said.

"What do you mean gone?"

"He left, escaped, he ran."

"He was here, right?"

"That's right."

"So how did he get away?"

I glanced up at Kimberly, who, while making a statement of her own to one of the officers, obviously overheard our conversation because she was looking at me with a face full of concern.

"There was a gun," I said to Telushkin, loud enough so that Kimberly could hear. "There was a sword fight, a scuffle, things happened. I don't know, one minute he was here and then, poof."

"Where the hell did he go?"

"Don't know for sure," I said, "though I heard something about the Cayman Islands."

Telushkin spun around in frustration, then turned to one of the dark suits and mumbled something. The suit said, "Search the ship," and then all the dark suits left the room and scattered.

Telushkin turned back to me, gestured toward the justice. "Was he involved?"

"He saved the day," I said.

"Son of a bitch. You know, Carl, I won't rest until I find him."

"And if my guess is right," I said, "that is going to leave you very very tired."

After he stormed out I said, "Can I go now?"

"Not yet, Carl," said McDeiss.

So I stepped over to the bar and sat on one of the remaining stools and watched the proceedings. Justice Straczynski with his arm around his wife, Alura Straczynski, still holding on to her precious notebooks, Colfax being jerked to standing, being led out, and Kimberly Blue, smiling hesitantly at me as she came my way.

"I guess I'm really in a poodle now," she said. "Are they going to arrest me for letting him escape?"

"Only after they pin a medal on you for capturing, single-handedly, a vicious double murderer."

"Did I do that?"

"Oh yes, yes you did."

"Did I do the right thing, V?"

"Kimberly, you did your thing, and from where I'm

standing, your thing is pretty damn terrific. When did you figure it out?"

"Just here, today. Ever since we talked that time, remember, I've been thinking about why he would hire me. And then when I read her journals and realized she was pregnant, and then when your friend Mr. Skink told me Mr. D was really Tommy, it all came clear."

"How did it feel to realize he was your father?"

"He's not my father. My father took care of me all his life, my father tucked me in at night and worked in his crummy little store to make sure I had a house and fabulous clothes. My father was the most brilliant man I ever knew. Mr. D was just a distant relative, but still, blood is blood."

"What about her?" I said, gesturing to Alura.

"I don't know."

"Don't expect much."

"I never do, V. But she's my mother, isn't she? That means something. There might be things I can learn from her."

"God, I hope not. So now that you've quit your vice presidential position, what are you going to do with yourself? Merry Maids?"

She lifted her hands, showed off her nails, shrugged.

"Why don't you think about becoming a lawyer? You would be a dynamite lawyer. What jury wouldn't grant you your every wish? I could talk to someone at my old law school, give you a leg up on the application process."

"Victor, that's sweet of you and all, but really now. Take a look at me. Do you see me in a stuffy blue suit, black shoes, bowing and scraping to judges over every little piddling legal point? I don't think so. Besides, from what I can tell about your finances, I wouldn't earn enough to keep me in the lifestyle to which I intend to become accustomed. Actually, I sort of like the vice presidential thing."

"Really?"

"I was thinking maybe business school or something? Maybe Wharton? Do you know anyone at Wharton?"

"No, but I bet he does," I said, pointing to the justice.

"Do you think he'd help me get in? Do you?"

"For sure," I said, though her brilliant smile told me she knew it already.

When McDeiss finally released us, with stern warnings about leaving the city or talking to reporters, I raced down those bare metal stairs, through the engine room, out the gangway, and onto the pier. It was crowded now with police and press and an ambulance, which scared the hell out of me. Bright lights, yellow tape, flashing reds and yellows. The perverse cheerfulness of a crime scene late at night. I ignored the shouts from the reporters, which was painful, believe me—free publicity being so . . . —and instead walked around like a fool, calling out for Beth. That's what I was doing when I spotted Skink chatting up a nice-looking police officer.

"Victor, come over here, you oughts to meet someone. This is Madeline. She's just out of the academy, full of vim and vinegar."

"Where's Beth?" I said.

"At the end of the dock," he said. "I'll take you in a moment." He leaned back toward the officer. "Sos like I was saying, the thing about detecting is observation. You always gots to be looking out for the telling detail. You never know what it is that will—"

"Can we go now?"

"Wait a minute."

"Phil."

"All right. Here, sweetie, my card. Give me a call and we'll have that coffee."

"Sure thing, Phil."

As we walked off to the end of the pier, Skink was rubbing his hands. "She's got a sweet smile, she does."

"You're impossible," I said.

"Just trying to be of assistance to the local constabulary, I am. You clear everything up in there?"

"It was Colfax."

"Never did like him."

"How'd it go out here?"

"Like pie. As soon as I ran into Kimberly and had a little heart to heart with her it wasn't nothing finding our girl. She wasn't even guarded, just tied up with rope and duct tape, and put belowdecks."

"She was okay?"

"She's tougher than both of us. How did our Kimberly do up there?"

"Amazing."

"It was she who insisted on going up, delaying everything to give me time to find Beth and make the call. Quite a girl, that. See I told you, I had a feeling about her from the start."

"Yes, you did."

He led me around the long warehouse on the pier to the rear of the great rusting boat sitting in the harbor. At the end of the pier stood a shadow, staring out into the water. Beth.

"You did well, Phil."

"I know it. Go on, now. She's been asking for you."

I gave him a glance and then walked slowly toward her. She didn't turn around to look at me when she said, "It was here, the boat he put me on. It was right here."

"I guess Eddie Dean sailed it away."

"You let him go."

"Kimberly let him go. But it was Colfax who took you on his own, without Dean knowing or approving. How are you?"

"Fine. Shaken but fine."

She turned and gave me a hug, a strong hug, stronger I think than she had ever given me before.

"I knew you'd come for me," she said.

"It wasn't me. It was Phil."

"I know."

"And Kimberly told him enough so he could guess where you were."

"I know, but it was you who came for me. When Colfax pointed that gun in my face and took me away I realized I wasn't as scared as I should have been. And it was because I knew you'd come for me."

"That's what partners do."

"I'm so glad you're my partner. We'll make it work, Victor."

"Okay."

"I don't care about the money. We'll sell cookies door to door if we have to."

"Okay, but we won't have to. Selling cookies, I mean. I took the last bit of money still left in Tommy Greeley's suitcase. Thirty thousand dollars."

"What are you going to do with it?"

"I thought you and I would pay a visit to Joey's mom and give it to her. She won't see a penny from the man who killed him, he'll be judgment proof. But I'd still like to give her something."

"Okay."

"Excluding our one-third contingency, of course."

Beth laughed. "Of course."

"Should last a few months. And then something will come in, I know it. Before we go to Mrs. Parma's, make sure you haven't eaten for a few days. Her veal is amazing."

"I won't. So when?"

"Soon, but not tomorrow."

"What's tomorrow?"

"Tomorrow?" I said. "First I'm getting Rashard Porter out of jail. Then I'm saying good-bye to my dad."

CHAPTER

75

I was late for the hospital, but I had one quick errand to run.

The bell tinkled with silvery merriment when I opened the door. The shop was small, bare, dusty. Its entrance was in an alleyway, you had to go down four steps to reach the door, the sign was too small to read from the street. You didn't just happen to wander into Bullfinch's Stamps and Coins, you came looking for something specific, and so I had.

Inside, the few shelves were stocked with old reference books, the counter was unmanned, with only a banker's lamp on its surface. A table to the side of the bookshelves had a pile of scrap paper and a ballpoint attached to a chain. I walked over to the table, examined the pen. A good thing the chain was there, wouldn't want anyone to walk off with the Bic.

"Yes, yes, what do you need?" said a man who appeared behind the counter, wiping his hands on a filthy towel. He was tall and stooped, his shirtsleeves were rolled up, his glasses were round, his mustache gray. He would have been the telegraph operator in a frontier town except the frontier was gone and everyone now had cell phones. "Are you here to buy or to sell?"

"Neither really," I said. "I'd just like some information."

"Public library has a very fine reference section. Eighteenth and the Parkway. Now if you'll excuse me, we're very busy."

I looked around at the empty store. "This won't take long."

"Why don't you come back when we're under less of a rush?"

"When will that be?"

He glanced at his watch. "February," he said.

"Are you Mr. Bullfinch?"

"No," he said. "That was my father. Good day."

"It is, isn't it?" I said. "Twenty-dollar Saint Gaudens gold piece."

He cocked his head. "What about it?"

"Worth much?"

"How can a question like that be answered, Mr. . . ."

"Carl."

"What year? What condition? Motto or no motto? Regular strike or proof? Please, Mr. Carl. The twenty-dollar Saint Gaudens is generally considered to be the most beautiful American coin ever minted. Let's say a regular strike in decent condition, you could sell it for three hundred or so, buy it for four-fifty or so, prices varying depending on the year, the mint, and, of course, condition."

"Three hundred thousand?"

He laughed. "No, Mr. Carl. There were seventy million issued between 1907 and 1933. They are beautiful but not rare. You seem disappointed."

"Is there a higher end market for the coins. Are some vastly more valuable than others?"

"As with everything. Recently a Saint Gaudens, once the possession of King Farouk of Egypt, sold for over seven million dollars, but that was truly one of a kind. It had historical value. But there is a more accessible higher end, if you're interested."

"Very," I said.

Bullfinch opened the gate of the counter, walked to the door, opened it, peered outside, then closed it, locked it, pulled down the shade. "One moment, please."

He disappeared into the room behind the counter and returned a few moments later with a flat black box. He placed it beneath the banker's lamp, switched on the light, lifted open the box's lid to reveal a surface of fine black velvet with a single coin atop it.

The coin shone in the light with the sweet glister of gold. About an inch and a third wide, it had a deeply sculpted figure of Lady Liberty striding forward amidst the brilliant rays of a radiant sun.

"May I touch it?" I said.

"No, you may not. Fabulous, no? This is a high-relief Saint Gaudens in excellent condition, rated at MS65. There were only eleven thousand of these issued, before the design was flattened for convenience. They didn't stack well, you see, and the banks complained."

"What's it worth?"

"If you had one like it, Mr. Carl, I would buy it from you for, let's say, thirty thousand dollars."

"And how much would you sell this one for?"

"More."

"I see."

"This is a business."

"It's quite beautiful."

"Yes it is. It is the finest coin in my stock."

"So, this is what is referred to as ultra-high."

Bullfinch snapped shut his black box, pulled it close to him, switched off the lamp. "That is not what I said. Good day, Mr. Carl, we are quite busy."

"So what is an ultra-high?"

"It is something not worth considering."

"Consider it for me," I said.

Bullfinch clutched the black box in his long fingers, leaned forward, lowered his voice. "I've never seen one, you understand."

"Go ahead."

"Saint Gaudens's original design called for something very unusual. He made a proof set, struck with nine blows from the minting press each. Nine, when normally there is only one. The result was spectacular, more sculpture than coin. Only twenty-four were struck, given to influential senators, to the president, a few notables. Twenty-four. They are very rare. Some of them are held by organizations never to be sold. Others have disappeared, a few disappeared in Philadelphia, the locations and purview completely unknown."

"How much?"

"Mr. Carl, why the interest?"

"How much?" I said.

"Again, condition is of paramount importance. But recently, those that have reached the market have sold for in excess of one million dollars."

"In excess?"

"Well in excess."

"Well, well, well," I said. "So four would be worth?"

"Now you're being silly."

"Yes, you're right. I am."

"You wouldn't, Mr. Carl, happen to know the whereabouts of such a coin?"

"Thank you for your help, Mr. Bullfinch."

"We could be of great assistance if you do."

"I'm sure you could."

"Would you like a card?"

"No, thank you," I said, as I unlocked his door. "If need be, I know where to find you."

"Good day, Mr. Carl."

"It is," I said, "isn't it?"

"This is the big day, Victor," said Dr. Mayonnaise, with an unseemly excitement in her voice.

"Yes, it is," I said.

"He's been waiting for you."

"I'm sure he has."

"Did you ever think this day would come? Did you?"

"No," I said. "Truthfully, I did not."

"The paperwork's been signed and everything is settled so you're free to take him home whenever you're ready."

"That's great," I said. "Just great."

"He'll need some care for a while. He's still weak, but he'll get stronger day by day."

"That's my father, like something out of *Godspell*. I want to thank you, Karen, thank you for everything. You were right about the medicine, you were right about Dr. Goetze. You're a hell of a doctor."

"I appreciate that, Victor. I really do. Not everything works out so well. We're going to miss him here."

"Really?"

"Oh, yes. Your father tells the most wonderful stories."

"Stories? What about?"

"About you. That time, at school, when you mistakenly put your underwear on the outside of your pants?"

"Oh, that one. The funny thing is that I was in high school at the time."

"Take care of him, Victor," she said.

"I'll try."

She was right, Dr. Mayonnaise, my father was waiting for me, sitting in a wheelchair, in his street clothes, a small suitcase on his lap. The surgery had gone off without a hitch, his recovery was labeled remarkable by the staff, his breathing was growing stronger every day as he worked out his newly efficient lungs by blowing a ball in a tube for exercise. The ball and the tube were going home with him so he could continue his rehabilitation.

"Where you been?" he said when he saw me.

"Running an errand," I said.

"They're making me sit in this wheelchair. I don't need no stinking wheelchair."

"They're afraid if you fall and break a hip on the way out you'll sue."

"And I would too, the bastards."

"I could sure use the work. How do you feel?"

"I hurt," he said. "I hurt all over."

"That's better than the alternative. I've been to the house and readied it for you, made it nice and cozy."

"It's never been nice and cozy."

"Until now."

Slowly I pushed him out the door of his room and down the hall. All the nurses stopped us and said good-bye, told him jokes. It was like there was a stranger in the chair, the way they were going on, someone who had charmed them all, had become like a favorite old uncle. How was that possible? At the last, Dr. Mayonnaise leaned over, gave him a little hug, said her words of encouragement.

"She's a nice girl," he said as we waited for the elevator.

"Yes, she is."

"You know, that cat thing. They got pills for that."

"So I've heard, but how do they get them to open their little mouths."

"You're going to have to grow up sometime," he said.

"Yes, I'm afraid I am."

In the privacy of the elevator I couldn't help from asking. "Dad, you know that box you were talking about. The one you buried. Do you have any idea where it is?"

"Why?"

"I'm just asking."

"Let me tell you something. There's nothing in there worth a damn thing. Nothing in there but blood and despair."

"Okay."

"It ruined enough lives."

"Okay. We'll talk about it later."

"No, we won't."

"Maybe now's not the time. But there is a map?"

"I didn't say that."

"No, you didn't. So, Dad. The girl in the pleated skirt. You never told me. What happened to her?"

"She left me," he said. "What did you think? What else was going to happen? She left me."

The elevator doors opened, I wheeled my father to the entrance. An orderly in blue scrubs was waiting for us at the door.

"I'll take the wheelchair for you, Mr. Carl," he said.

"Thank you," I said as I took the small suitcase off my father's lap. "All right, Dad, are you ready?"

"No." But even as he said it he took hold of my arm and pulled himself to standing. Slowly, together, we walked outside. It was bright outside and warm. My father put a hand up to his eyes and turned his face to the sun.

Later that night I was sitting alone, in my apartment, with a picture of the Grand Canyon in my hand. The picture was on one side of a postcard, the other side had a simple message: "Wish yous was here with us. Thanks." No signature, no name, but I knew who had sent it. Derek Manley. He

had picked up his boy and was driving cross-country, seeing the sights, trying to figure out his next move. It would
probably be witness protection all over again, but this time
starting over with his son. Good for him. But something
about the postcard was troubling me. It wasn't Derek I was
thinking of, it was myself.

I stared at the great mysterious landscape carved by the
Colorado River and tried to put it all together. It was as if
everything that had happened to me since Joey Parma had
called the morning of his murder had been leading me
toward one thing, yet I couldn't figure out what it was.
There was something in the confluence, something in the
gaps, something I was missing.

I suppose it is a common flaw, to believe yourself to be
an acute observer of humanity and yet be totally blind to
the circumstances of your own small life. Or maybe I am
the only one totally clueless. Because it took me a long
time, far longer than it should have. I had been thinking I
had unshackled myself from my past when everything I
had learned, everything that had happened, had proven
with utter clarity that I had not. You don't free yourself
from the past by ignoring it and hoping it goes away, because it won't, ever, it can't. The only way to free yourself
is to reach out to your past, try to understand it, fight to
embrace it no matter what the barriers.

I opened a beer and thought it through. It was there,
somewhere, in Joey Parma's failed life, in Tommy Greeley's pathetic search to regain what he believed he had lost,
in my father's story, in the justice's relationship with his
wife, in the buried box of coins, in Kimberly Blue's revelation, in the Zen proddings of Cooper Prod, in Derek
Manley's cross-country jaunt with his son, in the twenty
bottles of gin lined up in Mrs. Greeley's china hutch.
Twenty bottles of gin. "She left me," my father had said

his voice flat, devoid of rancor or pain. As if the telling of the story had pierced something in him, deflated something angry and ugly and he was left to say, simply, that she left him. She left him. He had said it before, I had heard it before, but never so calmly, never before without the pain. My dad, showing me the way, would wonders never cease? There is a statute of limitations in the law, maybe there ought to be one in the heart.

I reached for the phone, dialed a number I hadn't called in years but that I knew as well as my own. It rang, I was hoping it would keep ringing, but then the ringing stopped and a voice from far away and long ago answered.

"Hello?" I said. "Mom?"

ACKNOWLEDGMENTS

For their generous help with this manuscript, I wish to thank a number of persons. Barry Cosgrove, one of Cardinal Spellman's most illustrious alumni, gave me an intimate tour of his hometown, Brockton, Massachusetts, bought me a beer at the Lit, and told me all the lore surrounding Dee Dubs. John Pomerance hung around and was a general nuisance during our time in Brockton, especially in the bar, so I thought I'd mention him, too. Barry Fabius, M.D., examined, diagnosed, and treated Jesse Carl for me before he transferred the patient to Dr. Hellmann. Lloyd L. Reynolds, Commander USNR (Ret), was instrumental in giving me a history of, and a sense of what it feels like to be inside, the SS *United States* as it currently sits on the Philadelphia waterfront. Victor's references to the ship as a boat are not the commander's fault. The SS *United States* has recently been purchased by Norwegian Cruise Lines and, though it still sits as Victor describes, a seemingly ruined hulk on Pier 84, it appears to have a future as bright as its past. Much thanks also to Ronald Eisenberg, chief of the Law Division of the Philadelphia District Attorney's Office, for discussing with me the statute of limitations as it currently applies to Philadelphia. Many thanks also to Josh Marwell, Penn fencing class of 1978, for fixing my sabers. My editor, Carolyn Marino, has been an extraordinary partner, and I can't thank her enough for the kindness and wisdom she has shown me. I also wish to thank the entire crew at William Morrow, including Lisa Gallagher, Debbie Stier, Jennifer Civiletto, and Claire Greenspan for their tremendous enthusiasm and support. My literary agent, Wendy Sherman, has been unfailingly encouraging to my literary efforts. Finally, the most important support I have is my family, who give me more than they could ever imagine. Much gratitude especially to my mother, who continues to instruct me on grammar; to my children, Nora, Jack, and Michael; and to my partner and love, Pam.

WILLIAM LASHNER

FALLS THE SHADOW

The *New York Times* bestselling author returns with another brilliantly twisty tale that probes the dark side of the law—and man . . .

"Lashner is as impressive as anyone writing legal thrillers today."—*Washington Post*

New in hardcover from William Morrow
0-06-072156-1 • $24.95 ($32.95 Can.)

Available from HarperAudio
0-06-078534-9
6 Hours/5 CDs
$29.95 ($42.50 Can.)

Available wherever books are sold or call 1-800-331-3761 to order.

wm WILLIAM MORROW
An Imprint of HarperCollins Publishers
www.harpercollins.com

HarperAudio
Imprints of HarperCollins Publishers
www.harpercollins.com

AuthorTracker
Don't miss the next book by your favorite author.
Sign up now for AuthorTracker by visiting
www.AuthorTracker.com

FTS 0505